Rakkety Tam

A NEW TALE of REDWALL

REDWALL
MOSSFLOWER
MATTIMEO
MARIEL OF REDWALL
SALAMANDASTRON
MARTIN THE WARRIOR
THE BELLMAKER
OUTCAST OF REDWALL
PEARLS OF LUTRA
THE LONG PATROL
MARLFOX
THE LEGEND OF LUKE
LORD BROCKTREE
TRISS
LOAMHEDGE
RAKKETY TAM

THE GREAT REDWALL FEAST

THE REDWALL MAP AND RIDDLER
REDWALL FRIEND AND FOE
BUILD YOUR OWN REDWALL ABBEY

CASTAWAYS OF THE FLYING DUTCHMAN
THE ANGEL'S COMMAND

SEVEN STRANGE AND GHOSTLY TALES

BRIAN JACQUES

Rakkety Tam

A NEW TALE *of* REDWALL

Illustrated by David Elliot

PUFFIN

PUFFIN BOOKS

Published by the Penguin Group
Penguin Books Ltd, 80 Strand, London WC2R 0RL, England
Penguin Group (USA), Inc., 375 Hudson Street, New York, New York 10014, USA
Penguin Books Australia Ltd, 250 Camberwell Road, Camberwell, Victoria 3124, Australia
Penguin Books Canada Ltd, 10 Alcorn Avenue, Toronto, Ontario, Canada M4V 3B2
Penguin Books India (P) Ltd, 11 Community Centre, Panchsheel Park, New Delhi – 110 017, India
Penguin Group (NZ), cnr Airborne and Rosedale Roads, Albany, Auckland 1310, New Zealand
Penguin Books (South Africa) (Pty) Ltd, 24 Sturdee Avenue, Rosebank 2196, South Africa

Penguin Books Ltd, Registered Offices: 80 Strand, London WC2R 0RL, England

www.penguin.com

First published in the USA by Philomel Books,
a division of Penguin Putnam Books for Young Readers 2004
First published in Great Britain in Puffin Books 2004
1

Set in MT Palatino

Made and printed in England by Clays Ltd, St Ives plc

British Library Cataloguing in Publication Data
A CIP catalogue record for this book is available from the British Library

ISBN 0–670–91069–4

For Tim Moses, a colleague and a great friend.
Thank you for everything

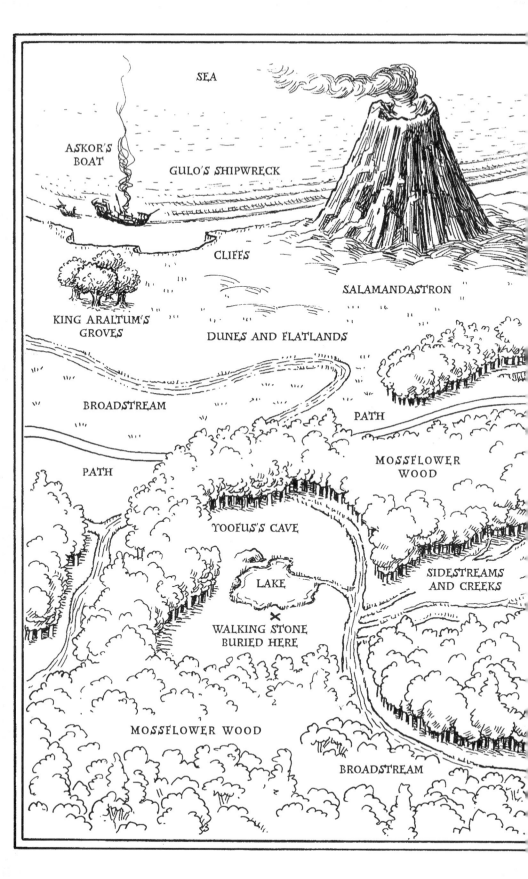

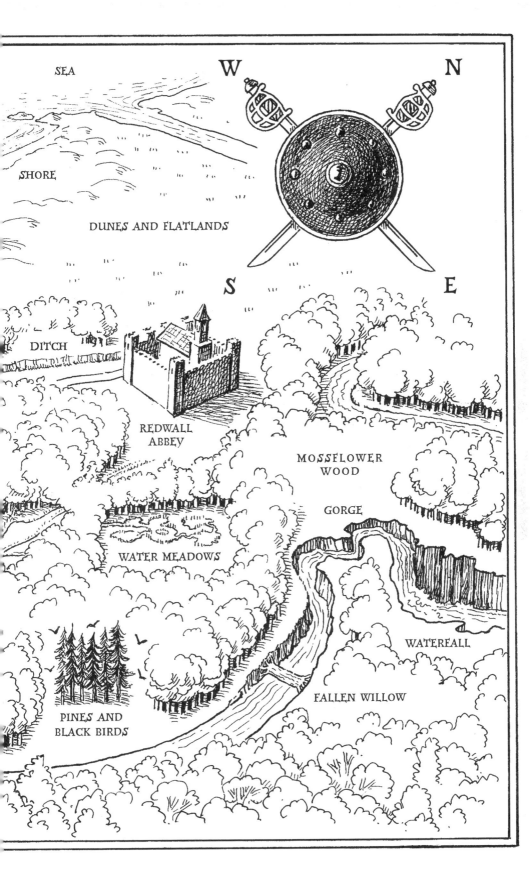

Prologue

My name is Melanda. I am the youngest creature ever to be appointed to the position of Recorder at Redwall Abbey. My teacher and mentor is a kind old mouse called Sister Screeve. She has retired from being Recorder now, taking up the job of Assistant Gardener to Brother Demple, a remarkable feat for one who has seen so many seasons come and go. She was the one who suggested that I should write a volume for our Abbey Archives about the time we now refer to as 'The Seasons of the Savage' – a fearsome title, I grant you, but one that I felt was appropriate to this narrative. I was not born at the time, so my research into the happenings was both long and painstaking. However, now that my work is completed, I would like to thank every-beast who contributed by providing their recollections of those harrowing events – all of the Redwallers, hares of the Long Patrol Regiment and others too numerous to cite here. I will not mention specific names lest I cause any offence by forgetting to include any one of my contributors.

My narrative tells of a time when our Abbey was in peril

from a beast none had ever encountered in Mossflower Country, a brutal and horrific barbarian on an insane quest for power and vengeance. But I will tell you no more than that for the present. I leave you to read on and judge for yourselves, my friends.

Melanda. Recorder of Redwall Abbey in Mossflower Country

BOOK ONE

'The warrior who sold his sword'

Rakkety Rakkety Rakkety Tam,
the drums are beatin' braw.
Rakkety Rakkety Rakkety Tam,
are ye marchin' off tae war?

A warrior from the borders came,
a buckler o'er his shoulder,
a claymore swingin' at his side,
there's no' a beast who's bolder!

O Rakkety Tam has sold his sword,
Ah scarce believe he's done it.
He swore an oath untae a fool,
who took his pledge upon it!

1

Shrieking like a thousand wild eagles, the blizzard drove mountainous grey, white-crested waves before it. The powerful ship thundered southward – mast timbers groaning, rigging lines thrumming and sails stretched to bursting point – leaving behind it the lands of ice and snow. A murderer was pursuing a thief. Gulo the Savage was hunting down his brother, Askor!

Lightning ripped through the racing storm clouds, illuminating Gulo's questing eyes. His fearsome claws, still stained with the blood of his father, dug deep into the bowrail as he peered out across the watery wilderness of peaks and valleys. Only he who had possession of the Walking Stone could rule the land of snow and ice. The once mighty Dramz had held it, this miracle which had been brought from the places beyond where the sun sets. He had also been the one who had set down the law: only the strong would inherit the Walking Stone. None was stronger than Gulo. To prove this, he had slain his father. But Askor, his brother, had stolen the Stone. Then, like a coward, he had taken to the Great Northern Sea to escape the wrath of Gulo the Savage!

With a hundred vermin warriors at his command, Gulo took up the chase in his big ship – though, in reality, he needed none to protect him. Strongest of the strong and wildest of the wild, Gulo could face daunting odds and emerge victorious. All his foes had fallen victim to his maniacal rage and awesome strength. He had but one remaining enemy in the world – his own brother. Gulo would not rest until he had sent Askor to Hellgates and had seized the all-important symbol of power, the Walking Stone!

Leaping and rearing like a wild stallion, the vessel plunged onwards. It would journey, untamed, running in sync with the surging currents – away from the land of ice and snow to warmer, more temperate coasts. Down to its fearless navigator's final destination . . . the very shores on the borders of Mossflower Country, where creatures dwelt who knew nought of what lies beyond the cold Northern Sea but were soon to witness the sight, the might and the ferocity of the beast known as Gulo the Savage!

2

In the course of a single night, winter folded the land into its earth-numbing embrace. Snow, that silent invader, fell deep and soft upon Redwall Abbey in Mossflower Country. Abbot Humble rose early from his bed in the cellars, as he always did, no matter what the season. The old hedgehog had ruled as Father Abbot for a long time. It still bemused him that he was the one chosen by all Redwallers as their leader. Humble had been a Cellarhog, born to the task, with an unsurpassed knowledge of ales, wines and cordials. Nobeast was more surprised than he, when two seasons after the passing of Abbess Furtila, the Council of Elders, backed by unanimous approval, had elevated Humble to the lofty position – Father Abbot of Redwall.

It had taken lengthy persuasion before the modest old Cellarhog accepted his new role and, even then, only under his personal conditions. He would never forsake his beloved cellars – all those barrels, kegs, casks and firkins filled with the good beverages. Having created, nurtured and cared for them, Humble would not hear of coming to live upstairs. The saying at Redwall was 'Humble is as Humble does'. By choice, the cellars remained his home. Old habits die hard, they say. This was clearly the case with

Humble. Even to this day, his first chore on rising was to check his cellars before tending to his business as Abbot.

Raking out the ashes from his little forge, Humble stoked up the burning embers with judicious amounts of broken barrel staves, seacoal and charcoal. He ambled around his cellarstock – tapping, wedging and checking the barrels. Satisfied, Humble looked in on Burlop, the present Cellarhog, whom he had trained up for the job. The stout young Cellarhog was still sleeping peacefully in a truckle bed tucked beneath an alcove. Humble smiled as he covered Burlop's footpaws with the eiderdown. Burlop was a good beast – trustworthy, diligent and strong as an oak. The Abbot took comfort in knowing that the cellars were safe in his care. Instinct told Humble that snow had fallen outside. He took a warm homespun cloak from the peg behind the door and left to make his way upstairs.

Friar Glisum was another early riser. The fat dormouse looked up from his work as the Abbot entered the kitchens. He waved a floury paw. 'G'morning, Father. Snow's thick on the ground outside.'

Humble returned the greeting as he stirred a cauldron of steaming oatmeal and began ladling out two bowlfuls. 'Morning, Glis. I'll take a spot of breakfast up to the east nightwatch, with your permission.'

The friar spooned honey over one bowl for Humble. He gave the other bowl a generous dash of hotroot pepper from a gourd shaker, murmuring half to himself, 'Carry on by all means, Abbot. I've put hotroot on Skipper's oatmeal, he sprinkles it on everything. Oh, wait a moment, I'll add some nutmeg to it.'

He grated the sweet, pungent spice over the bowl and stirred it in, winking mischievously. 'There, that'll keep the plank-ruddered rogue guessing!'

Humble left the kitchens, carrying a tray loaded with both oatmeal bowls, a small basket of hot hazelnut toast and two beakers of steaming coltsfoot-and-comfrey tea.

It was snowing heavily and still dark outdoors. Humble's sandalled paw printed tracks into the pristine surface of the white carpet as he rounded the south gable. Chuckling, he recalled his Dibbun days. ('Dibbun' is the name conferred upon all Abbeybabes.) He remembered dashing out into the first snow, with his little pals, to see who could make the first pawprints.

On top of the east wall's broad ramparts, Skipper of Otters stood cloaked, warming his paws at a fire in a strapped iron brazier. Turning, he spotted the figure with the tray, illuminated in a shaft of golden light from one of the rear Abbey windows. Blowing snowflakes from his lips, the burly otter shouted, 'Ahoy, who goes there – friend, foe or food?'

Abbot Humble's cheery reply rang back at him. ' 'Tis a friend, and bearing breakfast. Permission to come up?'

Skipper stamped his paws, chortling happily. 'Come on aboard, matey, afore I perish from 'unger!'

Bounding down the wallsteps, he took the tray from Humble, cautioning him, 'Mind yore step, Father. 'Tis slippy underpaw.'

The two friends stood on the ramparts of the Abbey, facing the snow-wreathed trees of Mossflower Wood. They warmed their backs on the fire and took breakfast together, watching the rising sun make scarlet flame patterns through the leafless branches.

Skipper spooned oatmeal down at an alarming rate, nodding toward the rising light. 'Here comes the good ole sun, what'd we do without it! Hmm, somethin' in this oatmeal, aside from 'otroot. An odd taste, wonder wot it is?'

The Abbot could not resist telling him. 'Friar Glisum said you wouldn't guess. Actually, it's nutmeg.'

Skipper wolfed it energetically. 'Very nice, I like it!'

The rising sun came up swiftly, bearded in a pinky fawn cloud. It shone like a ruby dipped in molten gold.

Skipper paused. 'Mother Nature's miracle. Ain't it a pretty sight?'

Shielding his bowl from the whirling snowflakes, the Abbot turned his gaze upon the beautiful Abbey. He shook his head in wonder. 'Redwall takes on a different face with each season, my friend. See how the light catches the stones?'

They both stood silent, viewing the ancient building through the falling snow. In the newborn day, its normally dusty red sandstone was turned to a pale roseate hue, reflecting sunlight from the belltower to the weathervane. Buttresses and arches stood out in deeper-shaded relief. Rear dormitory and hall windows blazed light from the risen orb of the sun, causing snowladen window sills to twinkle like powdered silver. Beyond the south lawns and the orchard, Redwall Abbey's pond was smooth under a thick sheet of ice. The entire scene was bordered by the walkways and battlements of the Abbey's broad outer walls.

Skipper placed a paw on his friend's shoulder, smiling. 'Aye, mate, 'tis a wonder to behold! An' to think that yore the great Father Abbot over it all!'

Humble blinked and put aside his bowl. Then he and Skipper began taking a leisurely stroll around to the west wall and the main gate. 'I was quite happy as a Cellarhog, you know.'

Chuckling, the burly otter replied, 'An' so ye still are. But you were the best beast for the job, an' you deserve it!'

When they reached the southwest walkway, a cry rang out from the path beyond the outer wall. 'Any brekkist to be had fer two pore beasts a-wanderin' pawloose in the freezin' winter?'

Abbot Humble beamed from ear to spiketip. 'Cousin Jem, I'd know that voice anywhere!'

Sheltering their eyes, they peered down to the path. Two aged creatures, towing a small cart, were trudging up from the south, the tracks behind them being obliterated by the downfall of white. One was a hedgehog, the other a mole, both cloaked and hooded.

10

Tipping his snout politely, the mole grinned up at them. He roared up in a deep bass voice, speaking in the quaint mole accent, 'Oi beg ee pardon, zurrs, but bee's you'm goin' to leave us'ns owt yurr 'til we'm both a-turned into snow-beasts?'

Skipper leaned out over the battlements. 'Well, scuttle me rudder, 'tis Hitheryon Jem an' Wanderin' Walt. Where've you two ole relics been for the last eight seasons? We'd give up 'ope of seein' ye again!'

Hitheryon Jem, the hedgehog, waved a mittened paw. 'Good wintertide to ye, Cousin Humble, an' to you, Skipper. We ain't sayin' another word 'til we're through yore gates an' eatin' good vittles in front of a blazin' fire. So look lively an' let us in, ye ole streamwhomper!'

Skipper led Humble along the west rampart and down the wallstairs. They both banged on the gatehouse door.

Still clad in nightshirt and bedcap, Brother Gordale, the mouse Gatekeeper, shuffled out, yawning and scratching. 'Brrr, snow. What's all the kerfuffle about? 'Tis scarcely day-break, can't ye sleep?'

Skipper began unbarring the main gates. 'Visitors, matey. Lend a paw 'ere, we've got guests!'

Snow was drifting against the bottom of the heavy oaken gates, making a crunching sound as the Redwallers tugged them open. The two visitors trundled their cart inside, then helped to close the gates and bar them.

Simultaneously, the main door of the Abbey building burst open. A horde of cheering, squealing Dibbuns stampeded out, roaring with delight at the sight of snow, a first experience for some of them. Within moments the Abbey grounds were a scene of chaos.

Abbot Humble raised his eyes resignedly to the sky. 'Oh, dearie me, let's get indoors quickly!'

Ducking snowballs, and avoiding sliding little ones, they made their way through the melee. Older Redwallers stood in the doorway, holding mufflers, mittens, scarves and hoods. Their entreaties were lost on the wild herd of Dibbuns.

'Come back here and get dressed properly!'

'You'll be snufflin' with cold if you don't put decent winter clothes on!'

'You'm cumm back yurr, this vurry h'instint, rarscals!'

'Put those snowballs down, please . . . Don't you dare!'

Volleys of snowballs were hurled by the rebellious pack of Abbeybabes. Trying to get inside the building, the Abbot and his friends were caught on the front steps with the Dibbun minders. Everybeast came in for a good pelting.

Humble faced the little ones, paws open wide. 'Now stop this, please! I command you to st . . . Ooooff!'

A well-aimed snowball caught him on the snout. More snowballs spattered across Skipper's back as he rescued the Abbot and pushed him inside. Still throwing, the Dibbuns retreated in the direction of the pond, intent on trying out the ice.

Skipper called to one of his ottercrew, 'Follow those villains, mate. Make sure none of 'em goes through the ice!'

Gordale slammed the Abbey door shut as a barrage of snowballs burst against it. He brushed snow from his night-shirt indignantly. 'Hooligans, rogues! The manners of young 'uns these days, really!'

Shaking snow from his habit sleeves, Humble chuckled at the old Abbey Gatekeeper. 'Forgotten your Dibbun seasons, Brother?'

Jem pulled snow from his headspikes. 'Aye, let the babes have their fun. Right, lead me to those kitchens. As the Abbot's cousin, I demand it!'

Walt was fully in agreement. 'Burr aye, let oi toast moi paws boi ee stove an' git summ brekkist in ee ole stummick!'

Friar Glisum put aside his ladle and shook the travellers' paws cordially. 'Enter, weary travellers. Come in and let me feed your bodies and warm your hearts. My kitchens are at your disposal!'

Walt winked at Jem. 'Boi 'okey, thurr bee's a creetur oi cudd dearly h'admire!'

Glisum seated them on a heap of dry sacks. They gasped with pleasure as the Friar opened his big oven, gesturing with a long paddle. 'Mushroom pasties with hot gravy, leek and carrot bake topped with yellow cheese, or maybe some fresh-baked crusty wheatbread? Murly, heat up some of that harvest vegetable soup we had for supper last night. There's a good little maid!'

A tubby little molemaid, in frilly apron and mob cap, curtsied. 'Zoop bee's cummen roight h'away, zurrs!'

Skipper gaped in awe as the guests shed their travelling gear and fell upon the food hungrily. 'Great seasons, 'tis a good job there's only two of ye, mates! 'Ow many famines 'ave ye lived through?'

Jem looked up from his second pastie. 'Too many, mate. We done nought but dream o' Redwall grub for eight seasons!'

Walt grabbed a crusty loaf. After tearing it apart, he began dunking it in the savoury onion gravy. 'Ho gurt h'Abbey vikkles!'

Virtually no conversation ensued as Hitheryon Jem and Wandering Walt applied themselves wholeheartedly to the good fare provided by Friar Glisum and his kitchen staff. Abbot Humble and the others knew they would have to wait for news of the comings and goings in other places until both guests had taken their fill. It had been a long time since the travellers' last visit, and the Abbey creatures were anxious to hear the news from places far beyond Redwall. As the kitchens would be busy with mealtimes, Humble ordered the fire to be banked up in Cavern Hole and two comfortable armchairs moved close to the hearth. His guests could rest there and talk in relative comfort and peace.

Much later in the morning, Jem and Walt vacated the kitchens. As they made their way across Great Hall, the main door opened. The Dibbuns finally had been rounded up and were being marched in for a very late breakfast. Sister Armel, the pretty young squirrel who was Infirmary Keeper, led the way. She was accompanied by her two helpers – Foremole Bruffy and Sister Screeve, the stout, cheery mouse who was Abbey Recorder. All three were trying to gain some semblance of order amid the excited little ones.

'Wipe those paws thoroughly on the mat, please! Stand in line.'

Sister Armel eyed a tubby mousebabe sternly. 'Mimsie, please take that snowball outside and throw it away.'

Mimsie waved cheerily to Humble. 'Goo' mornin', h'Abbit. I jus' gonna frow dis snowball 'way.'

Abbot Humble nodded understandingly. 'There's a good little maid, it's not nice to take snowballs in to breakfast.'

Mudge the molebabe called out helpfully, 'Hurr, cos snowyballs can't eat breffist. Can they'm, zurr?'

A hedgehog Dibbun named Perkle piped up. 'An' hysiggles can't not eat breffist, neither, can they?'

Mudge shook his head solemnly. 'No, they'm carn't, you'm gurt pudden-'eaded choild!'

Sister Screeve retrieved a long, pointed icicle from Perkle. 'Give me that icicle before you put somebeast's eye out with it.'

Skipper laughed at the antics of the Dibbuns, who, now that they remembered they were hungry, were anxious to be fed. They squeaked and bounced up and down as the helpers tried to keep them in line. They splashed about in puddles of melted snow which dripped from them.

The otter chieftain called to the helpers, 'Sister Armel, when you get that lot brekkisted, may'aps you'n Foremole an' Screeve might like to drop by Cavern 'ole to 'ear the latest news from Jem'n'Walt.'

Sister Screeve chivvied three latecomers into line. 'Thank you, I'll bring quill and parchment to record any important events. We'll see you down there shortly.'

3

An hour later, all Redwallers interested in hearing the news were gathered in Cavern Hole. They waited respectfully until Hitheryon Jem had sipped at a tankard of mulled October Ale. He smacked his lips appreciatively, glanced at the eager faces of his audience and then commenced.

'Well now, my good friends, those last two winters were so deep an' hard that me'n ole Walt here couldn't make it up to yore Abbey, but here we are now. Other seasons were fine – springtimes fresh, summers warm an' autumns agreeable. There weren't much to report on until this late autumn. Then we came across a mighty strange thing, didn't we, Walt?'

Putting aside his tankard, the mole blinked dozily in the warm firelight glow. 'Burr aye, et wurr strange an' h'odd, vurry h'odd!'

Sister Screeve dipped her quill into some ink swiftly. 'Strange and odd – in what way, pray tell?'

Jem gazed into the fire, as if reliving the incident. 'It were a sunny morn, but misty. We was rovin' along the tideline, southwest, a couple o' leagues from the mountain strong'old of Salamandastron. There on the shore we espied a small vessel, wrecked it were, an' washed up on the rocks. So, me'n Walt, we went to see wot we could do. Right, Walt?'

But the old mole had slipped off into a slumber, wooed by the fire and the comfortable armchair. Jem smiled, then continued with his narrative.

'Looks like I'm bound to tell this tale alone. Aye, 'twere a small craft, with a simple square-rigged sail, smashed to bits an' stoved in by the rocks. All that was in it was a few empty food sacks, a broken water cask an' some fish bones. But there were tracks aplenty, runnin' up the beach an' headed nor'east. We took a good look at them marks, made by a single beast they were. I tell ye, it made pawprints like we'd never seen, great, wide, blurry ones with deep curvin' clawmarks – bigger'n those of a badger. The claws were broader, more pointed, not blunt like a badger's but very sharp an' long. By the blurrin' o' the tracks, I figgered this must be a beast with long hair comin' from its paws. By the length o' the pawmarks, an' their depth, Walt reckoned that the thing'd be about the same size as a big male badger. Anyhow, we was thinkin' of makin' our way over to visit ye at Redwall afore winter set in. So seein' as the tracks went in the same direction, we decided to follow 'em, just to get a look o' this oddbeast.'

Jem paused to refill his tankard, giving the Abbot the chance to enquire, 'Did you not visit the mountain of Salamandastron at all?'

The wanderer nodded. 'Aye, we stopped there at the end o' spring season – that ole mountain fortress ain't changed a whit. Lady Melesme is still the Badger Ruler o' the western shores, she an' those hares send ye all their fond best wishes. Oh, I forgot to mention, Melesme's sendin' ye a gift.'

Brother Gordale leaned forward. 'A gift, for us?'

Jem took a draught of his ale. 'Do ye remember about four summers back, when she visited here with that troop of Long Patrol hares? Both yore bells were down for cleanin' whilst ye repaired the bellropes. D'ye recall that?'

Foremole Bruffy wrinkled his velvety brow. 'Ho aye, oi amembers et. Ee gurt badger lady sayed she'm missed ee sounds uv our bells. Hurr, she'm wurr gurtly fond of ee bellnoises.'

Skipper nodded. 'That's right, so she was. Lady Melesme said to me that if'n our bells were down, we should 'ave somethin' to mark the times o' day an' night.'

Jem winked at the otter. 'Well, she's sendin' ye a drum.'

Sister Screeve paused from her recording. 'A drum?'

The traveller explained. 'Hoho, but what a drum, marm! When I saw it, 'twas only half made. The drumskin was taken from a big dead shark. The hares found it washed up on the beach one mornin'. Melesme an' the hares were makin' the casin' from two great circles of elmwood, an' the ribbin' from sharkbone. I saw the hares at the forge, beatin' out gold an' silver to decorate the rim an' edges o' the drum. 'Tis goin' to be a drum the like o' which ye've never seen!'

Abbot Humble folded both paws into his wide sleeves. 'How kind and thoughtful of our friend Melesme. We must think of something to send her in return – perhaps a beautifully woven robe and a keg of sweet damson and elderberry wine. She was very fond of my wine when she visited us.'

Sister Screeve turned to Jem impatiently. 'Yes, yes, but on with the tale, my friend. Did you and Walt follow the tracks which ran up the shore?'

Jem took up the threads of his tale again. 'Oh aye, marm. We followed right enough. It looked like the beast were travellin' fast, though, as if 'twere in haste to get clear o' the coast. Walt'n me thought mayhaps the creature was bein' pursued, but we weren't in no rush, just followed at our own pace, slow'n'steady. Ole Walt an' meself, we've never hurried for nobeast. Those tracks was as clear as the snout on yore face, so we plodded on after 'em. The trail took us off'n the shore, up into the hills, o'er the clifftops. From there it were all trekkin' across heaths an' moorlands, fordin' rivers an' brooks'n'streams. It took quite a few days, I can tell ye. We made it into the southwest marches o' Mossflower Woodlands.'

Jem savoured the taste of his October Ale. 'Aye, 'twas of a nightfall when we reached the trees. Lucky we did, marm, cos it came on to storm somethin' fearful. So me'n ole Walt dug in under a rocky ledge for shelter. Huh, I wouldn't be out in a storm like that'n for anythin'!'

Sister Armel interrupted Jem. 'That big thunderstorm . . . but that was only five nights ago?'

The hedgehog nodded, holding out his tankard for a re-fill. 'Right ye are, pretty miss. Otherwise we'd have arrived at yore Abbey two days afore the snow. Findin' that beast cost us time.'

'So you did find the creature?' Abbot Humble enquired.

The traveller held his footpaws up to the fireglow. 'That we did, cousin. 'Twas the followin' morn when it 'appened. Neither of us was sure o' the trail, y'see – that storm'd washed out the tracks. Well, we was wanderin' along as best as we could, when ole Walt 'ears noises. A sort of gruntin' an' groanin' an' yowlin', like as if somebeast was in pain. So we goes towards the din, an' there 'twas, trapped under a big ole rotted sycamore that the storm musta blowed down. Got it right across its back, snapped the thing's spine, I reckon. 'Twas clear the beast was dyin'. It was built like a big male badger, though its limbs was thicker an' shorter. Strange-lookin' thing – pointed, weaselly snout, with a thick, bushy-furred body, blackish brown, with lighter stripes runnin' down both sides to a tail thicker'n a squirrel's. But you should've seen its claws an' teeth! I never seen such dangerous claws, or so many sharp fangs in one mouth. Made yore blood run cold t'see that animal, snarlin', growlin', screechin' an' tryin' to bite its way through a tree trunk ten times its size!'

Foremole Bruffy twitched his snout curiously. 'Boi 'okey! Wot did ee do, zurr?'

Hitheryon Jem shrugged. 'Wasn't alot we could do, really. As soon as it saw us, the beast roared an' yowled even louder. That fallen sycamore was a great ole woodland giant of a thing – a score o' creatures couldn't 'ave budged it. So me'n Walt tried talkin' to the beast. We told it we was friends an' didn't mean it no harm. Hah, it just bared its fangs at us an' said, "Nobeast is friend of Askor. Ye come near, I tear ye to pieces. Askor slays all enemy, everybeast is enemy!" '

Jem paused and looked around at his audience. 'Well, friends, I ask ye, wot were we t'do? Ole Walt threw Askor his canteen in case he was thirsty, but he flung it back at us. When I tossed him some food, he did the same thing. Can ye imagine it? Layin' there under a big fallen tree, dyin' of a broken back an' refusin' food, drink an' friendship. I lost patience with Askor an' told him he was a thick'eaded fool. He just gave a nasty laugh an' said, "Gulo will come. Tell him I say he will never find Walking Stone. Askor soon will die, then you can eat me"!'

A horrified gasp came from Sister Armel. 'Eat him?'

Jem clenched his jaw grimly. 'Aye, those were his very words, miss. Huh, I told him we 'ad no intention of eatin' him. Then he laughed, showed us those fangs of his an' said, "You are fool, not eat Askor? Weak fool. I am wolverine, all beasts are my enemy. Wolverine eat enemy, grow strong on their blood! When Gulo finds me, I will be long dead, not good to eat. You tell him, Askor wins, Walking Stone is mine forever. Gulo will never find Walking Stone." '

Abbot Humble was keen to hear more. 'What did you do then?'

Jem sat back. 'Nothin', we did nothin'. We knew his name was Askor an' that he was a wolverine, though we'd never heard o' such a creature. That beast must've been mad with the pain his broken back was causin' him, but it were more'n that. Askor wouldn't talk to us any more. He just lay there waitin' for death to take him. Mutterin' on about the one called Gulo an' sayin' how he'd never get his paws on the thing called Walkin' Stone. So I asked him to tell me more about Gulo an' the Walkin' Stone. Askor went quiet for a bit, then he spoke.'

Sister Screeve dipped her quill pen into the ink. 'Can you recall the wolverine's words?'

Jem continued. 'He said, "Gulo the Savage is my brother. Nobeast is more bloodthirsty and fierce than Gulo. We live in the lands of ice, beyond the great sea. Dramz, our father, ruled over all, even though he was growing sick and old. He was obeyed, as long as he owned the Walking Stone. It was his wish that, after his death, we would share the Walking Stone and rule together, but Gulo did not want this. He murdered our father and took the Walking Stone. It was I, Askor, who stole it from Gulo. The moment I did this, my life was in danger. Gulo had the white foxes and ermine on his side. I would be a deadbeast if I stayed in the lands of ice. But the Walking Stone was as much mine as his, so I stole a boat and sailed away. Gulo will come after me, as sure as night follows day. He would find where the Walking Stone is, then kill me and eat me. Not now, though – I will already be dead. Gulo the Savage will not find where I have hidden the Walking Stone. He cannot be ruler without it. Askor has won!"'

Jem paused. 'So I asked him where he had hidden the Walking Stone. I never expected Askor t'tell me, an' I'm not sure he did, but these were his exact words. Sister, ye'd best write this down while I can still remember.

"Where the sun falls from the sky,
and dances at a pebble's drop,
where little leaves slay big leaves,
where wood meets earth I stop.
Safe from the savage son of Dramz,
here the secret lies alone,
the symbol of all power, the mighty Walking Stone."

Jem glanced at the Abbot. 'A riddle if ever I heard one – eh, cousin?'

Humble nodded slowly. 'Aye, a very puzzling rhyme, Jem. Tell me, what happened then?'

Twirling dregs in his tanker, the old hedgehog quaffed the last of his ale. ' 'Twas a terrible thing to see. Askor reared up and shouted, "I defeated thee, Gulo. Me, Askor, I won! When next I see your face, I will laugh at you in the light of the fires at Hellgates." Then he gave a mighty roar and gripped the fallen trunk with all four paws. You should've seen the size o' that log, but I swear he actually lifted it a fraction! Then he slumped back an' fell dead, probably from the exertion an' the strain o' his broken back. We couldn't get him out for buryin', so me an' Walt covered his body over with loam an' dead leaves, leavin' Askor where he lay. Then we set out for Redwall Abbey. Ole Walt, bein' a rock o' good sense, made sure we covered our tracks well. Nobeast could have followed us, cos Walt's an expert at wipin' out a trail.'

Sister Screeve, looking alarmed, put down her quill. 'Do you think that the evil brother, this Gulo the Savage, will come here? Mayhaps he'll think that you and Walt found the Walking Stone and have taken it with you.'

Skipper patted her back reassuringly. 'Don't fret, marm. Jem'n'Walt knows all the skills o' woodcraft. I wager not even a hungry serpent could've followed 'em here. Ain't that right, Father?'

Humble trusted the otter chieftain's judgement. 'Skipper's right, Sister Screeve. No need for you or any other Redwaller to worry over such things. However, I'd be obliged if you didn't go speaking of the incident to others. No need to concern them unduly.'

Foremole Bruffy held a big blunt digging claw to his mouth. 'Hushee naow, zurrs'n'marms. Ole Jem bee's falled to sleepin'.'

Jem's head had dropped back upon the cushions. A

combination of food, ale and warmth had lulled him into a peaceful slumber. Removing the empty tankard from Jem's grasp, the Abbot lowered his voice. 'Poor weary travellers, they both look worn out. Leave them to their rest, friends. Let's go and see what mischief those Dibbuns are up to.'

Silently, the Redwallers tippawed from Cavern Hole. Skipper and Abbot Humble were last to leave. The otter chieftain latched the door gently, murmuring to Humble, 'No more fires on the walltops for a while, Father. I'll tell the wallguards to stay alert during the night, an' keep a weather eye peeled for anythin' unusual. No sense invitin' trouble by bein' unprepared.'

The Abbot patted Skipper's brawny paw. 'A good idea, my friend. I'll leave the arrangements to you.'

After breakfasting late, the Dibbuns had stampeded out into the snow again. Inside, the Abbey was relatively quiet. The dishes had been cleared away from Great Hall tables, and most of the elders had gone outdoors. Humble knew that they went on the pretext of watching the Abbeybabes, though mainly they wanted to join in the fun.

Humble wandered over the worn floorstones, stopping at the tapestry of Martin the Warrior. He it was who had fought to free Mossflower Country, and helped to build the Abbey, in the dim, countless seasons of long ago. Martin was the very essence and spirit of Redwall. Now his marvellous sword was displayed between two brackets over the tapestry. Humble gazed up at the figure of the heroic mouse whose likeness was woven lovingly into the huge ancient tapestry. His features were strong and resolute; his eyes – friendly, gallant and caring – seemed to follow wherever one went.

From outside, the Abbot could hear the distant merriment where everybeast was playing on the Abbey pond. It was a sound very dear to the old Cellarhog who had risen to be Father Abbot of Redwall. He whispered to

Martin, 'Don't let any ill fortune disturb the peace and happiness of our home – I beg you, Martin.'

Lanterns flickered on each side of the tapestry, which rippled slightly in an errant breeze from the open door. But the figure of Martin the Warrior did not stir. He stood steadfastly, guarding his beloved Abbey throughout the winter, as he had through time immemorial.

4

The territory of Squirrelking Araltum and Idga Drayqueen consisted of a sizeable grove of beech, hazelnut and various conifers that grew near the clifftops and shoreline, some two leagues south of Salamandastron. It was not far from where Walt and Jem had found Askor's wrecked boat.

Araltum was a fat, pompous and vain creature whose title, 'King', was one of his own making. He had also conferred the name 'Drayqueen' on his haughty and ill-mannered wife, Idga. They were, indeed, a well-matched pair. It was some twelve seasons since they had arrived and had enforced their authority over the tree groves. Araltum did this by hiring mercenary squirrel warriors, travelling pawloose fighters who pledged their swords in exchange for position and the benefits of life amid the fertile groves of fruit and nut trees which abounded in the Squirrelking's domain. It was no mean achievement for the royal couple to have established their rule. Their home and court was in the terraces at the centre of the groves. Araltum and Idga revelled in the setting of petty ceremonies, laws, acts and penalties, which were rigidly enforced by their officers.

One morning Idga Drayqueen awoke to witness the arrival of spring, a welcome event after the harsh, dark days of winter. The last snows melted and slid from bended

24

boughs under a warm, beaming sun. Birdsong echoed through the trees, backed by the rippling music of streams freed from their icy covers. The earth was renewing itself once more. With the new season came the initiation of a new ceremony, the Marking of the Marches! This was something which Araltum and Idga had planned throughout the tedious days and evenings of wintertide. It was to be a grand parade of the royal couple's boundaries, starting at the court, then spreading forth to circle the groves which marked their lands, and culminating back at the court with a grand feast. The entire affair would be punctuated with music, song and many high-flown speeches which the Squirrelking and his Drayqueen had written for themselves. This was designed to impress upon their subjects the power and magnificence of the royal pair. Idga and her servants had spent long winter nights making a banner, a large, florid thing. Truly a triumphal set piece, it was yellow, with blue chevrons on one side to denote the sea. Six green trees represented the land at the other side. Its centre was dominated by two huge, bushy tails, the symbols of king and queen.

At the opening of the new ceremony, the royal banner, which was now fixed to a long flagstaff made from yew wood, was presented to Araltum by Idga. Amid cheers and jubilant chants from the rank-and-file squirrels, Idga performed an elaborate curtsy and fell flat on her considerable rear end. A playful gust of wind caught the banner, causing Araltum to stagger about and to nearly be swept off his paws. Driltig and Chamog, two of his captains, saved the king from injury by taking charge of the billowing flag. As Idga was helped up by her servants, Araltum launched squeakily into his speech.

'Ahem! Er, let all who see this, our Royal Standard, bow their heads and wave their tails in respect. Yes, wherever our banner flies, it will inspire joy in the hearts of all . . .'

Dutiful cheers echoed forth from the onlookers as the king continued. 'And strike terror into the hearts of foebeasts, who are, er, rash enough to trespass upon these, my territories!'

More orchestrated calls of approval rang out among the crowd before Araltum concluded his speech. 'This flag shall fly a hundred, nay, a thousand seasons, as a symbol of my power! Let allbeasts know of the beauty and wisdom of Idga Drayqueen and her King, the fearless, the mighty, the magnificent . . .'

Here he raised his paws as his subjects shouted en masse, 'Long live Idga Drayqueen and Squirrelking Araltum!'

The procession wound off through the trees – Araltum swaggering in the lead, Chamog and Driltig slightly behind, bearing the new royal standard, and six other various captains and officials following. In their wake marched a score of singers and musicians, trilling the praises of their rulers in a song jointly composed by the royal couple.

'O mighty and magnificent,
upholders of our laws.
Thy loyal subjects call to thee,
protect us with thy paws.
O Araltum and thy Drayqueen,
so fair of fur and tail,
we bow to thee in honour,
and joyfully cry Hail!'

A huge, ancient chestnut tree, which held the court within its spreading limbs, had a small barred door set in the base of its trunk. This was the cell which held dissidents and malefactors.

Doogy Plumm peered through the tiny barred aperture and laughed. Then, in his strong Northern Highland accent, he shouted out, 'Ho ho ho! Will ye listen tae the dunderheads, all chantin' an' singin' tae that wee lard barrel!'

Doogy, a short, thick-bodied squirrel, was no lightweight himself. He turned to his fellow prisoner – a tall, powerful, sinewy-built beast. 'Och, Tam, mah beauty, don't ye wish we were oot there, havin' sich a braw time, caterwaulin' the auld eejit's praises? Will ye be grieved tae miss the braw feast for their majesties?'

Rakkety Tam MacBurl unfolded himself from a small bunk and stretched lazily. 'Nay, Doogy, I'd sooner miss a dozen feasts than have to bow'n'scrape around that little toad, singin' foolish ditties that him an' Idga penned between them!'

Tam's accent was not as broad as Doogy's; he was a Borderer and not from the Highlands. Doogy scrambled down from the stool he had been perched on and threw himself on the bunk. 'Ah, Tam, Tam. Why did we ever roam south tae pledge our blades tae sich a pair o' fools?'

Tam laughed drily. 'Because it seemed a good idea at the time, wee Doogy Plumm. Ye have to take the bad with the good.'

Doogy scratched his tail. 'Aye, an' there hasnae been much o' the good lately.'

Tam rattled the cell door to attract the attention of the guard who was posted outside. 'Hi, Hinjo! When are they goin' to let us out o' here? We're famished for the want of food!'

Hinjo had served with both Tam and Doogy and was friendly toward them. He shrugged apologetically. 'Sorry, Tam, I've got my orders. Both of ye have got to stay there until the ceremony and the feast are finished. Then I'm to march ye up to the court, where the royal pair will decide what punishment fits yore crimes, mate.'

Rakkety Tam's face was the picture of roguish innocence. 'Who, me? What crime am I supposed to have committed?'

The guard shook his head, chuckling. 'Yore an insubordinate rascal, Cap'n MacBurl. What did ye think Araltum was goin' t'do after ye called him a waddlin' ole windbag an' refused to carry the royal flag in his new ceremony? Tam, yore the best warrior the King's ever had, but ye can't insult him like that an' get off free.'

Doogy scrambled back up on to the stool, next to Tam. 'Ah never said ought aboot the blitherin' oaf!'

Hinjo guffawed loudly. 'Of course ye didn't, Doogy, but ye did call Idga Drayqueen a fussy-bustled ole branch-burster! I think that might've had somethin' to do with ye bein' in there, eh?'

Doogy Plumm wrinkled his nose. 'Ach, but we was only sayin' what everybeast was thinkin'.'

Hinjo leaned on his spear as he explained to Doogy, 'Aye, but no matter what everybeast is thinkin', they keep it to theirselves. You two are the first to say it out loud. Why don't ye go an' take another nap? When all the celebrations are done with, you'll be sent for. Take my word for it, mates, I've got my orders.'

Further argument was useless. Tam and Doogy lay heads to paws on the little bunk and tried to slumber, each with his own thoughts. Both beasts had left the Northlands to come south in the winter of the famine. Starvation, or death by bands of predatory vermin, killed off many squirrels that winter. Neither Tam nor Doogy had any close family, but both were young warriors with a sense of adventure. They had met up on the road whilst trekking south to the warmer climes. Straightaway they had taken to each other and had become the closest of comrades. Together the two squirrels had lived through a series of perils and scrapes but had come through it all, still side by side.

Tam and Doogy had been spotted by Araltum's scouts as soon as they had walked into his territory. The Squirrelking immediately knew that these two young warriors were the best he had ever seen. Initially, Tam and Doogy had been flattered by the cordial welcome and the attention lavished upon them by the royal couple. In Araltum's kingdom were rich and fertile copses and glades, food grown in abundance everywhere and balmy coastline climate for most seasons – a whole different world compared to the hard life of the Northlands from whence Tam and Doogy had come. Soon the two companions had pledged their word and swords in the Squirrelking's service. Both had risen swiftly in the ranks – Tam being made Royal Champion, with the faithful

28

Doogy always at his friend's side. Having fiercely repulsed any foebeasts who attacked, soon there were few large vermin raids of any kind. After a while, the names Rakkety Tam MacBurl and Wild Doogy Plumm had become bywords for courage and fearlessness.

With the passing of seasons, Araltum's land became safe and secure, no longer a satisfying place for active warriors. Tam and Doogy, still young and wild, became disenchanted with having to enforce the trivial, and oft times piffling, petty regulations made by Araltum and Idga. The day before the new ceremony brought things to a head. Now they were imprisoned by the same laws that they had upheld. Things would never again be the same between Tam, Doogy and the royal squirrel rulers.

Tam and Doogy whiled away the hours, dozing fitfully. At midnoon Hinjo tapped on the door. Doogy sat up, rubbing both eyes with his tailbrush. 'What's goin' on oot there? Can ye no' let a body take a wee rest – away wi' ye!'

This time the spearbutt rapped the door sharply. Hinjo's voice was loud and urgent. 'Come quick! Idga Drayqueen wants to see ye both. Somethin's gone badly wrong. I don't know what 'tis, but yore both to follow me at the double!'

Rising unhurriedly, Tam began wrapping on his woven heather tartan of brown, green and dusty lilac – first around his waist, in a kilt, then across his chest and over one shoulder so that it draped down, cloak-like, upon his back. He winked roguishly at Doogy, who was also dressing.

'Idga wants t'see us, that's nice. I wonder if she's saved us some cake an' wine. Dearie me, we can't dash up there lookin' like a pair o' ragamuffins, Doogy!'

Hinjo unbolted the door and opened it hastily. 'Will you two put a move on! Yore needed urgent, now!'

Doogy Plumm was setting a small eagle feather in his cap. He spat on one paw and preened his tail slowly. 'Och, the poor wee Queenie, tell her we'll drop by tae chat wi' her as soon as we're lookin' braw an' saucy.'

Hinjo pleaded. 'Come on, mates, please, or she'll have my hide. Tam, will ye move yoreself?'

Tam cinched his broad belt tight and set his cap at a jaunty angle. 'So then, Doogy my friend, d'ye think we look fit enough to be presented to Her Majesty?'

His companion threw up a smart tail salute. 'Aye, like a pair o' lassies ready tae dance a reel, sir!'

Rakkety Tam bowed gallantly to Doogy. 'After you, sir. Quick march, left right, left right, tails up, shoulders back, eyes front!'

They marched out in perfect step, leaping together up into the big old chestnut trunk.

A wide platform of limbs and boughs connected the chestnut with several large trees nearby. This formed the royal court, which at that moment was in a state of chaos. King Araltum was wrapped in a blanket, dishevelled, shivering and wailing. Idga Drayqueen had gone into a swoon, lying flat on her back and gasping for breath. Several of her servants were fanning her with ferns and dabbing her paws with rose water. Squirrels were running hither and thither – some hiding, others gathering up their belongings.

Tam marched straight up to Araltum, questioning him sharply, 'What in the name o' seasons has been goin' on here?'

Regardless of not being addressed by his title, the king sobbed, 'I was attacked, invaded, assaulted! Barbarians, hooligans, monsters! They've stolen our Royal Banner!'

The courtiers and servants set up a concerted moan. Doogy roared at them, 'Will ye shut that wailin' up!'

Idga Drayqueen raised a tearstained face, blubbering, 'Oh oh, my poor love! What have those murderers done to you? We'll all be slain in our beds. Wahaaaaah!'

Tam turned on her contemptuously. 'Silence, marm, an' try to behave like a queen. Your husband's alive an' well. Where did all this happen, Driltig?'

Nursing a bruised paw, Captain Driltig muttered brokenly, 'Down at the west fringe, near the clifftops.'

Tam nodded to Doogy. 'Get down there fast, mate. See what's gone on, then report back t'me!'

Doogy took off like an arrow, zinging through the foliage. Turning his attention to the trembling king, Tam tried to make sense of all that was going on. 'Tell me what you can. What did you see?'

Araltum blurted out squeakily, 'There were hundreds of them . . . white vermin. They surrounded us. Then that thing, that Gulo, attacked without warning. I was almost killed! D'you hear me, almost killed!'

Araltum collapsed, weeping hysterically. Tam gave an irate snort. Grabbing hold of Driltig, he hauled him upright. 'Make your report, Captain. Come on, smarten up!'

Driltig could not meet his interrogator's gaze. He rubbed his bruised paw, babbling like a beast in a trance. 'It was a nightmare! One moment we were marching out of the trees and on to the western fringe. Me an' Chamog were carryin' the flag, the others were singin' an' playin' flutes . . . Suddenly they ambushed us, out of nowhere – a great mob of wild vermin, white foxes an' ermine stoats. The leader was called Gulo, they were yelling his name. 'Gulo! Gulo!' They hit us like lightnin' – rippin', slayin' an' slashin'. We never stood a chance. I dropped the flag. Then me an' Pinetooth over there, we seized the King an' rushed him up into the trees. That's when I hurt my paw. We went like the wind, our creatures screamin' an' dyin' back there. We could hear those vermin roarin' an' laughin' like madbeasts. I'll never forget it as long as I live, never!'

Driltig slumped down, weeping. The older squirrel, Pinetooth, was an experienced campaigner. He sat silent, ignoring a bleeding wound to his shoulder. Tam looked to him.

Pinetooth shook his head. 'I can't tell ye any more'n he did, Tam. It all happened too fast!'

31

Tam nodded. 'Ye'd best get that wound seen to, mate.'

Pinetooth glanced at his injury as if just noticing it. 'One of the vermin slashed at me with a blade shaped like a sickle. I was lucky, though, I escaped. That Gulo beast got Cap'n Chamog first. Pore beast, he screamed like a babe!'

Idga Drayqueen had sufficiently recovered to complain at Tam. 'My poor Araltum, almost killed! And where were you while all this murder was taking place, eh?'

Rakkety Tam lost his temper and bellowed at her, 'Locked in the guardhouse because I wouldn't play your stupid little games, marm. Don't ye remember? Where's me'n Doogy's weapons o' war – you had them confiscated.'

Pinetooth went to a concealed place amid the branches. He dragged forth a big sack with its neck tied shut. Tearing it open with his teeth, he upended it. Tam grabbed the belongings that had been taken from him – his trusty weapon, a claymore, with a hefty double-edged blade and a basket hilt; his dirk, the long dagger used by Northerners for close fighting; and his Sgian Dhu, a small, keen skinning knife with a black handle and an amber cairnstone set on top. Tam thrust the claymore into the side of his belt, the dirk at the back, beneath his cloak, and the Sgian Dhu behind a hackle of feathers set into his cap. Last, he picked up his buckler, a small, round fighting shield, slinging it behind his left shoulder.

'Now I feel properly dressed. I'll hold Doogy's gear here until he gets back.'

It was some time before Tam's partner returned. Buckling on his three blades and picking up his shield, Doogy spoke quietly to Tam. 'Ah tell ye, mate, it was a massacre!'

Tam showed no emotion. 'Were there no wounded on either side? Did ye not catch sight o' the vermin?'

Doogy shook his head. 'Nary a sign of 'em, but they left tracks aplenty. There was no' one of our fighters alive.'

Tam pointed at Idga and Araltum. 'Doogy, you an' the rest bring these two along. 'Twill do them good to see the results of their playactin'. 'Tis safe enough to return there now. I'll go ahead an' look at the vermin tracks whilst they're still fresh.'

As Tam swung off through the trees, Araltum protested, 'He can't talk to me like that, I'm a king!'

Doogy dragged Araltum up, whipping the blanket off him. 'Yore nought but a blitherin' auld bloater. Get movin'!'

Idga Drayqueen called out indignantly, 'You common little beast! I'll have you thrown back in the guardhouse for your impudence. Guards, seize him!'

As nobeast moved to hinder him, Doogy scowled fiercely at Idga. 'Ah don't want tae hear anither word out o' ye. Now move that fat tail, ye wee biddy, or ah'll move it for ye!'

5

Rakkety Tam was casting about the area where the attack had taken place. He peered over the cliffs down to the far shoreline. Two boats lay wrecked on the rocks – a small craft, which the pounding waves had reduced to splinters, and a big, four-masted vessel. This latter ship was holed at the bowline, close to its prow, where it had been driven headlong on to the treacherous reef.

Doogy arrived with the royal couple and the other squirrels. He indicated the big wrecked four-master. 'Yon's the ship the vermin must've come in, though ah'm thinkin' 'twill be no use tae anybeast now.'

Tam's eyes hardened. 'Aye, an' they won't be able to repair it once we put torches to it, Doogy!'

He turned to the carnage, which Idga and Araltum were pointedly trying to ignore by gazing in another direction. 'This was a massacre indeed, Doogy. By the tracks, I'd say there were about fivescore vermin who did the slaughter. Mostly foxes an' stoats, though I see the big-pawed one, their Chieftain, leadin' away over the clifftops.'

Doogy strained his eyes north and east. 'Och, they must've been fair speedy villains. There's no' a sight of 'em anyplace!'

Tam faced Araltum. 'How many were with ye at the start of yore ceremony?'

The king shrugged airily. 'How should I know?'

The squirrel warrior glared at him in disgust. 'Aye, an' why should you care, now that yore skin's saved! Pinetooth, can ye recall what the numbers were?'

The older squirrel did a quick mental estimate. 'Countin' the singers an' musicians, I'd say about thirty.'

Idga Drayqueen snapped her bark fan shut moodily. 'Really, what difference does it make? They're all dead now!'

Tam scratched his brush as he viewed the slain squirrels. 'There's not one carcass of a foebeast among these. They're all our creatures. Thirty, ye say, Pinetooth? Well, how d'ye account for the fact there's only eighteen lyin' here? Countin' yourself an' Driltig, that makes ten missin'.'

The old squirrel leaned on his spear. 'Are ye sure, Tam, only eighteen?'

Tam gestured. 'Count 'em yourself, mate. Doogy, go an' cast an eye round the edge of the trees to the north, will ye?'

Idga Drayqueen began weeping in genuine distress. 'Oh, that beautiful banner! It took me and my servants almost a full winter season to make it. Is it lost forever, my dear?'

Araltum patted her paw. 'There, there, my pet, don't you fret. Tam will get it back for us.'

Gritting his teeth, Tam managed to bite back the insulting words he was about to issue. Just then he heard Doogy hail him from afar. 'Will ye come an' take a look at this, mate?'

Striding off along the fringe, Tam came upon his companion some distance away. Doogy was swatting flies from the grisly site. Holding a paw over his mouth, he muttered, 'Och, the poor beasts, ah reckon there's little more than their heads left. 'Tis an awful thing tae see, Tam.'

His friend paced carefully about, identifying the remains. 'There's Chamog an' Eltur, Birno an' Rofal, this one could be

35

Girtan. Well, that's the other five captains. The rest look like singers an' flute players. See these two, Doogy – they couldn't have had more'n fourteen summers between 'em. We're dealin' with the lowest kind of barbarian brutes here. These squirrels have all been eaten! See, there's bones'n'fur scattered everywhere!'

Grim-faced and shaken, the two warriors returned to the main gathering.

Araltum asked peevishly, 'Did you find my Royal Standard? Was it damaged or torn? Your Drayqueen spent a lot of hard work making that bann–'

The king's back slammed hard against a tree under Tam's furious charge. Araltum's eyes popped fearfully wide as the warrior squirrel had him by the throat, his dirk blade almost in his mouth.

Tam's voice was ice-cold. 'Ye vile little worm! A score an' a half o' yore creatures are lyin' murdered, an' all ye can do is whine about a stupid flag. I should slay ye an' leave ye here to rot with these poor creatures!'

This statement seemed to cheer Doogy Plumm up no end. 'Go to it, Tam. Carve the wee lardbucket's head off!'

The warrior flung Araltum down on his fat tail, casting him a hate-laden glance. 'I'm sore tempted, Doogy, but that'd only make us as bad as the vermin who killed our comrades. The only thing stoppin' me is that I pledged my sword an' my oath to Araltum, aye, an' ate his bread in good faith!'

Massaging his throat, the king rose, sneering. 'That's right, Rakkety Tam MacBurl. I'm still your king, and you're still bound to obey me!'

Doogy drew his claymore, grinning like a disobedient young one. 'Ach, 'twas a silly thing we did, but ah've a mind tae alter the rules. Let me slay him for ye, Tam.'

The warrior placed his dirk across his friend's blade. 'Put up yore sword, Doogy Plumm. Without our word, we're nothin'. Araltum, what would it take to release us from our bond to ye?'

The king smirked. 'Why should I release my two best warriors? What price could you two offer? Hah, you're nothing but a pair of raggedy-backed swordbeasts. No! You shall serve me unto death as your oath decreed.'

Idga Drayqueen interrupted, speaking imperiously. 'We'll free you if you return our Royal Standard to us!'

Araltum stamped his footpaw down hard. 'Never!'

Idga turned upon her husband. 'You mean you'll let those vermin steal away our lovely banner – the one I worked my paws to the bone to make? Oh, you brute!'

Doogy shook his head sadly, sympathizing with her. 'Och, yer right there, mah Queen, after all the braw work ye put intae that flag. Yer hoosban' mustn't care a whit for ye, the heartless wee beastie!'

Araltum put a paw around Idga's shoulders. 'But I do care for you, my love. Don't upset yourself so!'

The drayqueen shook off his paw and began weeping. 'Go away, you nasty creature! I'll never speak to you again if that's all the thanks I get for a full winter's stitching. You're despicable!'

Doogy patted the queen's paw comfortingly. 'Aye, there's nought worse tae have than a despicable king, marm. 'Tis a wonder how ye put up wi' him.'

Araltum slumped against a tree. Knowing he was beaten, he glared sullenly at Tam and Doogy. 'All right, all right! Bring back our Royal Standard and I will release you both from your bonds. Once that banner is back here with us, you can go to the very stones of Hellgates for all I care, both of you. But not until then!'

Tam stared hard at the royal couple. 'We have your word?'

They nodded, speaking together. 'You have our word!'

Doogy looked north across the clifftops. 'Then we'll no' be hangin' aroond here tae waste time. Are ye ready, Tam?'

The warrior squirrel sheathed his dirk. 'Aye, as ready as I'll ever be. Grab some vittles, Doogy, an' let's away.'

Idga forced a smile at Tam. 'Er, when will we expect to see you both back with our standard?'

Tam shrugged. 'A season or two, who knows? If we don't return, ye'll know the vermin have slain an' eaten us.'

Araltum stepped back, horrified. 'Eaten you?'

Doogy winked cheerfully at him. 'Aye, eaten us. Go an' take a peek at yore Cap'ns an' singers yonder. Ye'll note there's nought left o' them but their heads an' a few wee scraps o' fur'n'bone. It shouldnae be much bother buryin' them. 'Tis the least ye could do for beasts that served ye well an' died for ye!'

'Whooooahhhhh!' Idga gave a great swooning moan and fainted in a heap.

As Tam and Doogy marched off, their last sight of the despicable royal taskmasters was Araltum trying to heave his wife's considerable bulk upright while courtiers rubbed her paws and dabbed rose water upon her brow.

Tam winked at his friend. 'Ye've a fine way with words, Doogy Plumm, there's no doubt about that!'

His faithful companion's tough, scarred face beamed with pleasure. 'Och, now ye come tae mention it, mah grannie allus said I was a braw silver-tongued beastie. Have ye no' seen me charmin' wee birdies from out the trees?'

Tam shot him a sideways glance. 'No, not yet. Let's see if we can go an' charm the royal flag off those vermin with our blades, my bold Doogy. But first we'll go down to the seaside an' do a spot o' ship-burnin' to cheer ourselves up. Nought like a good fire, eh?'

Late-afternoon sun cast long shadows as they climbed down the cliffs toward the big vessel perched on the tideline rocks. Both were unaware that, through the hole smashed into the forward bow, wickedly glittering eyes were watching them.

6

Arflow revelled in the freedom of the open sea. This was the young sea otter's first journey without the constraints of his parents. To date, his life had been spent in the north-western coastal waters, never venturing far one way or the other. Last spring, Arflow's family had been visited by distant relatives, a small group of sea otters from the southern coast. Arflow enjoyed their company immensely, especially that of the four young ones who were about his age. Sad when his newfound cousins departed at midsummer to return down south, Arflow promised to come and visit them the following spring. At first, his parents would not hear of their only son, not yet fully grown, going off all that way to the southern coast alone. Arflow nevertheless persisted with his request, despite the unlikelihood that his parents would give in. But at the start of this spring, a miracle happened: the birth of a little sea otter maid to his mother. Named Matunda, the baby kept both parents busy night and day; accordingly, Arflow stepped up his pleas to go and visit his cousins. He finally won out one evening when his mother and father were worn out, swum ragged by the antics of little Matunda who, as they complained, was more lively than a sackful of sardines! Arflow's request was granted, but with a hundred provisos, which included the young otter's promise to get the proper rest, navigate by the sun and stars, stick to the coast, make his supplies last and mind his manners with others, plus, of course, all the usual things that mother and father sea otters go on about. He agreed to everything without hesitation.

Arflow had been swimming since early morning. Now, at late noon, the golden orb of the sun had not far to sink before it touched the western horizon – a league and a half past the mountain fortress of Salamandastron. He lay on his back and drifted on the calm surface of the ebbtide, happily reflecting on what a glorious day it was to be young and alive! Arflow looked out to where the waters changed from a light opaque green to a deep aquamarine blue in the west. Though starting to tinge a delicate peach in the distance, the sky was still bright periwinkle blue overhead, dotted with small puffball clouds, their undersides shot gold from sunrays. The young sea otter wriggled with delight at the seabirds wheeling and calling above. He giggled as a cormorant winged nearby, splashing him as it dived headlong into the gentle swell. Sheer exuberance flooded over Arflow. He broke out into a sea otter song which he had learned from his father:

'Sing hi yo ho, let every creature know,
I'll swim where e'er I choose to go,
on rippling wave or tidal flow.
Oooooooh, no lark's as blithe as me!

Sing hey make way, let nobeast bar my way.
To frowning faces I will say,
cheer up and smile now, come and play.
Oooooooh, be happy on this day!

Don't cry, 'tis I who laughs at misery,
so young, so full of life and free,
with all the seas to roam and see.

Oh, Moooother Nature, list to me, I thank thee
    gratefully!'

Arflow dived, swooped up and sprang from the water,
throwing himself high into the air and landing back with a
resounding splash. Then he heard the drum. *Boom boom!*
Boom boom! Boom bumpitty bumpitty boom!

He peered landward at a group of creatures marching
along the shoreline. Arflow barely distinguished the distant figures as hares. They were banging a big drum and
singing a marching song as they strutted along the beach.
Raising a webbed paw, he shouted a greeting, despite
knowing they were too far off to hear. That did not bother
the young sea otter: they were happy, and so was he.

Suddenly, without warning, things went amiss. In the
distance, other dark shapes, a host of them, appeared. Who
they were, Arflow could not tell. For a moment, the hares
tried to resist the newcomers, but they were outnumbered
by more than ten to one. The invaders surrounded them
and hurled themselves upon the small band of hares.
Screams and agonized cries rent the air, accompanied by
shouts and howls. Even from that distance the sea otter
could hear them.

Boom! The drum sounded once. Then there was silence as
the dark shapes settled on the fallen hares like crows upon
carrion. Arflow did not know what was happening, but he
sensed that something very bad and wicked had taken
place on the shore. Shock and worry beset him after the
terrifying swiftness of the incident.

Recovering himself hurriedly, he turned on his stomach
and altered course immediately. Cleaving the sea like a
blade through satin, Arflow sped back in the direction of
Salamandastron. Whatever had occurred, he felt it impera-
tive that Lady Melesme, the Badger Ruler of the mountain,
should know. All creatures who were not vermin looked to
the fortress and its Badger Ruler, who commanded the

army of hares known, and famed, as the Long Patrol. They were sworn to protect the western coastlands, and all about, from harm by foebeasts. Urgency had replaced Arflow's previous euphoria. The scenic glories of evening's approach and the joy he had been revelling in were forgotten. He concentrated all his energy into swimming, faster than he had ever moved, towards the distant mountain which stood in the fading light like a giant, purple-shaded sentinel, guarding the shores.

7

Springtime had made its welcome presence felt at Redwall Abbey. Brother Demple, the skilful mouse who managed most of the cultivation besides serving as Abbey Beekeeper, was arranging seedlings in the vegetable gardens. Everybeast knew that Demple possessed a knowledge of the earth and an unsurpassed talent for growing things. Hitheryon Jem was helping Demple to bed and water the tiny plants. Both creatures knelt on moss-padded sacking, carefully arranging drills of scallions.

The Abbey Gardener watched Jem, nodding approvingly at the old hedgehog's work. 'You like doing this, don't you, friend?'

Wiping soil from his trowel, Jem straightened his back. 'Indeed I do, Brother. I often think I'd have done better as a gardener, instead o' bein' just a pawloose rover. Tell me, why've ye kept some o' these scallion sprigs back instead of plantin' 'em all at once?'

Demple bedded another seedling in, covering its delicate roots. 'Because they'd all grow at once, and we'd have a wonderfully useless bumper harvest. No, Jem, 'tis better to plant vegetables at different times. Then, when we need some, they can be fresh-picked, leaving us room to grow more. Otherwise, our storerooms would be overfilled.'

He waved a paw across the vegetable gardens. 'See, beet-roots, leeks, lettuce, carrot, onion and cress. But never too many growing at one time, that's the trick.'

The wise mouse waved his trowel at two Dibbuns who looked as if they were ready to dash right through his produce. 'Be careful to walk around the border! Now, how can I help you two rascals, eh?'

Demple remarked under his breath to Jem, 'Sometimes I wish we could plant our babes like seedlings. At least it would stop them from charging through my drills like little ploughs.'

Mimsie and Mudge skirted the plants, calling out, 'Bruvver Dimples, Fry Glis sended us. We gotta fetch herbers an' 'tatoes an' coddyflowers, cos he's makin' a veggible bake wivva crust on it!'

The kindly Brother smiled. 'Stop there, me and Mister Jem will take you to the storeroom to get them.'

Holding the Dibbuns's paws, Jem and Demple walked the babes back to the Abbey. Jem raised his spiky eyebrows at the molebabe. 'Mudge, you should've gone to the stores in the first place. Our stuff isn't ready t'be picked yet.'

Mudge gave him a cheerful grin. 'Hurr, us'ns bee's only h'infants, zurr. Ow'm uz apposed to know that?'

Jem looked down at the velvety little head. 'Didn't the Friar tell you to get his supplies from the storerooms? I'll wager he did.'

Mudge smote his brow with a tiny paw. 'Moi gudderness, so he'm did, zurr! But oi aspeck uz furgot to amember thart. Us'ns only got likkle brains, so uz h'offen furgets all kinds uv fings.'

Jem nodded sympathetically. 'I know exactly wot you mean, mate. It happens to us old 'uns, too. I get like that a lot lately.'

They were getting the supplies out of the storeroom when Abbot Humble entered. 'Hello! What are you two rascals up to, eh?'

44

Mimsie scowled. 'Us not rakkles, we get veggibles for Glis!'

Humble patted her head. 'Oh, right, there's a good little maid. I forgot, we're having a special supper tonight to honour our moles. Should be good fun, eh, Demple?'

Molebabe Mudge wagged a stern paw at Humble. 'Nought funny abowt ee supper. Et bee's a gurt honner to bee ee moler, loike oi!'

Humble shook Mudge's tiny paw. 'My apologies. I'm sure it is a great honour to be a mole, and you, my friend, are a shining example of a wonderful molebabe!'

Mudge scratched his snout and shuffled his footpaws, a sure sign of embarrassment displayed by Dibbun moles. 'Noice uv ee to say so, h'Abbot zurr. Thankee!'

As the babes continued selecting their supplies, Humble remarked to his wandering cousin, 'Jem, I was wondering if you could recall the lines that Askor related to you, the rhyme about the Walking Stone. Do you think you could remember his exact words?'

Pursing his lips, Jem stared at the ceiling, as if seeking inspiration there. 'Hmm, somethin' about the sun fallin' from the sky an' dancin'. No, I'm sorry, I seem to 'ave forgotten it.'

Mudge left off nibbling a sweet young carrot. 'Hurr hurr, you'm furgettin' to amember jus' loike oi. Yurr Jem, you'm a dozy ole pudden 'ead, hurr hurr!'

Jem made a stern face at the molebabe. 'Don't be so cheeky to yore elders, ye young rip, an' leave those carrots alone!' He turned to the Abbot. 'Why do ye wish to know the rhyme?'

Humble shrugged. 'Just because it's a puzzle, I suppose. The idea of a Walking Stone intrigues me.'

Jem selected a cauliflower and plucked off a few of its outer stalks. 'Hmm, that puzzle had me wonderin' too, Cousin. Ahah, wait a moment! Screeve wrote it down at the meeting in Cavern Hole. She did, I remember now!'

Humble's eyes gleamed with pleasure. 'What a splendid

Recorder we have. Once Screeve makes another copy, Brother Gordale and I will get down to studying it. Mayhaps you and Walt would like to help us?'

Jem agreed instantly. 'Aye, we'd love to 'elp out. Me'n Walt dearly likes a good riddle to solve, though we ain't learned as you Abbeybeasts. Shall we be startin' today?'

The Abbot shook his head. 'Oh, good gracious no! We've got to attend the mole festivities tonight. All our Redwallers will be rehearsing their party pieces. I hope we shall see you and Walt doing something – a song, a dance, a poem. Even a trick would be acceptable.'

Jem scratched his spikes thoughtfully. 'Well, it's been awhile since we was called upon t'do such things, but I'm sure we can oblige. I'll go an' speak to Walt if'n you'll excuse me, Cousin.'

Wandering Walt was down in the cellars with Foremole Bruffy and his crew. They were drinking daisybud-and-dockleaf tonic whilst tracing back through their ancestry. This was a pursuit beloved of moles. Though they were never quite truthful and were given to inventing tales, it was all in good fun.

Ole Jarge, an ancient, grey-backed mole armed with an ear trumpet, pulled a series of bark sketches from his belt wallet. He pointed to each in turn. 'Naow, this 'un wurry Burby Longseason, ee'm wurr moi gurt-gurt-granfer's gurt-granfer. They'm sayed Burby cudd fall in ee barrel of 'tober ale at brekkist an' drink ee'm way owt afore supper, hurr aye!'

Laughing uproariously, the molecrew stamped the floor with their hefty footpaws, evidently vastly amused at anybeast who could perform this feat. They refilled their tankards and drank deep, waiting for a mole to cap Ole Jarge's tale.

Jem felt he was intruding on the all-mole gathering. He backed out, politely tugging his headspikes. 'Er, you'll excuse me, friends. Beg pardon . . .'

A fat, homely molemum bustled him to a seat. 'Nay nay,

zurr Jem. You'm welcum as ee bumbly bee in ee rose garding. Set ee daown, ee'm 'edgehog bee's only ee mole with a spoiky 'ead!'

Some of the molecrew fell over backwards with laughter at this remark. Jem found himself seated next to Walt, a large tankard of the fizzy tonic thrust into his paw. It tasted odd but rather pleasant, and it made Jem become quite giggly.

The moles continued with their stories. One jolly-looking fellow took the floor. 'Hurr, moi ole granmum, she'm lived close by ee gurt mountain. So oi sez to 'er, "Granmum, 'ow long've ee lived yurr?" An' she'm sayed, "Since this yurr mountain bee'd only a likkle hill. Oi jus' woked upp one mornin' an' et'd growed thurr in ee noight!" '

The moles were now in paroxyms of laughter, rolling about on the floor and gripping their sides. Jem giggled helplessly, even though most of what was being said went right over his head. Clearly, the jolly atmosphere was having a marked effect upon him.

Walt tapped his friend's shoulder. 'Bee's you'm wanten to see oi, Jem?'

Wiping away mirthful tears, the hedgehog managed to control himself. 'Aye, Walt. My cousin the Abbot wants to know if you'n I would like to 'elp him an' Gordale solve that puzzle Askor gave us. But not tonight, we'll do it tomorrow.'

Walt nodded vigourously. 'Boi 'okey, us'ns will, Jem. We'm allus been fond o' rigglers an puzzlers!'

Satisfied that his friend was willing to lend assistance, Jem withdrew from the cellars, leaving the molecrew to their yarn telling. As he went out the door, he heard Walt setting up more gales of merriment with his contribution.

'Yurr, you'm knows moi mate, Ole Jem. Well, ee'm got a cuzzen who'm bee's his Father, hurr hurr hurr!'

Giggling and chuckling, Jem made his way to the room that he and Walt had been allotted for their stay at the Abbey. The travelling hedgehog, fond of any sort of party, was eagerly looking forward to the evening's event. Jem sorted through his belongings to choose something appropriate for the festivities. After the long time he'd spent wandering with only Walt for company, this celebration with so many of his Redwaller friends was very welcome.

That evening, Burlop Cellarhog and Sister Armel stood guarding the door to Cavern Hole. It was to remain closed until Foremole Bruffy gave the word. A line formed along the corridor and down the stairs. Redwallers accompanying Dibbuns, all dressed in their festive best, waited, though not too patiently. There were cheers as Abbot Humble came down the stairs with his cousin Jem. Humble was garbed in a pale-green habit girdled with a thick, cream-hued cord. Jem had on a red tunic and a short cape of blue, silky fabric. Everybeast shuffled sideways to make way for them. Humble solemnly tapped three times upon the door.

Foremole's voice sounded from within. 'Who'm bee's a-knocken' on this yurr door – be ee a moler?'

The Abbot answered as custom required. 'No mole am I, but a Redwaller true, Father of this Abbey. I am come here with my friends, good creatures all. We are here to honour our trusty moles!'

Opening the door wide, Foremole Bruffy stood on the threshold. He had on a flowing cloak of rich brown velvet and a crown fashioned from buttercups, daisies and pale-blue milkwort. In his right paw he bore a wand of willow branch with fuzzy catkins growing from it. Smiling from ear to ear, the mole chieftain intoned a traditional poem.

'Yurr bee's moi 'eart, an' yurr bee's moi paw.
Wellcum, an' henter ee thru this door.
Friends of'n ee bee's friends o' moine,
us'll all 'ave ee gurt ole toime!'

The Redwallers flooded into Cavern Hole, which was lit by coloured lanterns and decorated with spring flowers and streamers of coloured ferns. Moss-padded wall ledges provided seating all around. Three long tables were placed in an open square to leave room for the performers.

A barrel of last summer's strawberry fizz was on tap, along with October Ale, pale cider and rosehip cordial. The food was mainly good solid mole fare – deeper'n'ever turnip'n'tater'n'beetroot pie, leek and celery soup, spring salads and several enormous cheese-crusted loaves stuffed with chopped hazelnuts and mushrooms. For dessert there were inevitable mounds of hunnymoles, bowls of candied chestnuts and a huge, dark fruitcake decorated with preserved plums and damsons.

No sooner was the supper served than the entertainment commenced. To the music of flutes, tiny drums and a peculiar instrument called a molecordion, the small band struck up a paw-tapping family quadrille. Two rings were formed – the outer one by molemums and grandmums, the inner one by Dibbuns holding sticks. The elders began sticking out first their right, then their left footpaws, whooping and whirling around in a clockwise circle. The Dibbuns circled in the opposite direction, their little faces concentrating seriously as they tapped the floor skilfully between the elders' footpaws.

The sound of *tap tap tap, rap rap rap* resounded as the pace sped up. Gruff whoops and infant giggles rang out, the sticks missing footpaws by a hair'sbreadth. Clapping in time to the dance, a group of fine bass and baritone moles began singing.

'Oi pray ee zurr doant 'it moi paw,
furr if'n ee do, et will be sore.
Thump ee stick down on ee floor,
an' us'ns will be 'arpy.
Rumpitty tum ho rumpitty tum,
moles bee's 'aven so much fun.
No likkle 'un will strike 'is mum,
cos they'm luvs 'em so gurtly!'

49

Twice more they danced, each time tapping and rapping more rapidly until the sticks and paws moved in a blur. The entire ensemble took a bow to hearty applause. Then there were calls for a time-honoured request. 'Foremole, do the poem with Abbot Humble. Do the poem!'

Humble and Bruffy, both modest creatures, were coaxed out on to the floor, shaking their heads and protesting.

'Oh no, please, surely you don't want to hear that old thing, do you?'

'Burr, oi doant thinks as 'ow oi can amember ee wurds!'

In the end, however, they had to concede to the roars of encouragement. Foremole stood up on a stool, striking a noble pose. Humble circled him slowly and began reciting.

'Here am I, the Abbot of all Redwall,
I rule my Abbey with voice and paw.
And who are you, sir, standing there?
Pray tell me now, for I'm not sure!'

Foremole spread his paws wide and shouted, 'Oi'm a mole!'

Everybeast chorused, 'He's a mole!'

The Abbot looked surprised, then continued.

'I have a Friar who's an excellent cook,
'tis said he wrote a recipe book,
and two stout mice, our bells to toll,
and you, forsooth, what is your role?'

Foremole looked at the audience as he repeated, 'Oi'm a mole!'

The onlookers shouted even louder, 'He's a mole!'

Humble shook his head, as if he had not heard.

'I have a Keeper who guards our gate,
and another who tends our bees,

and a healer to care for any who ail,
but you're not one of these!'

Foremole merely pointed to himself as the crowd howled,
'He's a mole!'

The Abbot scratched his headspikes and looked bemused.

'We've a Cellarhog who brews our drink,
and a Recorder with both quill and ink,
and guards who pace our Abbey wall,
so what do you do, tell me all?'

Foremole smiled at his audience, who rose to their paws
with a deafening roar. 'He's a mole!'

Before the Abbot could reply, Foremole Bruffy held up
his paw commandingly. Silence, apart from stifled giggles,
fell. He came down off the stool and faced Humble boldly.

'You'm got summ faithful creatures, zurr,
but none as true h'as oi.
'Twas moles built cellars under yurr,
an' if'n ee arsks these uthers whoi,
they'm'll tell ee gurtly wot's moi role . . .'

The Redwallers, who had been waiting for this final line
with unconcealed glee, stood and bellowed en masse, 'Cos
there's nobeast can dig a hole like a mole!'

Humble and Foremole bowed and sat down to wild applause. Smiling and shaking paws, they refused pleas for an
encore.

Outside, the spring night was tranquil, with scarcely a
breeze to ruffle the leaves. Twinkling pinpoints of stars
dusted dark velvet skies. In solitary splendour, an apricot-
hued crescent moon hung over Redwall Abbey, casting

gentle shadows on the ancient stone. From the woven tapestry, the figure of Martin the Warrior stood gazing out between flickering sconces, watching over his citadel of safety and friendship. Whilst far off to the southwest, murder and evil were being committed by a band of vermin, led by a strange beast that had come from the lands of ice beyond the great sea.

8

Two ermine who had been left behind to repair the big ship
upon the rocks watched Rakkety Tam and Doogy Plumm
advancing through the dusk. In the ship's bow, the vermin
hid, peering through the hole which had been smashed
through the hull on its waterline. It was not difficult to see
the two squirrels, since they were both carrying lighted
torches. Neither of the ermine knew anything about ship
repairing, but they were forced to comply, knowing that
disobedience to their savage leader meant instant death.
From the gloom of their hiding place, they watched the
squirrels move closer.

Drawing his sickle-curved sword, the more hefty of the
two ermine licked the blade, grinning wickedly. His companion, a tall, thin beast, whispered a warning. 'Don't slay
'em straight off. They lives on the coast 'ere prob'ly. Two like
those'd be bound t'know about pluggin' the 'ole in this craft
an' makin' 'er seaworthy.'

The hefty one sniggered. 'Aye, mate, good idea. Why
should we do all the toil? Let these oafs fix the ship first,
then we'll skin 'em, nice'n'slow. I claim the liddle fat 'un.
'Tis long seasons since I tasted a fine plump squirrel.'

His companion nodded his head. 'Right, I'll take the

other. Huh, wonder wot those two idiots are doin', wan-derin' round the shore at this hour?'

Eyes shining with anticipation, the hefty ermine mur-mured, 'Who cares? Nice of 'em t'bring fire along. We won't need t'put flint to steel'n'tinder to make a roastin' fire.'

Moving closer to the edge of the hole in the ship's hull, he whispered to his partner, 'Let's go an' welcome 'em!'

As Tam and Doogy reached the ship, the two ermine sidled out on to the rocks with drawn swords. Doogy's paw dropped to the basket hilt of his claymore. 'Weel now, will ye lookit, we've got company!'

Tam slid the dirk behind his shield, hiding it from view. He raised his voice, addressing the vermin cheerily. 'A good evenin' to ye, sirs. Is this your vessel? Dearie me, in a bit of a mess, ain't it?'

The hefty ermine swaggered forward. Tossing his sword in the air, he caught it skilfully. 'Aye, she's got a hole in the bows, as ye can see. But it ain't nothin' that you two bump-kins can't fix up fer us, is it?'

Doogy smiled disarmingly. Ignoring the ermine, he addressed Tam. 'Will ye no' listen tae that saucy auld wind-bag! He thinks we're ship repairers!'

Tam wedged his torch between two rocks. 'He's certainly a hardfaced rogue, Doogy. He called us bumpkins. I think we'll have to repair his manners.'

The thin ermine brandished his sword, snarling, 'Shut yore mouths an' surrender those weapons. D'ye know who yore talkin' to? We're two warriors who serve Gulo the Savage. Do as yore told an' we might let ye live!'

Doogy stuck his torch alongside Tam's. 'Och, ye great string o' seaweed, ah dinna care who yore Chieftain is. Nobeast talks tae Wild Doogy Plumm like that!'

Without further ado, a fight to the death commenced. The thin one swung his blade at Doogy's head, but the little Highlander moved with a speed which belied his girth. Leaping forward, he swung his claymore in a single, mighty arc. It smashed the blade from the vermin's paw, following through across his throat and despatching him with a single blow. The hefty one closed with Tam, trying to spike him from overhead with a downward sweep of the curved blade. Tam whipped his shield up over his head, deflecting the blow. In the same instant, Tam's dirk took the shocked vermin through the heart in an upward thrust.

Showing no great concern, Doogy enquired as he cleaned his blade, 'Did he do any damage tae yore buckler, Tam?'

After inspecting the shield's centre boss, Tam shrugged. 'Only a wee dent. This old shield's taken enough of them in its time. Let's search the ship in case there's any more foe-beasts lurkin' about.'

Climbing through the rift in the hull, they held up their torches and gazed around. Doogy pulled a face, covering his nose with his tail. 'Land's sakes, Tam, the smell in here's enough tae knock a body flat! Ah wonder who Gulo the Savage is – yon vermin spoke his name as though we ought tae know him.'

Tam bent to examine a locker, which proved to be empty. 'That's the one Driltig mentioned. He'll be their leader, the beast who goes around eatin' other creatures. He's the lad we'll have to meet up with if we're to get Araltum's banner back.'

Grimacing with distaste, Doogy turned over some mouldy seabird feathers and fishbones with his bladepoint. 'Aye, well mind ye speak tae him politely. Ach, there's nae much of any use here, Tam. Let's be rid o' this stinkin' hulk!'

Exiting the ship, they heaved the slain ermine carcasses through the holed bow, tossing the lighted torches in after them. Night was fully fallen as Tam and Doogy watched flames and smoke rising. Fire shot up the rigging and through the sails like a hungry beast, sending sparks crackling into the dark sky. Using the light, Tam cast about until he found pawprints.

'They must've doubled back this way after raiding the groves. There's a whole army here, headin' off north along the shore. Well, Doogy, do we follow 'em now or leave it until dawn?'

Sitting down on some dry sand, Doogy held up his paws to the blaze. ' 'Tis a shame tae be wastin' sich a braw fire, Tam. Let's take a wee bite o' supper an' sleep here, where 'tis warm an' upwind o' the sparks, eh?'

Supper was merely a few apples and some cheese, which they stuck on the points of their swords, toasting them in the glowing prow timbers.

Having eaten, Doogy wrapped his cloak about him, grunting contentedly. 'Mercy me, aren't we livin' the life o' kings, Tam. A braw fire in the hearth, a floor o' sand, a roof o' sky an' toasted apples'n'cheese – what more could ye ask for, eh?'

Tam wiped melted cheese from his swordtip, imitating his friend's thick Highland brogue. 'Och, yer easy pleased, mah wee Doogy. We've no' got a pretty maid tae sing us tae sleep!'

Doogy gathered a swathe of his cloak about his face like a headscarf. He began twittering in what he fondly imagined was a maidenly voice. 'Och, ye saucy great beastie! Dinna fret, ah'll sing ye a wee lullaby!'

Tam groaned in mock despair. 'Spare me that, Doogy. Ye look like a boiled pudden, an' ye sound like a toad trapped under a rock!'

He lay back and tried to sleep whilst his friend serenaded him in a gruff bass voice which bore no resemblance to any young maid's.

'Oh a beetle maid sat in a glade,
an' she lamented sadly,
"Mah love's gone off tae fight the bees,
ah'm feared that he'll fare badly.
Those bumbly bees are fierce wee things,

wi' stripey shirts an' wee small wings.
Their bottoms carry nasty stings,
they're feisty aye an' buzzy!"

Och, mah Berty Beetle looked so stern,
he didnae think 'twas funny,
when ah said that ah'd no' kiss him,
'til he brought me some honey.
He took his club from off the shelf,
an' said tae me so gravely,
"Ah'll fetch ye honey back the noo,"
an' he marched off right bravely.

'Twas some lang time 'ere he returned,
mah poor love injured sorely.
Ah spread him wi' some liniment,
an' listened tae his story.

Alas, poor me tae love a fool.
Did naebeast tell this fellow,
those bees that don't wear fuzzy shirts,
are wasps striped black an' yellow?

Wi' a hey an' a hoe an' a lacky doodle don,
midst all this shameful fuss.
'Tis not just birds who live in trees,
an' not just bees that buzz!'

Tam was snoring before Doogy finished his ballad. The
sturdy Highland squirrel glanced huffily at his companion.
'Well, thank ye for those sounds of appreciation. Ah'll bid
ye a guid night, an' hope that some sparks get blown on to
yore unfeelin' tail!'

Scraping sand together into a pillow shape, Doogy laid
down his head, allowing slumber to soothe his injured
dignity.

Two hours before dawn, both the friends were sound
asleep, wrapped in their cloaks and warmed by the glowing

57

embers not far away. Neither had time to wake, or even stir, when dark shapes pounced on them, swiftly cudgelling them senseless. Tam and Doogy were bundled up in their cloaks and lashed on to long spearpoles, then hurried off north along the beach.

9

Driftail and his gang of eight were all River Rats, robbers and bullies, no strangers to violence, assassins all. They scoured the rivers and streams far and wide, stopping wherever the pickings looked good. Their strategy was simple – they hid among the waterways, ambushing defenceless travellers, lone wanderers and small families. Any creature who could be easily intimidated became their victim. Of late, life had not been very lucky to the River Rats; prey was seemingly thin on the ground. They were forced to work for a living, fishing the waters and grubbing along the banks for berries, fruit and any edible vegetation. At the moment, they had camped on the inlet of a high-banked broadstream, which wended its way over the heath and flatlands, southwest of Mossflower's vast woodlands.

Dawn was rising as Driftail climbed the sloping bankside to watch for movement amid the scrub and gorse. Behind him, the others were lighting a fire and scratching about to put together some kind of breakfast. Four were trawling the waters for stray fish whilst the others gathered wood and dug for roots. Driftail's stomach gurgled sourly; he had not eaten for a day and a night. Rising spring dawn in all its beauty was lost on the rat leader. He had seen sunrises come and go, most of them hungry ones of late.

Suddenly, his keen eye caught a stirring. Wandering about a flat rocky patch, a stone curlew strode warily in pursuit of insects. The bird pecked at something, lost it and called its soft plaintive cry. *Coooooeeeee!*

Driftail could not believe his good fortune. Unwinding the sling from about his lean waist, he selected a few pebbles from his pouch. Crawling stealthily along on his stomach, he tried getting closer to the curlew for an easy shot. The bird froze momentarily, then began walking again, as though it sensed it was being hunted. It paced off in the opposite direction from Driftail, not yet frightened enough to leave the flat rocks where the insects lived. Driftail moved forward a little more, loading a pebble into his sling. Then he crouched and began whirling it. The curlew, immediately hearing the disturbance, did a short hop-skip and winged off into the air. The River Rat leader let the sling wrap around his paw, mentally cursing the lost breakfast. Just then, spying a white fox, he fell flat amid the scrub and watched it approach from the west, oblivious to his presence.

Driftail swiftly backshuffled to the streambank. Sliding down the side, he hissed urgently to his gang, 'T'row sand onna fire quick! Arm you'selfs, a lonebeast comes diss way!'

A moment later, all mundane activities had ceased. The rat gang – armed with a motley assortment of weaponry: broken knives, sharpened sticks and stone-topped clubs – crouched below the banktop behind their leader.

Runneye, a rat with a leaking squint, peered over the rim at their intended prey. 'Worra sorta beast be that 'un, Drift?'

Driftail grabbed Runneye's tail and pulled him down. 'Dat's a foxer, funny white 'un. Gorra curvity sword anna likkle bag o' vikkles too!'

One of the gang ventured a peek over the banktop. 'Mebbe dat foxer be good wirra sword, an' not frykind?'

Driftail hauled the speaker down and cuffed him scornfully. 'Gerraravit! On'y one foxer, they's lots of us, we'll lay 'im flat! Dat curvity sword an' de nice belt wot foxer's wearin', dey mine, y'hear?'

He slitted his eyes, glaring fiercely at the gang until they lowered their gaze. Knowing the prizes were his without question, he loaded his sling with a rock the size of his paw. 'We all shares de vikkles out.'

The white fox was close to the bankside when Driftail popped up and launched his stone, striking the fox on the side of his jaw. He did not fall but clapped a paw to his face, staggering about half stunned.

Driftail howled triumphantly, 'Quicknow, gerrim!'

The gang charged out and mobbed the white fox, dragging him down. A blow from Runneye's club finished the job, knocking the fox unconscious. They bundled him down the bank to the stream's edge.

Driftail dashed down the slope in time to kick one of the gang who was wielding a rusty knife. 'Mud'ead, not killim yet, I want words wid diss one!'

Whilst the rats fought over the fox's small ration bag, Driftail relieved his captive of the belt and sickle sword. Grabbing some tough vines, he bound the prisoner's paws together and slung water over the fox's head to revive him.

It took awhile for the strange creature to come around. He struggled briefly with his bonds, then looked up at the ugly, grinning faces surrounding him.

Runneye sniggered nastily. 'Heeheehee, gotcha self inna big trouble now, pretty white foxer!'

Elbowing Runneye out of the way, Driftail leaned down and drew the sickle-shaped sword. 'Wot name be yer called, foxer?'

The captive glared at Driftail but maintained his silence.

The River Rat tapped the point of the blade on the fox's chest. 'Ya be dumb, or jus' shoopid, eh? I be Chief round 'ere! When I axe question, yew answer quick, or I skin yer slow. Wherra ye commed from, foxer? Speak!'

61

The prisoner stared levelly, unafraid of the rat. 'From the land of ice, across the great sea.'

Driftail had never heard of or seen a great sea. He kicked the fox savagely. 'Ha, fibba lie! How yew comed, who yew comed wid – eh, eh?'

The white fox replied flatly, 'We came in a great ship, a band of us one hundred strong, led by Gulo the Savage.'

Driftail sensed a note of contempt in his captive's voice. He kicked the bound fox several times more. Then he strutted around the streambank, doing a bad imitation of the fox's voice for the benefit of his gang. 'Ho yes, I come onna big shippen, wid a strong band of hunnerd, an' Glugo der Sanvage. Hah, we be scared, eh?'

Hoots of derision came from the River Rat gang, taking a cue from their chief's disbelief of the fox's explanation.

One of the rats began pretending that he was all of a tremble. He knelt down by the bound fox, wailing piteously, 'Waaaaah, I be reel frykenned. Save me, save me!'

The fox waited for the jeering to die down before he replied, 'So ye should be feared, stupid fool!'

Driftail struck him across the face with the flat of his sword. 'Yew gorra smart tongue, foxer. Afore I chop it off, tell me, where be all dese hunnerd beast an' yore big Glugo now, eh?'

For the first time since his capture, the white fox smiled. He stared over Driftail's shoulder at the top of the bank. 'Right behind you, rat!'

Boom! Boom! Boom! Boom! Driftail and his gang whirled around at the sound. White foxes and ermine, all armed to the fangs, lined the banktop. Two of them bore a large elaborate banner between them; another two were positioned on each side of an ornate drum. Standing between them, beating the drum, stood a beast straight out of nightmare – Gulo the Savage. He exuded power and ferocity. With eyes glittering insanely and saliva dripping from his bared fangs, he struck the drum one more time. *Boom!* As he pointed the drumstick at the rats, his army swept down on them, chanting, 'Gulo! Gulo! Gulo! Gulo!'

Petrified with fright, the small River Rat gang was swiftly surrounded. This army looked more vicious and numerous than they could imagine. Gulo stalked past them disdainfully, followed by two of his captains – a white fox, Shard, and an ermine, Dirig – and four guards. Further up the bank, they set the stolen standard up and laid the drum flat, where Gulo could sit on it.

Closely guarded, the River Rats were forced to sit on the stream edge, well away from Gulo. They were left to ponder their fate in silence. Anybeast who tried to look up, or whisper, was soundly beaten with spearbutts. After a while, Zerig, the white fox whom they had held captive, came among them.

He seized Driftail by the ears, dragging him free of the rest. Yanking the belt from the rat leader and retrieving his sword, he gestured upstream. 'Lord Gulo will see thee now!'

Now that a fire had been lit for him, Gulo perched on the rim of the drum, holding a bulrush stalk over the flames. Spitted on it was the very curlew which had eluded Driftail but had not been so lucky when one of Gulo's ermine had brought it down with a well-aimed arrow. Not bothering to have the bird plucked, Gulo was roasting it. A rank stench of burning feathers hung on the air. The wolverine savage glanced up as Zerig thrust Driftail into his presence. The four guards shoved the rat into a kneeling position within reach of Gulo, who continued his cooking as he eyed the trembling River Rat. Gulo the Savage was well aware that he created this effect in lesser beasts.

Driftail's eyes began flicking back and forth. Betraying his fear, he almost leapt up at the sound of Gulo's harsh, grating tones. 'What are ye doing around here, rat? What name do ye go by?'

Driftail strove to keep the shrillness of panic out of his

voice. 'We lives onna water, fish an' get roots to eat. I be called Driftail . . . Lord.'

The rat's voice faltered as Gulo stared at him. Taking the curlew from the fire, Gulo tested it with a long, sharp claw. 'Driftail, eh? Ye ever see one like me passing hereabouts?'

The rat shook his head vigourously. 'No, no, never see'd one like you afore round 'ere – on me life, no!'

After pulling the bird off its spit, Gulo took a bite, his wicked fangs ripping through burning feathers and bone into the still raw meat. Without warning, he lashed out with the thick bulrush spit, whipping it into Driftail's face as he roared, 'You lie, rat! Where is the Walking Stone? Speak!'

Tears spilled from Driftail's eyes as he nursed his stinging face. 'Lord, I not lie. Wot be Walkin' Stone?'

The bulrush whistled through the air, again and again, each time followed by Driftail's pitiful screeching. Gulo the Savage threw aside the broken rush stalk. Digging his claws into the rat's narrow chest, he dragged him forward. Bringing his face close to Driftail's ear, Gulo rasped, 'I'll ask ye again, rat, an' this time ye'd best tell me what I want to hear!'

Driftail's face was a mask of frozen agony as his interrogator's claws pierced his hide. Gulo hissed, 'The beast who was like me – when did he pass by here?'

Driftail was not stupid; he knew he had to say something to keep himself alive, so he resorted to a lie. 'Aaaaargh! T'ree, no, four night ago, diss beast pass 'ere, goin' to d'east!'

Gulo tightened his cruel grip. 'The stone he carried with him . . . of what size was it?'

Driftail quickly reckoned to himself that, if anybeast were to carry a stone on a long journey, it could not be too huge. He babbled on, hoping to buy himself some time. 'Not bigga stone, only der size of, er, er, apple!'

Gulo's voice dropped to a whisper. It sounded like a blade scraping across glass. 'Those who lie are bound to die!'

Runneye and the other rats, having heard the screams, huddled together in alarm. The same white fox, Zerig, came with the four guards. He pointed to Runneye. 'Bring this one next!'

Lifted clear off the ground, Runneye was borne away, whimpering, 'I never did no'tink! Driftail be's Chief!'

The River Rat was flung roughly to the ground, landing facedown, not daring to look up. However, he was compelled to obey the voice of his captor.

'Look at me, rat, I am Gulo the Savage!'

One terrified glance from Runneye told him all. The rat was staring into the face of a living nightmare. An image flashed through Runneye's mind of an unfledged sparrow facing a serpent. Gulo's sadistic nature revelled in tormenting those he held helpless. 'What name be ye called, rat?'

Gulo watched, amused by his victim's stammering. 'R . . . R . . . Runneye.'

The wolverine spat out fragments of scorched feather. 'Tell me, what do ye eat?'

It was a strange question. Runneye tried to compose himself and answer as best he could. 'Fishes, bird egg, mebbe bird if'n we catch 'im. Most time jus' der roots'n'berries.'

Gulo leaned forward. The smile that crept over his evil face was not a pleasant sight. Runneye caught a whiff of his fetid breath as the savage whispered, 'Do ye know what is the best of food? Can ye tell me what Gulo and his warriors like to eat, can ye guess?'

Puzzled, the River Rat shook his head. 'No.'

The wolverine bared his awesome fangs. 'We eat anybeast that moves. Birds, fish, snakes . . . rats.'

Runneye's good eye widened as he mouthed the word 'R . . . rats!'

Gulo nodded, his savage eyes glittering insanely. Runneye gave a strangled moan and fainted with fright.

The wolverine kicked the senseless rat. 'Take this weak fool and feed him to my warriors. Bring the next one here!'

The handsome white fox, Shard, who was Gulo's leading

captain, was standing behind the drum. He leaned over and spoke respectfully into his master's ear. 'Methinks we will learn nought from these creatures, Lord. Thy power over them is so terrible that they cannot talk. Soon ye will have slain them all.'

Gulo growled impatiently, but he heeded Shard's counsel. 'So, what would thy method be, Shard?'

The white fox had his answer ready. 'Let me question the rats, Lord. 'Tis clear they have not seen thy brother, nor do they know what the Walking Stone is. Mayhap I will get some information from this one when he revives. Then thou can do what thou wilt with the rest. Just allow me to try, O Savage One.'

Gulo picked a fragment of feather from between his fangs. 'If they know nought of Askor, or my Walking Stone, how can the brainless idiots tell thee anything?'

Shard spoke soothingly to placate his ferocious master. 'One may catch more birds with honey than with stones, Lord. I have my ways. Oftimes creatures will tell me things they thought they did not know. Mayhap the rats know not thy brother or the Stone, but methinks they would know where a beast carrying such treasure would go, to hide it. 'Tis better finding out such information than merely slaying and eating them, eh?'

Gulo had always been a beast of swift action, never of deep thoughts. He paused a moment, weighing his decision before staring at his captain through narrowed eyes. 'Thou art cunning, Shard, but foxes were ever cleverbeasts. Canst thou find out such things for me?'

The fox bowed. 'I live only to serve the mighty Gulo!'

Throughout the remainder of the day the wolverine rested, eating and taking his ease, letting his clever captain take care of future planning and strategy. Gulo knew that if any scheme did not please him, he could change it to suit himself at a single stroke.

Shard sat with his mate, Freeta, who watched him with

calculating eyes. 'So then, is the Savage still devouring everything that moves, or has he started using his brain and not his fangs?'

Shard gave a swift glance around, making sure nobeast was party to their conversation. He tapped his forehead. 'Nay, 'tis I who is Gulo's brain. He is merely a dangerous weapon which must be controlled. I will need thy help to question the rats. We must learn more about this warm land of plenty, this place is a paradise.'

Freeta agreed. 'Aye, far better than the lands of ice beyond the great sea. Tell me what I must do to aid thee, Shard.'

Eventide fell softly over the flatlands in a wash of crimson and purple. Gulo the Savage lounged by his fire, picking over the bones of a pike. He looked up expectantly as Shard approached. The white fox hunkered down, slightly out of the wolverine's reach; it was always wise, Shard had learned through experience, to take such precautions in the presence of Gulo.

Casting aside the pike bones and licking his claws, Gulo half-closed his glittering eyes. 'Well, what news do ye bring me, Captain?'

Shard made his report. 'It is as ye said, O Savage One. The rats know nought of the Stone or thy brother. But in the early winter two beasts, a hedgepig and a burrower, were espied, travelling northeast into the woodlands which lie ahead. Betwixt them they pulled a cart.'

Gulo came instantly alert. 'What was in this cart?'

Shard shrugged eloquently. 'Who could say? They had entered the woodlands before the rats could catch up with them. Those two beasts were the only creatures who moved through this territory since the rats have been here. Mayhaps we could hazard a guess – yon cart could have contained Askor, fleeing thy wrath, hiding from view with the Walking Stone.'

Gulo yawned moodily. 'I grant thee, 'tis possible, but

67

where would they be going, and why should they be hiding Askor and taking him with them, eh?'

The white fox explained his reasoning. 'Ask thyself, what resistance could two lowly creatures put up against a wolverine? As to whence they have gone, the rats all know of such a place. 'Tis a great stone fortress called Redwall. They say many great treasures are stored within its walls. The rat thou ordered slain, Runneye, he knows exactly where 'tis to be found. A good thing we did not slay him, Lord.'

Gulo, ignoring his captain's object lesson, was clearly excited. 'The rat can take us there?'

Shard touched his sword hilt, smiling thinly. 'He loves life too much to refuse.'

Gulo showed his fangs as his claws began working eagerly. Shard noticed the insane light burning in his eyes. 'Ye did well, Shard. We will go to this place of treasures. What did ye say 'tis called?'

The white fox repeated the name. 'Redwall!'

10

Pain was the first thing Rakkety Tam MacBurl wakened to. His head was one massive ache, and his limbs could not move. Upon opening one eye slowly, Tam found himself lying bound to a pole on the floor of a lantern-lit rock cavern. He tried to rise but fell back, the pole clattering against the stone floor.

Behind him, a voice sounded. 'I say, chaps, this tall rascal's awake, wot!'

From someplace close by, Doogy could be heard, regaining his senses volubly. 'Yerrah, ye cowards, sneakin' up on a body an' bludgeonin' him. Get these ropes off mah paws!'

Another voice rang out. 'I do believe the little fat villain's awake too!'

Paws grabbed hold of Tam and Doogy, dragging them roughly over to the rock wall and propping them up in a seated position. Over a score of hares gathered around them. Tam held his silence until he could make sense of the situation they were in, but not so Doogy.

Furious, the small Highlander roared at an older hare – a sinewy, athletic-looking beast with a battered face, who was wearing a green tunic with three stripes affixed to the sleeve. 'Did ye no' hear me, ye great flappin', cloth-eared clod? Ah told ye tae get these ropes off'n me!'

The hare avoided his gaze, setting his eyes right ahead. 'Sorry, mate, h'I can't do that h'until Lady Melesme sees ye.'

A tall, elegant hare, much younger than the other, stepped forward. He was wearing a red tunic and had a long rapier belted about his waist. Placing a footpaw upon Doogy, he pushed him flat.

'Get down on the floor, like the confounded, murderin' snake you are, sirrah!'

Though he was tightly bound, Doogy managed to slew around. His teeth clashed as he snapped at the hare's footpaw, causing him to dodge backward as the prisoner ranted, 'Ah'm no murderer, an' ye've no right tae call me a snake, ye great snot-nosed rabbet!'

The hare raised his footpaw to kick Doogy. 'How dare y'-call me a rabbit! I'll teach you a lesson . . .'

He was wrenched clean off his paws and hurled to one side by the older, green-tunicked hare, who berated him. 'Nah, nah, young master Ferdimond, try to be'ave yoreself like a h'officer an' a gentlebeast, sir!'

The young hare, Ferdimond De Mayne, argued back vociferously. 'Bad show, Sarge. You shouldn't be takin' the side of that bloomin' assassin! We've lost eight comrades good'n'true to the likes of that confounded worm. I'm going to knock his bally block off, first chance I get. You see if I don't, wot wot!'

Tam interrupted, calling out indignantly, 'That should be easy to do, he's unable to defend himself. Doogy's right, we're not murderers!'

Suddenly the sergeant bellowed, 'Stand fast allbeasts for the Lady Melesme!'

The Badger Ruler of Salamandastron strode in among them. Melesme was no longer young, but she was an imposing creature. Tall and powerfully built, she looked every inch a ruler, though clad only in a simple homespun smock with a forge apron belted over it. Turning her dark, liquid eyes upon the sergeant, Melesme spoke in a voice which boomed around the cavern.

'What's going on here, Wonwill?'

Sergeant Wonwill took a smart pace forward and saluted. 'Marm, we h'apprehended these 'ere squirrels near the spot where the slaughter took place. They was loiterin' round by a burnt-out ship, so we took 'em in for questionin', marm.'

Melesme beckoned, and Arflow the young sea otter was escorted through the gathering of hares. The badger indicated both captives. 'Have you seen either of these before, young 'un?'

Arflow shook his head. 'No, marm, it wasn't them.'

Tam decided it was time to speak his piece. 'I could've told ye that! It couldn't have been us who did whatever was supposed to have been done. We were chasin' after the Gulo beast an' his white vermin, on the orders of Araltum Squirrelking an' Idga Drayqueen!'

The Badger Ruler raised her heavy eyebrows. 'But you two have the look of warriors. How did you come to be taking orders from those two overblown little idiots? Fortindom, Wilderry, release them!'

Two capable-looking hares, with medals and stars on their pink tunics, marched out. Whipping out their sabres, they sliced through the bonds with a few masterful strokes.

Tam and Doogy stood up, massaging the life back into their numbed paws. Knowing they were in the presence of a Badger Ruler, they bowed courteously. Tam elected himself spokesbeast for them both.

'I thank ye, marm. I'm Rakkety Tam MacBurl, an' this is my friend, Wild Doogy Plumm. We serve Araltum an' Idga because we pledged our oath an' our swords in their service. The only way we can be freed from the bond is to take back an' return their Royal Banner, stolen by the vermin.'

Melesme issued a mirthless grunt. 'Royal Banner, indeed! Is that what those two idiots are up to these days? I've had them watched since they came to my groves. Oh, they're no harm to honest beasts, so I've let them be, but I don't want to ally myself to fools. What is this Royal Banner thing, Tam?'

The warrior squirrel's jaw tightened. 'Just a symbol, marm, part of their silly pomp an' ceremony. What matters more is that a lot o' squirrels, some of 'em our friends, were massacred when the Gulo beast stole the flag. Araltum an' Idga care more for the return of it than the lives of their subjects. We'll get the flag back, but me an' Doogy are more concerned with settlin' the score.'

Doogy's teeth gritted audibly. 'Aye, lady. Guid warriors cannae rest 'til those dirty slayers are paid out in steel for their crimes, ye ken?'

Melesme nodded. 'Well spoken, sir. But tell me, who is this Gulo beast? Have you seen him?'

Tam answered. 'No, marm, but we've seen his tracks, an' they look like no other creature that ever walked this land. The pawprints are as big as those of a grown badger, but this beast has huge, curved claws, though the fur is so long that it blurs the pawmark. One other thing I must tell ye, the Gulo beast an' its followers, about a hundred of 'em, feed off the flesh of their victims. We've seen the evidence, marm.'

The Badger Ruler looked grim. 'I know this – we lost eight fine young hares to them. There was little left by the time my Long Patrol got to the spot. Also there is a drum, we made it for Abbot Humble of Redwall Abbey, as a gift. That has gone the way of your flag. Though such a thing cannot compare with the death of our hares, nonetheless, it is a point of honour that we take back this drum and give it to its rightful owner.'

There were heartfelt murmurs of agreement from the hares. Melesme held up a huge paw, restoring silence. 'I have scouts out following the Gulo beast's tracks. At dawn, a force of one hundred fighting hares will leave Salamandastron. They will track the vermin and their chief until they face them. It is my command that they send those evil murderers, everybeast of them, to Hellgates!'

She turned to the two squirrels. 'Will you be joining in the hunt?'

Doogy nodded. 'Ah'm thinkin' ye'll have tae be marchin' at the double tae get at yon vermin afore we do. Eh, Tam?'

Ferdimond De Mayne pawed at his rapier hilt. 'Indeed, sah, an' I say ye'll be eatin' our flippin' dust if ye try to keep up with the Long Patrol. Wot wot!'

A shout of agreement came from the hares but was quickly stifled by a stern bark from Lady Melesme. 'Silence! Stop this foolishness! You officers and any other of my warriors will answer to me if you do not work together with our two friends. Is that clear?'

Captain Derron Fortindom and Lancejack Wilderry drew their sabres and saluted, replying together, 'Crystal clear, marm!'

Melesme beckoned Sergeant Wonwill forward. 'You are older and more experienced than any. I want you to keep an eye on these younger bucks. Understood?'

The scar-faced veteran touched a paw to his eartip. 'My 'eart'n'paw, marm, h'I'll keep the young rips in line. H'attention, Long Patrol! Ye've got less'n three hours to rest, provision h'an choose yore weapons. At crack o' dawn I wants to see ye on parade, smartly turned out an' fit t'march. Brigadier Crumshaw'll be on the square, so ye knows wot to h'expect. Dismiss!'

Tam approached Melesme. 'Marm, we need our blades.'

She stopped Ferdimond from walking off. 'De Mayne, return these warriors' weapons, please.'

There was still a rebellious glint in Ferdimond's eye, but he complied with the order promptly. Tam accepted his shield and blades from the hare, but Doogy was out to rankle him.

'Och, mind ye dinna slice yore paws on mah claymore, laddie. 'Tis a sword for braw beasties, no' a fancy-talkin' rabbet like yoreself who carries a bodkin!'

73

Ferdimond threw Doogy's gear on the ground. 'Get 'em yourself, treewalloper. Just call me rabbit one more time, an' y'see this rapier? I jolly well promise ye it's no bodkin, an' it'll chop the insolent snout off ye!'

Doogy belted on his claymore, grinning broadly. 'Oh, dearie me, ole fellow, ole chap, ye've got me all scairt stiff now. Ach, away with ye, rabbet!'

They stood glaring at each other until Sergeant Wonwill stepped between them. 'Nah, nah, you gennelbeasts, break it up! You 'eard Lady Melesme's h'orders, be'ave yoreselves!'

Tam pulled Doogy away. 'Come on, mate, let's find someplace to get a spot o' shuteye for a few hours. What's the matter with ye, Doogy? Just ignore Ferdimond!'

The little Highlander followed Tam reluctantly. 'Yon taffy-nosed buck is strokin' mah tail the wrong way. Ah'll have tae teach him some wee manners, so ah will!'

Tam led his friend down to a grotto, thickly carpeted in dry grass and soft moss. He waved a paw under his nose. 'Listen t'me, Wild Doogy Plumm. If yore bound to cross blades with that hare, then wait until we're clear of here. I won't have ye abusin' Lady Melesme's hospitality. Now curl yore tail up an' get some sleep!'

The sergeant appeared with two steaming beakers which gave off an aromatic scent. 'Get this down yore throats afore ye go t'sleep, buckoes. H'it'll do the bumps on yore noggins a power o' good. Mister Doogy, pay no 'eed to young De Mayne – that un's perilous an' lightnin' fast with a blade, but Ferdimond's young an' ot'eaded like you, so steer clear of each h'other.'

Tam eyed the sergeant's battered face curiously. 'Thankee, Sarge. Ye don't mind me sayin', but all ye carry is a slingshot. Is that yore only weapon?'

The hare winked and held up his paws. 'Weapons, mate? These is my weapons. I'm a boxin' hare. The ole slingshot's good for long-range hittin', but fer close work there ain't nothin' better'n these two trusties!'

74

Doogy sipped his fragrant cordial, feeling the headache recede immediately. He inspected the sergeant's clenched paws. 'A boxin' hare, eh? What manner o' beastie is that, Sarge?'

Wonwill dropped into a fighting pose, lowering his brows and circling with both paws. Like lightning, he shot out a right, then a left, the air whistling around him as he danced lightly, ducking and weaving, throwing punches. 'I was born to box, that's me trade. Y'know why they calls me Wonwill, no? Then I'll tell ye. If'n me right don't get ye, then me left one will. Left or right, mates, either one will set ye on yore tail. Wonwill, see?'

Doogy was mightily impressed. 'Ah wouldnae mind learnin' how tae box, Sarge. Mayhap ye'll give me some wee lessons sometime, eh?'

Wonwill relaxed, dropping his guard. 'Per'aps I will, mate, when I ain't busy lookin' arter the young Patrollers. Mark my words, they ain't h'experienced, but they're Salamandastron born'n'bred. All made o' the right stuff, an' perilous brave. I've just got ter stop 'em knockin' the stuffin' outta one another. Know wot I mean?'

He gave Doogy a wink. 'I'll bid ye a goodnight now.'

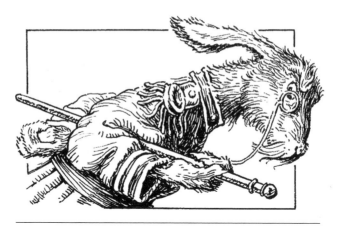

11

Following their few hours of sleep, both squirrels woke refreshed, with all aches and pains banished. Tam tickled his friend's ear, and Doogy leapt up.

'Top o' the mornin' tae yeh, Tam. Ah'm feelin' braw an' sprauncy the noo. Yon cordial did me a power o' good!'

Just as Tam was about to reply, a fat, smiling hare entered the grotto, bearing a tray of breakfast which he placed between them. Unshouldering two filled haversacks, he saluted comically. 'Mornin' chaps, wot! Name's Wopscutt, Corporal Butty Wopscutt. In charge of the jolly old supplies an' provisions. Tuck doncha know, vittles for the use of!'

Doogy returned his friendly smile. 'Mah thanks tae ye. Vittles for the use of what?'

Butty did a scut twirl and waggled both ears. 'For the use of eatin', o' course. That's the way we talk here, wot. I'd shift my tail if I were you, old Crumshaw's takin' the parade. Wouldn't keep him waitin' if I was you, chaps. No sir, not his nibs, he'd have your tails for tea an' your guts for garters. So quick's the word an' sharp's the jolly old action, wot wot!'

The tubby corporal marched off without further ado. After belting his blades on, Tam hefted his shield and fixed the Sgian Dhu in his cap. 'Up ye come, Doogy Plumm, this is the life for us. Marching with real fighters who know what they're doin' an' do it right!'

Brigadier Buckworthy Crumshaw was a fine figure of a hare – from his eye monocle, to his bristling moustache, to the highly polished buttons on his freshly brushed pink tunic, down to the short swagger cane he carried. The brigadier was smart as paint, and old school to the rigid backbone. He squinted ferociously through his monocle, taking in the fivescore ranks of Long Patrol hares, all standing stiffly to attention. That was when he caught Tam and Doogy creeping up, trying to slip into line unnoticed.

Crumshaw pointed his stick at the latecomers. 'Parade at first light o' dawn means just that, an' not two flippin' blinks of an eye later, laddie bucks. Sergeant, are these two laggards supposed t'be with us? Get 'em fell into line immediately!'

Wonwill saluted and bounced forward a pace. 'Sah! They is with us, sah! Mister Rakkety Tam MacBurl h'an' Mister Wild Doogy Plumm. Ye'll have to h'excuse 'em lollygaggin' an' loiterin', sah. We had to boff 'em over the brains an' knock 'em cold to capture 'em last night, sah!'

Tam and Doogy fell in on the left flank of the first rank. The brigadier circled both squirrels, his sharp, monocled eye inspecting them. 'Harrumph! Well, at least you chaps have the look o' seasoned warriors – very good, very good. Eyes front! Seen any action have ye, wot?'

Both squirrels knew a good officer when they saw one. Doogy kept his face straight as he barked out, 'Aye, we've fought tae get porridge in the breakfast line an' wounded several bad cooks. Sah!'

Tam added another old campaigner's jest. 'An' both our blades can peel onions, though we never shed a tear about it. Sah!'

A faint smile hovered around the brigadier's moustache. 'Well said! You two rogues will fit the bally bill fine. So, remember, your mothers might've loved ye, but I don't. It'll be march 'til your paws drop off, sleep where ye drop an' blood'n'vinegar for supper. Do I make myself clear, you horrible squirrels?'

Doogy replied, 'Clear, sah! 'Twill be a wee life o' luxury!'

Morning sunlight sparkled off the sea. As a warm breeze ruffled the dry sand above the tideline, the ranks stood fast until Lady Melesme appeared at the main cave entrance. The Long Patrol waved blades, bows, slings, axes and javelins, hailing her with their wild war cry. 'Eulaaaaaliiiii-aaaaaa!'

She held up a paw, then addressed her warriors. 'Find the vermin who murdered our young hares. Take no prisoners!'

Sergeant Wonwill bellowed out the marching orders. 'H'atten . . . shun! Patrol will form off h'in columns of five! Look to yore dressin', eyes right! By the left, quick march!'

Away they went, with paws pounding up sandy dust as the sergeant shouted, 'Present colours!'

A pennant-shaped green banner, centred with a white representation of the mountain fortress, was raised as they paraded past Lady Melesme. Two hares set up a march beat on small snare drums, and a hundred lusty voices began singing a regimental marching song.

'Farewell, dear mother, I've been sent,
to march away from here,
along with my good regiment,
an' a bullyin' Brigadier.

What a sight to see! Don't cry for me!
I'm a hare that's fair, I do declare,
I'll follow the drums most anywhere!

The dear old Sergeant tucks us up,
he sings to us so nicely.

78

He's pretty as a buttercup,
dressed in a frilly nightie.

What a sight to see! Don't cry for me!
I'm a hare that's fair, I do declare,
I'll follow the drums most anywhere!

I'm choked by dust, me paws are split,
me back is broke in two.
I have one wish an' this is it,
to stay at home with you.

What a sight to see! Don't cry for me!
I'm a hare that's fair, I do declare,
I'll follow the drums most anywhere!'

The march progressed northeast from Salamandastron, cutting at an angle across the shore into the dunes. It was a warm day, and the pace was kept up briskly. As they slogged up the sandhills, Tam winked at Doogy. 'This is better than prancing around the groves, wonderin' what new tricks an' fancies Idga an' Araltum are up to, eh? Hah, just listen to the Sarge givin' those greenpaws a bit of his mind.'

Wonwill was haranguing the slower marchers in typical sergeant fashion. 'Step lively now, ye bunch o' ditherin' daisies – left, right, left, right! Flummerty, sort 'em out, that's your left! Pick up those paws, you 'orrible little h'animal. Straighten that back, missie, think 'ow lucky you are. Out for a nice walk on a lovely day, eh! Folderon, wipe that smile offa yore face, missie, an' stop flutterin' yore lovely eyelashes at young Flunkworthy, or I'll 'ave yore scut for supper! Keep up at the back there – chins in, chests out, shoulders back, eyes front. That's the ticket, me buckoes!'

Doogy chuckled at the dismayed faces of the three back rankers. 'Flunkworthy, Folderon an' Flummerty, eh, the awkward squad. Poor wee beasties, they dinna know the sergeant's all bark an' no bite tae the young 'uns.'

Tam spat out sand kicked up by the front rank. 'Aye, but they'll learn soon enough. 'Tis one thing goin' for a walk an' another keepin' pace with a regiment.'

It was midnoon before the brigadier gave orders to call a halt, and that was only because he was waiting on reports from the forward scouts. They set up camp where dunes and sand gave on to the heath and flatlands.

Tam and Doogy sat with Wonwill and Corporal Wopscutt, resting whilst they dined off haversack rations. Crumshaw had given orders that no fires were to be lit. The food was plain but nourishing – thick slices of chestnut and barley bread with wedges of yellow cheese, washed down with mint-and-pennycloud cordial.

Ferdimond De Mayne was sitting with another group close by. His voice could be heard clearly as he directed remarks at Doogy.

'Haw haw haw! Wild Doogy Plumm, eh? What sort of a bloomin' name is that for a chap, wot? Fat little braggart with a silly great tail who wears a flippin' skirt. No wonder he's jolly well wild. Haw haw haw!'

Doogy reached for his claymore, growling, 'Ah'll put a button on yon lanky toad's lip. That'll teach him tae mock mah kilt!'

With a firm paw, the sergeant prevented Doogy rising. 'Stay put, mate. Pay no 'eed t'young De Mayne. Only a fool rises to the bait of h'another fool.'

Tam had a grip on his friend's shoulder. 'He's right, Doogy, let it be. The time'll come when you'll face him, but not right now.'

The little Highlander thumped his paw against the ground. 'Aye well, it cannae come soon enough for me, ye ken!'

Further discussion was cut short by the arrival of two young hares, the scouts Kersey and Dauncey, a twin brother and sister. The brigadier joined his sergeant's group, beckoning the scouts to sit with them.

'Strewth, here's the best young gallopers we've had in many a season, wot. Corporal Wopscutt, bring 'em vittles an' something t'drink. Well, chaps, how did the reccy go?'

Dauncey was still panting as he threw a salute. 'Phew! Followed the vermin tracks nor'east, sah . . .'

Kersey continued as her brother paused. 'Still the same bunch of villains, sah, with that odd-pawed beast leadin' 'em . . .'

Then it was Dauncey's turn. 'They were at a high-banked stream yesterday. Seems they captured some River Rats – Driftail's bunch it was, sah . . .'

The brigadier's monocled eye swivelled to Kersey. 'Our old foe Driftail, eh? How did ye know 'twas him?'

Kersey pulled a digusted face. 'We found his blinkin' head, sah. Dreadful thing t'report, but the vermin ate the River Rats!'

Dauncey duly followed his sister. 'All save two, sah, whom they took along with 'em when they broke camp. Good golly gosh! Fancy scoffin' a gang o' scummy rats, filthy vermin, wot!'

Crumshaw polished his monocle studiously. 'I wouldn't shed any tears over those blighters, young 'un. They've done their share of slayin' in the past. A few less for us to bother about, wot! Where d'you estimate the vermin's present position, miss?'

Kersey pointed. 'Still goin' slightly east, sah, but cuttin' off sharp north into Mossflower Woodlands. They should reach the tree fringe by evenin'.'

The twins fell upon the food and drink which Butty had brought them. Wonwill exchanged glances with Crumshaw. 'Puts 'em a day an' some hours in front of us, sah.'

The direction his scouts had given suddenly dawned on the brigadier. The monocle dropped from his eye. 'Great wallopin' weasels! Turnin' sharp north – that can mean only one thing. Those vermin are bound t'run smack into the blinkin' Abbey!'

Tam had never visited the place, but he knew what Abbey Crumshaw was referring to – 'Redwall Abbey'.

Doogy shrugged. 'Oh, that Abbey. Och, we came doon by followin' the shoreline, so we never got tae see it.'

Brigadier Crumshaw sprang upright. 'Well, yore goin' t'see it afore yore much older, laddie. We leave straight-away, Sergeant. Break camp! You two gallopers, go on ahead at the double. Report back t'me when ye find where the vermin entered the woodlands. We'll probly make it to the broadstream with a forced march late this evenin'. We'll sally forth at dawn an' cut down their lead, wot!'

Within an incredibly short time, Tam and Doogy found themselves on the march again – packs on backs, blades belted, kicking up a column of dust upon the flatlands in the ranks of the Long Patrol. Wonwill brought up the rear with Butty and Lancejack Wilderry.

There was little humour in the sergeant's tones as he exhorted the marchers. 'Move yoreselves now, pick 'em up an' put 'em down at the double! Speed up now, lef' right, lef' right, there ain't no room for stragglers in the Patrol. Stir yore idle selves!'

One of the old stagers hastened them on with a speedy chant.

'I'm chewin' dust because I must,
as long as I've got mates to trust,
we'll march on 'til our paws are bust,
cos we've been given orders!

So on we roll, the Long Patrol,
forget your bed an' drinkin' bowl,
cos if you stop, yore in a hole,
the Sergeant's right behind ye!

Left right, march he'll say,
over the hills an' faraway,

82

from crack o' dawn to end o' day,
good mateys an' companions!'

Even the best of them were weary and pawsore when they
reached the broadstream banks at late evening. Stumbling
with fatigue, the regiment scrambled down the steep slopes,
eager to find the best sleeping places. Camp was set up and
two big fires lighted on the brigadier's orders. Crumshaw
reasoned that, if the twin blazes were sighted, the vermin
might do an about-turn. This would mean the Long Patrol
would be under attack – a far better situation, from his
viewpoint, because the hares were armed and ready, but
Redwall Abbey was not.

Tam had become separated from Doogy in the rush down
the bankside. Both he and Corporal Wopscutt were about to
cool their paws in the shallows when they were distracted
by angry shouts. Turning, they hurried back to a crowd of
hares who had gathered to witness the hubbub.

It was Doogy and Ferdimond at each other's throats with
drawn swords.

Ferdimond was yelling at the onlookers who were
packed tight about them both. 'Make space there, so I can
swing me bally blade!'

Doogy was trying to raise his claymore, but he was so
tightly hemmed in that his nose was nearly pressing against
Ferdimond's chin. 'Swing yore bally blade, eh? Ah'll swing
yore bally ears from mah belt as soon as ah get room tae do it!'

Tam pushed forward into the press, but he was pulled to
one side by Wonwill, who had the brigadier with him.

Crumshaw winked at Tam. 'Leave this to us, MacBurl.
That's an order, stay out of it. There's a good chap, wot!'

Wonwill bellowed in his best parade-ground manner.
'Teeeeeen . . . shun! Stand fast all ranks, offisah present!'

The hares fell back and came to attention as Tam followed
Crumshaw and Wonwill through to the centre. The tough
sergeant immediately pulled Doogy and Ferdimond apart.
'Nah then, wot's all this 'ere, you two, eh?'

Ferdimond saluted with his long rapier. 'Point of honour, Sarge, private dispute doncha know!'

Wonwill faced Doogy. 'Wot've you got t'say for yoreself, Mister Plumm?'

The highland squirrel bared his teeth. 'Ah've got nothin' tae say, Sarge. Mah claymore'll do the talkin' for me. But that fancy talkin' fop'll no' be round tae trip me up from behind again when ah've finished!'

The brigadier came smartly forward, his moustache bristling. 'Put those blades down immediately! Rules an' regs of our regiment don't permit duels, private or public! Listen t'me, buckoes. If one of ye was to slay the other, I'd be forced to sentence the winner to death for killin' a comrade. Quince, Derron, you will disarm these hotheads!'

The two captains sprang in and confiscated the blades. Crumshaw cocked a monocled eye at Wonwill. 'Well, Sergeant, 'pon me scut, these two look as if they ain't goin' to kiss an' make up, wot! Looks like they've got plenty o' vinegar still in 'em, eh? What d'you suggest?'

Wonwill elbowed the pair further away from each other. 'H'it's my opinion they're bound to 'ave at each other, sah. May'aps they should settle their spat like proper gentlebeasts. Could h'I suggest the noble art, sah?'

Behind his monocle, the brigadier's eye twinkled. 'Capital idea, a little exhibition, eh wot! Purely nonvindictive an' in the true spirit o' the sport. Carry on, Sergeant, read 'em the rules!'

Crumshaw drew a line in the bank sand with his swagger stick and stood back. Wonwill called Doogy and Ferdimond up to scratch. 'Ready, young sirs? Place yore right footpaws on the line an' face each other. Forepaws well clenched now, that's the style! Yore goin' t'give everybeast a boxin' display. No bitin', gougin' or scratchin'. When I says fight, ye both go to it. But when I says 'alt, youse stop. H'agreed?'

Doogy and Ferdimond were eyeing each other fiercely,

milling their forepaws in tight, small circles as they both snarled, 'Agreed!'

Wonwill's battered features creased into a grin. 'Thankee kindly, young sirs. Ready? . . . Fight!'

Doogy's paw shot out. *Thud!* He caught his opponent a punch right to the nosetip. The hare staggered slightly, then countered with a stinging blow to his adversary's right eye. Undeterred, the small Highlander brought forth an upper-cut which rattled his foe's jaw. Then Ferdimond connected with a left that made Doogy's ear ring. Both fighters continued at it, hammer and tongs. A lot of hares were shouting for Ferdimond, but just as many joined Tam in cheering Doogy on. There were cries of advice and encour-agement from both sides as the combat raged back and forth.

'Tuck yore chin in, old lad, watch the blighter's left!'

'Give him the jolly old one-two, that's it!'

'Bang away at his tuck basket, that'll wind the blighter!'

'Duck an' weave, keep jabbin' away with that right, mate!'

They pounded away relentlessly, footpaws never leaving the line. Doogy's right eye was almost swollen shut, and Ferdimond's nose looked like an overripe damson plum. The hare whipped out a pile-driving left, but the squirrel ducked it, looping a superb right to his opponent's chin.

Whump! Ferdimond was knocked off the line, flat on his scut.

Wonwill leapt in, shouting, 'H'alt!'

Leaning over Ferdimond, he put the question, 'Are ye finished, Mister De Mayne?'

The hare spat out a tooth, jumping upright like a coiled spring. 'Finished? I've only just bloomin' started, wot!'

Wonwill watched as he came forward to paw the line again. 'Righto, fight on!'

Ferdimond floored Doogy with a left cross to the head.

Another halt was called as the sergeant questioned Doogy. 'Mister Plumm, 'ave ye taken h'enough, sir?'

Quick as a flash, the highland squirrel was up, grinning crookedly. 'Ach, away wi' ye, Sarge. Ah've got the poor lad right where ah want him tae be. Oot o' mah way!'

They battled on, neither giving any quarter. A simultaneous barrage of punches from both sides sent the two contestants down. Staggering up and blowing for breath, they swiped out wearily at each other until they both collapsed again.

The sergeant had filled Doogy's shield with streamwater. He winked at the brigadier, who nodded knowingly.

Splash! Wonwill drenched the pair. As the two gasping opponents sat up, the sergeant beckoned them upright to paw the line. 'I 'aven't called an 'alt yet, sirs! Ye wanted to fight, so stop malingerin'. H'up off yore hunkers an' fight!'

Bone tired, they hauled themselves upright and fought on. Everybeast had fallen silent now. They looked on as the two exhausted battlers raised leaden paws and swiped away. Most of the punches were only hitting mid-air; twice, in fact, the weary rivals found themselves back to back, actually peering about for each other. Tottering around, they tripped over their own paws and finally collapsed in a heap.

Satisfied, Brigadier Crumshaw signalled Wonwill, who called a final halt. 'Well, sirs, 'ave ye both 'ad enough now?'

Ferdimond had trouble lifting his head to reply. 'I've had enough if he has.'

Doogy raised a swollen paw. 'Aye, an' ah've had mah fill if'n he has.'

Crumshaw stepped in, helping the sergeant to stand them upright. Joining both their paws, he concluded, 'Well fought, chaps! A good scrap, I'd say, without havin' to wipe each other out with swords, wot! Take a bow!'

Both the Long Patrol and Tam gave the fighters three rousing cheers.

The brigadier patted both their backs. 'Absolutely top-hole! I hope this has solved any small differences ye may have had in the past, wot! Now, shake paws like two good eggs, then clean yoreselves up in the stream, eh?'

Doogy and Ferdimond shook paws as best they could. The young hare grinned lopsidedly. 'Sorry for what I said about you, old lad. I was wrong. You, sir, are a true flippin' warrior!'

Doogy attempted a wink, but both his eyes were swollen. 'Och, yer no' sae bad yoreself, matey. 'Twas all mah fault, ye'll have tae excuse me for bein' so touchy, ye ken!'

Holding each other upright, they staggered into the stream to the accompaniment of hurrahs and backslapping.

'What a go! Well fought, you two!'

'Here's to two perilous beasts, wot!'

'Rather, that scrap'll go down in Long Patrol annals!'

'Aye, never seen one like it in me blinkin' life!'

Tam squatted by the fire with Wonwill. 'Haha, just look at Doogy, wipin' Ferdimond's nose. They seem happy enough now, eh Sarge?'

The old veteran smiled. 'Like the Brigadier said, better'n seein' 'em carved to death by swords. A good 'ealthy boxin' match h'is just the ticket for clearin' the air, Tam!'

Crumshaw, who had joined them, sniffed the night air with relish. 'Only one thing better'n the smell of a stream-bank on a springtime evenin' – skilly an' duff for supper, wot wot!'

Corporal Butty Wopscutt, assisted by the haremaids Folderon and Flummerty, were cooking away industriously. Tam took in the savoury odour from the cooking fire. 'Hope it tastes as good as it smells, sah.'

Crumshaw stirred the fire with his swagger stick point. 'Young Wopscutt's the finest cook we've ever had, a real treasure, that 'un. An' he ain't put off by those pretty gels! By the way, Tam, that comrade o' yours, Doogy wotsisname, quite a game feller, put up a superb fight. I've a feelin' we're goin' to need chaps like him before the season's out.'

Tam watched Doogy and Ferdimond splashing in the stream. 'Aye, yore right there, sah. Goin' up against the Gulo beast an' his vermin, we'll want good warriors to conquer beasts who are so savage that they eat their enemies!'

12

On the morning following the moles' celebratory supper, young Burlop Cellarhog was up and about his duties before Abbot Humble awakened. Burlop busied himself in the cellars, selecting a new barrel of October Ale. Having found the one he had marked out, the young hedgehog upended it, single-pawed. He began knocking a spigot through the centre bung so the liquid could be tapped. Humble emerged from his bed in the corner, fastening the waist cord of his habit.

The stout young Cellarhog touched his headspikes apologetically. 'Father Abbot! I'm sorry, did my noise wake you up?'

Humble stifled a yawn, smiling at his protégé. 'Certainly not, Burlop. I merely slept a bit late after last night's mole supper. What a pleasant evening it was, eh?'

Burlop gave the spigot a final knock and set a tankard under it. ' 'Twas most enjoyable, Father, though the moles and our creatures finished off a barrel of the October Ale. I'm just replacing it. Would you care to taste a sip?'

He stood back respectfully as Humble sniffed round the barrel staves, tapping his paw on the lid several times and then listening, as if for an answer. Burlop always deferred to his Abbot's expertise. Humble turned the spigot tap, allowing a measure of ale to gurgle forth into the tankard. He spilt a drop on his paw and held it up to a lantern, checking on its colour and clarity. Burlop looked on anxiously as the Abbot took a sample mouthful.

The old hedgehog rolled the ale round his palate, then swallowed it slowly. Beaming happily, he smacked his lips. 'Excellent! Marvellous judgement, young Burlop! Of all the October barrels within our cellars, you could not have chosen a finer one!'

Burlop bowed low, allowing his spikes to stand up and then letting them fall back flat several times – the typical hedgehog way of receiving a great compliment. 'Thank you, Father. I learned all I know from you, and I'm always ready to heed your wise counsel.'

Humble gazed fondly over the top of his spectacles. 'I wouldn't trust my cellars to any hog but you, friend. Now, what was I about to do, eh?'

'Go up to breakfast perhaps?' Burlop suggested helpfully.

The Abbot scratched his chinspikes reflectively. 'Hmm, yes, but there was some other business also. Ah, I remember now! I've got to get Brother Gordale, my cousin Jem and old Walt together. Today we begin trying to solve the rhyme puzzle. If anybeast comes looking for me, please tell them I'll either be in the kitchens or the orchard.'

Burlop helped Humble with his overcloak. 'Certainly, Father.'

Humble stared around the kitchen passage at those being served with breakfast. None of the three he wanted was there.

Sister Armel, the pretty young Infirmary Keeper, approached him cheerfully. 'Good morning, Father Abbot. Are you looking for somebeast?'

Humble accepted a plate of hazelnut and honey turnovers from Friar Glisum absently. 'Er, good morning, Sister. Have you seen Gordale or Jem or Walt about?'

Armel put aside her tray. 'No, but I'll soon find them for

you. There's quite a few still abed after last evening's festivities. I'll give them a call.'

Humble began loading up his tray. 'Oh, thank you, that would be a help. Tell them I'll have breakfast set up in the orchard. We're supposed to be solving that rhyme puzzle today, you know.'

Sister Armel's big brown eyes lit up. 'May I help you, Father? I'm very good at puzzles.'

Humble chuckled. 'Of course you can, pretty one. A young head might prove a welcome addition to us elders.'

The orchard was carpeted with pink and white petal blossoms, shed by the many apple, pear, plum, cherry, damson and almond trees.

Brother Demple, the mouse who was Abbey Gardener, put aside his trowel as he saw Humble approaching with a heavily laden tray.

'Good morning, Abbot. Doesn't our orchard look pretty today? Here, let me help you with that tray.'

Humble willingly allowed the sturdy mouse to assist him. 'Thank you, Brother Demple. My word, I didn't realize one tray could be so heavy. There's breakfast for three there.'

Demple took up the tray. 'Thank goodness for that. At first I thought it was all for you, Father!'

He guided Humble to a sunny corner where he had set up a potting bench. 'Friends for breakfast, eh? What's the occasion?'

Humble sat on the bench alongside the tray. 'We've arranged to try and solve a puzzle.'

Demple rubbed his paws together eagerly. 'I love a good puzzle. D'you need any help?'

The Abbot smiled, eager to accept such a ready offer. 'By all means, be my guest – the more the merrier. Ah, here they come now.'

Gordale arrived with Walt and Jem. Slightly behind them came Armel, with Skipper's niece Brookflow. The fine, strong ottermaid had brought along an extra tray piled high with more food. Brookflow, or Brooky as she was known to all, was a jolly creature, possessed of an infectious laugh. Carrying the heavy tray on one paw, she waved with the other.

'Yoohooeeee! I heard there was a riddle t'be worked out, so I worked myself in. Is it all right if I join these other duffers, Father? Hahahaha!'

Humble raised his paws in mock despair. 'Come on, you beauty, come one, come all! Soon we'll have everybeast in the Abbey here!'

Breakfast was shared out, as there was plenty for everyone. In the middle of it, Humble smote his forehead and groaned. 'Sister Screeve has the written copy, and I forgot to invite her along. What was I thinking of?'

Yet even as he spoke, Screeve entered the orchard, waving a parchment, the one she had recorded the rhyme on. 'Friar Glisum told me you'd be here, Father. Hope you've not started without me!'

Brooky giggled into a scone she was demolishing. 'Teeheehee! How would we manage that? I think old Screeve's gone off her rocker. Teeheeheehee!'

Jem looked over the rim of an oatmeal bowl at Brooky. 'You could do yoreself a nastiness, gigglin' an' vittlin' like that, marm!'

Breakfast was taken in leisurely fashion, chatting, laughing and gossiping. Wandering Walt tapped his digging claws on the bench impatiently. 'Yurr, b'aint us'ns apposed t'be solven ee riggle t'day?'

Sister Screeve spread her parchment upon the ground. 'Thank you kindly, sir. If Miss Brookflow can stop her merriment for just a moment, I'll read the rhyme. Are you finished, miss?'

The jolly ottermaid stifled her mouth with both paws. 'Whoohoohoo . . . Oops! Sorry, Sister, just once more. Whoohoohaha! There, that's better. Right, let's get on with unpuzzling the riddle, or unrizzling the puddle. Whoohaha . . .'

Brooky looked about at the stern faces. 'Sorry.'

Screeve took up where she had left off. 'As I said, I'll read the poem, er rhyme. Right!

Where the sun falls from the sky,
and dances at a pebble's drop,
where little leaves slay big leaves,
where wood meets earth I stop.
Safe from the savage son of Dramz,
here the secret lies alone,
the symbol of all power, the mighty Walking Stone!'

Brother Gordale scratched behind his ear. 'Well, where do we start with all that jumble?'

'At the beginning, I suppose. Hahahaha . . .' Humble silenced Brooky with a stern glance over his glasses.

Then, suddenly, he mellowed. 'An excellent idea. Very logical, too, miss. Where the sun falls from the sky. Anybeast got an idea where that may be?'

Walt answered. 'Hurr that bee's in ee west, whurr ee sun be a-setten every h'evenin', zurr.'

Demple swept the horizon westward. 'That's a massive area. Any way we could narrow it down?'

Whilst they sat thinking about this, Gordale quoted the second line. 'And dances at a pebble's drop.'

Armel fidgeted with her apron strings. 'Maybe it carries on to link up. What's the next line?'

Sister Screeve supplied it in her precise tones. 'Where little leaves slay big leaves. Dearie me, I'm really puzzled now!'

Brooky interrupted her. 'Well, if the entire thing is a puzzle, yore supposed to be puzzled – that's why puzzlers write 'em. Haha, we're looking for a Walking Stone, and nobeast's ever seen one. I wouldn't recognize a Walking

Stone if it fell out of a tree and hit me over the head. Oh, ha-hahahoohoo!'

Screeve wagged her paw severely. 'Really, Brookflow, you aren't helping the situation by sitting there laughing!'

Armel, very fond of her ottermaid friend, spoke up in her defence. 'Don't be too hard on Brooky, Sister. She has a point, you know.'

Gordale shrugged. 'Right then, Sister Armel. Perhaps you'd like to tell us – just what *is* her point, eh?'

Armel's pretty face creased in a frown of concentration. 'Er, we, hmm, er . . . Maybe if Walt and Jem described the area where they found the dying beast, we might gain a clue from it.'

Humble agreed. 'Sounds reasonable to me. This Askor, the beast who died, it's likely he may have concealed the Walking Stone not far from where the tree fell on him. Jem, Walt, could you recall anything special about the place?'

Wandering Walt wrinkled his nose. 'Nay, zurr, it bee'd loike many bits o' furrest we'm parssed throo t'gether. B'aint that so, Jem?'

The old hedgehog shook his grizzled spikes. 'Gettin' old ain't no fun. I fergits a lot o' things now'days. It were some-place in sou'west Mossflower Woodlands, I'm sure o' that. Aye, an' there was a big ole rotten sycamore a-layin' there, that was the one wot fell on Askor. More'n that I'm a-feared I can't say, friends.'

Sister Screeve pushed the written rhyme under Jem's snout. 'Mayhap this'll jog your mind. Try to recall if you noticed any of these things – a place where the sun falls from the sky, where it dances at a pebble's drop, where little leaves slay big leaves . . .'

Brother Demple suddenly exclaimed, 'That's it . . . ivy!'

Jem stared at him curiously. 'What's that supposed t'mean, ivy?'

Demple's explanation shed the first tiny ray of hope on the riddle. 'Plants and growing things are both my hobby and my life as a gardener. So I ignored the rest of the puzzle and concentrated on the one line, "Where little leaves slay big leaves." Father, do you remember that old willow tree, down by our Abbey pond, on the south side? The tree I had to chop down about ten seasons back? It was an ancient, weak old thing, with ivy growing all over it – right from the ground, around the trunk, through the branches, until the whole willow tree was covered thickly in ivy vines and creepers. Not a single leaf could grow there as a result of that ivy. It had been strangled.'

Humble remembered. 'Ah yes, poor thing. Nobeast likes to see a tree felled, but it was becoming a danger, especially to our Dibbuns. I recall I took some of the branches to use as caulking for small casks. There was a lot of ivy though.'

Demple smiled triumphantly. 'You see, a clear case of little leaves slaying big leaves. Jem, can you or Walt recall seeing such a tree near the scene, one all choked by ivy?'

Hitheryon Jem pondered a moment, then laughed aloud. 'Hohoho! The wasp, Walt, remember the wasp?'

The old mole rubbed his stubby tail ruefully. 'Bo urr, oi b'aint likely to furget ee likkle villyun!'

Jem warmed to an account of the incident. ' 'Twas the day we found Askor, but earlier on. We'd just sat down to take a bite o' brekkist. I sat on the cart shaft, but ole Walt, he sat down with his back agin a tree. Aye, 'twas a big sycamore, there's quite a few in that neck o' the woods. But this'n 'ad been gripped by the ivy, just as you described, Brother Demple. From root to crown that tree was wrapped thick in the stuff. Walt should've knowed better, cos 'tis a common fact that wasps are very partial to ivy, somethin' in the scent of the leaves I've been told. Well, he'd no sooner sat down when out buzzes a wasp an' stings pore ole Walt right on the tail!'

Brooky could not resist breaking in. 'That's a story with a sting in the tail! Oh heeheehee!'

Walt glared at the jovial ottermaid. 'Et wurn't funny, marm. Waspers are vurry 'urtful beasts. Oi 'ad to bathe moi tail in ee pond an' rub et wi' dockleaves!'

Gordale spoke. 'You mean there was a pond close by?'

Jem's memory began coming back. 'Not a pond – it were more of a lake, bigger'n yore Abbey pond, a peaceful stretch o' water. We filled our canteens there.'

Sister Armel had enjoyed her breakfast in the orchard. She sat back in a sun-dappled corner, surrounded by friends, listening to Jem and the others discussing the problem. Though she had risen bright and alert that morning, her eyelids began to droop. A feeling of warm tranquillity enveloped her, the voices receding into a soothing hum. A different voice was calling to her, echoing along the corridors of her mind, gentle but firm.

'Armel, listen to me. Do you know who I am?'

A golden haze stole into her imagination. Through it drifted a figure she recognized immediately. 'I know you, sir. You are Martin the Warrior!'

The warrior's face was strong and kind as he smiled. 'And I know you, Sister Armel. That is why I choose you. Hear me now.

My sword must be carried by maidens two:
one who sees laughter in all, and you.
Bear it southwest through Mossflower Wood,
to he who pursues the vermin Lord.
The Borderer who is a force for good,
that warrior who sold and lost his sword.'

The image of Martin began to fade, but Armel heard his parting words quite clearly.

'Wake now, Armel. Tell them of the Abbey pond.'

Though she was not aware of it, her meeting with the warrior had lasted a mere moment. Jem was still speaking of the lake he had recalled.

Armel came wide awake at the sound of her own voice

speaking. "Where the sun falls from the sky, and dances at a pebble's drop." That's your lake, Jem.'

The wandering hedgehog stared at her curiously. 'How d'ye know that, Sister?'

Armel had forgotten Martin's visit, but she replied to Jem's question instantly. 'Oh, that's simple, really. When I was only a Dibbun, I often sat by the Abbey pond on summer afternoons. I could see the image of the sun on the water – it looked like gold. Many's the time Brooky and I threw pebbles at the reflection to see if we could hit it. The ripples caused by our pebbles made the sun on the water dance.'

Brooky broke out into laughter again. 'That's right! Oh, you are an old cleverclogs, Armel. No wonder they made you Infirmary Sister. But I was the best pebble chucker – I hit the sun more times than you did. They should've made me Abbey Pebble Chucker. Hahahahaha!'

She looked around at the stern faces, and the laughter faded on her lips. 'Oh, you lot are about as funny as a boiled frog!'

The Abbot polished his spectacles studiously to avoid smiling at the irrepressible ottermaid. 'Well, friends, the pieces of our puzzle are beginning to fall into place. In fact, I've just solved a line myself!'

Sister Screeve glanced up from her writing. 'Pray tell, Father.'

Humble repeated the lines. ' "Where wood meets earth I stop, safe from the savage son of Dramz." Where does wood meet earth naturally? At the base of a tree, where else!'

Sister Screeve scanned her notes. 'Right! So what have we got so far? We're looking for a sycamore tree overgrown by ivy, not far from a lake. This Walking Stone, whatever it is, has been buried at its base, safe from the savage son of Dramz, whoever he may be!'

Jem rose stiffly. 'If I remember rightly, Dramz is the father of Askor, the one who was slain by his brother, Gulo the

97

Savage. Dramz was the owner o' the Stone, but when he died, Askor took it an' ran. When we found Askor, he said that Gulo was chasin' 'im t'get 'old of the Stone. But that was last winter, an' we ain't heard o' Gulo ever since. I wonder why? Ooh, my ole back's playin' me up. If'n you'll excuse me, Cousin, I think I'll take a warm bath an' have a nice liddle liedown on a soft Abbey bed. Too many seasons sleepin' on rocks out in the weather, that's my trouble.'

Abbot Humble stood up and took Jem's paw. 'I'll walk with you as far as the Abbey. Mayhaps the rest of us might meet after supper this evening. We can talk further then. Come on, Jem, we're growing old together.'

The meeting broke up. Everybeast went off about their chores, which were many and varied in a place the size of Redwall Abbey. Old Walt had a split in his footpaw, which he, like Jem, attributed to long seasons of outdoor wandering. Armel asked him up to her Infirmary, where she kept some herbal salve to treat minor injuries. Brooky strolled up to the Infirmary with Armel, whilst Walt, who did not hold with sickbays and treatments, sat in the orchard, screwing up his courage to pay a visit.

As the young squirrel and her ottermaid friend walked through Great Hall towards the stairs, Sister Armel had the strangest feeling. She turned in the direction of the tapestry, and there, gazing straight at her, was Martin the Warrior's likeness. Then the mission he had entrusted to her suddenly dawned upon Armel. She gripped her friend's paw.

'Brooky, come with me. We've got to talk with Abbot Humble straightaway!'

13

Yoofus Lightpaw was a water vole. Chubby-faced and snub-nosed, with long, glossy, chocolate-brown fur, he was also a dyed-in-the-wool, incorrigible thief. Stealing was a compulsion with Yoofus, and he was very good at it. Although by nature he was an excellent little fellow – unfailingly kind, thoughtful and so generous that he would share his last crust with any creature in need – this did not alter the fact that Yoofus Lightpaw was the most expert thief in all Mossflower Woodlands. His wife – a dear, plump, homely creature named Didjety – was forever upbraiding him for his thieving ways, though secretly she was rather proud of her husband's extraordinary skills.

'Yoofus Lightpaw, ye dreadful ould beast,' she would say, 'sure you'd rob the very stars from out the sky if they weren't nailed up there an' ye could reach them!'

Yoofus always took this as a compliment. Hugging and kissing her fondly for making such remarks, he'd often reply, 'Arrah, Didjety me darlin', us Lightpaws was ever the same. As me ould granny used t'say while she robbed the supper off of the table, "Don't fuss yoreself, me pretty sugarplum pie, an' I'll go out an' borrow somethin' grand for ye!" '

Yoofus and Didjety lived in a neat bank burrow by a lake,

the very one where Wandering Walt had cooled his wasp-stung tail. Their home boasted an exceedingly well-disguised entrance, which would hardly merit a second glance from the outside. Inside, however, was a veritable treasure cave. From wall to wall, across the ceiling and over the floors, it was draped, hung and adorned with the trophies of the water vole's highly questionable enterprises. There were pictures, musical instruments, plates, bowls, jugs and jewellery. Everything – from carved tailrings to woven paw bracelets, necklets, brooches and headbands – shone and glimmered in the rainbow hue of many patterned lanterns. All in all it was a wondrous dwelling to behold.

Yoofus roamed far and wide in search of plunder. He was well versed in woodland lore and knew the movements of most creatures throughout the green fastness of copses, glades and ancient tree groves of Mossflower.

It was a still, sunny noontide when the water vole, scouting the southwest woods, spotted a magpie nest. Yoofus liked nothing better than thieving from a thief; magpies were known to steal bright objects to decorate their nests. He hid behind the trunk of an elm and settled down to scrutinize the bird's abode.

After a short while, Yoofus was rewarded by the flash of black-and-white plumage as a large, handsome magpie flew out from the nest. He watched it winging its way between the trees gracefully, its wedge-shaped tail and fanlike wings weaving amid the foliage as it headed toward the southwest fringes.

Unlooping a coil of tough climbing rope from his middle, Yoofus murmured, 'An' a fond goodbye to ye, sir. Don't hurry back now!'

Robbing a magpie nest could be a dangerous task. Big and strong, these birds were fierce predators and totally ruthless with anybeast trespassing in their nests.

The magpie was almost out of sight when an arrow

zipped upward, transfixing it. The bird fell to earth in an ungainly jumble of feathers, letting out a single harsh squawk. Overcome with curiosity, Yoofus rewound the rope about his waist and ran in the direction where the magpie had fallen. Acutely aware that danger was about, the vole-thief went cautiously. He was almost at the spot when he noted movement in a fern bed. Yoofus dropped behind a shrub, his paw going to the small dagger in his belt. Apart from a stonesling, this was the only armament he carried.

Four ermine, their fur patching from white to light tan with the lateness of the season, emerged from the grove of tall ferns. Each was armed with a short, curved bow and quiver of arrows. One of them retrieved the magpie's limp body, remarking to another, 'That leaves only thee to get a bird, Grik. So far we have taken a woodpigeon, a starling and this magpie twixt us three. Woe betide thee if Lord Gulo sees thee returning empty-pawed!'

Toting their bag of dead birds, the three ermine moved off, leaving the unfortunate Grik to hunt alone. Yoofus shadowed the ermine on his quest for prey. Grik got lucky suddenly. Ignorant of the ermine's presence close by, a song thrush trilled out its rapture from the branches of a witch hazel. Grik, who was not a proficient archer, shot the bird by pure fluke, slaying it with his first arrow. Flinging the thrush across his shoulder, the ermine set off back to camp, with Yoofus Lightpaw hot on his unsuspecting heels.

Shortly thereafter, the water vole was perched in a huge, high barberry shrub, studying the vermin camp. Other creatures may have been fearful at the sight of a hundred assorted ermine and white foxes, but not Yoofus. He saw the warriors of Gulo as a source of valuable loot. Many of them wore bracelets, pawrings and necklets of amber, gaudy shells and coral. There was also a goodly selection of weapons in evidence. Yoofus determined to bring his wife Didjety a few trinkets, bracelets and such. For himself, it was mainly a big blade he coveted, a sword. Never having owned one, the vole dreamed of roaming the woodlands, sporting a decent blade at his side.

Yoofus settled down to await the coming of darkness. When the vermin were asleep, and the camp quiet, he would go to work. The thief rubbed his paws in anticipation.

Gulo the Savage gnawed on a partly cooked dove. Close by, tied with a rope running from their necks to a stake, were the two remaining River Rats, Runneye and Bluesnout. Cringing on the ground, the pair scrabbled, fighting each other for the scraps tossed to them by the wolverine.

He eyed them disdainfully. 'So then, scum, how far off lies the Redwall place?'

Runneye had to think for a moment. 'On'y be notfar now, Lord – aye, notfar I t'ink.'

The wolverine frightened them badly as he leaned forward, baring his fangs, his open mouth half-filled with meat. 'Tell me again, what manner of beasts be those within its walls? How many strong are they, eh?'

Bluesnout whimpered. 'Jus' woodlan' beasters, Lord, not warriors – jus' mouses, moles, 'edgepigs, an' not many. Dey be peacelike, never fight you, Lord!'

Gulo leaned back on the drum where he was seated, fondling its decorated rim. He chuckled wickedly. 'Woodland creatures, not many in number an' peaceable. Methinks I like the sound of it. What say ye, Shard?'

The white fox captain reserved his judgement. ' 'Tis fortunate for us, but only if the rats speak truly, Lord.'

The savage's eyes narrowed menacingly. 'Wisely spoken, Shard. I have it in mind that thou shalt take a score and scout out the Redwall place in secret. Only then shall we know the real truth.'

He leered cruelly at his two rat captives. 'If ye have lied to Gulo, I have a special punishment reserved for ye – one that will last many days and nights!'

102

Runneye and Bluesnout wept openly, pleading with Gulo.

'No lie, no lies, us speaks true, Lord!'

'Us tellya der troo't, pleeze don't 'urt us, Lord!'

Gulo's predatory eyes glittered as he stroked his captives' heads. 'Hush now, cease thy whining. Live on in misery until my Captain returns. Then we will see how to treat thee. Shard, go swiftly. We will follow on behind and await thy report. Travel by night an' day.'

The captain bowed. 'Thy wish is my command, O Mighty One!'

Peering steadfastly between the thorns and the yellow blossom clusters of the barberry, Yoofus saw night descend. He had seen a creature like Gulo before – in fact, he had watched it die beneath a fallen sycamore trunk. The water vole had witnessed Wandering Walt and Hitheryon Jem covering Askor.

Yoofus had not been close enough to hear what went on between Gulo, Shard and the two rats. It did not concern him unduly; he was a thief, not a spy. What otherbeasts did was no concern of his. He was interested only in himself and his wife.

Campfires burned low, and the vermin ceased eating and quarrelling. Sentries were posted at four corners of the encampment. The volethief marked their positions to ensure that the guards would be no hindrance to him. When the last of Gulo's creatures was huddled by the fires, slumbering soundly, Yoofus left the barberry bush and drifted like a wraith into the camp. Silent as a moonshadow, he slid past two heavy-lidded foxes propped up against the bole of an elm. He heard the captive rats whimpering softly, forced to sleep sitting upright, their necks bound tight against the stake. Yoofus allowed himself a moment's satisfaction. He hated River Rats, all of whom he considered bullies and murderers.

Scanning the slumbering group for the best targets, the

103

volethief chose four ermine who were sprawled around a small heap of glowing embers. A cauldron rested on the remains of the fire. Yoofus took a quick peep at its contents – half-stewed birds, still with their feathers on. He wrinkled his nose in disgust. What a pack of primitive beasts these vermin were!

First he lifted a tailband of blue-coloured cord, with coral beads strung on it, from an ermine. What sort of poor creature had this once belonged to? Moving on to the next vermin, he artfully unbuckled a belt of eelskin studded with amber drops. Didjety would be pleased with that! The next sleeper yielded a silver ring with a purple mussel pearl set on its shank. Very nice finding scum who had taste in other places besides their mouths, he told himself. Then he espied the banner! A white fox, sleeping apart from the rest, had it spread over him like a sheet.

Yoofus quivered with delight. What a find! Didjety would have many uses for such a fine object, perhaps as a wall curtain, a bedquilt or maybe a cloth to grace their dining table. The banner was attached by its four corners to a pair of spearpoles. The volethief drew his little knife and snipped through the hanging cords. When next he tickled the fox's nose lightly, the creature released the banner and snuffled, scratching the offending itch. Yoofus took the opportunity to remove the flag, slowly and gracefully. Then things went awry. The fox sneezed. Though still half asleep, it sat up blinking at him, muttering, 'What be ye doing with yon fla–'

That was the furthest the vermin got. With eye-blurring speed, Yoofus seized a flagpole and whacked him squarely between the ears. The fox sat bolt upright for a moment, staring at him. Then the whites of its eyes showed, and it fell back, poleaxed. With his paws stinging from the impact, Yoofus placed the cracked pole aside carefully.

'Ah well, me ould foxie, ye'll sleep tight now, I'm thinkin'. Sure I'm sorry, but 'twas all I could do, y'see. Otherwise ye'd have wakened every rascal in the camp.'

The thief was bundling the banner up when he spotted the fox's sword, thrust through the belt at its side. Yoofus raised his eyes joyfully to the sky. 'Dame Fortune, me ould tatercake, may the sun always shine on ye. By all that's good'n'grand, a sword of me very own!'

Taking the fox's belt, he strapped it on with the sword hanging from it and struck what he fancied was a gallant stance. 'Ah, well ain't I the fine picture of a villainous vole!'

The sentries were now slumped against the elm, snoring industriously. Yoofus tippawed past them, saluting cheerfully. Away he went, with the swordpoint scraping the ground and the banner almost tripping him as it draped down over his back. Out on the trail once more, and clear of the camp, the irrepressible volethief broke into song.

'O, 'tis my belief that t'be a thief,
is a terrible thing t'be.
I tell ye straight that a thief I'd hate,
if he stole anythin' from me!

Come derry fol day folero,
an' chase me around the tree!

I'm bound to thieve though I never grieve,
when I lay me down to rest.
Cos I love the job an' I like to rob,
'tis the trade that I knows best!

Come derry fol day folero,
I'll bet ye don't catch me!

I've tried t'be good for I knows I should,
but 'tis hard for me ye see.
I'm more than willin' t'be a villain,
an' I can't help bein' me!

O come derry fol day foloooooooo,
now 'tis my turn to chase you!'

The following morn dawned warm but grey and misty, shrouded in fine drizzle. Captain Urfig, the white fox whom Yoofus had felled on the previous night, was wakened by an agonizing pain in his head. He touched the lump between his ears, groaning as fresh pangs lanced through his skull. Then the enormity of what had happened hit him like a thunderbolt. Images of the small, dark-furred creature, standing over him and swinging forcefully at his head with the flagpole, flashed before him. Then a brilliant starburst, followed by enveloping blackness, was all he could remember. Urfig struggled upright. His paw instinctively reached for his sword, but it was gone! Something between a whine and a sob escaped the fox's lips as he caught sight of the two poles and the severed cords on each side of him. The banner, too, was gone!

Gulo the Savage had entrusted him, as a high-ranking captain, with the flag. Urfig knew that his life was at an end. The wolverine would surely slay him for the loss of his standard – unless . . . ? Unless Urfig could think of an excuse that would satisfy his ruthless master. He tried to ignore his injured head, frantically seeking an alibi. There was no way that Gulo would accept the true explanation: his flag taken by some little woodlander? Never! Urfig wandered about distractedly until his eyes lit on the tracks Yoofus had left – scrapemarks where the swordpoint had dragged behind the vole and a blurring where the flag tassels had swept along with it. Urfig suddenly saw a ruse that might spare his life. It was a desperate chance, a wild gamble, but it had to be taken swiftly.

Gulo had becomed accustomed to the fair weather of this new land, but he was not a lover of rain, or even drizzle. On his orders, his guards had erected a canvas over a low tree limb. There he sat, gazing sourly into a smoky fire, awaiting the arrival of better conditions.

Nobeast was more surprised than the wolverine when

Urfig came hurriedly staggering out of the mist. Scattering the fire, he lurched into the awning, knocking the canvas loose.

Collapsing in a heap, the captain gasped hoarsely, 'Askor, it was thy brother, Askor, Lord!'

Gulo sprang up. Grabbing the captain, he pulled him from the wreckage and hauled him upright. 'My brother – where, when? Speak, fool!'

Urfig did not have to put on an act. Genuinely terrified, he babbled out a reply. 'I was almost killed, Lord, knocked senseless. I have just awakened and come here, straight to thee! During the night, Sire, thy brother Askor came. He stole my sword and thy banner! He knocked me over the head with a pole, sire . . .'

Gulo shook the fox like a rag, covering his face in spittle as he bellowed, 'Was it really Askor? Which way did he go?'

Urfig pointed a trembling paw in the direction taken by Yoofus. 'Truly, 'twas thy brother, Lord. Methinks he went that way, north.'

Dragging the captain along by his ears, Gulo yelled out orders. 'Guards! Guards! To the north! Find me a trail!'

Yanking Urfig close, he brought him eye to eye. 'The Walking Stone, did he have the Walking Stone?'

The hapless captain, up on tippaws, felt as though his ears were being pulled out by the roots. 'Mighty One, I did not see, it happened so swiftly!'

The ermine Garfid, who was Gulo's best tracker, was down on all fours, examining the ground. 'Over here, Sire. I see marks!'

Gulo was quivering all over as he knelt beside the tracker. 'What do ye see? Tell me, are they those of that brother of mine?'

Garfid glanced over the wolverine's shoulder and caught the nod from Urfig's frightened face. The tracker was no fool; he took the wise course, knowing death could be the result of an unfavourable answer to his ruthless chieftain.

107

'Only mighty beasts such as thee can leave a deep claw-mark, Lord. The blurring of the edges means that the creature had long-haired paws like thine. The drizzling rain has not helped this trail, but it looks very like thy brother's marks, Sire.'

Gulo the Savage threw back his head, letting out a great screeching howl of triumph. 'Yaaaaheeeeegh! I knew it, 'tis Askor! We go north, now. Now!'

14

Tam sat on the streambank with Doogy, Ferdimond and Wonwill. It was long gone dawn, and no cooking fires had been lit. They breakfasted on hard oatcakes and apples, with streamwater to wash them down.

Doogy blew rainwater off his swollen nose. 'Ach, 'tis no' much of a day tae be goin' on with!'

Wonwill chuckled drily. 'Wot, complaints already, Mister Plumm? Ye've not been with the Patrol more'n a day or two an' lookit the fun you've 'ad. A nice liddle stroll of a march, a fight, an' now yore moanin' about the beautiful mornin' an' a free drizzlewash. Ye don't know yore born, mate!'

Ferdimond gazed gloomily out at the prevailing mist and rain. 'Lucky old us, wot. I say, Sarge, where's the Brigadier got to?'

Wonwill cocked a paw behind him. 'Saw 'im go up t'the top o' the bank yonder. I've gotta feelin' Brig Crumshaw'll be wantin' me shortly.'

As if in answer, the brigadier's voice called from the banktop. 'Sergeant Wonwill, d'ye mind attendin' me, please?'

The hare's tough features broke into a grin. 'See, I told ye! C'mon, buckoes, let's see wot the h'officer requires.'

Brigadier Crumshaw waved his swagger stick at the flatlands in front of them. 'Y'see this, confounded mist an' blinkin' drizzle too. Can't abide the blitherin' stuff. Right, Sergeant, quick's the word an' sharp's the action, wot! Can't mope around here waitin' for gallopers all day, eh?'

The sergeant was aware of his officer's plan. He saluted. 'H'exactly, sah, just as y'say. H'I take it ye want the Patrol up an' marchin', sah. But wot about young Kersey an' Dauncey, sah?'

Tam shouldered his shield. 'We'll prob'ly meet up with 'em on the march.'

Crumshaw pointed his stick at Tam. 'Well said that, chap! Brisk march'll get the miseries out of us, wot! Maybe the blinkin' weather'll buck up soon.'

The Long Patrol were glad to form ranks and march off, even though their paws squished on the damp grass.

Doogy trudged along looking thoughtful. 'Suppose those wee gallopers – Kersey'n'Dauncey is it? – suppose they miss us in all this mist?'

Wonwill kept his eyes straight ahead. 'That's a thought, Mister Plumm. Mister De Mayne, sah, would ye oblige us with h'a song? Sing out good'n'loud so the gallopers will 'ear ye. That should do the trick.'

Ferdimond coughed and tried to look distressed. 'Actually I've got a bit of a jolly old frog in me throat this mornin', Sarge. Couldn't some other chap do the singin'?'

Wonwill grinned mischievously. 'Nah, nah, young Ferdimond, h'orders is h'orders, let the frog do the singin', eh?'

The young hare had quite a fair tenor voice, which rang out nicely as he rendered an old barracks room ballad.

'When I joined the regiment my comrades said to me,
there is one beast we fear more than the foe.
An army marches on its stomach, so 'tis plain to see,
that fool we call the cook has got to go!

O the cook! O the cook!
If words could kill, or just a dirty look,
he'd have snuffed it long ago, turned his paws up
   doncha know,
he'd be gladly written off the record book!

What a greasy fat old toad, that assassin of the road,
we tried to hire him to the enemy.
But they smelt the stew he made, mercy on us they all
   prayed,
we'll surrender, you can have him back for free!

O the cook! O the cook!
He could poison a battalion with his chuck.
I've seen him boilin' cabbage, an' the filthy little savage,
takes a bath in it to wash off all the muck!

He made a batch of scones, big grey lumpy solid ones,
the Sergeant lost four teeth at just one bite.
Then an officer ordered me, sling them at the enemy,
an' those that we don't slay we'll put to flight!

O the cook! O the cook!
He's stirring porridge with his rusty hook.
Playin' hopscotch with the toast, he's the one that we
   hate most,
tonight we're goin' to roast that bloomin' cook!'

A shout came from out the mist. 'What ho, the Long Patrol!'
   The brigadier called in reply, 'Gallopers come in an' make your report!'
   Kersey and Dauncey came bounding out of the mist. Slowing to the march, they told the tale, each in turn. Kersey went first.
   'Followed the vermin to the woodlands, sah! They entered Mossflower at the southwest fringe, on a track twixt some alders an' buckthorns.'

Dauncey followed his sister with hardly a break. 'We got jolly close t'the blighters, sah. Some nasty-lookin' bits of work among that bloomin' bunch. Guess what? We saw the Gulo beast too. My word, what a blinkin' horror! Hate to bump into him on a dark night, wot!'

Fixing his monocle rigidly upon the pair, the brigadier fumed. 'Confounded, perilous young buffoons! My orders were that ye kept a safe distance from those murderin' cannibals. They ain't green behind the ears, y'know. You could've both been captured an' eaten alive!'

Kersey pouted airily. 'Catch two gallopers like us, sah? Fat flippin' chance. All those clods would catch'd be mouthfuls of our dust!'

Brigadier Crumshaw looked as if he were about to explode. His moustache bristled as he thundered at the gallopers, 'Silence! Insubordination in the bally ranks, wot! Sergeant, place these insolent young blighters on firewood gatherin' an' potwashin' duties as of now!'

Dauncey gave a snort of disbelief. 'But, sah, that's not fair!'

Crumshaw bellowed at the unfortunate pair, 'Enough, I say! One more word from either of you malcontents an' I'll have ye clapped under close arrest an' marched back to Salamandastron to cool your paws in the guardhouse! I'm relievin' you of scoutin' an' gallopin' duties until ye learn to follow orders correctly. Wot!'

Sergeant Wonwill kept his eyes front as he spoke to the downcast twins. 'No arguments. You 'eard the h'officer, young 'uns, off y'go now. Report to Corporal Wopscutt. 'E'll show you yore chores.'

Kersey and Dauncey saluted before marching off stiffly, tears of hot indignation burning bright in their eyes. The brigadier watched their retreating figures with a fatherly eye.

'Hah, young pair o' buckoes, wot! One day they'll make splendid officers an' perilous warriors, mark m'words. But they've got to learn some jolly hard lessons first if we're to keep 'em from bein' slain. Right, Sergeant?'

Wonwill's tough face mellowed. 'Right y'are, sah, though ye can't 'elp feelin' sorry for the young rips. But who's goin' t'take their place as gallopers, sah?'

With a sweep of his swagger stick, Crumshaw indicated Tam, Doogy and Ferdimond. 'These three ruffians I fancy, wot!'

Wonwill could not help a passing glance at Doogy's solid little figure. 'Hmm, 'ardly cut out for gallopin', sah.'

Tam interjected. 'Maybe not, Sarge, but I don't think the Brigadier's lookin' for gallopers. Things could get a bit sticky keepin' tabs on a hundred vermin. We'll need beasts who've seen a bit of action, good stalkers who can use their judgement. Eh, sah?'

The brigadier's swagger stick tapped Tam's chest. 'Took the words out o' me mouth, MacBurl. You an' Plumm here have been around the trees a few times, I can tell. As for young De Mayne, he could jolly well benefit from the experience. He'll do all the gallopin' needed at a pinch.'

Doogy saluted the brigadier with his claymore. 'Ah take it we're tae be the braw new scouts for a wee while. Ah'm wonderin' whether tae be flattered or battered, sah.'

Crumshaw smiled briefly. 'Draw ration packs from Corporal Wopscutt an' go to it, you chaps. Report back this evenin'. We'll meet up by those alders'n'buckthorns young Kersey mentioned. That'll be all for now. Dismissed!'

Three sets of footpaws pounded the mist-shrouded flatlands, headed northeast for the woodlands. Ferdimond was way out in front, with Tam a close second and Doogy trying gallantly but struggling at the rear.

After a while, the little Highlander slowed to a jog. Clutching a paw to his side, he called out to the hare, 'Will ye no' slack off a wee bit, ye lang-legged hairpin? Ah wasnae built for dashin' aboot like a scalded frog!'

Ferdimond decreased his pace, grinning at Tam. 'I say, I can't see little barrel bottom in this blinkin' mist. Where d'you supposed he's got to, wot?'

Tam caught up with Ferdimond and took hold of his paw. 'Not so fast, mate, the woods won't run away. They'll still be there when we arrive.'

Doogy came out of the mist, panting like a bellows. 'Och, there ye are, ah thought ye'd got lost. Ah'll walk in front an' ye can follow me at a respectable pace.'

Ferdimond chuckled good-naturedly. 'Oh, how can I soar like an eagle when I'm surrounded by waddlin' ducks, eh?'

Winking slyly at Tam, Doogy stuck out his footpaw and tripped the young hare. Obligingly, he helped Ferdimond up. 'Ah'd go easy if'n I were ye. More haste less speed, mah auld grannie used tae say.'

The hare brushed dew from his tunic. 'Wise creature, your old grannie. Point taken, old lad.'

Doogy did an elaborate bow. 'Thank ye, old boy, old lad, old chap, wot wot, an' toodly blinkin' pip, eh!'

Tam walked alongside them, laughing. 'You sounded just like Ferdimond then, mate.'

Doogy straightened his cap, tugging at his eartips. 'Aye, well ah've decided tae become a hare, ye know.'

Ferdimond scoffed. 'You, a bally hare? Right, then I'll be a Highland squirrel. How'd that suit ye?'

Tam shook his head. 'Go on, let's hear ye then.'

Ferdimond adopted Doogy's truculent swagger comically. 'Och the noo, ah like a wee stroll tae the woods on a misty day, cos ah cannae dash aboot like yon wee hare.'

He looked at them trying to keep their faces straight. 'Come on, you chaps, how did I do? The truth now!'

Tam burst into gales of laughter as Doogy complained indignantly, 'Ach, if ah sounded like that ah would've swam oot intae the sea an' drownded mahself long since!'

Ferdimond replied huffily, 'Really, is that a fact? Well, if I sounded like you did tryin' to imitate me, I'd have begged that Gulo chap to scoff me pretty sharpish!'

They continued ragging and making good-humoured fun of one another as they marched. The mist began lifting in the early noon, and Tam spotted the treeline ahead. 'Keep it down now, mates. We don't need to advertise our presence to any foebeasts who might be around. We'll split up now and circle in from three ways. Doogy, take the left, I'll take the right. Ferdy, you go straight in but keep yore eyes peeled, mate. See you both by that big old alder tree yonder. Good luck.'

They reached the alder with no untoward happenings. Tam picked up the vermin trail. 'They went this way. Can you track these marks, Ferdy?'

The hare unsheathed his long rapier. ''Course I can. They look pretty plain t'me, Tam. But why d'you want me to track, wot?'

Doogy could not help sounding slightly self-satisfied. 'Because, mah lanky friend, we'll be takin' tae the trees. Us squirrels are fair speedy beasts up in yon foliage. Bein' a groundcrawler, you'll have tae stay down here, auld boy!'

Tam sprang up into the buckthorns. 'Don't worry, we'll keep in touch with you. The mist is gone now. We can see more from up here. Take care, Ferdy.'

Doogy chuckled maliciously. 'Aye, an' don't ye go trippin' up an' fallin' over now.'

The woodlands were still and eerily silent as Ferdimond made his way forward. There was neither wind nor breeze, but the drizzle had collected on branch and leaf. It plopped and dropped in the stillness, until Ferdimond was wet through. But he followed the trail dutifully until he came into a glade, where Tam and Doogy were waiting for him.

The young hare looked around. 'Feathers everywhere! They must've slaughtered quite a few birds, confounded savages!'

Tam ran his dirkpoint through the ashes of a fire. 'This ain't properly out, see? Look at the half-finished bird there, and the broken eggs, too. It looks to me like these vermin left here in a big hurry, eh, Doogy?'

His companion picked up a broken shell necklace and a pouch of slingstones. 'Aye, ah wonder why they went in such a haste, Tam.'

The warrior squirrel began climbing into a nearby oak. 'I don't know, but I'm going to find out. Doogy, you stay here and keep yore eyes open. Ferdy, time for ye t'do a spot of gallopin'. Make it back t'the patrol an' tell the Brigadier what's happenin'. It may be important.'

Tam dropped his shield to the ground so he would not be impeded. A moment later he was whipping through the middle terraces to the north. As he travelled, it was quite easy to track the vermin trail below. Gulo and his band had pushed forward heedlessly, breaking twigs, flattening shrubbery and generally leaving a broad path. It was well into noontide when Tam heard the vermin up ahead. A little further and he would have them in sight. He halted in the broad limbs of a chestnut tree to catch his breath and check his blades. Tam knew that when he reached the vermin, silence would be essential. Wrapping his plaid cloak into a tight bundle about his shoulder, he adjusted the claymore in his belt so that it could be quickly drawn.

There was a faint rustle of leaves from above, in the top branches of the chestnut. Before Tam could raise his eyes to look up, he was hit forcibly by a descending object and knocked out of the tree.

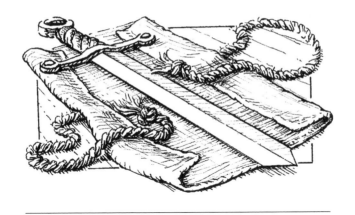

15

Abbot Humble was playing make-believe tea with the Dibbuns. He enjoyed being with the little ones, joining in their games and listening to their baby talk. Mimsie the mousebabe served him with an invisible platter, supposedly full of goodies.

Humble beamed delightedly. 'Oh my, these look nice, I like fresh scones!'

Mimsie scowled. 'They not sconeses, them's cream an' stawb'y cake wot I jus' maked!'

The Abbot apologized. 'Oh, I'm sorry. My old eyes aren't so good any more, you know. Cream and strawberry cake, my favourite! Have we got some sweet cordial to drink with it?'

Perkle the hogbabe passed him an imaginary beaker. 'No, Farver, this bee's boiled nekkle h'ale!'

Mudge the molebabe winked broadly at Humble. 'Yurr, zurr, but doan't ee tell Sis h'Armel. She'm say Dibbuns shuddent drink boiled nekkle h'ale.'

Humble nodded seriously. 'I won't breathe a word, promise. Boiled nettle ale, eh? Mmmm, tastes good, I like it!'

Perkle squeaked out a warning. 'Farver, 'ide it quick. Sis Armel bee's comin'!'

Sister Armel and Brooky came hurriedly into the dormitory, where the Abbot was playing with the Dibbuns. The pretty Infirmary Keeper could not keep the urgency out of her voice. 'Father Abbot, I must speak to you immediately in private. It's very important!'

Humble carried on pretending, putting both paws behind his back as if hiding the boiled nettle ale. 'Right, Sister, just give me a moment, please.'

He whispered to the Dibbuns, 'You'd better go and have tea down on the lawn so that Sister Armel doesn't see the ale.'

Touching paws to snouts secretly, the Dibbuns nodded. They loaded the make-believe meal on to a make-believe trolley and began solemnly trundling it away.

Brooky called after them, 'Save some o' that boiled nettle ale for us, you greedy villains!'

As the Dibbuns clattered out of the dormitory, giggling mischievously, Humble turned to the squirrel and ottermaid, shaking his head. 'Cream and strawberry cake with boiled nettle ale? Whatever next! What can I do for you, young Armel?'

The pretty squirrel explained her sudden visit. 'When we were in the orchard, solving the puzzle, I suddenly felt drowsy. It must have been only for a moment. Father, I don't know whether you'll believe this, but Martin the Warrior appeared to me.'

Humble looked into Armel's innocent brown eyes. 'Why should I doubt you, my child? Did our Warrior speak?'

She nodded emphatically. 'He did, though I completely forgot I'd even seen him until a short while ago. Brooky and I were passing through Great Hall when I saw Martin's picture on the tapestry. Then it all came back to me like a flash!'

The ottermaid laughed. 'Oohahaha! Very exciting, isn't it?'

Humble silenced her with a mild glance. 'Tell me, Armel, what did Martin the Warrior say to you?'

Armel remembered everything clearly. 'He said he knew me, and that was why he chose me. Then he spoke these lines.

My sword must be carried by maidens two:
one who sees laughter in all, and you.
Bear it southwest through Mossflower Wood,
to he who pursues the vermin Lord.
The Borderer who is a force for good,
that warrior who sold and lost his sword.'

Humble folded both paws into his wide habit sleeves. 'Did he say any more?'

Armel sighed. 'No, Father, that was all. What should I do?'

The Abbot pondered for a while, then made his decision. 'Go and find my cousin, Hitheryon Jem. Brooky, you will seek out your uncle Skipper. Bring them both to the gatehouse. We need to discuss this matter urgently.'

Jem was rather grumbly as he followed Armel across the sunlit lawns to the gatehouse. 'Great seasons, ain't there no rest for a poor ole body? I'm scarce out of a good warm tub an' into a clean robe when I'm bein' marched outdoors through the grounds. A beast of my seasons could catch cold, y'know!'

Armel patted his paw as they came to the gatehouse door. 'Oh, I'm sure you'll take no harm, sir. It's not me who wants you here, it's your cousin, the Abbot.'

Jem opened the door. 'Humble? Oh, that's different, missy. Why didn't ye say?'

The young Sister smiled. 'I did, but you probably forgot.'

Skipper and Brooky were already there, as was Humble and Gordale the Gatekeeper. Friar Glisum arrived unexpectedly, bearing with him a sliced pie of damsons and honey with a container of his own special pear and redcurrant wine.

119

He popped his head around the door with the air of a conspirator, commenting, 'Hope you don't mind me joining you. I saw you all hurrying here, and it made me rather curious.'

Humble beckoned him inside. 'Come in, Friar. Sit down there and listen carefully, all of you. Sister Armel has something to say. Sister?'

Armel took a deep breath and recounted her experience. When she had finished, the Abbot looked from one to the other. 'Well, what do you think, friends?'

Skipper of Otters was first to venture an opinion. 'I was 'oping that all last winter an' right through the spring, 'til now, that this wouldn't 'appen, Father, but it looks like it must be, eh, Jem?'

The old hedgehog answered sadly, 'Aye, Skip. This Abbey's a sizeable buildin', stickin' out like a bandaged paw twixt the woodlands an' flatlands. Stands t'reason that any vermin gang in this part o' the country is bound to sight it.'

Brother Gordale caught the hedgehog's drift. 'You mean that creature Gulo the Savage and his followers?'

Humble went to the little gatehouse window. There he stood, gazing out at the sunlit lawns and the Abbey building. 'We were hoping, Skipper and I, that maybe they'd miss us somehow and go off on a different course. But if I read Martin the Warrior's message correctly, it seems that Redwall is in danger. Why else would he send us this warning through Sister Armel? One thing, though. Before we go any further, I must ask. Are we all agreed to act upon this?'

Brooky's sudden laughter made Gordale jump. 'Whooohahahoo! We'd be real puddenheads if we didn't.'

Skipper silenced his niece by treading on her rudder. 'Young Brookflow's right. She's noisy, but right. So then, Father, what d'ye suggest?'

Humble placed a paw on the otter chieftain's shoulder. 'I say we should carry out Martin's words to the letter. That is, if Armel and Brooky are willing to undertake the task. As to anything else, I tell you truly. I am only a Cellarhog who was fortunate enough to become Father Abbot of Redwall. As such, I am concerned with its safety, and all the creatures within who are under my care. I know nothing of the ways of war or defence. I have always entrusted those matters to you, Skipper.'

The burly otter bowed slightly. 'Thankee, friend, I wouldn't 'ave it any other way. Now then, Sister Armel, will you carry out the task Martin has sent ye? An' you, too, Brookflow, cos yore the one who sees laughter in all, an' yore a maid too. So?'

The Infirmary Sister took Brooky's paw. 'I'll go if you come with me.'

The sturdy ottermaid giggled with embarrassment. 'Heeheeheehee, just you try and stop me!'

Skipper ruffled his niece's head fondly. Unwinding a sling from his waist, he gave it to her with a full pebble bag. 'Take good care o' this, ye scallywag. 'Tis me best sling. I want ye to take good care o' Sister Armel too!'

Brooky helped herself to a slice of the friar's pie. 'Nice sling, nunky Skip. Of course I'll take care of Armel. If I don't, you can load me into this sling an' chuck me out the attic window. Hahahahaha!'

Armel gave her a playful shove. 'Don't worry, Skip, we'll look out for each other. When do we go?'

Jem looked up from the deep armchair he was occupying. 'Travel by night is best. Stick to the shadows on the pathside an' don't make any noise. Me'n ole Walt should be goin' along with ye by rights, but the seasons are weighin' too 'eavy on us now, an' we'd be slowin' ye down, missy.'

Skipper bit his lip, looking a bit worried. 'I could hunt out a few o' my otter mateys. Them stayin' close by both of ye wouldn't go amiss. Couple o' big coves with javelins.'

However, Armel would not hear of this. 'Definitely not, but thank you, Skip. Martin was quite clear who should go: "My sword must be carried by maidens two, one who sees laughter in all, and you." I would not risk disobeying the word of Martin the Warrior. We will leave tonight after supper. The directions are also quite clear – southwest through Mossflower Wood, until we find the Borderer who is a force for good. Right, Brooky?'

The ottermaid nodded cheerily. 'Correct. We're out to deliver Martin's sword to this Borderer cove. 'That warrior who sold and lost his sword.' Bit careless of him, wasn't it? Hope he doesn't lose Martin's sword. Hohohohoho!'

Skipper glared at Brooky so fiercely that she quailed. 'Don't even think of it, Brookflow!'

Supper that evening was served in Great Hall, the tables laid out beneath Martin's tapestry. Both maids were the centre of attention. It seemed that every Redwaller wanted to give them gifts, either knowledgeable information or equipment for their journey.

'Yurr, marm, take ee moi likkle dagger, h'it bee's gurtly sharp. An' take ee moi ole granfer's cloak too!'

'Remember now, if ye see any vermin, don't stop to talk with the nasty sly brutes. You just run off, fast as y'can!'

Humble cast an amused glance at Armel. 'I think you and Brooky will leave here with more information than your heads can carry, and more clothing, food and weapons than your paws can bear, eh, Sister?'

Armel put aside a lucky pebble, which had been donated by Mudge the molebabe. 'Aye, Father, but everything is given in friendship and with good heart. How can we refuse them?'

Wandering Walt whispered to her, 'Doan't ee fret, marm. Give 'em all to oi. Oi'll give ee h'all ee gifts back on yore safe return, hurr aye.'

Brooky interrupted. 'Thankee, Walt. How's the footpaw, still split? Maybe it'll split altogether. Then you'll have three footpaws. Hahahaha!'

Old Walt chuckled. 'Nay, marm, oi spreaded et with ee h'ointment from Sister's affirmery. 'Tis foine now. Oi'm gurtly taken with ee affirmery medicines, they'm gudd.'

Armel took a quick peep at Walt's footpaw. 'Well done, sir! Perhaps you'd like to fill in as Infirmary Keeper while I'm away?'

The ancient mole beamed with pleasure. 'Thankee gurtly, Sister. 'Twould be noice to 'old such an 'igh posishun!'

Brooky raised her goblet to him. 'Listen, everybeast, this good mole is our new healer. From now on, he will be known as Sister Walt. Hahahahaha!'

Foremole Bruffy called out, 'Yurr, Sister, can ee cure moi blister? If'n ee do, oi'll give ee a gurt kiss. Hurrhurrhurr!'

Walt scowled. 'Burr, then oi'll raise anuther blister, zurr, roight on ee skull!'

Good food and merry banter went back and forth. Humble waited until there was a lull in the proceedings before he signalled to Skipper. The otter chieftain went to the tapestry. Standing upon a tall chair, he took the sword of Martin from its two brackets above the tapestry. A hush fell over all as he laid the blade on the table in front of Armel.

The Abbot addressed her in a voice which could be heard by every Redwaller present. 'This is the sword of Martin the Warrior, made by a Badger Lord in the fires at Salamandastron. It is said that the blade was forged from the metal of a star which fell from the skies. This sword has always stood as a symbol of truth, honour and justice at Redwall. I place it in your care, Sister Armel. You must promise to bring it back here when its task is fulfilled.'

Apart from a red pommel stone, the sword hilt was a plain black grip, serviceable and strong. Armel laid her paw upon it, gazing in awe at the legendary blade. This was fashioned with a centre channel and double edges, keen as ice in midwinter, running to a point which shimmered like a searing flame.

The blade was as old as forgotten dreams and as lethal as death's shadow.

Armel's voice was hushed, yet it echoed round Great Hall. 'Father, it is a strange thing for a maid who knows only about healing, and caring for the sick, to be bearing such a weapon. But I will deliver it to the warrior whom Martin has spoken of. When the sword has served its purpose, I swear upon my life that I will return it to you, here in this room at Redwall!'

Amid applause and cheers of approval, Humble embraced the young squirrel, whom he had seen grow from infancy to a well-loved member of his Abbey. Tears dewed in his eyes for the unknown dangers she might be facing.

16

Slow-drifting cloudbanks masked a buttercup-hued half-moon in the spring night. Somewhere off in the distant trees a nightjar churred its nocturnal melody. At the south wallgate, Skipper withdrew the bolts of the little door in the wall. The mouse Gatekeeper, Brother Gordale, eased the door back on its well-oiled hinges.

Skipper patted his niece's cheek affectionately. 'Be a good young maid now, an' watch out for Sister Armel an' that sword. D'ye hear me?'

Even Brooky knew that this was no time for laughter. She pressed her uncle's big paw. 'Don't worry, I'll keep an eye on 'em both.'

Humble assured Sister Armel, 'We'll be watching every day for your return. Go now, and may good fortune smile upon you both.'

The little walldoor closed quietly as two hooded and cloaked figures ventured off into the darkness.

Armel and Brooky went quickly over the small area of grassland which skirted the south wall. They headed for the path which curved through Mossflower Wood. Outside of the Abbey, everything looked different without the blessing of sunlight.

Armel shuddered. 'I've only been outside the Abbey a few times, and then not far – either gathering herbs or for picnics when I was small. It feels very lonely out here with just each other for company.'

Brooky stifled a titter, trying her best to sound confident. 'You stay close t'me and you'll come t'no harm, pal. I've been twice to the north shores in the summer with Uncle Skip and his crew. I'm used to this sort o' thing, y'know.'

She tripped on a rock and went headlong into a pile of broom. Armel could not help chuckling as she took hold of Brooky's paw. 'Up you come, mate. Are you all right?'

The stout ottermaid shot up immediately. 'Right as rain, thankee! Though I wish that moon'd keep still an' stop dodging behind the clouds. This cloak's a nuisance too. Can't take a step without it tripping me!'

They made the path without further incident and followed it south for a while. Armel began getting used to the dark. 'Watch the ditch on your right side, Brooky. Hold on a tick while I fix this sword.'

Brooky helped her friend adjust the sword, which was wrapped in a sheath of soft barkcloth. She fixed it so that the blade hung flat down Armel's back beneath her cloak, away from prying eyes. The ottermaid took charge of both their foodpacks, toting them easily over one shoulder. 'I'll carry these. You take care of the sword, pal.'

Armel smiled gratefully. 'Thanks, mate. Friar Glisum said that he thought up some travelling rations specially for us, stuff that doesn't need cooking. He said there's a full meal in each piece. Oh, and Burlop Cellarhog gave us a flask of a recipe he's invented to save carrying too much weight.'

Brooky flexed her shoulder. 'Feels light enough. What is it?'

Armel explained. 'A syrup made from boiled-down fruit juices and honey. Burlop said you only have to add water to it and it'll make a sweet, nourishing drink. Good, eh?'

The ottermaid commented doubtfully, 'I'll let you know

after I've tried it. Hadn't we better cut off west into the trees? This path runs mainly south.'

Armel agreed. 'Good idea, but how do we cross the ditch?'

Brooky suddenly regained her sense of fun. 'The best plan would be to jump over it, cos we can't very well jump under it. Hahahaha, here goes!'

She took a short run and jumped, making the other side with ease. 'See that, Armel! I should've been born a bird really, I just flew over. Your turn now – ready, steady, jump!'

The squirrelmaid took a short run at the ditch, but at the crucial moment of jumping, her footpaw became snarled in her cloak hem. With a small cry of dismay, she plunged headlong into the ditch.

Her otter friend came swiftly to the rescue. 'Oh, bad luck, pal. Stay there, I'll get you out!' She slid down into the ditch, which was deeper than she had thought it would be.

The moon came from behind the clouds, throwing a pale light down to illuminate the scene. Armel was flat on her back, almost rigid with fright as she called out, 'Brooky, stand still, don't move!'

There was no water in the ditch, just a deep layer of damp leaves and weeds. Right between the two travellers, a snake reared its head out of its scaly coils, hissing venomously. 'Thrrrrttsss!'

Wide-eyed with horror, Armel whispered, 'Brooky, I think it's an adder. What do we do now?'

The ottermaid had been studying the reptile carefully. Slowly she took the ration packs from her shoulder. As she did this, Brooky appeared to be striking up a conversation with the snake. 'Well, are you an adder?'

Its head swivelled to face her. 'I am death to all-beastssssss!'

Brooky seemed quite fascinated by this declaration. 'Are you really? Well, what can we do for you, Mister Death?'

The snake slithered toward Brooky, its forked tongue flickering. 'I like to eat thingssssss!'

As soon as the reptile had its back to her, Armel began inching her paw slowly towards the sword hilt. However, there was no need for any action on her part because of what Brooky did next.

The ottermaid smiled engagingly at the snake. 'You like to eat things . . . haha, don't we all! Listen, we've got lots of nice vittles with us. Why not try some?'

She swung both the ration packs with lightning speed. *Whap! Smack! Thunk! Wallop!* Four hefty blows landed forcibly on the snake's head, leaving it slack-coiled and totally senseless.

Armel struggled up and ran to her friend. 'Oh, Brooky, I thought the adder was going to kill you! How wonderfully brave you were, attacking it like that!'

The young otter looked up from the packs, which she was checking for damage. 'Hahahaha! Wonderfully brave, my grannie's apron! You great, fluffy-tailed buffer, don't you know the difference twixt an adder an' a grass snake? Huh, Mister Death, eh!'

Armel stammered, 'B . . . but I didn't know, I thought it was poison!'

Brooky scoffed. 'Just look at its back, the thing hasn't got a diamond pattern. Adders have diamond patterns along their backs. Grass snakes only have markings on their sides. Look.'

She wiped the unconscious reptile's back off with her cloak hem. There, beneath the layer of ditch mud and rotten leaves, was the black V-marked head and zigzag marks of an adder.

Brooky thought this was hilarious. 'Oh hahahahoohoo! Silly me, it was an adder after all. Well, the food looks all right, so there's no harm done, really – except to Mister Death there. He'll have a headache that should last him until midsummer. Let's get out of this slimy place. I've never liked hanging about in ditches.'

Armel joined in the spirit of the thing. Nobeast could stay

gloomy for long in the company of the happy otter. 'Neither have I. Let's leave Mister Death to his nap.'

Laughing together, they climbed out of the ditch and headed into the woodlands. They had not gone far when Brooky halted, scratching her ear. 'How will we know we're going southwest? I'm not too bright on all that northing and southing business.'

Armel reassured her. 'It's quite simple, really. The sun rises in the east, you see, so if you have it directly at your back, you'll be going west. South is off to the left if west is straight ahead, so we take the middle course and we'll be travelling southwest. Get it?'

Brooky shook her head. 'I'm still as baffled as when you started explainin'. So you be the pathfinder, and I'll deal with any hungry snakes that we come across!'

They trekked all night until the dawn sunrays told them they were on the right track.

Armel rubbed her eyes. She was feeling quite tired. 'Walk by night and rest by day, that's what we were told. So let's make camp, have a spot of breakfast and a nice little snooze. Does that sound like a good idea?'

Brooky grinned from ear to ear. 'Do you hear me objectin'? How about camping at the base of that big elm over there?'

They spread their cloaks and opened the ration packs. Armel opened one parcel that contained two wheaten loaves. She bit into one, passing her friend the other.

'Mmm, this tastes good! Look, it has cheese, mushrooms, carrots and onions baked inside. What's yours like?'

Brooky took a healthy mouthful from her loaf, which was sweetened ryebread. 'Haha, this is full of thick honey, chopped hazelnuts, cooked apple and blackberry. Good old Friar Glisum, he's given us two courses in two loaves. Tell you what, we'll swap when we're halfway through 'em. Then we'll have had main meal an' dessert together.'

Armel found one of the drink flasks and two beakers. 'I'll go and find some water to mix with Burlop's fruit syrup. There might be a stream or a spring nearby.'

The squirrelmaid was not gone for long. Brooky was dozing gradually. She opened one eye when her friend returned. 'Well, did you find some water?'

Armel slumped down beside her. 'No, couldn't see any around, but I did find something.'

The ottermaid's eyelids began drooping. 'What was that?'

Armel yawned. 'The path from last night. It runs straight with the direction we're going. We've been struggling along through the woodlands all night, not knowing that the path was hardly a stone's throw away. It must run southwest for quite a bit. So, Miss Puddenhead, who said that we should take to the woods because the path goes straight to the south?'

The ottermaid imitated a snoring sound. 'Not me, must have been you. Don't disturb me, I'm asleep!'

Armel lay down, shielding her eyes from the sunlight. 'It was you, you great, fat-tailed fibber. Goodnight!'

Brooky wrinkled her nose. 'Heeheehee, don't you mean good day?'

Armel smiled. 'Don't speak to me, I'm not talking to you!'

Brooky snuggled down into her cloak. 'I'm not speaking, I'm sleeping. Don't wake me, please. Heeheehee!'

The day was both warm and pleasant, heralding a fine summer to come. Butterflies and wood moths fluttered noiselessly through the tranquil woodland glade. Bees droned soothingly amid small blossoms of white campion, whitlow grass, sweet woodruff and blackberry. By mid-morn the ground was dry and sunkissed. Partially shaded by the foliage of the big elm, the travellers enjoyed their first sleep outside the protection of Redwall Abbey. Morning drifted serenely into noontide, shifting the shadows as the sun began its descent from midday zenith.

Brooky, the more volatile of the two, awoke around midnoon, with sun shining in her eyes and an inquisitive yellow brimstone butterfly fluttering about her half-open mouth. The ottermaid blew it away and tried to resume her slumber. The combination of daylight and a growing thirst, however, kept her awake. She looked across at Armel, still sleeping peacefully, wrapped loosely in her cloak.

Brooky sat up, yawning loudly and heaving gusty sighs. The moment she saw that the sounds were making Armel stir, she began complaining. 'Oh, it's not a bit of use, I can't sleep any more!'

Her friend awakened, blinking. 'Why, what's the matter?'

The ottermaid cast aside her cloak and stood up. 'Cos the flaming sun's in my eyes, I'm being trampled on by all sorts of insects and my tongue's like a baked sandal. I'm thirsty, aren't you?'

To her surprise, Armel arose and began folding her cloak. 'Aye, let's go and find some water. I could do with a drink.'

They broke camp and walked to within sight of the path, heading southwest alongside the ditch.

Before long, Brooky stopped. She held up a paw. 'Listen, can you hear the sound of water? Come on, pal, it's coming from down that way!'

It was an underground rivulet, trickling out of the ditchside. Armel tested the water; it was clear and cold. She filled both their beakers about a quarter full with Burlop Cellarhog's fruit syrup, then topped them up with the water.

Brooky stirred hers with a twig and took a good swig. 'Hahahaha, good old Burlop. Delicious!'

Armel also found the taste of the mixture very pleasant. They each drank two beakers before their thirst was satisfied. Both travellers, feeling quite refreshed at last, were ready to continue their journey.

Brooky suddenly vanished momentarily, then returned carrying a long, thick branch. 'Haha, this is the very thing we need! No more falling down ditches and fighting adders for us, pal. Watch this!'

Pushing one end of the branch down firmly into the bed of the ditch, she vaulted across on to the path. 'Hohohoho! Clever young me, eh? Come on, miss, your turn!'

She pushed the branch back to Armel, who took a tight grip on it and swung herself easily over the ditch. The squirrelmaid was both surprised and pleased with herself. 'My goodness, I am getting quite daring! What would Abbot Humble have said if he could've seen me leaping a ditch?'

Brooky patted Armel on the back. 'He'd have said well done! Right, let's step out now. We've got plenty o' daylight left, and it's a good straight path.'

Between them the pair covered a fair distance. The shadows were starting to lengthen as they marched down the path, with Brooky singing out in a fine melodious voice to keep them in step.

'There was an old otter who lived down a well,
the truth of this tale I can readily tell.
His wife an' ten young 'uns lived with him as well,
an' they dwelt there together for quite a long spell.

Left right! Two three! March along in step with me!
Such an odd situation did ever you see!

Then one frosty morning there came a good mole,
he waggled his tail as he peeped down the hole.
'Come down,' cried the otter, 'an' live here with me,
for 'tis cosy an' warm an' the rent is quite free.'

Left right! Two three! Down went the mole and his
    familee,
his wife an' his grandpa an' mole Dibbuns three!

The very same evenin' there came a poor mouse,
who the wind an' the rain had washed out of his house.

The otter took pity an' cried out, 'Come in,
you won't take up much room, cos ye look pretty thin.'

Left right! Two three! The mouse went down right
    happily,
with five uncles, six aunts an' a pet bumblebee!

Then who should turn up but a fat little flea,
he stood all alone there a sad sight to see.
He called down to the otter, 'Move over a bit,
cos I see a small space there where I might just fit.'

Left right! Two three! That's a tale my mother told to
    me,
but I made up the bit about the flea, cos I'm a bigger liar
    than she!'

The white fox Captain Shard and his twenty assorted foxes
and ermine were sitting on the ditch side, sucking woodpigeon eggs. Ferwul and Brugil, two of his forward scouts,
had come across a number of nests, visible through the
boughs of a sessile oak. The birds flew off when they began
climbing the tree, leaving their nests and clusters of eggs at
the vermin's disposal.

Shard's mate, Freeta, pierced an egg deftly with her claw
and sucked it dry. Tossing the empty shell into the ditch, the
vixen winked slyly at Shard. 'A good spot to camp for the
night, methinks?'

Shard chose a fresh egg. 'Aye, but Lord Gulo ordered that
we should travel both night and day to reach the Redwall
place.'

Freeta snorted scornfully. 'Lord Gulo, eh? Is Lord Gulo
here watching thee? Look at those weary beasts! Ye need
some rest too. One night here will make little difference,
Shard. Gulo need never know.'

Shard picked a piece of grit from between his pawpads.
'Thou art right. We rest here tonight and continue on the
morrow.'

He raised his voice to the ermine scouts. 'Ferwul, Brugil! Take bows and arrows, go to those nests ye found an' see if the birds have returned. The rest of ye, find someplace close by to rest until dawn.'

Both scouts went forward up the path to where they had found the nests in the oak. The rest of the vermin sought out sleeping places, grateful for the break they had been given. Shard was about to settle down in some ferns on the woodland side of the ditch, when the two ermine scouts came scurrying back. Both of them held paws to their mouths as a sign for everybeast to stay quiet.

Shard leapt the ditch in a single bound. He hissed to the pair, 'What is it?'

Ferwul rubbed her paws gleefully. 'Captain, two creatures, maids, comin' hither – a streamdog an' a treemouse. We saw them before they saw us!'

Shard gave orders in a hoarse whisper. 'All of ye, down in the ditch. Be silent an' look to thy weapons. Two beasts are coming. I want them taken alive!'

Armel and Brooky had finished singing, but they were still stepping along very well.

The squirrelmaid unwrapped her cloak and put it on. 'It's not as warm as it was this afternoon. When shall we sleep, d'you think?'

Brooky shrugged. 'When we feel tired, I suppose, though we might as well keep going until we do.'

A slight sound from somewhere on the path behind them caused Armel to look back over her shoulder. Four ermine – two carrying spears, the other two with shafts notched to their bowstrings – stood on the path, watching them. She tugged at Brooky's paw. 'Look what's behind us . . .'

The ottermaid did not have to: four white foxes, armed with sickle-shaped swords, came out of the ditch to block their forward path.

Brooky whispered out the corner of her mouth, 'I don't

have to, pal. Look what's in front of us. Listen, when I give you a nod, we'll cut and run into the woods!'

A voice sounded, close to the ottermaid. 'Too late, streamdog. One move an' ye are both deadbeasts!'

More vermin emerged from the ditch and the woodlands, surrounding Armel and Brooky. Captain Shard stepped out. 'Take them and bind them tight!'

BOOK TWO

'The warrior who gained a sword'

Rakkety Rakkety Rakkety Tam,
the drums are beatin' braw.
Rakkety Rakkety Rakkety Tam,
Are ye marchin' off tae war?

An' who will stand wi' Rakkety Tam,
tae win the King's Royal Banner?
Wild Doogy Plumm the Highlander,
of rough an' ready manner!

Those fighters o' the Long Patrol,
have vowed tae give no quarter,
a-roarin' blood'n'vinegar,
when chargin' tae the slaughter!

17

As he was knocked from the tree, Tam glimpsed a fierce, gold-rimmed eye. Then powerful talons locked into the folds of his plaid cloak and great wings beat at his face. He was being attacked by a large bird. Together they whirled downward in a welter of feathers, fur and kilt. Fortunately, a lilac bush broke their fall. As they crashed into it, Tam managed to grab his sword, but only by the blade. The warrior squirrel and the bird rolled from the bush, fighting wildly. Tam pushed his free paw against the bird's throat, trying to stop its fearsome hooked beak from going for his eyes. He slammed the claymore's basket hilt hard over his adversary's head, gaining himself a moment's relief. Hurriedly he tore the cloak from his shoulders and flung it over the bird's head, muffling its angry shrieks. Tam rapped the sword hilt sharply down on his assailant's skull. Once, twice, thrice! Disentangling himself, the border squirrel scrambled upright just in time to see two vermin charging at him – a white fox wielding a sickle-curved sword and an ermine brandishing a spear.

Having heard the commotion, the fox and the ermine had dropped back from the rear of Gulo's band to investigate.

Now the border warrior's blood was up. He sprang at the fox, battering it backwards with his long heavy blade, whereupon it withered under his relentless force. After sweeping the fox's blade aside, Tam swung, cleaving the vermin from ears to neck with one mighty stroke.

Spear poised, the ermine charged Tam from behind, but found himself confronted by the big bird, who had rid itself of the enveloping cloak. As the ermine ran by, the bird struck savagely with beak and talons, bringing the beast screeching to the ground. The ermine wriggled over, raising its spear for a killing thrust. But Tam turned like lightning, his blade slaying the vermin with a single blow. Panting and aching all over, the border warrior looked down at his dead enemies, then stared up into the questioning eyes of a huge male goshawk.

The bird clacked its black-tipped beak together abruptly. 'Eekrah! Why vermin kill vermin?'

Tam kept his claymore at the ready, lest the hawk renew its assault upon him. 'I'm no vermin, they are my enemies. Why did ye attack me? I was doin' ye no harm!'

The goshawk preened its barred chest feathers. 'Hahaaak! Tergen thought you vermin. No talk now, more vermin come soon. Hide, hide, come!'

Judging this to be sensible advice, Tam followed Tergen. The goshawk hobbled along swiftly with an odd hopskip-ping gait. One of its wings hung awkwardly, brushing the ground. They made their way through the undergrowth until they reached the big bird's hideout. This was a ledge beneath a low hill, surrounded by ferns, vacated by some creature who had dwelt there long ago.

Tergen winced as he settled down. 'Grraaahak! All vermin must die. See what they do to this bird with arra!'

Moving aside the hanging wing with his beak, Tergen displayed a festering wound with a broken arrow shaft still in it, right where the wing connected to his body. 'Vermin arra shoot me out of sky. Hurtzzzzz! Tergen not fly now. Garreeeh! But this bird still hunt vermin!'

Tam felt both pity and an instant comradeship with the courageous goshawk. Tergen was clearly a born fighter. 'Let me try an' get that arrow out for ye, mate. Then we'll see if that wing still works. By the way, my name's Tam, Rakkety Tam MacBurl.'

The gold-rimmed eyes widened approvingly. 'Aaaa-rrrrik! Burl be good name. You pull arra out, Burl. Then Tergen fly again, kill many vermin. Yeeeekaaarrrr!'

For the next few hours, Tam busied himself with removing the broken arrow shaft. It was no easy task and exceedingly painful for the hawk. However, Tergen bore it stoically, gritting out continuously, 'Cheekaaargh! Slay all vermin! Kill, kill!'

Tam finally accomplished his grisly chore. He held up the barbed shaft for the goshawk to see. 'There, that's the best I can do for ye. I know little of healing. Even if I had a fire, hot water, herbs an' dressin's, I still wouldn't own the skill an' know-how. Well, how does it feel, Tergen?'

Tam could see that it caused him pain. Squinching his fearsome eyes, the goshawk tried flexing the wing. 'Pachaaah! This bird not fly again, Burl!'

Tam patted the hawk's long talons sympathetically. 'Don't give up hope yet, mate. That was only a rough job. You come with me. I'll take ye to my friends, a band of hares called the Long Patrol. I'm sure one of 'em will know how to treat injuries.'

Tergen swivelled his head, showing the white stripes on each side. 'Long 'trol, eh? This bird see harebeasts many times when I hunt far'n'wide. Hear them too. They say wot wot!'

Tam could not resist a chuckle. 'Oh, they say that quite a lot. Come on, mate!'

Obeying Tam's orders faithfully, Doogy had stayed at the deserted vermin camp, but the small Highlander was not gifted with patience. Sitting about, idly twiddling his paws, did not suit him well. Therefore, the Highlander was vastly relieved when Ferdimond returned with the Long Patrol. In Doogy's estimation, Brigadier Crumshaw, who had been made well aware of the situation, looked to be doing very little.

Fuming with impatience, the squirrel complained to Sergeant Wonwill, 'Sittin' aroond here on our tails an' waitin'! Is that all we've got tae do, Sarge?'

Wonwill knew the brigadier's mind from long experience. He tried to clarify things for Doogy. 'Steady on, Mister Plumm, we've got some tired an' hungry troops 'ere, y'know. The Patrol 'ave gone without vittles an' made a double-forced march to get 'ere. They needs feedin' an' a short rest. As for yore mate, Tam, the Brigadier reckons 'e'll be back to report soon. If'n 'e ain't come by the time everybeast is fed'n'watered an' rested, then we'll take up the trail agin, sharpish!'

Still fretful at the delay, Doogy wolfed down a bowl of leek and mushroom soup, realizing that he, too, had not eaten in some time.

Corporal Wopscutt refilled Doogy's bowl, continuing the attempt to talk some sense into the disillusioned squirrel. 'Weary paws an' empty tums ain't much perishin' good to any chap – particularly if you have t'go scoutin' on the double after rascally crowds o' vermin, wot! Imagine what'd happen if we caught up with 'em an' had to charge straight in t'do battle against the blighters. Hah, that'd be a right old how d'ye do!'

But Doogy would not be appeased. 'Ach, yer all sittin' aboot like a bunch of auld biddies. There's only me who cares what happens tae mah mate Tam!'

He was immediately rewarded by the sound of Tam's voice hailing the camp. 'Hallo, the Patrol! Tam MacBurl comin' in with a wounded friend. Put up yore blades!'

The border warrior strode in with Tergen hopskipping behind him. Passing Doogy on his way over to the brigadier, Tam collected his shield. He glared at Doogy with mock severity. 'Had a good nap an' a fine feed, Doogy Plumm? Huh, ye lead a hard an' desperate life, sufferin' back here!'

The Highlander was delighted to see Tam back safe, but he masked his feelings by scowling darkly. 'Och, will ye no' look at what the wind blew in? Ye took yer time, MacBurl! An' who pray is the scruffy auld featherbag dancin' aboot behind ye?'

Doogy skipped back a pace as Tergen's beak snapped close to his nose. The hawk eyed him dangerously. 'Yekkaaah! Burl want this bird to slay the little fat one?'

Further exchanges of welcome were cut short by the brigadier's arrival. He waved his stick. 'Ah, there y'are, Tam. What's to report, eh, buckoe?'

The warrior informed the brigadier of what had taken place. Crumshaw listened intently, then paced back and forth, twirling his moustache as he planned the next move. 'Hmmm, I'd say the villains are headin' for Redwall, wot! We've precious little time to dillydally. Our task has become a jolly sight more important than recapturin' a drum. Immediate action's what's needed. Sergeant, are ye listenin' to me orders?'

Wonwill snapped to attention. 'H'I'm h'all h'ears, sah!'

The brigadier scratched a rough sketch on the ground with his swagger stick. 'Righto, these are the moves! The Patrol's right here, yonder is the Abbey, an' there's the vermin, someplace twixt the flippin' two. Now, our job is t'get ahead of the foe an' reach Redwall to defend it. Tam, I want ye to take Plumm an' De Mayne. Your task is t'get to Redwall first, before the vermin or the Patrol. You must warn our friends of the danger in case they're attacked before we arrive. I know I'm askin' a blinkin' lot, but if I'm any judge o' gallopers, you're the lads who'll do the job. You'll have to travel like the bloomin' clappers. Well, chaps, are ye game?'

In answer, Tam passed his shield to Crumshaw. 'Ye can return this t'me later, sah. I'll be at Redwall waitin' for ye to arrive with it. Can ye find somebeast to fix up this goshawk's wing, sah? Tergen's taken a bad wound. I did what I could, but I'm no great healer, sah.'

143

Tam winced as the hawk's beak rapped his paw. 'Gaaar-raaat! This bird go with you, Burl. Plenty time for fix wing when all vermin are killed!'

One glance at the fury in the bird's wild eyes told the brigadier that nobeast could hold him back. 'Er, harumph! Looks like you've picked up an extra galloper, laddie, an' a jolly perilous one at that, wot!'

Tergen nodded in agreement. 'Yeeehaak! Wot wot!'

The twins, Kersey and Dauncey, marched up with soup and a flagon of cold cider.

'Corporal Wopscutt's compliments, sah!'

'Food for the galloper before he sets off, sah!'

Tam and Tergen ignored the soup but each took a gulp of cider. Tam wiped a paw across his mouth. 'Tell Butty thanks, but we've no time for vittles. Ferdy, Doogy, let's get underway for the Abbey!'

Brigadier Crumshaw peered through the dust cloud the four left as they dashed off. 'Forward the Buffs, that's the spirit, wot! Now then, Kersey'n'Dauncey, dispose of that tucker. I've got work for you two young rips!'

The twins gulped the soup and slung aside the bowls.

'Work, sah, for us?'

'Command away, sah!'

The monocled eye flicked from one to the other. 'Find the quickest way to Redwall Abbey for the Patrol, one that'll take us away from the path an' the vermin. I want to surprise the scoundrels when they reach Redwall. Well, don't stand there with your jaws flappin'! I'm promotin' ye back to gallopin' scouts. Don't disappoint me this time, d'ye hear?'

The two young hares beamed, shoving their chests out fit to burst and saluting several times.

'You can jolly well rely on us, sah!'

'Rather! Y'won't regret this, sah! Thanks absolute bags!'

Sergeant Wonwill's stentorian bellow rang round the camp. 'Come on, ye sloppy idle creatures. Let's 'ave yew formed up in ranks ready t'march h'immediately, if not sooner! Front an' rear markers, meself an' Derron! Flankers'll be Wopscutt an' Wilderry! Nah then, me lucky babes, yore goin' to double-march so blinkin' 'ard that yore paws'll push 'oles inter the rocks. Straighten up those backs, look smart! Anybeast droppin' or losin' a weapon on the march will be on a fizzer! Do yew 'ear me, Folderon, Flunkworthy an' Flummerty? Don't answer that question – eyes front, ye blushin' beauties! Long Patrol! By the right . . . Quick double . . . Maaaaaaarch!'

Brigadier Crumshaw marched out sprightly, ahead of the flag. It was a straight, rapid pace, and he had forbidden all noise and singing for obvious reasons. However, as the commanding officer, he sang a little verse from an old song he had learned during his young seasons in the ranks. Unaware of the smiling faces behind him, the youngest of whom thought that brigadiers and officers were born full blown, with resounding voices and moustaches, Crumshaw smiled to himself as he recalled his younger days, singing away.

'To Hellgates or to glory, away we march in style.
Each warrior hare without a care,
we'll see ye in a while.
No time for tears or droopy ears,
or blades to lay and rust.
As off we roll, the Long Patrol,
an' stragglers eat our dust!'

18

Yoofus Lightpaw was really enjoying himself. He lay flat on the high bough of an alder, watching Gulo the Savage and his vermin band scouring the woodlands beneath. The water vole was not only an expert thief but also a clever tactician. He knew that when he left the vermin camp carrying the objects he had stolen, the white foxes and ermine would be on his trail. So Yoofus left them a trail, not back to his dwelling on the lakeside but to a clear track to the east. It delighted him to play games: he would leave marks of the swordpoint scraping and the banner brushing. From his various secret spots throughout Mossflower, Yoofus would watch them getting more frustrated. Little did he realize that the trail he was leaving resembled that of a wolverine!

Fools and idiots – thinking that they were tracking him to his home! As long as they followed, Yoofus Lightpaw would lead them on a merry trail, and whenever they halted at night, he would sneak into their camp and steal some more booty.

Yoofus watched the vermin, figuring out his next move whilst murmuring softly to himself. 'Ah, come on now, ye great thick-headed gobeens! I'll be drawin' rings around ye, an' ye'll never know how t'play me game. Sure, I think a little jaunt over the ditch an' across the ould path is called for. That'll wear yore paws down a bit. Ye'll sleep all the better for it tonight, while I'm robbin' ye!'

After the vermin had moved on, Yoofus came down from his perch. He could hear Gulo berating his creatures threateningly. 'Gaarrr! Addlepates, bumblers! Find that trail, or ye'll be leaving a trail of your own blood if ye try my patience further!'

Yoofus cut off in an arc, crossing the ditch and path ahead of the vermin scouts. He artfully laid fresh marks on the east side of the woodlands, scarring one or two trees with his stolen sickle blade and bruising some low bushes whilst dragging the flag over the grass. Then he backtracked to the path, shinned up a thick crack willow tree and peered at the leading scouts, who were blundering about only a few spearlengths short of the ditch. Snapping the string on one of his purloined necklaces, the crafty water vole tossed shells and coloured stones down on to the path. He saved a few of the biggest beads and placed them in the tongue of his sling.

Grik, the ermine tracker, was foraging a few paces ahead of the rest when an amber bead struck him lightly on the footpaw. 'Over here, he passed this way, look!'

The white fox captain, Urfig, rushed past Grik, scrambling his way over the ditch and on to the path. 'Look, shells and beads! These are off my necklet. Dirig, hurry an' tell Mighty Gulo that I have found the trail again. Methinks it goes east into this forest!'

In a short time, Gulo and his beasts were into the east forest, discovering the clues which Yoofus had left them.

The volethief descended from the willow, chuckling. 'Off y'go now, ye ravin' eejits, run y'selves ragged around the trees. Sure I'll pay yez a call tonight, while yore all asleep!'

Yoofus recrossed the path and climbed down into the ditch. He settled down in safety to take a nap. Scarcely had he closed his eyes when he heard the sound of somebeasts coming down the path from the north. Keeping low, the water vole peered over the ditch edge.

147

Armel and Brooky had rope halters about their necks. Ferwul and Brugil, the two ermine scouts, were leading them. The squirrelmaid and the ottermaid were well hemmed in by Captain Shard and the rest of the vermin. The group halted, right opposite where Yoofus was crouching in the ditch.

Staring at the signs of recent disturbance on the path's other side, Brugil seemed slightly bewildered. 'Lord Gulo has taken the others east into these woodlands. But I thought that he was going to the Redwall place.'

Ferwul muttered under her breath, 'Aye, an' I thought we were ordered to go there also.'

Shard's mate, Freeta, clipped the ermine scout's ear sharply. 'Thou art not here to think. Lord Gulo will wrest all the information he needs from these two – they are from the Redwall fortress. See how they are garbed alike?'

The white fox captain cut in abruptly. 'Cease squabbling and lead on, you scouts. We go to join the Mighty Gulo!'

Shard let them go forward into the trees while he hung back with Freeta, whispering to her, 'Say nought to Gulo, or anybeast, about this!'

Drawing his cloak back slightly, he revealed the cloth case enclosing Martin's sword, which he had snatched from Armel.

The vixen touched her muzzle slyly. 'The sword is far too valuable for others to see. It is our secret!'

Then Shard and his mate proceeded to follow the rest of the vermin gang east into Mossflower.

Yoofus relaxed. He sat down and took some food from a small wallet he carried on his belt. The volethief munched on his rations whilst he analysed what he had just witnessed. Yoofus often held conversations with himself; he found it easier to think that way.

'Ah now, the fox was right, indeed. Those maids both come from the Abbey. I've seen them meself when I've visited there t'borrow some o' the grand ould fruit from their orchard. Sure they're cunnin' things, those foxes. I wonder what the big 'un had under his cloak? Well, no matter, I'll find out this very night, when I pays him a visit. But 'tis a bit o' shuteye I'm needin' now, just to keep me wits sharp after dark.'

The little thief was never troubled by conscience. In a short time he was snoring like an innocent Dibbun, wrapped snugly in the flag, curled up on the ditch bed amid last autumn's leaves, far from the questing vermin.

It came as a rude awakening when the point of a claymore tipped his nose. Two tough-looking squirrels, a hare and a hawk were standing over him.

Ever the quick-witted one, Yoofus smiled up at them. 'Ah, isn't it a grand ould day, t'be sure, sirs? Don't mind me now, I'll not block yore way. Just step over me tired carcass an' carry on t'wherever yore bound!'

Doogy Plum hauled him upright. 'Och, ye saucy wee maggot, where did ye get yon flag, eh?'

The thief's agile brain was racing as he quickly put two and two together. He replied glibly, 'Ah, 'tis not some coloured scrap o' cloth yore after. We'll discuss that later on, me friend. I think that you fine buckoes are on the trail o' the dreadful-lookin' beast they calls Mighty Gulo. Sure that's a fine hifalutin' name for any ould murderer, isn't it?'

Tam smiled at the thief's audacity. 'Aye, we'll talk about the flag later. Now, what about this Gulo? Surely you've seen him.'

Disengaging himself deftly from Doogy's grip, Yoofus answered, 'Ah, ye'd be right there, sir. As true as me name's Yoofus Lightpaw, I've sighted the villain – him an' his whole army o' boyos. An' I'll tell ye somethin' else too. They've got with 'em two prisoners, River Rats, an' haven't they just captured another two pore creatures, an otter an' a squirrel like y'self, sir. Both maids, from the Abbey of Redwall!'

Ferdimond's jaw tightened. 'Two Redwall maids? The dirty scum! Which way've they gone, Mister Lightpaw?'

149

The water vole winked. 'If ye come with me, sir, I'll show ye, so I will!'

Before they could stop him, the little thief had bounded out of the ditch, across the path and up into the high branches of the crack willow. Drawing his sickle sword, he danced about on the tree limb, waving the flag and brandishing his blade.

'Put a paw near me, any of ye, an' I'll rip this flag to bits an' carve cobs of anybeast who tries t'get up here! I'm a desperate character when me fur's stroked up the wrong way, so keep yore distance!'

Tam signalled his friends to stay in the ditch. 'Leave this to me, mates!'

Standing at the foot of the tree, he called up to Yoofus, 'Listen, friend, we don't mean ye any harm. I'd like to have that flag, but there's something of greater importance. We must free the two maids from those vermin. They're slayers, an' they eat the flesh of other creatures. I'd be grateful for your help, Yoofus.'

The water vole sat down on the branch, shaking his head. 'Flesh eatin's a terrible wicked thing. I'm no murderer, just a thief. I'll tell ye what, though. Fair exchange is no robbery. I'll give ye back yore flag an' help ye to get the maids free, but we'll call it a trade, see?'

Tam nodded willingly. 'That sounds fair enough, but what d'ye want us to trade with?'

Yoofus wrinkled his nose coyly. 'Sure I'll throw in this fine curvy sword too. How'll that suit ye?'

Tam shrugged. 'Ye still haven't told us what you want to trade from us. Tell us what it is.'

The water vole dropped to a lower branch. 'That's a grand ould sword yore carryin', sir, a good big straight 'un, wid a fine fanciful hilt to it . . .'

Doogy scrambled out of the ditch. 'Ach, he wants yer sword, Tam. Ye cannae part wi' that!'

Tergen hobbled on to the path. 'Kreeeek! No give sword, Burl. I kill that beast!'

Ferdimond nibbled at his lip. 'But what about the maids?'

Yoofus pointed at the hare. 'Isn't he the wise one now! Give me the sword, an' ye'll be gainin' yore flag, the lives of the two prisoners an' me sword into the bargain. Either that, or ye get no flag, an' those cannybals will serve the maids up for supper. Now what's it goin' t'be? Make up yore mind!'

Tam tossed the sword up into the tree. 'Here, catch!'

Yoofus caught it neatly by the basket hilt. Then he descended through the branches, grinning. 'Ah, that's the stuff! Goodbeast yerself, sir. So, here's yore flag an' this grand ould curved sword. I'll lead ye to where the maids will prob'ly be.'

But Tam had other views on the subject. 'No, Yoofus. I want ye to keep the flag an' that curved blade, 'tis not to my liking. Here's what ye must do. Go with my friends, Tergen an' Ferdimond, to the Abbey of Redwall an' wait there.'

The goshawk and the young hare protested.

'Yaagaaah, this bird stay with Burl. Kill lots of vermin!'

'I say, Tam old lad, can't I come with you, rescuin' maids an' all that? Bet I'd be jolly good at it, wot!'

The border warrior would not hear of it. 'No! Doogy an' I stand a better chance doin' this alone. We don't need Yoofus, either. The tracks are clear enough. Our mission was to get through to Redwall and warn them of the vermin. I know the Brigadier would like to see us savin' the two prisoners also. He put me in charge, so that's my decision. Doogy an' I go after the captives. You three get along to the Abbey. Now go!'

Surprisingly, the three went without further argument. Doogy patted his friend. 'Och, yer a fine figure o' command, Tam, but what ails ye? Partin' with yore claymore like that, an' allowin' that scruffy wee robber tae toddle off with yer blade an' flag. That's no' the Rakkety Tam ah'm used tae!'

The border warrior drew his dirk, testing its edge. 'The banner an' the blade are safe, mate. Yoofus has Ferdy an' the goshawk to keep an eye on both my goods an' him. Don't fret, Doogy Plumm, 'twill all work out. Now rid yoreself o' claymore'n'shield. Our smaller blades are more fitted to the job ahead. We'll hit the vermin camp when 'tis still an' dark tonight.'

Hiding his sword and shield in the shrubbery, the stout Highlander grinned with anticipation of the action to come. 'Hoho, that's more like the Rakkety Tam ah know!'

Clenching their small Sgian Dhus in their teeth and holding their dirks ready, both warriors set off into the silent woodlands.

19

Flames from the vermin campfire illuminated the face of Gulo the Savage, giving him a malevolent look. The wolverine's eyes glittered like twin stars of evil omen in his brutish head as he sat upon the drum in the gathering twilight. Gulo's mood had not improved: his scouts had once again lost the trail which, he was convinced, belonged to his brother. Foxes and ermine crowded about the far side of the blaze, anxious to maintain distance from their cruel chieftain. Laying huddled about midpoint between the vermin and Gulo were Runneye and Bluesnout. Gaunt, exhausted and terrified witless, the two River Rats had been roped tight by their necks to a stake.

An ermine guard approached Gulo cautiously. 'Lord, Captain Shard has returned with his scouts. He brings captives.'

The white fox marched in at the head of his contingent. He was wearing Martin's sword as Armel had worn it, down the back of his cloak, tied to his shoulders. Standing partially out of the firelight, Shard bowed stiffly to the wolverine.

'Mighty One, I have taken prisoners, two creatures from the Redwall place. Knowing thy wisdom, I brought them straight to thee. These two should have good knowledge of their fortress, its strengths and weaknesses.'

Had Gulo captured the Redwallers, he would have slain them first, leaving it too late for questions later. He knew Shard was merely flattering him, but the white fox was his best and most intelligent captain. 'Ye did well, Shard. Where are these two?'

Armel and Brooky were thrust forward. Both caught their breath at the barbaric sight of the wolverine. Armel shuddered as the beast's eyes roved over them both. Gulo's paw banged down on the drum, startling them. It was hard not to show fear in the presence of such a monster.

The wolverine glared at them from beneath hooded eyelids before he began his interrogation. 'My Captain tells me ye are both from Redwall. 'Tis true?'

Armel whispered bravely to her otter friend, 'Tell him nothing.'

Gulo acted as if he had not heard the remark. 'So, a riverdog and a treemouse, eh? Tell me thy names.'

Though Brooky was trembling, she shouted at Gulo, 'We will tell you nothing!'

Gulo smiled. A chill ran through the ottermaid at the sight of his bared fangs. Rising from the drum, Gulo walked a slow circle round the two Abbeymaids. 'I like to see courage in a beast. 'Tis admirable but foolish. At dawn you will tell me all I want to know – How many creatures dwell within Redwall? What warriors are there who could resist me and my fighters? What would the easiest entrance to your fortress be for us?'

Armel echoed her friend's words. 'We will tell you nothing!'

The wolverine returned to the drum, perching on its edge. Now was the time to put into action the strategy he had learned from Shard when they had dealt with Driftail's gang. He held up a paw, as if forbidding either of them to speak further. 'I do not want ye to tell me anything right now. But at dawn I will come and speak to ye again. Then

154

ye will gladly tell me all. Why? Because I am Gulo the Savage from the lands of ice and snow beyond the great sea. Heed me now!'

Armel and Brooky watched in trepidation as Gulo gave orders to some of his ermine. 'Bring the rats hither!'

Runneye and Bluesnout were loosed from their stake and dragged into Gulo's presence, both stricken dumb with fear.

The wolverine cast a glance in the Abbeymaids' direction. 'Look at these rats! See ye how frightened they are? They are not brave like thee, because they know what I can do. Gulo and his warriors eat their enemies. Anybeast who offends Gulo is his enemy. Take them from my sight!'

The two River Rats were flung to the mass of vermin at the other side of the fire. They only had time for a single despairing scream before the beasts of Gulo fell upon them en masse.

Gulo turned to his captives and shrugged. 'Ye have all of tonight to think of answers to my questions. Shard, guard them closely until the dawn.'

Just beyond the firelight, Armel and Brooky were bound to the broad ancient trunk of a two-topped oak. Both had been stunned into horrified silence by what they had witnessed.

It was some time before Armel whispered to her friend, 'I can't believe this is happening to us!'

The ottermaid strained against her bonds, but they were too securely tied. 'If only my Uncle Skip knew what a fix we're in. He'd do something to help us. Oh, I'm sorry, pal. I'm not being very helpful, am I?'

A tear fell from Armel's eye, but she could do nothing to stop it from running down her face. 'Just keep talking, Brooky. The sound of your voice comforts me. At least we're together.'

Two ermine had been left to guard the prisoners. One of them kicked at Armel's footpaw from where he lay. 'Silence! Save thy talkin' until dawn.'

The other ermine sniggered wickedly. 'I'm hopin' ye

won't talk at dawn. Methinks streamdog an' treemouse won't be as stringy as River Rat!'

Armel kicked back at him, but he was out of range. 'Rotten scum, dirty coward!'

Brooky struggled with her bonds. 'Aye, why don't you untie me, you miserable toad! We'd see who'd get eaten then!'

The ermine rose, licking the blade of his sickle sword as he confronted the ottermaid, taunting her. 'Heehee, but I ain't about to untie thee. So what will ye do now, streamdog – eh, eh?'

Shard, who had been seated closer to the fire, crept up and dealt the ermine a sound smack over the ears. 'Thou art here to guard these prisoners, not to bandy gossip with them. Cease thy prattling!'

The ermine stood to rigid attention until Shard went back to his seat by the fire. Then he slumped down on the ground alongside the other sentry and fell silent.

Tam and Doogy lay in the bushes, a short distance from the sentries who stood guard at the camp edges. They had circled the area until both were behind the fire, facing the backs of Gulo and Shard.

Tam pointed with his dirk, whispering, 'The big old oak, that's where they've got the two maids tied. D'ye see it, Doogy?'

His friend moved position slightly before responding. 'Aye, ah see it right enough. That's one o' the lassie's cloaks stickin' oot frae the ropes. They're bound tae the other side o' the tree, Tam. What's the plan?'

The border warrior studied the lay of the land for a while. 'First we'll have to let them settle down. There's vermin still movin' about. When the fire burns down lower, that's when we'll move. If we could make it up into that hornbeam yonder, we could jump into the upper branches of the oak where they're tied. Just one problem – that sentry.'

Doogy peered at the back of the perimeter sentry, an ermine, leaning against the hornbeam trunk. He was armed with a spear.

The Highlander shrugged carelessly. 'Och, that rascal's nae problem, mate. Ah'll deal with him whilst we're layin' here waitin'.'

Tam watched Doogy slip off quietly and circle in on the sentry. He heard the vermin give a soft grunt, then saw him lean back against the hornbeam trunk.

A moment later Doogy was back. Cleaning the blade of his small dagger on the grass, he murmured, 'Ah've propped him up on his spear. He won't be complainin' aboot gettin' a good long sleep!'

Armel could tell by the slump of Shard's back that he had fallen asleep by the fire, which now was only white ash and glowing embers. Gulo was sleeping further away from her. She could see him stretched out on the ground with his back to the heat. Both of the ermine sentries were also deep in slumber – one curled up almost nose to tail, the other flat on his back, snoring throatily.

The squirrelmaid tried for the fourth time to reach the ropes with her teeth, but all she got was a straining pain in her neck. She sighed. 'If I could only get my teeth into these ropes. How are you doing, Brooky?'

The ottermaid gritted quietly, 'I've rubbed my paws raw trying to get 'em free. Huh, that Shard creature certainly ties a tight knot. He knows the ropes all right! Armel, did you hear that – "knows the ropes"? I actually made a joke, but it doesn't seem very funny right now.'

'Ssshh! Don't make a sound, either of ye.'

Brooky whispered to her companion, 'Did you say something?'

The voice sounded again. 'No, it was me, marm. Look up, but don't say anything. We're friends!'

Gazing upward, both Abbeymaids found themselves staring into the faces of Tam and Doogy.

The Highlander smiled. 'Now hauld yer wheesht, lassies. We're here tae get ye away back tae yore Abbey.'

Both squirrels dropped noiselessly down behind the oak, where they could talk unobserved. Tam whispered to the captives, 'Be quite still now, don't make any sudden moves. Just tell me, how many are guardin' ye?'

Brooky hardly moved her lips as she replied. 'Only these two laying down not far from us. They're both asleep. The beast they call Gulo is over to the left of the fire. I think he's asleep also. There's a fox sitting by the edge of the fire – keep an eye on that one. His name's Captain Shard. He looks like he's asleep, but you never can tell. He's a sly one. That's all.'

The ropes which had been stretched about the oak trunk at neck height suddenly fell slack. Tam and Doogy crept around to face Armel and Brooky. Tam whipped through the ottermaid's bonds with his small dagger.

As Tam handed over his knife to Brooky, he instructed her carefully. 'Free your friend, then move quietly around to the back of this tree and wait for us. Give us your cloaks. We'll need them for the two guards.'

The Abbeymaids did as they were bidden. They had to wait only a brief moment before the two squirrel warriors returned. Doogy began retying the ropes that had been stretched around the tree, whilst Tam spoke reassuringly to the liberated prisoners. 'My friend is binding the guards to this tree. I hope ye didn't mind us borrowing your cloaks. We've dressed them up to look like you two, in case any-beast wakes during the night. Now let's get away from here as quick an' silently as possible.'

Brooky suddenly halted at the sight of the sentry leaning up against the hornbeam, but Doogy urged her onward. 'Dinna be feared, lassie, he'll no' be botherin' ye!'

Neither Abbeymaid had ever encountered a slain crea-ture before. The ottermaid crept gingerly past the dead ermine. 'You mean you killed him . . . and the guards?'

Doogy raised his eyes skyward, as if seeking patience.

'Marm, they're vermin! The foebeasts, ye ken? Would ye sooner be back there, roped tae a tree?'

Armel shook her head. 'Please forgive our foolishness. We are more than grateful that you and your friend saved our lives.' She placed her paw upon Tam's. 'I'm sorry. We'll take the time to thank you properly back at the Abbey. Oh . . . wait!'

Tam gazed into the most beautiful eyes he had ever seen. 'What is it, miss? We can't wait, we've got to go, fast!'

The squirrelmaid shook her pretty head. 'I must go back for the sword. That fox Shard took it from me. It's hidden under his cloak!'

Tam barred her path back to the camp. Puzzled, he enquired, 'Sword, what sword? What are you talking about, miss . . . ?'

'Armel,' she replied. 'My name is Sister Armel. Who are you, sir, and where do you come from? Please answer me!'

Tam was frankly bewildered, but Sister Armel fascinated him. 'My name's Rakkety Tam MacBurl, an' he's Wild Doogy Plumm. I'm from up north, the border, but Doogy's a Highlander. Why?'

Armel's eyes shone with joy. She seized Tam's paw. 'The Borderer who is a force for good! Tell me, why aren't you wearing a sword, Mister MacBurl?'

Tam was bewildered by her question. 'Er, I had to give it up in exchange for something. Why, Sister? Is it important?'

Armel pressed on with her interrogation. 'It's vital, sir. Would you say that you'd lost your sword?'

Doogy interrupted. 'Aye, marm, ye could say that, but we don't have time tae stand here gossipin'. Move yersel', Tam, afore the vermin come after us!'

Normally Tam would have heeded his friend's warning, but something he could neither explain nor understand was urging him to listen to the squirrelmaid. 'You go, Doogy. Take the ottermaid with ye. I must hear our friend out. We'll catch up with ye shortly.'

The Highlander shook his head at Tam's attitude. 'Ah

159

hope ye know what yore doin', mate. We'll await ye near the path, where ah left mah shield an' claymore. Good luck tae ye both!'

When the Highlander and the ottermaid had gone, Tam turned to Armel. 'Doogy's right, Sister, we shouldn't stay long here. So, please, tell me what this is all about.'

Realizing the urgency of the situation, the squirrelmaid tried to explain briefly. 'In a dream, I was told by a long-dead warrior to take his sword and search for he who pursues the vermin lord. His exact words were "The Borderer who is a force for good, that warrior who sold and lost his sword." That white fox, Captain Shard, he stole the sword from me. Mister MacBurl, I think you are the warrior who can get it back.'

The border warrior's heart melted at the hope shining from the maid's soft brown eyes. He smiled. 'You can call me Tam. I'll get that sword for ye, Sister, but ye stay out of the way when we get back to the vermin camp. Here, take my little dagger, ye may need it.'

Armel took the Sgian Dhu, which fitted her paw perfectly. 'Thank you, Tam. You may call me Armel.'

He winked boldly at her. 'Lucky me, I've lost a sister and gained a friend. Right, let's go an' get this sword, Armel!'

Nothing had stirred in the camp since Tam and Armel had left. Vermin slept around the bed of glowing embers that had once been the campfire. Gulo the Savage lay on one side, facing away from the white ashes, his mouth lolling open as he emitted hoarse, rasping snores. Shard sat bent almost double, his shoulders rising and falling beneath his cloak.

Tam peered from behind the double-topped oak, assuring himself that nobeast was on the alert. Armel crouched alongside the warrior, pointing out the white fox captain.

'He's the one. Look, I can see the sword! It's hanging from his shoulders by a cord. Abbot Humble had the sword wrapped in a soft cloth sheath. See the tip of it sticking out beneath the fox's cloak, on the left side?'

Tam nodded. 'I can see it now, Armel. Listen, get up into this tree. We'll travel faster by branch-hoppin' if they come after us.'

The squirrelmaid began climbing into the lower boughs. 'I was brought up in an Abbey, so I mightn't be very good at what you call branch-hopping, Tam.'

Tam flattened himself upon the ground, drawing his dirk. 'Don't fret, you'll learn. I'll be with ye.'

He slid forward carefully, feeling the heat of the glow upon his face. Keeping his eyes on Shard's back, the warrior crawled up behind him. Reaching out, he touched the sword wrapping, testing it with a gentle tug. Then he froze! Shard moved in his sleep, mumbling incoherently as he pawed at his back. Tam figured that the cord must still be holding the sword to the fox's shoulders. It was not in his nature to kill a sleeping beast, even one of Gulo's vermin. With this in mind, there was only one course of action. Reversing his grip on the dirk, he took hold of it by the blade. Standing up straight, Tam brought the heavy bound handle cracking down on his enemy's head.

Shard had a thicker skull than the border squirrel had reckoned with. The white fox captain stood up, letting out a howl of pain. Tam struck him again harder; this time the manoeuvre worked, but not before an ermine awoke, shouting, 'Guards! Guards! Attack!'

The ermine came dashing around the glowing fire remnants toward the intruder, grappling to free the sickle sword from his waist sash. Tam sprang into action. Catching the fox as he fell backward, the squirrel heaved him bodily upon the ermine, sending them both crashing into the fire pit.

Leaning forward, Tam slashed at the rear of the fox captain's cloak, ripping it wide and severing the retaining cord of Martin's sword. He grabbed it and dashed to the oak as an uproar broke out behind him.

Gulo was bawling, 'Yaaaaargh! Cut him down, get him!'

Bounding up into the oak branches, Tam rapped out orders to Armel, who was waiting wide-eyed with fright. 'Jump! Go for the hornbeam!'

She hesitated a moment, then felt herself pulled out into space as the warrior took her with him, guiding her encouragingly. 'That's the way, mate. Grab that big limb. Now swing yoreself an' drop down into that elm on the right. Good, keep goin', on to that yew. Fall across one of the lower branches. Now swing – hup, two, three – straight into the willow. That's the stuff, Armel. Yore learnin' fast!'

Elated by her newfound agility and pleased with Tam's praise, Redwall's Infirmary Sister went looping and hurtling through the leafy terraces.

Tam continued guiding her. 'Now run up this sycamore branch and bounce. Push yoreself out. Use that thin elm branch to throw yoreself forward into the beech. Keep goin', I'm right behind ye. Don't stop, we'll soon be at the path!'

Tam allowed Armel to learn her natural rhythm before he glanced back at the howling crowd of vermin coming through the woodlands. He looped the covered sword around one shoulder, beckoning her to continue. 'Carry on, I'll be with ye in a tick!'

There were three frontrunners among the vermin, two foxes and an ermine. Another fox was close behind them, rushing to catch up. Tam dropped from the beech, landing on the ground by an aspen. It was a slim, many-branched tree, and very flexible, its lower boughs almost sweeping the grass. He seized the end of a thick, whippy branch and pushed at it, running forward as it bent. The aspen limb was bowed round in an arc. Tam held it a moment until the three front-running vermin were almost upon him. Then he let go of the bough. It came back at the runners like a thunderbolt.

Whooooosh! Craaaaack! Poleaxed by the force, the trio were knocked flat. Tam raced to them. Grabbing one of the ermine's spears, he flung it at the fox who had been catching up on them. Unable to stop until the spearpoint met it halfway, the fox fell without a sound, never to rise.

Doogy could hear the yells of the pursuing vermin. Standing on the path with Armel and Brooky, he called out, 'Haway the braaaaw! Over here, laddie!'

The wild war cry of the Borders and Highlands came back at him from the woodlands. 'Haway the braaaaaaw! Here's a MacBuuuurl!'

Tam came hurtling through the branches and bounded on to the path. He quickly pulled the dirk from his friend's belt so that he was double-bladed and ready. 'They're comin' on fast, mate, but in small bunches! Armel, you an' yore friend get goin' with all speed for Redwall. Keep going an' don't look back. Go on!'

The squirrelmaid took one glance at the bloodfire in Rakkety Tam MacBurl's eyes and decided that this was not a time to stop and argue.

Doogy began laughing wildly. 'Aye, we'll see ye back at yore Abbey, lassies. Dinna fuss yerselves aboot us!'

Armel seized Brooky's paw. 'Do as they say!'

Both maids sped off northward up the path to the Abbey.

The first six vermin to reach the path saw the two retreating figures in the early dawn light. One of them was a white fox captain named Zerig. He pointed at Armel and Brooky with a spear. 'Stop them!'

Tam and Doogy burst from the ditch, roaring, 'Haway the braaaaaaw!'

They threw themselves ferociously upon the vermin, fighting like madbeasts. Tam took two ermine with a flying thrust from both his dirks. Doogy belted a fox in the throat with a clenched paw, felling an ermine with a swing of the claymore. Zerig was dashing back into the woodlands when Tam threw a dirk which pinned him to a willow. Doogy was countering a fox's sword when Tam retrieved the dirk and called to him, 'Haway now, buckoe, they're comin' in force!'

The Highlander despatched his opponent with a neat lunge as Tam reached his side. Over twoscore more vermin came bursting out of the trees. Seeing six of their own lying slain, they hesitated fractionally. That was all the squirrels required. Taking to their heels, the pair dashed off northward.

Bulling bush and beast from his path, Gulo burst amid his warriors, bellowing, 'Kill kill kill! Chaaaaarge!'

The vermin thundered on to the path after the two squirrels.

Tam and Doogy sped on abreast. Looking back fleetingly, Doogy glimpsed the mob of vermin racing madly to catch them up. He frowned. 'How far tae this Redwall Abbey, d'ye reckon?'

Tam kept his eyes on the path ahead. 'I don't know, mate, just keep goin'. I can see Armel an' her friend way up ahead.'

The small Highlander winced as an arrow zipped by his head. 'Och! Ah hope 'tis soon, cos those murderers mean business!'

'Yore always complainin', Doogy Plumm. Save y'breath an' run!'

Doogy's paws were hitting the path like pistons. 'Run? What d'ye think ah'm doin', dancin' a jig?'

Tam grabbed the front of his comrade's belt and speeded up his pace. 'There's the Abbey, don't start flaggin' now!'

He risked a backward glance at their pursuers. The vermin were gaining upon them. Gulo, who was not built for sustaining a fast run, was shambling along at the rear.

Skipper was watching from the southwest wall corner of the Abbey, shouting frantically, 'Gordale, get the gates open! Sound the alarm bells! Arm some able-bodied beasts an' get them to the gates!'

The otterchief bounded down the wallsteps, still calling orders as the Abbey's twin bells boomed and clanged out into the bright early morn. 'Burlop, 'elp Gordale with the gates! Demple, tell Foremole to get 'is crew to the threshold fast!'

Boom! Clang! Boom! Clang! The Matthias and Methusaleh bells tolled out their brazen warning throughout Redwall. Creatures poured from the Abbey building, armed with the first thing that came to paw – window poles, broom handles, kitchen pans, knives and barrel staves. Skipper, Gordale and Burlop swung the front Abbey gates open, then dashed out on to the path, bellowing encouragement to the two Abbeymaids.

'Armel, Brooky, hurry please!'

'Come on, mates, not far t'go! Run! Run!'

'Don't look back, there's two of 'em catchin' you up!'

As Skipper ran to meet them, both maids fell panting into his strong paws.

Armel gasped out urgently, 'That's Tam and Doogy, they're friends!'

Tergen and Ferdimond shot by her. The goshawk was screeching, and the young hare had his rapier drawn.

'Yeekaaaar! We come, Burl, we come!'

'C'mon, don't dawdle, you chaps! Let's get this bally gate shut, wot!'

They grabbed the squirrels' paws, pulling them along the final few paces and rushing them into the Abbey grounds. Skipper had Armel and Brooky inside. Tam and Ferdimond helped him to slam the heavy oaken gates shut. Doogy and Burlop barred them hastily, thrusting the thick, greased timbers into their holders. Willing paws hurried the two Abbeymaids off to the main building as Skipper unwound his sling. 'Up on the walls everybeast!'

The Long Patrol were marching on the double over the western flatlands when the brigadier sighted the Abbey and heard the bells. Even from far off he suddenly made out the figures speeding along the path to Redwall. Throwing caution and order to the winds, he raced forward, wielding his swagger stick like a drum major. 'Long Patrol, chaaaaaarge!'

165

Swords, lances and spears flashed in the spring morning as the regiment broke ranks, thundering toward the Abbey with their blood-curdling war cry ripping through the air. 'Eulaliiiiiaaaaaaa!'

Crowding the battlements, the Abbey creatures set up a joyful cheer at the sight of a hundred gallant hares charging to their aid.

'Hooray for the Long Patrol!'

'Give 'em blood'n'vinegar! Redwaaaaaallllll!'

The forty-odd vermin who had been in pursuit of Tam and the escapers stopped running. They were strung out all along the path. Gulo the Savage was a reckless fighter, but he was not a complete fool. With the rest of his force back at the camp, the wolverine knew he was heavily outnumbered.

He sought out the white fox, Captain Urfig. 'All those with bows, tell them to release a volley. Then follow us into the woodlands, back to the camp!'

Urfig swiftly gathered a dozen archers, positioning them at the edge of the ditch. They notched shafts to their bowstrings, sighting on the oncoming hares. Sergeant Wonwill was with the frontrunners. Though unable to halt the headlong stampede, he ran up front for all he was worth with Crumshaw alongside him, both calling orders amid the war cries.

'Archers t'the front ahead, slow down!'

'Slow down an' fall flat! Attention to the h'officers!'

Most of the veterans heeded the commands, throwing themselves flat in the dewy grass. Some of the younger element, however, fired by the wild rush and eager to distinguish themselves in battle, actually increased their speed, rushing headlong at the enemy. Foremost among these were the twin gallopers, Kersey and Dauncey. A volley of shafts shot from the vermin bows, humming and zipping like maddened hornets. Crumshaw threw himself forward. An arrow pierced his shoulder as he hit Kersey, knocking her flat. Dauncey halted abruptly. For a few moments the young hare scout stood swaying, gaping at the two shafts buried in his chest, then fell slowly into a kneeling position. Wonwill pushed himself into a somersault, reaching the stricken hare and holding him closely. Then the sergeant lowered him gently back upon the ground.

The young galloper stared up into Wonwill's battered face questioningly. 'Eulalia, sah, charge to the bells. Elali . . .'

Dauncey's head fell to one side as his eyes clouded over.

The vermin archers were fitting more shafts to their strings. Looking about, Captain Urfig saw that they were alone on the path and that the hares were rising to renew their charge.

The vermin captain shouted out urgent orders. 'Shoot quick an' retreat back into the woodlands!' He whirled about as a roar came from the battlements.

'Haway braaaaaaw!' Rakkety Tam MacBurl and Wild Doogy Plumm were climbing down the Abbey walls, as only two skilful squirrel warriors could. Doogy had his claymore between his teeth; Tam had his jaw clamped around the sword of Martin. The vermin broke and fled, but the two warriors were hard on their paws. Urfig panicked and ran the wrong way. Four others in his vermin gang – two foxes and two ermine – went with him, leaping into the ditch. Doogy threw himself in behind them. They turned to run, but Tam had raced down the path ahead of them. Dropping himself down into the ditch, the border warrior now faced all five of his foes.

Skipper, Ferdimond and Tergen were unbarring the gates when Yoofus scuttled up, waving Tam's claymore. 'Let me at the dirty ould villains. Sure I'll carve their tails from their throttles!'

Skipper ran out to stop him. 'You'll stay be'ind me. There might be vermin still about out there – easy now.'

Doogy sat on the ditchtop, clipping at daisies with his claymore. He greeted them mournfully. 'Ach, I never even got tae raise mah blade. Tam did for 'em all afore I could get goin'. Ye'll have tae find me a sword like that 'un. 'Tis a braw, bonny blade!'

Tam came walking back up the ditch bed, cleaning the sword on his kilt. He stared at it in wonder, reflecting aloud, 'I tell ye, this thing felt like a lightnin' flash in my paw. The beast who forged this blade knew what he was doin'. I'll stake my name on that!'

20

Abbot Humble and his team of Redwallers helped the Long Patrol carry their wounded into the Abbey. He walked alongside the stretcher on which the brigadier was being carried.

Humble held the hare's paw. 'I can't thank you enough for coming to our rescue the way you did, sir.'

Crumshaw's jaw tightened as he was jolted slightly. 'Don't mention it, Father. All in the line o' duty, y'know.'

Captain Fortindom and Sergeant Wonwill carried the body of Dauncey between them. Ferdimond De Mayne came hurrying over to place a comforting paw about the shoulders of Dauncey's twin sister, Kersey.

'There, there now, old gel, what can one say? Your brother went down bravely. He was a perilous warrior, wot!'

Kersey was dry-eyed and tight-faced, obviously in deep shock. A kindly molewife intervened to take care of her. 'You'm leave thiz yurr young 'un to oi, zurr. Cumm ee with oi, moi dearie. Ee bee's needen a gurt rest.'

Sister Armel and Brooky were assisting a hare who had an arrow protruding from his footpaw. As they came through the gate, Tam joined her, still carrying the sword of Martin. 'Armel, how are you?'

She nodded at her patient. 'Much better than this poor hare, thank you. I heard how you leapt the Abbey wall and slew five of those brutes single-pawed. It was a very brave thing to do, Tam.'

Shuffling awkwardly, the border warrior chuckled. 'You've been listening to rumours – Doogy was with me. We scaled down the wall. It's not hard t'do when you know how. As to slayin' the five vermin, well, I was just in the right place at the right moment.'

Doogy scowled as he trundled past, trailing his sword. 'Och, if he fell doon a well, he'd come up wi' a cake in his paw. Next time yer passin' oot braw swords, lassie, dinna forget tae save one for the bonny han'some Highlander!'

The pretty squirrelmaid passed the wounded hare to them. 'I will, sir, if you can find me a bonny handsome Highlander! Will you and Tam help this patient up to my Infirmary? Come on, I'll show you the way.'

When they arrived at the Sister's sickbay, there were other casualties waiting besides the Abbot and Brigadier Crumshaw. Though he was the most seriously wounded, the brigadier refused to be treated until all his injured creatures had been seen to.

He chatted with Tam as he waited. 'Heard all about ye, MacBurl. From what I'm told, you're a brave an' perilous fighter, wot! Six o' the blaggards an' ye put paid to 'em all, single-pawed, by jingo!'

Tam corrected him. ' 'Twas only five, sir, an' I was just doin' my duty. I was very sorry to hear about young Dauncey, he was a gallant young galloper. I hope I got the scum who slew him, sah.'

The brigadier heaved a great sigh. 'Young life like that, wasted. My fault, really. I should've kept the rascal on cookhouse duties. But who knows? Maybe his luck would've run out in a different way. Ah me, I tell ye, Tam, the Long Patrol is a hard an' dangerous life for anybeast.'

Abbot Humble nodded in agreement. 'Indeed it is, Brigadier. But where would the peaceable creatures be without their protection? We'd have been long ago overrun and enslaved, or killed by vermin.'

Tam rested his chin on the pommel stone of Martin's wondrous sword. 'Aye, yore right there, Father, an' so are ye, sir. We all choose our different paths. Some are born gentle, whilst others are destined to be warriors. Look at Doogy an' me – all we've ever lived by are our blades. We could no more live quietly in an abbey than Abbot Humble could take to the sword. None of us was forced to do anything against our will. Poor young Dauncey, he was just one of the unlucky beasts. He loved gallopin' an' fightin' with the Patrol. If he had to die, I don't suppose he'd have had it any other way. It could happen to any warrior. Our fates are in the wind!'

Sister Armel brought her trolley of dressings and herbs across to where Crumshaw lay. She eyed Tam curiously. 'You're quite a deep thinker!'

Doogy looked up from a roll of bandage he was playing with. 'Aye, lassie, ye ken he learned all his deep thinkin' from me. Ah had a fearful job tryin' tae teach him!'

She slapped Doogy's paw and took the bandage from him. 'Do something useful, Mister Plumm. Take hold of the Brigadier's paw. Tam, would you take his other paw, please? You'll have to hold him still whilst I remove that arrow.'

The Highlander took a grip on Crumshaw's paw. 'Och, yon Sister's a fearsome creature, Tam. She's a braw pawslapper too!'

Smiling, Armel ignored the jibe. She worked skilfully on the wound, explaining as she went. 'Luckily the arrow went right through. If I break the shaft, it pulls out easily from the back, see? Hmm, there's no broken bone in there, it's a clean injury. I'm not hurting you – am I, sir?'

Holding the barbed point and the broken arrow up to his monocle, the brigadier shook his head. 'Not at all, m'dear. Wish I could jolly well steal you away t'be the healer at Salamandastron. Pretty gel like you, who knows what she's

171

doin'! Not like old blood'n'fluff Hackworthy, the hare who's the present sawbones. Hah! Saw a young chap go to him with an ingrown pawclaw one time. D'ye know what the confounded buffoon did? Pulled two o' the poor beast's teeth out, wot wot!'

Armel stifled a giggle. 'I've packed the wound with boiled stream moss, some sanicle leaves and curled dock leaves. We'll bandage it firmly but not too tight. Drink this cordial, it's made from motherwort and gentian root. It will ease any pain and help you to rest.'

Tam winked at the Infirmary Sister. 'That must have took some deep thinking to learn all about herbs an' dressin's, eh?'

The pretty young squirrelmaid answered modestly, 'Not really, just a lot of bitter experience and hard concentration. Now, shall we escort the wounded down to lunch? I'm sure you'll enjoy Redwall cooking.'

Brigadier Crumshaw leaned on Tam and Doogy, chortling. 'By the left! Redwall scoff! I've visited here before, doncha know. Finest vittles anywhere! Makes our tucker taste like stale haversack rations an' hardtack. Lead on, sweet Sister, point us to the blinkin' trough!'

However, before anybeast could eat, there was a burial to attend, that of the unfortunate galloper Dauncey. Foremole Bruffy and his crew had seen to the digging arrangements. It was a quiet little spot at the corner of the southwest wall, shaded by an old cherry-plum tree which had rooted itself into the base of the wall. Kersey, unable to bear watching her twin laid in his grave, sat stone-faced by the fire in Cavern Hole, attended by the homely molewife.

After the burial, the hares of the Long Patrol sang a short verse as a farewell to their comrade.

'Now the sunny glades are silent,
where our fallen warriors lay.
As in memory we treasure

172

all the brave who marched away.
Through the dusty seasons rolling,
o'er our passing out parade,
how we laughed and sang together,
Oh your face 'twill never fade.'

Most of the younger hares broke down in tears as Sergeant
Wonwill stepped forward and placed the galloper's empty
despatch purse and belt on the flowerstrewn mound.

The brigadier wiped something from his eye, replaced
his monocle and addressed his command. 'Vigilance in
battle, alertness on the march! Somethin' everybeast o' the
Long Patrol must bear in mind. Obedience to the officers'
orders an' strict attention to the advice of veteran comrades,
vitally important! I say vitally, because if ye adhere t'these
rules, it may save your life. This young galloper lost his life.
I don't want to witness any more lives, particularly young
'uns, lost needlessly. You march to the warrior's way, learn
those ways well an' burn 'em into your minds. You'll all
get your chance to avenge the memory of young Dauncey
in the comin' days. That'll help him to rest easy, knowin'
his friends are continuin' the fight against evil an' brutal
vermin. That's all I've got to say. Sergeant!'

Wonwill threw a smart salute. 'Sah! All ranks t'the mess,
an' remember yore manners in front o' these kind creatures.
Dismiss!'

Nobeast could ever be gloomy for long at Redwall Abbey.
The newcomers were made heartily welcome by the Abbot
and his creatures. Friar Glisum and his helpers had the
kitchens working to capacity. With his ample past experience in feeding hares, the good Friar was aware of the huge
appetites they possessed and was well prepared to cater to
the Long Patrol.

Glisum bustled about his kitchens, checking everything
for quality and quantity. 'Salad, we need mountains of good

spring salad! Chop more carrots, add extra radishes! Borty, that little few stalks of celery won't be nearly enough. Go and get some more from Brother Demple, lots more!'

Borty the mole tugged his snout. 'Aye, zurr, an h'oill fetch ee gurt load o' waterycress, an' scallions an' leekers, too. Yurr, Mudge, bring ee likkle cart an' lend oi a paw!'

Skipper strolled into the kitchens, dipping a paw into a big wooden bowl and licking it with relish. 'Hmm, that tastes nice, though it'd be better with a dash of 'otroot pepper in it.'

Glisum raised his ladle threateningly. 'Away, you great plank-ruddered marauder! That's my own special recipe – rosehip vinegar and almond-oil salad dressing with grated dandelion bud. Anyhow, what are you doing in my kitchens, eh?'

The otter chieftain stole a hot scone from a tray which had just come out of the ovens. He retreated to the door, jiggling it between both paws. 'Abbot says to tell ye lunch'll be out on the lawns. He said to serve it buffet style, cos he wants a full banquet supper laid out in Great Hall this evenin'.'

Glisum threw up his paws in despair. 'Well, this is a fine time to be telling me that! Ulba, please run down to the cellars right away. Tell Burlop to bring up the trestle with the folding legs. Have it set out on the lawn, not too far from the steps. Everybeast sits on those steps when we have lunch out there. Now, what next? Mushroom and onion gravy for the pasties, hazelnuts for the fruit slices, damson glaze for the pear flan . . . Cheese! I knew I'd forgotten something, ripe yellow cheese for the grilled chestnut dip.'

21

Despite the last-moment rush, the buffet lunch went off smoothly. Glisum's prediction proved correct, with everybeast seating themselves on the broad, sun-warmed steps which fronted the Abbey building's main door.

Foremole Bruffy remarked to Humble as they shared a pastie, 'Stan' on moi tunnel, zurr. H'oi never see'd owt loiken it in moi loife. They'm hurrs bee's gurt vikklers!'

The Abbot watched Corporal Wopscutt wolfing his way through a mound of salad and swigging pale cider furiously. 'Indeed, they don't seem to stint themselves at mealtimes. "Perilous scoffing," I've heard them call it. I remember, in old Friar Furdle's time, he used to say, "I'd sooner feed a hare half a day than a full season." Furdle certainly had a point there.'

Tam and Doogy brought their laden platters from the table and sat beside Armel and Brooky. The border warrior dipped a grilled chestnut in melted cheese and bit into it. 'No wonder you like Abbey life, Armel. This lunch is superb!'

The Infirmary Sister sipped at her beaker of plum cordial. 'I'm glad you like it. What's the matter with your friend up there, doesn't he like company?'

Tergen was perched on a dormitory window sill, making inroads to a sizable slice of pear flan.

Doogy nodded in the goshawk's direction. 'Och, he cannae get away from the wee ones. As soon as yore Dibbuns found out he wasnae goin' tae eat them, they all wanted tae play wi' him.'

Tam took up the matter of the goshawk with Armel. 'I don't know how Tergen got up there, he has an injured wing. See, the one that flaps down by his side? He was wounded by a vermin arrow. I was wonderin', Armel, with your knowledge of herbs an' healin', could you do anything for him? 'Tis a sad thing to see a bird like that hobblin' about, unable to fly.'

The pretty Sister readily agreed. 'Indeed it is. Bring him up to the Infirmary later, I'll see what I can do. You do travel in some odd company, Tam – a wounded hawk and a thief! By the way, I haven't seen Yoofus about. Where d'you suppose he's got to?'

Sitting close by, Brother Gordale could not help overhearing the conversation. He tapped Tam's shoulder. 'Pardon me, but I saw the water vole ye call Yoofus. As soon as lunch was served, he filled himself a platter and went off down to the south wall. Mayhaps he's a trifle bashful around others.'

Doogy questioned the mouse Gatekeeper. 'Was he carryin' a bundle an' sword like mine, sir?'

Gordale thought for a moment. 'Yes, he was actually . . .'

The Gatekeeper got no further. Tam and Doogy were off and running down to the south wall.

When Doogy saw the small south wickergate hanging ajar, he stamped his footpaw down. 'Ah knew it! The saucy wee robber, he's made off with yore claymore an' the flag. Ach, I'll love tae get mah paws on the thievin' rascal!'

Tam closed the wickergate and bolted it. 'So would I, mate, but he's long gone now. I'll find him sooner or later, an' I'll mend his thievin' ways for him. I just hope he doesn't fall into the clutches of Gulo an' his vermin first.

You wouldn't wish that on anybeast, not even a thief. Ah well, back to lunch, Mister Plumm.'

The small Highlander shook his head in mock sadness. 'Dearie me, 'tis a hard an' sore life we lead, Tam. Ah wonder what supper's goin' tae be like, eh?'

After lunch, Tam and Doogy were called to the gatehouse, where the brigadier, Sergeant Wonwill, Abbot Humble, Ferdimond and Armel awaited them. Sister Armel and Skipper met them at the door.

The otter chieftain nodded briefly to Tam. 'Wot's all this about, matey?'

Tam ushered them inside. 'Council o' war, prob'ly.'

Crumshaw waved his swagger stick at the border warrior. 'Well-guessed, MacBurl, that's exactly what it is. We can't rest inside Redwall, eatin' these good creatures out o' house'n'home, with a hundred of the perishin' foebeasts wanderin' the woodlands outside. Bad form, wot!'

Humble settled both paws into his wide sleeves. 'So, Brigadier, what action do you propose?'

Crumshaw looked at the broad linen sling which was holding his wounded shoulder still. 'Not a jolly great lot I can do with this blinkin' thing hamperin' me. I was hopin' for some sensible suggestions.'

Ferdimond De Mayne pawed at his long rapier hilt. 'I say we march out tomorrow an' give the blighters a spot of good old Long Patrol blood'n'vinegar, sah!'

The brigadier was watching Tam closely. 'An' what d'ye say, buckoe?'

Tam had his answer ready. 'Well, I'd say we're pretty evenly matched against the vermin, as regards numbers. But if we march out to find 'em an' fight 'em, that leaves the Abbey unprotected, so we need a proper plan.'

Wonwill tapped Ferdimond's ear. 'I 'ope yore lissenin', young blood'n'vinegar, there's experience talkin' for ye!'

He winked at Tam. 'My 'pologies for h'interruptin', sah. I could tell ye had a plan.'

Tam outlined his suggestions to the group. 'First, we've got to split the Patrol, half to stay here an' defend Redwall. They'll be commanded by the Brigadier. Doogy an' I will take the others out to fight the vermin.'

Sister Armel looked alarmed at the suggestion. 'But, Tam, you'll be outnumbered two to one, and those vermin are vicious brutes!'

Humble chided her mildly. 'Don't be so hasty, Sister, hear him out first. You were saying, Tam?'

The warrior squirrel continued. 'I'm not talking about meeting Gulo an' his mob head-on in a charge. We'll use hit an' run tactics, small, swift raids, pickin' the enemy off a few at a time. Never stoppin' in one place for long. We'll be like hornets, stingin' the great beast, then disappearin', always drawin' them further away from the Abbey.'

Crumshaw rapped the table with his stick. 'A capital tactic, sah! Duck an' jolly well weave, hit 'em where it hurts, then vanish like smoke. That's the ticket, wot wot!'

Tam outlined his strategy further. 'Aye, but I'll need somebeast who knows the territory like the back of his paw to help us. Skipper?'

The burly otter nodded. 'That's me, mate! When d'we leave for this liddle jaunt?'

Tam pondered for a moment before answering. 'I think the best time would be late tonight, while the supper is still bein' held. We'll slip out by the east wallgate. One thing, though – the hares will have to leave their regimental tunics behind. Father, d'you think ye could lend 'em somethin' to wear? Stuff that wouldn't stand out so brightly in the woodlands?'

Humble rose from his armchair. 'I'll have a word with Foremole Bruffy. He knows about that sort of thing.'

The meeting broke up. Crumshaw and Wonwill stayed behind to go through the roster and decide who would go with Tam and who would stay behind at Redwall. Tam and

Doogy helped Armel to entice the goshawk for treatment at the Infirmary.

Tergen expressed reluctance to have his injured wing attended to. 'Naaaaar! Wing get better by itself, Burl. Not go to 'fermery. Haf knifes up there, cut this bird's wing off!'

Armel decided the best tactic was ridicule. 'Well, dearie me, you great big Dibbun! Haha, Brigadier Crumshaw had a worse wound than yours, and he got treated without a murmur. I've never used a knife to cut anybeast. I'm here to heal, not to injure. Right, Doogy?'

The small Highlander agreed. 'Aye, right lassie, but if'n yon auld featherbag is too feared tae be made better, what can ye do, eh?'

Tam winced as the hawk's powerful talons latched on to his paw. Tergen glared icily at Doogy and Armel. 'Yeehok! Take this bird to 'fermery, Burl, wot wot!'

The goshawk proved to be a worthy patient. He perched on a bed end, nibbling candied chestnuts which Armel kept in a big jar for her Dibbun patients.

As the Sister worked on the goshawk's wing, she explained to Tam the significance of the sword she had given him. 'Have you seen the picture of Martin the Warrior on the tapestry in Great Hall?'

Tam passed Armel the bowl of verbena water she had requested. 'Aye, he looks like a mighty warrior. No wonder, too, with a sword like this.'

The Sister cast a quick glance at the sword, which had seldom left Tam's side since he had been in charge of it. Then she proceeded with her account to the warrior squirrel. 'It is countless seasons since the days of Martin, but his legend, and that of the great sword, lives on. We learned at Abbey school that the hilt of the sword was the one which originally belonged to Luke, Martin's father. A Badger Lord named Boar the Fighter made the blade in his forge at Salamandastron. It is said that the metal came from a fallen star. There is no steel keener or stronger than that blade. The sword of Martin the Warrior belongs to Redwall Abbey and must always return here, though at special times an outstanding warrior may be chosen to wield it when danger threatens us. Martin appeared to me in a dream, proclaiming that you were the one he had chosen, Tam.'

Doogy selected a candied chestnut mournfully. 'Och, are ye sure yore Martin dinnae mean me, lassie?'

Tam picked up the sword. Swinging it in a flashing arc, he clipped the candied chestnut that his friend was holding neatly in half. He twirled the blade back and forth, watching the sunlight from the window playing along its edges as it cleaved the air.

'Great seasons o' slaughter, what a weapon! The balance and lightness, the way it fits my paw. I could face any ten vermin armed with this sword!'

Armel rapped Doogy's paw as he reached for another chestnut. 'Mister Plumm, those are only for injured Dibbuns!'

Tergen cackled as he grabbed another from the jar. 'Kraahahaa, an' wounded birds who be not feared!'

The banquet supper that evening was a splendid affair. Redwallers sat cheek by jowl with Long Patrol hares, chattering and laughing as they did justice to the culinary triumphs of Friar Glisum and some of Burlop's best cellar produce. The centrepiece was a huge meadowcream trifle garlanded with pink rosebuds of almond icing. Soups, dips and salads took up the border of the table. Behind them came pasties, turnovers, tarts and flans; closer in were the crumbles and cakes. As each course was completed, the dishes were removed and the next course brought forward. Burlop presided over a side trestle which was lined with drinks – from October Ale and pale cider, to cordials and squashes, with mint and fragrant herb teas. Even the ravenous hares were sated after a while, yet there was plenty left, and always new dishes being ferried in by helpers with trolleys.

A variety of entertainment was provided by numerous of the banquet attendees: a mole did some magic tricks; a trio of mousemaids danced an intricate reel, which involved weaving multicoloured ribbons into a plaited circle; then a party of Dibbuns performed a high-kicking jig, their little faces screwed up with concentration as everybeast called out encouragement to them.

During a lull when the tankards and beakers were being refilled, Tam and Doogy obliged with a sword dance from their northern home. They received great applause, but had to warn some enthusiastic Dibbuns about attempting to imitate them.

Banging their tankards on the tabletops, the Long Patrol called to Wonwill and Crumshaw.

'I say, sah, how about you an' the Sarge givin' us a ballad?'

'Yes, give us that jolly one about Algy an' Bobbs!'

'Aye, clear the floor there for the Brigadier an' the Sergeant. Give order please, you chaps!'

Crumshaw and Wonwill got up, much to the delight of the younger hares. They sang an old Salamandastron barracks room ballad, waltzing about paw in paw with a dignified air.

'Old Algy an' Bobbs an' me,
received the official call,
to attend A.S.A.P.
at the Regimental Ball.
All togged up in our best,
weren't we a sight to see,
combed an' brushed an' polished,
old Algy an' Bobbs an' me!

Honour an' bow to your partners,
chaps of the Long Patrol.
Whirl'n'curl'n'twirl your tail,
as round the floor we roll.
All the pretty ladies, lookin' for company,
an' didn't we oblige them,
old Algy an' Bobbs an' me!

Refreshments then were served,
an' Bobbs slipped on a flan.
He bumped the Colonel's daughter
headfirst into a pan.
Then Algy slung a pudden,
hit the Major's bride-to-be.
An' the Sergeant fired a crumble
at Algy an' Bobbs an' me!

O pass me a trifle smartly,
with a cherry on top for luck.
It smacked the Quartermaster,
he was bowled out for a duck.
Lathered in cream an' howlin',
'Arrest those bloomin' three.'
We wound up in the guardhouse,
old Algy an' Bobbs an' me!'

Finishing with a swirl and a flourish, the brigadier and the
sergeant bowed and curtsied to hoots of applause from the
rankers.

The banquet continued as Foremole Bruffy signalled to
Skipper. 'Ee garmunts you'm arsked for bee's ready in ee
kitching, zurr.'

Those who had been picked excused themselves and
went to get kitted out. Shortly after, they emerged, clad in
simple, short smocks of subdued brown and green. Their
blades had been smoke-blackened over a fire by Friar
Glisum.

Brigadier Crumshaw looked them over. 'Stap me, ye look
like a right crew o' rogues, wot!'

Wonwill saluted. 'Beggin' yore pardon, sah, but they
h'aint goin' out for no dress parade!'

With his good arm, Crumshaw clasped his faithful
sergeant's paw firmly. 'Let's hope they come back safe, wot.'

Tam's fifty hares took a moment to bid goodbye to their
comrades and the friends they had made at Redwall.

'Well, toodle pip, old lad, an' chin up, wot!'

'Hah, you lucky toads have got the hard job, stoppin' back here an' scoffin' all that super grub, eh?'

'Aye, we'll be thinkin' of ye. Give 'em a few biffs for us, will you?'

Kersey, who had been sitting in the background, presented Ferdimond with Dauncey's sling and pebble bag. 'Take this along with you, and watch out for yourself.'

He bowed gallantly. 'I'll be lookin' out for you when I come back, if I may?'

A faint smile creased Kersey's lips. 'Thank you, Mister De Mayne, that would please me.'

Armel gave Tam a small satchel. 'This is a few herbs and dressings in case you're wounded, Tam.'

He winked at the pretty squirrelmaid. 'I'll use 'em to bandage up Doogy's mouth if he starts grumbling. Stay safe now, and don't worry about me.'

The border warrior turned to salute the brigadier. 'All present an' correct, sah. Ready t'move off!'

Crumshaw smiled at Tam. 'I knew I could count on ye, MacBurl. Right, forward the buffs, eh wot! True blue an' never fail, that's the ticket!'

Skipper tweaked Brooky's nose lightly. 'Behave yoreself now, missy. Don't ye go whoopin' an' laughin' an' upsettin' everybeast while I'm gone.'

The ottermaid hugged her uncle tightly. 'Right ho, Skip. I'll cry in the night an' keep 'em all awake until you get back.'

Brother Gordale opened the east wickergate, patting each one on the back as they stole off silently into the night-shrouded woodlands. He bolted the door shut, remarking to Sister Screeve, who had accompanied him, 'Well, there they go, luck and fortune go with them.'

The Recorder mouse shuddered, drawing her cloak close. 'Thank the seasons that Redwall has such brave allies!'

22

Gulo the Savage was in a killing rage, the proof of which was laid out in front of him. Every white fox and ermine who served the insane wolverine stood in horrified awe, staring at the torn remains of the four vermin whose responsibility had been to guard the camp on the previous night. Gulo had personally killed them. He had literally destroyed all three, using only his fangs and claws. So overwhelming was his anger that he had also vented it on the carcass of the fourth sentry, the one whom Doogy had put paid to with his blade. Gulo's warriors stood to rigid attention, scarcely daring to breathe as he prowled amongst them, berating everybeast with his increasing wrath.

'I am Gulo the Savage, son of Dramz, greatest and fiercest in all the lands of ice beyond the great sea! Yet I am served by fools, knaves and idlers! Scouts and trackers who are so blind and stupid that they cannot follow the trail of my treacherous brother, Askor, the coward who fled from me, the thief who stole the Walking Stone! Idiots who call themselves warriors, who let my banner be stolen and allowed valuable captives to slip away. Tremble! Aye, shake like aspens before the storm, all of ye!'

Shard, the white fox captain, his cloak in tatters, crouched beside the drum, whimpering in pain. All down one flank he had lost his snow-white fur in the hot embers of the fire; dried blood matted his skulltop where Tam had hit him with the dirk hilt. Shard looked like a pitiful remnant of his former self, completely cowed and in searing agony from his injuries.

Gulo eyed him contemptuously. 'And thou, my clever Captain, have ye a solution? What is the answer to all of thy Lord's woes, eh?'

Shard knew that to speak would be to invite his own death. He lay quivering, with downcast eyes, before his master. Perching upon the drum's rim, Gulo leaned down with his mouth close to the captain's face. 'One more mistake, Shard, just one, and I will build me a fire to finish off roasting thee properly. Yes?'

The white fox spoke without daring to look at the insane eyes that were appraising him. 'Yes, Mighty One.'

Gulo patted the fox's injured flank, making him quiver in anguish. 'Good, now listen to my commands. Ye will come with me. We will march straightaway to the Redwall place. There ye will take all of my fighters and gain entry. I want everything! My banner, the Walking Stone and Askor, ye will deliver them unto me. Is this understood?'

Gulo grabbed Shard by both ears, wrenching his face upward as he repeated his final word. 'Understood?'

Swallowing the huge lump which seemed to have arisen in his throat, the fox stammered, 'To h . . . hear is to obey, Lord!'

The wolverine gave Shard a swift kick, releasing him so that he fell flat. Gulo the Savage snarled, 'Go then, and obey!'

Early morning sunlight dappled through the tree foliage, casting a mottled pattern of light and shadow upon a quiet waterway in the woodlands. Just as Tam and his company were about to cross it, Skipper raised a paw for silence.

Doogy whispered to the otter chieftain, 'What is it, the vermin?'

Skipper shook his head. 'No, mate, stop here an' be quiet, all of ye. I'm goin' to take a look.'

The two squirrels and the band of hares watched as Skipper slid into the water and sped off beneath its clouded surface. He was lost to sight for a few moments, then emerged further upstream, close to the bank.

Ferdimond twitched his ears in puzzlement. 'What the dickens is he up to, Tam?'

The border warrior clamped a paw over the hare's mouth. 'Hush and watch! Skipper knows what he's doin'.'

The otter floated slowly forward. Then he shot his paw into a shallow bank hole, yelling, 'Gotcha, me buckoe!'

Yoofus Lightpaw's yells were smothered by the water as he was dragged back through the stream by his tail. Skipper hauled him unceremoniously up on to the bank. 'Lookit wot I just found!'

Shaking his flattened fur back into its usual untidy ruffle, the water vole smiled impudently up at Tam. 'Ah, top o' the mornin' t'ye, Mister MacBurl, sir, an' a grand ould day it is, t'be sure. Wasn't I just comin' back to the Abbey to report to yore goodself now!'

Tam whipped out his sword and placed the point at the neck of the thief. 'Where's my flag an' my claymore? Speak or die!'

Yoofus pushed the blade away casually. 'Now isn't that a daft thing t'be sayin'! Sure, if I never spoke, an' ye killed me, then ye'd never get yore goods back. That's a fact, cos ye'd never find 'em now, would ye?'

Skipper chuckled at the little thief's audacity. 'You got to admit, he's right there, mate!'

Yoofus switched his attention to Tam's sword, his eyes shining with admiration and desire. 'Ah, will ye look at that now! Sure that's the grandest ould sword I ever clapped eyes on, so 'tis. I could do ye a fine trade for a blade like that!'

The border warrior's voice left the water vole in no doubt that he had said the wrong thing. 'I warn ye now, my light-pawed friend. If ye so much as look at this sword the wrong way, you'll surely die, an' ye have my oath on that!'

Avoiding Tam's icy stare, Yoofus swiftly changed the subject. 'Sure I'd have thought ye'd other things on yore mind than standin' gossipin' here like ould frogwives. D'ye not know that the great beastie an' his crew are on the trail to attack Redwall?'

Ferdimond grabbed the front of the water vole's tunic roughly. 'How d'you know that, you flippin' fibber?'

The volethief wriggled in the hare's grasp. 'Unpaw me, ye great lanky lolloper, that's me favourite weskit yore ruinin'!'

Doogy squeezed the hare's paw, making him release his grip. 'Let's hear wot the wee rascal has tae say, Ferdy.'

Yoofus straightened his tunic indignantly. 'Where would you lot be without a fine creature like meself to help ye, eh? When I left Redwall, I sez t'meself, sure, an' why not pay the ould vermin camp a visit? There might be stuff there I could pick up before I wends me way home. So, up into the trees by their camp I went. Everybeast always looks for water voles in water, but no one ever thinks o' lookin' up in trees for 'em. That's the secret of me success, d'ye see.'

Skipper gave him a light cuff with his tail. 'Well, I caught ye in the water. Now stop wofflin', mate, an' give us yore news smartish!'

Yoofus continued promptly. 'Well now, the things I saw an' heard there! The ould Gulo monster himself was madder'n a toasted toad. Didn't he only kill about four of his own gang. Then he gave 'em all a right hard down the banks tellin' off about wot a lazy daft lot they were. Mind you, he's no great wisebeast himself. Gulo thinks that the banner an' somethin' called a walkin' stone an' his brother Askor are all at Redwall Abbey. Huh, a walkin' stone, I ask ye? Well, t'cut a long story short, him an' the other gobeens are marchin' to the Abbey to conquer the place.'

Tam could see that Yoofus was telling the truth. 'When did this all take place? Tell me quickly!'

187

The water vole scratched his chin. 'Er, 'twould be just about dawn. I left the vermin right away. Wasn't it meself that was on the way back to warn ye at Redwall? But now I found ye so cleverly, I can tell ye that they're comin' this way, an' they'll be crossin' this stream afore the mornin's much older.'

Lancejack Wilderry glanced up and down the stream. 'Jolly good spot t'make a stand an' stop 'em crossin', wot?'

Tam was of a different opinion. 'Not with the odds at two to one, they'd rush us. Give me a moment to think, mate. You take the rest back a bit an' hide in the bushes. Skipper, Yoofus, I want a word with ye, but we'll have to make it short. Doogy, find a lookout spot up in that elm. Let me know the instant ye can see them comin'.'

Wilderry crouched alongside Butty Wopscutt behind a wild privet. He glanced nervously ahead at the streambank. 'Blinkin' long moment MacBurl's takin'. Wish he'd hurry up!'

The jolly corporal reassured him. 'Steady, old chap. Rakkety Tam knows wot he's doin'. Aye, an' Skipper ain't no duffer. An' as fer that Yoofus, he's sharper'n the point of a thistle. Leave it to them, buckoe. Tam's the officer o' the day now.'

Shard was limping hurriedly along through the woodlands with his mate, Freeta, and the ermine tracker Grik at his side. The main body of vermin were marching behind.

The white fox captain gritted his teeth. 'Unhhh! 'Tis as though the fire is still burning my flank. I need a poultice for it.'

Grik gestured ahead. 'Methinks there be water up yon, a stream mayhaps. There'll be damp moss an' soothin' mud aplenty for thy wound, Captain.'

Freeta chanced a look back at the ranks behind. 'Where's the mighty Gulo, pray tell? I don't see him.'

Gathering his tattered cloak around him, Shard winced. 'Didst thou not hear him? Gulo is behind the last rank. He says he will slay anybeast who takes a rest or a backward pace. That beast has neither pity nor mercy. Yea, he is truly named the Savage. I hope somebeast slides a blade twixt his ribs whilst he sleeps!'

The ermine tracker kept his face on the trail ahead. 'I'll pretend I never heard thee, Captain. Gulo is too strong and fierce for anybeast among us to bring him down. He lives an' thrives on the blood of others.'

Freeta beckoned the tracker forward. 'See if thou canst find the stream, Grik.'

When the tracker was far enough ahead of the two foxes, Freeta murmured, 'The great sword thou took from the Abbeymaid, I wager Gulo could be felled by such a blade.'

Shard, still rankling at his injuries and seething with hatred for Gulo, muttered, 'Aye, an' twill be the first thing I'll seek once we are within the Redwall place!'

The vixen motioned him to silence as Grik came loping back. 'I was right, the stream is not far, Captain!'

The rest of the vermin were right behind Shard as he reached the streambank. He limped into the shallows, about to bend and drink the water, when a sharp, growling voice from the shrubbery on the opposite side roared out, 'Where is my brother Gulo?'

Shard's paw shot down to the curved sword at his side. A javelin whizzed out of the bushes, causing the white fox captain to fall with a splash, the weapon protruding from his neck. Foxes and ermine pushing from behind stumbled to a halt in the crimsoning waters, shocked by the rough shout from the concealment of the other bank.

'Gulo! Where is Gulo?'

The wolverine leader came dashing forward, knocking aside his creatures who were trying to back off from the stream. Having heard the voice, Gulo called back, 'Askor, I cannot see thee!'

A snarling reply echoed back at him. 'Aye, but I see thee, brother!'

Ever quick in action, Gulo could move surprisingly fast

for one of his bulk and size. He saw the foliage rustle and grabbed an ermine that had its back to him. Shoving the unlucky beast in front of him, Gulo saw the point of a second javelin emerge from the ermine's back. He dropped flat with the dead vermin on top of him. Heavy slingstones whipped by overhead, one or two of them finding targets among the confused vermin ranks. Then there was silence.

Gulo flung aside the slain beast he had used as a shield. Scrambling up, he saw the bushes rustle and heard the pounding of retreating paws from the other side of the stream. He quickly shouted out orders to his vermin gang. 'East, they are going east. Ford this water an' follow them!'

Zerig, one of Gulo's fox captains, led the band into the water. They waded warily across, expecting another salvo of missiles at any moment.

Gulo thrust Shard's body callously to one side as he followed on, roaring, 'Get Askor! I will reward the beast who brings me his head!'

Gulo's warriors ran through the leafy woodlands giving chase, but they were not charging headlong. Nobeast wanted to be among the first to encounter another wolverine. Gulo was fast, but not as quick on the run as the more agile ermine and foxes of his command. When he caught up with the main band, he saw that they had stopped. Grik the tracker was bent over the trail, studying it. Although Gulo's first impulse was to kick the ermine and urge the others forward faster, he refrained from doing so; he had never been fond of prolonged rushing. With his own sides heaving, Gulo just stood over the tracker. 'Well?'

Grik straightened up and made report of his observations. 'Lord, they number only fifty, an' they are running east. But here, see, three have cut off to the north.'

Captain Zerig backed off a touch from the panting wolverine. 'That is why we awaited thy orders, Mighty One.'

Gulo did not have Shard to counsel him, but he was not

above making the effort to think for himself. The vermin leader called Zerig to one side. 'Only fifty, eh? Then these are my orders. Zerig, thou wilt take half of my force to the Redwall place. Try to gain entrance there by night, but do not charge it. I will follow my brother and these others.'

Zerig saluted with his spear. 'And the three who went north, sire, what about them?'

Gulo made a quick decision. 'Send Dirig and three others after them. Tell him to try and take them alive. Go!'

The three who had gone north – Doogy, Ferdimond and Yoofus – had halted in an open space. It was pleasant, with short, bright green grass dotted about with patches of moss.

The hare twiddled his ears at Doogy. 'I wonder how many vermin are followin' us, wot?'

The Highlander found a stone to hone his blades. 'Ah've no idea, Ferdy. There may be none if they never spotted our trail. Ask that wee scamp, 'twas his plan.'

Yoofus was busy making an acquaintance with Doogy's Sgian Dhu, polishing the blade lovingly. 'Ah sure, don't get yore ears in a twist, Ferdy me ould son. Those vermin aren't bad trackers, if'n ye leave 'em a plain enough sign. Well, 'tis meself that laid the tracks, so the daft scum'll be along soon, ye can rely on it. Doogy darlin', what's a grand strong warrior like yoreself doin', carryin' a little toy knife like this now?'

The Highlander snatched his blade back. 'Ye thievin' wee maggot, keep those fiddledy paws off mah Sgian Dhu! Anyhow, what are we hangin' aboot here for?'

Yoofus wrinkled his snout comically. 'We're layin' a trap, ye fuzzy-tailed omadorm.'

Doogy sheathed the small blade in his cap. 'A trap, in this pretty wee clearin'?'

Yoofus nodded sagely. 'Right enough, I know this neck o' the woods well. Y'see that pretty wee clearin', as y'call it? Well, ye'd be advised to stay away from it. Ah, I'm wastin' me breath on the likes o' you two, the vermin'll be here soon. Listen, why don't ye go an' hide behind that big ould log yonder? Go on, off with ye! When the vermin arrive, don't make a sound, just sit an' watch the fun. Now I'm off on a secret route, known only to the greatest thief in Mossflower, that's meself. I'll see ye anon.'

The volethief vanished off among some willows to the right. Taking his advice, Doogy and Ferdimond sat down behind a huge, rotten beech trunk which had fallen many seasons back.

Ferdy flicked a wood beetle from his footpaw. 'I say, what d'you suppose that Yoofus chap is up to, wot?'

'Don't ask me, mate, just check your paws'n'whiskers tae make sure he's no' robbed 'em. Hist! Here they come!'

The ermine Dirig halted at the clearing edge, remarking to the other three ermine as he scanned the ground, 'The tracks end here. Take a look aro . . . oooww!' A well-aimed slingstone bounced off his snout.

Yoofus Lightpaw stood at the other side of the glade, waving cheerily at them. 'Now then, ye stinkin' deadnettles, I can smell ye from here. Wait'll I tell yore mammies about ye not takin' a bath, ye filthy ould reprobates. Sure here's another stone. I won't be wantin' it back, it'll be contagious once it's hit ye!'

He whipped another pebble off, catching an ermine on the ear, and a swift third shot numbed the other ermine's paw. Seeing the impudent little water vole, jigging about and laughing as he fitted another pebble to his sling, sent the ermine into a howling rage. Drawing their weapons, they dashed forward, roaring, 'Chaaaaarge! Kill! Kill!'

Their view being blocked by the tree trunk, Doogy and Ferdimond hurried out to see what was happening. But there was no sign of the foebeasts; apparently they had vanished.

Yoofus called over to them. 'Stand right where y'are, mates. I'll be with ye in a tick!'

True to his words, before long the water vole emerged

from the willows, laughing at their astonishment. 'Heehee-hee, you should see yore faces. Well, did ye like me trick? Sure 'twas grand, wasn't it? Go on now, ye loved it!'

For a moment Doogy raised his eyes to the sky, as if expecting to see the vermin there. Then the whole thing dawned upon him. 'Och, ye canny wee rascal, ye lured 'em intae a swamp!'

Ferdimond gazed, dumbfounded, at the tranquil green glade. 'Good grief, is that really a blinkin' swamp?'

Yoofus flicked a pebble into it. There was a faint plop, and then the small stone was lost to view forever. 'Oh, 'tis a swamp all right, mate. I nearly lost me life in it one time, when I was about yore age. Don't let it fool ye like it fooled the ould vermin. If'n ye took four paces from where we stand, straight ahead, nobeast'd ever know where ye vanished to, that's a fact. Ah well, 'tis a good job I knew me way around it. Come on now, I promised Skipper we'd meet up with him an' the others at the water meadows where me friends the Guosim live.'

Doogy carefully backed away from the deceptively calm clearing. 'Guosim? What's Guosim?'

The water vole threw up his paws in despair. 'Do ye know nothin' at all? Guosim are a grand ould tribe o' shrews. Their name tells it all. Take the first letter of each word – Guerilla Union Of Shrews In Mossflower. Guosim. That's what it stands for, ye fluffy-tailed clod!'

Ferdimond adopted a superior air. 'Guosim, eh? I've heard of 'em, old lad, never seen one o' the blighters, though.'

Yoofus beckoned them onward. 'Ah well, 'tis meself who'll have to further yore eddication. Follow me!'

It was past high noon. The Highlander and the hare had to hurry to keep up with the water vole as he led them through the vast woodlands on a tortuous route.

Ferdimond was prone to grumbling, as is the case with hungry hares. 'Strewth, I'm bally well famished! Doesn't this chap ever stop for a mouthful o' scoff?'

Doogy, who possessed a healthy appetite, was in

agreement with his friend. 'Aye, ah could manage a wee gobful o' vittles mahself.'

Yoofus glanced back at them in mock pity. 'Will ye listen to yoreselves! Famished, is it? Hah, if I was carryin' half the fat youse two have between ye, I'd be hard put t'stand up straight. Stay quiet now, there's the bulrushes ahead. Stick close t'me.'

Yoofus threw back his head and gave forth with a long ululating call. 'Logalogalogaloooooog!'

Doogy tapped his shoulder. 'Ah thought ye told us tae be quiet, an' yore makin' enough racket tae wake a stone!'

The volethief shushed him as an answering call came back at them. 'Logalogalogalogaloooooog!' Four Guosim shrew warriors – small, scruffy-furred beasts – emerged from the tall reeds and bulrushes. Each one wore a brightly coloured bandanna tied around his brow and had on a waistcoat plus a broad-buckled belt through which was thrust a short rapier.

The eldest shrew, a tough-looking patriarch with a trim grey beard, shook tails with Yoofus, who grinned cheerily. 'Ah, 'tis me ould friend Log a Log Togey. Have ye any more liddle grandshrews since I last met ye?'

Togey patted his ample stomach. 'Two score an' two at the last count, mate, but there'll be more by summer. How would ye like feedin' as many mouths as that, eh?'

He eyed Doogy and Ferdimond, then smiled a welcome. 'Yore mates are all here. Come this way, but be careful where ye put yore paws. My water meadows are well booby-trapped, as the vermin have found out!'

Water squished from the marshy reed margin as they filed along behind Log a Log Togey. Doogy's paw shot to his claymore as he glimpsed the coat of an ermine through the tangle of reeds.

One of the younger shrews assured him, 'Save yore blade, mate. That 'un's a dead 'un, see?' He drew back the jumble of vegetation, revealing a drowned ermine with a hefty log hiding its head.

The young shrew winked at Doogy. 'They always fall for the seesawin' log trick. Step on one end, an' the other end swings up an' belts 'em. Step over that tripcord – ye see it, that thing wot looks like a thick weed? Yore a goner if ye put a footpaw on that!'

The Highlander did not trouble the shrew for an explanation of the tripcord's workings but made sure to avoid it studiously.

They mounted a disguised jetty as the reeds thinned out, where a long narrow Guosim logboat was waiting.

Ferdimond gazed around at the water meadows. 'I say, this is a jolly nice place. Goin' for a paddle, are we?'

They sat in the logboat as Guosim shrews plied their oars expertly through the mighty maze of small islands, reedbeds and weeping willows. Doogy had never seen anything so magical or pretty. Huge water lilies and spikes of milfoil carpeted the surface; dragonflies with iridescent wings and pastel-hued butterflies were everywhere. Ferdimond trailed his paw in the water until a shrew cautioned him, 'Pike swim round here, mate!'

The logboat nosed gently beneath a bower of overhanging willows, which hemmed three low islands at the centre of the water meadows. The Guosim oarsmen tied up the logboat at a massive deck of floating logs spanning the inner pool. From beneath leafy awnings, their friends emerged to greet them.

Tam waved to Doogy. 'Well, look what the breeze blew in! Did ye smell the food cookin', Doogy Plumm?'

Scrambling from the logboat, Doogy returned the wry greeting. 'Aye, ah did, so ah hurried here afore some Border beastie ate it all up. How are ye, mate?'

Tam spread his paws expressively. 'Oh, still livin' the hard old life an' knockin' myself about. And you?'

Doogy shrugged. 'Didn't even get the chance tae draw mah blade. Lost four vermin in a swamp, though. Hi there, mate!'

Butty Wopscutt was bouncing a shrewbabe on his lap. 'Mister Plumm, I've saved ye a place over here.'

Guosim cooks served everybeast a fine meal. There was a delicious watercress soup, followed by watershrimp dumplings and watermeadow salad, with apple and rhubarb crumble for dessert – all this topped off with hazelnuts, Guosim cheese and shrewbeer, which was dark, foamy and slightly sweet-tasting.

Ferdimond sat back with a satisfied sigh. 'First-rate tuck, wot! A chap couldn't grumble at scoff of that bloomin' quality, eh, Yoofus?'

Picking his teeth with a bulrush spike, the volethief nodded. 'Sure 'twas a grand ould spread. Me stummick rejoiced at it!'

Ferdimond made his report to Tam and Skipper, telling them of how Yoofus led the vermin into the swamp.

Then the otter chieftain related the progress made by the main force. 'When they were chasin' us, I thought of these water meadows. We were in the area, so I led 'em on, knowin' how much me ole mate Togey loves vermin.'

The Guosim chieftain banged his tankard down. 'As long as I'm Log a Log, there'll be no vermin scum comin' into my territory to loot an' murder. My ole dad was slain by vermin, an' two of my brothers, but that was in the days when I was only a shrewlet. From wot Tam tells me o' that brute Gulo an' his crew, I say 'tis a crime to let the sun rise on such rotten villains. Eatin' otherbeasts? The filthy, dirty cannibals. Ugh! It don't bear thinkin' about. They need t'be wiped from the face o' the land. Pity we only slew six of 'em today!'

Tam tapped the tabletop with his dirk blade. 'Aye, even Gulo the Savage retreated from those reeds once he saw how things were goin'. I wonder where he is now.'

Log a Log Togey put aside a shrewbabe who was trying to chew at his beard. 'We'll find out soon enough when my scouts bring word. So, what's the next move?'

Tam gestured with a sweep of his blade. 'Tell me, what other foes do ye have in the neighbourhood?'

The Guosim chieftain frowned thoughtfully. 'Plenty I could think of, Tam. That's why us Guosim are born fighters – we have to defend our land an' our families. Let me see now, there's the marshland toads an' lizards over to the east. A band o' River Rats, though they usually never stop in one place . . .'

A young shrew wife, who was nursing a sleeping babe, spoke up. 'What about those black birds in the pine groves? They're a bunch of robbin' murderers! Sometimes you can't leave a little 'un out in the open when those savages are about!'

Togey smoothed his beard. 'Oh yes, the crows an' rooks. We don't mess with them, only when they fly over the meadows lookin' for prey. Then we gets out the bows'n'-arrows to drive 'em off.'

A plan began forming in Tam's mind. 'Where are the pine groves, Togey?'

The Log a Log pointed southeast. 'About a day's march over that way. Guosim keep clear o' the pines, there's just too many of those big black birds. If ye wandered around in that area, they'd think ye was out to rob their nests an' attack ye. I tell ye, there'd be little chance o' gettin' out o' the pine groves alive!'

Tam grinned wolfishly. 'Right, that's what we'll do then!'

Yoofus looked aghast. 'Ye mean, go into the pine groves?'

It was Doogy's turn to look superior. 'Och, ye wee pudden-headed robber! Lissen now, an' get yore own eddication completed. Rakkety Tam MacBurl's got a braw brain for plannin'. Tell him, mate!'

The border squirrel outlined his scheme. 'We've got to get Gulo to take his vermin into those pine groves. He doesn't know about the big black birds.'

The slap of Skipper's rudder was audible upon the log deck. 'Great streams'n'rivers, matey. 'Tis a masterful plan!'

Tam disentangled a shrewbabe from his footpaws and

stood up. 'Maybe it is, but it needs more thought yet. I'm goin' to put my mind to it, an' anybeast who comes up with a workable idea, well, I'd be pleased to listen to it.'

Evening drew softly over the water meadows, bringing the warm spring day to a close. Guosim logboats, plied by sentries, patrolled the area. Lanterns lit the covered boardwalk as everybeast took their ease. Shrewparents laid their little ones down to slumber in wicker cradles which were suspended from the thatched ceiling. Guosim warriors and Long Patrol fighters sat swapping yarns and sipping shrewbeer. Log a Log Togey's eldest daughter strummed on a stringed instrument, called a shrewbec, accompanying herself to a lullaby.

'When the sun slips o'er the treetops,
then small birds fly off to nest.
Feel the peace lie on the meadows,
'tis a time that I love best.

Slumber on, little one,
I am ever near.
Drowsily, lean on me,
dream small dreams, my dear.

All the jewelled stars a-twinkle,
watch the clouds drift through the night.
Sail upon thy boat of dreaming,
to the rays of dawning's light.

Slumber on, day is gone,
by thy side I'll lay.
Fear no harm, rest in calm,
'til the golden day.'

Doogy yawned as he remarked to Yoofus, 'Och, ye could live here forever with no' a thing tae bother ye.'
He was about to continue eulogizing when he saw that

the water vole was snoring peacefully. The Highlander chuckled. 'Just like a thief, eh? Stolen off tae sleep!'

Ferdimond had a mischievous glint in his eye. 'Look at the little curmudgeon. I say, I've just thought of a super wheeze. See that empty cradle hanging over yonder?'

Skipper caught on right away, grinning broadly. 'Good idea, Ferdy. Come on, Doogy, Butty . . . lend a paw over here, will ye!'

The four companions carefully lifted the sleeping water vole. They tippawed over the log floor, carrying Yoofus between them, and laid him gently into the hanging cradle. The little thief snuffled a bit but carried on slumbering.

Doogy added a humourous touch by sliding a shrewdolly between his paws and a shrewbabe's bonnet upon his head. 'Och, doesn't the wee darlin' look sweet? Ah've never seen such a bonny bairn, the robbin' wee scruffbag!'

Tam, who had been sitting outside, suddenly came striding in. 'I've got it! Listen, here's the plan for tomorrow . . .'

23

Tergen did not like wearing a splint upon his wing; it irked him and hampered his movement. The goshawk was highly disappointed that Sister Armel had not cured him instantly, giving him back the power of flight. He trundled about the Abbey grounds, brooding and grumbling to himself as he shrugged his good wing.

'Kruuuurrrrk! This bird never fly. Tergen no use to anybeast now. Huh, vermin be glad of that!'

Armel sat on the gatehouse steps with Abbot Humble and the brigadier, watching the hawk. Humble felt a certain sympathy with the wounded bird. 'Poor Tergen. It must be very hard for him, being grounded like that. I wish I could help him in some way.'

Sister Armel, however, did not share Humble's view. 'I'll tell you, that bird's trouble, Father. He's got no patience at all. Oh, he'll fly again, I'm sure. The wing just needs lots of rest, then plenty of exercise.'

The brigadier polished his monocle. 'I've seen some of my hares actin' like that after they've been injured. That chap needs something to occupy his mind an' make him feel jolly well useful again, wot!'

Armel sighed wearily. 'I've tried everything I could think

of. I made Tergen a sickbay assistant, but all he did was eat the rest of my candied chestnuts and lay on the beds. Then I introduced him to Friar Glisum as a kitchen helper. He said the kitchens were too hot and he couldn't breathe. Next came a spell with Ulba molewife, minding Dibbuns, but he was short-tempered and frightened the little ones. So, Brigadier, what would *you* do with that goshawk?'

Crumshaw toyed with his moustache. 'I see what y'mean, Sister. Hmm, what t'do with the chap. Hah, I've just thought o' the very thing – discipline!'

He rose smartly and paced off, wagging his swagger stick. 'I say, you there, Turfill, or whatever y'flippin' name is. Come with me! Liven y'self up now, laddie bird, I've got a job for you, wot!'

The hawk's gold-rimmed eye glared icily at the brigadier. 'Karrraaa! This bird be named Tergen. What job you have, eh?'

Crumshaw marched up the west wallsteps, explaining as he went. 'Rampart sentry, ideal for a bird like y'self, wot! Nobeast has an eye as jolly well sharp as a hawk. Eyes like a hawk – you've heard the expression, wot? Need somebeast I can rely on to patrol these walltops regular. Keep an eye out for those confounded vermin, should they come skulkin' about. Well, are you up to the task, wot wot?'

Crumshaw was forced to back off a pace as the goshawk advanced. For a moment the hare thought Tergen was about to attack him. Then the wonder occurred: Tergen raised his good wing and saluted, his chest swelling proudly. 'Greekah! Brigadier Wotwot is right. This bird have good eyes, see all. Tergen will do job for Brigadier Wotwot!'

The hawk ambled along the walltop to the south, stopping at each space between battlements and peering down avidly. The other hares on walltop guard kept well out of the fierce-looking goshawk's way.

Crumshaw stumped down the gatehouse steps and

resumed his seat with Humble and Armel. 'Well, he seems to be fairly happy up there. Peculiar blighter, though. Seems t'think my name's Brigadier Wotwot. Can't think how that notion got into his head. Can you, Father?'

Humble was hard put not to burst out laughing. 'What, er, I've no idea at all, Brigadier!'

Three of the hare wallguards excused themselves as they came hurrying down the steps. The brigadier rose indignantly. 'Just a tick! Where the dickens d'ye think yore off to, wot?'

Young Flummerty threw him a hasty salute. 'Beggin' y'pardon, sah, but that bird chased us from our posts. Said he didn't need us cos he could see everything!'

The monocled eye halted the trio where they stood. 'Oh did he, indeed? An' you three shrinkin' violets take that as an excuse to disobey orders, wot? Now get back up there t'your posts at the double, an' if ye get any blinkin' arguments from that bird, tell him it's me, Brigadier Wotwot, who's givin' the orders round here!'

A moment later, the hawk was leaning over the parapet, calling down to Crumshaw, 'Yikhaah! They stay up here with this bird, I teach 'em to stand watch proper. You right, Brigadier Wotwot!'

Giggles of uncontrolled glee greeted this announcement.

Crumshaw rose huffily and marched off, muttering, 'Must see what the grubslingers have cooked up for afternoon tea. Brigadier Wotwot, indeed! Who ever heard of such foolishness, wot wot!'

Captain Zerig and his vermin watched the Abbey walls from the tree fringe beyond the sward which fronted the south wall. Freeta, the mate of slain Captain Shard, crouched alongside Zerig. She viewed the high red sandstone construction doubtfully.

'If we were birds, 'twould be easy to fly over those walls.'

Zerig replied as he studied the situation. 'Aye, 'twill be a hard task, but we must do it, or face Gulo. He will not want to hear excuses.'

The vixen spat viciously. 'Speak not to me of that savage! Shard might yet have been alive were it not for Gulo. But I will have my revenge someday, I swear it!'

Zerig chewed on a milky stem of grass. 'Brave words, Freeta, but 'tis not likely that Gulo will ever be defeated by anybeast, or even tenbeasts. Forget him for now, our problem lies before us. What would thy mate, Shard, have done if he were here? I recall he was ever a crafty and wise captain.'

Freeta dropped her voice so the rest of the vermin could not hear. 'I am as sly as Shard. He often came to me for counsel. I think we should wait until dark, then send two reliable beasts to scout the place for openings.'

Zerig looked at Freeta with a newfound respect. 'A sensible plan, but which ones would ye send?'

After casting an eye over the vermin warriors, she beckoned forth two. 'Fargil, Graddu, attend Captain Zerig. He would speak with ye.'

Two big, white, well-armed foxes crept forward. Zerig eyed them approvingly. 'When darkness falls, I want ye to scout around the outside of this place. See if ye can find any weakness, a spot where we might enter in secret.'

Both foxes merely nodded, then went back to rest among the trees.

Freeta whispered to Zerig, 'They are a silent pair, but good. More reliable than ermine.'

Zerig lay back, closing his eyes and enjoying the sun. 'We will see.'

The two hares, Cartwill and Folderon, were pacing the north wall together, as far away from the goshawk as they could get. Cartwill's stomach made an ominous rumble. He held a paw to his mouth politely.

'Pardon me! Time for afternoon tea, ain't it? I'm famished!'

Folderon peered expectantly at the Abbey door. 'Chin up, we should be gettin' relieved soon. Oh corks, what does that flippin' hawk want now, eh?'

Tergen was signalling them from the south wall, waving his good wing to attract their attention.

Cartwill groaned. 'Another one of his confounded lectures about havin' eyes as sharp as a hawk, prob'ly. Come on, we'd best stroll over there or the nuisance won't give us a moment's peace.'

They marched along the west wall, calling to the goshawk.

'Not to fret, old lad, we're keeping the old peepers peeled.'

'Rather, not missing a bally thing!'

Tergen glared at them. 'Kuuuurk, shushushh, you be hushed!'

Folderon dropped her voice. 'Why, what's up?'

Tapping his talons on the south parapet, the goshawk whispered, 'Sssshuuuuk! You stan' here, don't move. This bird must go to speak with Wotwot.'

He stumped off down the steps, leaving both young hares bewildered and rather indignant.

Cartwill's ears stood rigid. 'Well, of all the bloomin' cheek, where does he think he's off to? Leavin' us here like two frogs in a flippin' bucket!'

Folderon watched the hawk hopskipping off over the lawns. 'Stole a march on us there, crafty old featherbag. I'll bet he's gone for afternoon tea!'

Brigadier Crumshaw and Sergeant Wonwill were taking tea in Great Hall with Burlop and Abbot Humble when Tergen came hurrying in.

Wonwill looked up from spreading a scone with greengage preserve. 'Looks like the 'awk 'as somethin' to report, sah!'

Crumshaw put aside his beaker of mint-and-rosehip tea. 'Ah, our hawkeyed sentry, wot. Everything hunky-dory on the ramparts, old chap, wot wot?'

Tergen helped himself to an almond slice. 'Karrak! Every-thin' not hory-dunky, Wotwot. Vermin are outside, good job you got eyes of hawk to see 'em!'

Crumshaw came promptly upright, moustache bristling. 'Vermin, y'say? How many, where, when did ye spot 'em, wot?'

Tergen preened his feathers calmly. 'Wotwot, not get ears in flap! Listen to this bird. In trees by south wall I see vermin hidin'. Yaaaark! They think nobeast know they there – huh, I spot white fur easy. No hurry, vermin just hidin', restin'. Not attack, not do anythin' yet. I think maybe twoscore, maybe fifty.'

Humble stared anxiously at the brigadier. 'What do you suggest we do, friend?'

The old campaigner regained his composure. 'Hmm, nothin' for the moment, Father. The bird's right, they won't attack right off in broad daylight. Eh, Sergeant?'

Wonwill put aside his scone. 'Aye, sah, they'll wait h'until night-time. I'd better git our lot on the h'alert.'

Crumshaw cautioned Humble and Burlop, 'Not a peep to your Redwallers, mum's the word. Don't want a fewscore rascals upsettin' peaceful creatures. We can deal with the blighters, believe me!'

Tergen grabbed some scones and another almond slice. 'Yeehaaak! This bird go back on walltop. I watch vermin close, but they not know I spy on 'em!'

Crumshaw picked up his swagger stick. 'Very good! Sergeant, turn the troops out, slings an' bows'n'arrows. Tell 'em to keep their ears down below the battlements. Don't want the enemy t'know we're aware of their presence yet. We'll be ready when they make a move. Father, I suggest you keep all Redwallers indoors for the rest of the day, an' more especially the night, wot wot!'

Humble nodded to his young Cellarhog. 'Come on, Burlop, let's find Brother Demple. He'll help us to get everybeast inside – though they'll think it strange, being called in on such a fine afternoon.'

Burlop lent the Abbot his paw for support. 'Then we'll have to think of an idea, Father, something to make them want to be indoors. What about some sort of contest, with prizes for the winners?'

The Abbot brightened up. 'An excellent scheme, Burlop. Do you know, it's been a while since we had a riddle competition. That's always good fun!'

The young Cellarhog guided his Abbot outdoors. 'I've got a keg of strawberry fizz we can use, and I'll ask Friar Glisum to bake up some goodies. We'll hold the contest down in Cavern Hole.'

Wonwill watched them trundling paw in paw across the lawn outside. 'A riddle competition, eh? I'd like to 'ave a go at that, sah.'

Crumshaw breathed on his monocle and polished it. 'Oh, for the carefree life, Sergeant. But duty calls, eh?'

The craggy-faced Wonwill saluted. 'H'indeed it does, sah!'

Westering sunrays painted the walls of the Abbey like a deep blushing rose in the lengthening shadows; larks trilled their evening song as they descended to the flatlands beyond the ditch. All around the ramparts, hares crouched below the battlements, bows and slings close to paw.

Young Folderon sniffed and wiped a paw across her eyes. The sergeant nudged her lightly. 'Nah then, missy, wot's all this?'

She blinked furiously. 'Beg pardon, Sarge, but I was just thinkin', what a glorious sundown! Day endin' an' all that. A pack of vermin villains waitin' in hidin'. Makes you wonder how many of us'll live to see the dawn, if the worst comes to the worst, if y'know what I mean?'

The kindly Wonwill passed her his kerchief. 'Oh, I don't think much'll 'appen tonight, young 'un. Ye'll still be 'ere to stuff yore face at brekkist tomorrer. Now dry up an' stop reddenin' those pretty eyes.'

*

Down in Cavern Hole, the Redwallers were eagerly watching Sister Screeve, who had devised most of the riddles, questioning Hitheryon Jem. 'Now, I want you to tell me, who would be saying this? "Why Myrtle, me dear, ouch ouch! How nice to see you, ouch!" "Likewise, dearie, ouch! And how's your family? Ouch ouch!"'

Jem answered without hesitation. 'Marm, that's two ole hedgehog wives huggin' each other.'

Screeve ticked her parchment. 'Correct! Now stand over there, Jem. Next, please!'

Mudge the molebabe strode boldly up. 'Yurr naow, marm, you'm doan't arsk oi any 'ard riggles. Oi'm only ee h'infant!'

Screeve gave the molebabe a pretend scowl. 'I don't have any favourites, my questions are all hard. Right, answer this. You are a mole, and he isn't a mole – he's not your father, yet you call him Father. Who is he?'

Mudge stood gnawing his digging claw. 'Urm, urm . . .'

Sister Armel whispered in the molebabe's ear. He grinned, replying, 'Hurr hurr, that bee's ee h'Abbot, marm!'

The Recorder ticked her scroll. 'Very good! We all call the Abbot by the title Father. Correct, stand over there!'

Mudge waved at Humble. 'Oi daon't call ee Farther, zurr. Oi allus calls ee h'Abbot, duzzent oi!'

Humble smiled absentmindedly as he murmured to Burlop, 'It should be almost dark outside now.'

The young Cellarhog patted his elder's paw. 'Don't worry yore 'ead, Father. The Long Patrol will take care of everythin'. Come on, up ye go, 'tis yore turn.'

'Here's your riddle, Father.' Sister Screeve chuckled, then continued. 'Oh, I've got this name all mixed up! It says "Read well baby" on my parchment. What should it say?'

Humble looked distracted. His mind was on the vermin and the hares outside. 'I'm sorry, Sister, I've no idea.'

Armel encouraged him. 'Oh, come on, Father, it's easy. What do we call this lovely place where we live?'

Humble answered without thinking. 'Redwall Abbey. Why?'

Wandering Walt applauded loudly. 'Well done, zurr, that bee's ee h'answer. Redwall Abbey!'

Screeve pointed her quill at Armel. 'Any more helping with answers, Sister, and it's straight up to bed with you!'

The Dibbuns roared with laughter at the idea of an Infirmary Sister being sent off to bed like a naughty babe.

Darkness had descended outside. Captain Zerig signalled the two scouts from the shelter of the trees. 'Go now, an' take care ye are not discovered.'

Checking their weapons, the big, hard-eyed foxes made for the south wall in utter silence. Skilled at the art of concealment, they both moved like drifting cloud shadows over the grassy sward, using every hump and hollow as they crept towards the outer ramparts.

Tergen murmured to the brigadier as he observed their every move, 'Kyuuurh, they come now. Two foxes – one will go to the left, the other right. Other vermin stay hidden.'

Crumshaw kept his head low. 'Scoutin' the Abbey out, eh? Sergeant, take Folderon with ye, go t'the left. Cap'n Fortindom, you take Cartwill an' take the fox on the right. I want at least one of the scum alive. I intend sendin' their leader a stern warnin'. Off y'go!'

Both Graddu and Fargil stopped at the south wallgate. They tested it and found the small wicker door locked tight. Then they parted company, searching the high walls for possible pawholds to climb and checking the earth at the wall base for soft soil or possible tunnels.

Captain Derron Fortindom was renowned in the Long Patrol for his skill with the sabre. He had fought honourably in many campaigns. Removing his cloak, he watched Cartwill easing open the locks on the small east wallgate. Fortindom slid out into the surrounding woodland, murmuring to Cartwill, 'Lock this door an' stay inside, young 'un. Open it only when y'hear my voice again.'

Cartwill gripped his javelin eagerly. 'But, Captain . . .'

Derron Fortindom shook his head. 'Those are my orders, obey 'em!'

Cartwill barred the gate, then hurried up the east steps to join some others who were spread out along the walltop.

Kersey, the runner who had lost her twin, gritted her teeth. 'I'd give that scum what for if I was down there now!'

Another hare reassured her, 'Don't fret, mate. The vermin ain't been born who could cross blades with Cap'n Fortindom an' live t'tell the blinkin' tale!'

Fortindom still had the sabre belted to his side. He leaned casually against a sycamore trunk, almost invisible in the darkness, watching as Graddu, inspecting the walls, drew closer. He allowed the fox to pass him by a few paces before stepping out into the open to address him.

'Tut tut, all alone, wot. You must be a bold 'un! Where's your gang, scumface?'

Graddu whirled around to face him, curved sword in one paw and a short axe in the other. He began circling Fortindom, bared fangs showing in an evil grin. 'A big rabbit, all to myself? Such luck! I had to share the last one I ate, down upon the beach!'

Fortindom drew his sabre and moved, countering his circle. 'Aye, it took enough of ye – a hundred to eight, wasn't it? Sssssdeath!'

The hare captain moved like chain lightning, his sabre flashing up and across. The severed axe handle fell to the ground, almost in unison with the stricken fox. Fortindom wiped his blade upon Graddu and stepped over his carcass. Cartwill came dashing down the steps with Kersey close behind. They wrestled the doorlocks open and stood staring at the captain in dumb admiration.

He pulled Cartwill out into the woodlands, rapping an order at Kersey. 'You, miss, bar the door. Come with me,

Cartwill. We'll go around the outside in case the other one's runnin' away from Sergeant Wonwill. We may be able to cut the vermin off. Step lively now!'

The hares on the west wall stood with Folderon and Wonwill, peeping over the battlements as they monitored the progress of the remaining white fox along the outer walls.

When the sergeant heard the main gates rattle slightly, he whispered to the hares around him, 'Quick'n'quiet's the drill now, mates. We got to take this vermin alive. Stick to my h'orders now, young 'uns.'

Fargil the fox had his curved sword through a gap in the centre of both gates, using it as a lever to release the long wooden bar. Then, without warning, the gates opened, swinging inward. Fargil found himself facing a lean, grizzled Wonwill and ten young hares. Instinctively he turned to run, but Captain Derron Fortindom already had a sabre point to his throat. 'One move, sirrah, an' ye'll be crowmeat!'

Sergeant Wonwill knocked Fortindom's blade aside. 'Brigadier's orders, Mister Derron. Put up yore sabre, sah. This 'un's mine. Sentries, form a ring!'

Swiftly, the hares made a circle around Wonwill and the big fox. Holding up his paws to show he was unarmed, the sergeant addressed the hulking Fargil. 'Yore a big, tough-lookin' murderer. Come on, let's see wot ye can do! An unarmed beast should be about the right mark for the likes of a bully like you!'

Fargil had his curved sword ready, but he pulled a long dagger from his belt, charging at Wonwill double-bladed. The sergeant skipped to one side, his clenched paw punching the fox's shoulder twice.

Rap! Rap! The dagger clattered upon the path. With his numbed paw held limply by his side, Fargil let out a bellow of pain, swinging his sword back in an effort to cleave his opponent's skull.

Whoooofff! The wind was driven from him by a hard right to his stomach. The fox was bent almost double. Crouching, Wonwill delivered two hard uppercuts to the vermin's face. Stepping on the swordblade, the sergeant trapped it against the ground. He grabbed Fargil, hauling him upright by the ears. 'H'up ye come, me bold buckoe. Let's see wot sort of a shape ye can make!'

Fargil's fangs almost bit the tip of Wonwill's nose, but the hare's forehead shot forward like a battering ram. *Crack!* Minus a few teeth, the big fox lay stretched unconscious in the centre of the circle.

Wonwill kicked aside his enemy's blade, staring woefully at Fargil. 'Huh, I was just gettin' into me stride when he goes an' lays down on me. Vermin – no backbone, no grit, eh!'

The young hares applauded him lustily.

'Oh, well-hit, Sarge. That taught the blighter a lesson, wot!'

'Rather! Big clod didn't know his bottom from breakfast when ye decked him. Y'must have a head like a bloomin' boulder, Sarge!'

Fortindom stirred the prone fox with his sabre. 'Nice job, Sergeant, but personally I wouldn't soil me paws on scum like that. A blade's the only cure for vermin, wot? Righto, chaps, drag him inside an' close the gates. I suspect old Crumshaw will want a word with him when he wakes up.'

Down in Cavern Hole, Burlop had tapped his keg of strawberry fizz. He poured out beakers for one and all, whilst Sister Screeve and Jem distributed Friar Glisum's fresh-baked pies and tarts. The riddle contest had ended with a unanimous decision that everybeast should share in the prize. Abbot Humble was still looking worried and pre-occupied when Sergeant Wonwill entered, accompanied by several young hares.

Humble immediately accosted him. 'Any news of the vermin attack, Sergeant?'

The veteran saluted smilingly. 'Bless yore 'eart, Father, there ain't no need t'worry. Brigadier says for you to rest easy. The h'emergency is h'over!'

The home-loving Abbot heaved a huge sigh of relief. 'Seasons be praised! Would you and your hares like to share supper with us? There's plenty for all, Sergeant.'

Wonwill accepted the invitation gratefully. He enjoyed the unexpected treat as Dibbuns gathered around him, exclaiming, 'Sarjin', we haved a riggle concert!'

The sergeant took Mimsie the mousebabe on his knee. 'Ye don't say, missie, a riggle concert! Wot's that?'

Sister Armel refilled his beaker with fizz. 'She means a riddle contest, Sergeant. It was good fun.'

Perkle the hogbabe climbed up with Mimsie, who gazed up at Wonwill's leathery features. 'Joonow h'any puggles or rizzles, Sarjin?'

Sister Screeve interpreted. 'Perkle is asking if you know any puzzles or riddles, Sergeant. Well, do you, sir?'

Wonwill was captivated by the Abbeybabes. With no family, outside of the regiment, he found the little ones an endless source of wonder and delight. 'Oh I knows 'undreds of 'em, beauty. Shall I sing one for ye? I h'aint no great singer, but I'll 'ave a try.'

Humble intervened. 'Don't bother the Sergeant, Perkle. He's had a hard evening. I expect he's tired.'

But Wonwill reassured the Abbot, 'No, no, Father. Singin' for the little 'un's no bother. I'd sooner be 'ere singin' for the babbies than out there knocking the stuffin' out o' vermin. Right, 'ere goes!'

The sergeant sang an old tongue-twister, which was new to the Dibbuns, but all the older Redwallers joined in each chorus heartily.

'There once was a frog an' his name was ole Glogg,
He lived in a log on top of a bog.
He loved plum pudden an' gooseberry pie,
but if anybeast dared to come near him he'd cry.

Frog bog log Glogg! Pudden an' pie he'd loudly cry!
Wot a hard terrible life!

To his abode down the road came a toad,
bearin' a load as she puffed an' blowed,
"I'm tired of this bundle atop of my head,
I'm almost half dead but I'm fit to be wed."

Frog bog log Glogg! Pudden an' pie he'd loudly cry!
Abode road toad load! Head dead fit t'be wed!
Wot a hard terrible life!

He took both her paws an' pulled her indoors.
She swept the floors an' did all his chores.
Her bundle came open, ten tadpoles jumped out,
"Oh good day to ye, Dad." They all gave a great shout.

Frog bog log Glogg! Pudden an' pie he'd loudly cry!
Abode road toad load! Head dead fit t'be wed!
Dad! Dad! The frog's gone mad!
Wot a hard terrible wife!'

Abbot Humble patted the sergeant's back. Amid the cheers
and whoops, he called to Wonwill, 'Thank you, friend, and
all your gallant hares, thank you for everything – from
everybeast in this Abbey!'

24

Morning brought with it a sky of light-washed blue, with not a cloud to cross the sun's passage. Already Captain Zerig was awake. He bit into a hard green apple, pulled a wry face and spat out the mouthful of sour fruit. He threw the rest of it at Freeta, who was still sleeping. She sat up, rubbing her face. 'What was that for?'

The fox captain pointed to the open sward between the south Abbey wall and the trees where the vermin lay. 'See thy scouts, the two who were so good an' reliable?'

Fargil was stumbling on all fours through the grass with the slain Graddu tied across his back. Freeta kicked some nearby ermine into wakefulness. 'Rouse thyselves an' help them, quickly!'

They scurried out and dragged the two big foxes back into the woodlands. Vermin crowded around, severing the bonds from the pair. Thrusting his way through the onlookers, Zerig's contemptuous glance shot from the carcass of Graddu to Fargil, who was lying on his back. Zerig shook his head at the sight of Fargil's battered face. 'Well, tell me how this befell thee?'

The big fox mumbled from between his swollen lips, 'Water!'

The white fox captain returned his plea with a sharp kick. 'Report first, an' tell me all. Speak!'

Fargil stumbled through the events of the past night haltingly. When he reached the account of his fight with Wonwill, Zerig stopped him scornfully. 'Do ye mean to say that a single rabbit did this to thee with only his paws, whilst ye were fully armed?'

Fargil sobbed brokenly. 'Aye, Captain. They are called hares, not rabbits. He could have slain me, but he spared my life to bring ye a message from their leader, one they call the Brigadier.'

Freeta came forward, administering the beaten fox a few sips of water from her canteen. 'Say on, what did this Brigadier hare tell thee?'

Fargil managed to sit up shakily. 'He said that if we stay in this place we will all die. His warriors have sworn vengeance on Lord Gulo and all who follow him. Captain, he gives ye until the setting of the sun to be gone from Redwall Abbey!'

Zerig thrust his chin forward belligerently. 'Or what?'

Fargil repeated Crumshaw's words as accurately as he could. ' "Or he shall meet ye on the west flatlands to give ye blood'n'vinegar, with no surrender." Then one, a Captain like thee, also said to make sure I told thee this. He said that whether we stand and fight, or choose to run like cowardly scum, the hares of the Long Patrol will not rest until we are all staring at Hellgates through dead eyes, an' our bones lie bleaching in the sun.'

A hush fell over the vermin. Fargil and Graddu had been two fearsome fighters, but now one lay dead and the other was reduced to a beaten and pitiable creature.

Sensing the mood of his followers, Zerig drew his curved sword and tested its edge by licking the blade, an obvious show of bravado. 'Hah! Threats mean little to the warriors of Lord Gulo. We came not from the lands of ice beyond the great sea to be frightened by the words of rabbits!'

Fargil stood upright. He began pacing to the left, towards the path, his voice rising as he replied to Zerig's boast. 'Those beasts are not rabbits, they are hares, fighting hares! Ye did not face them, Captain, I did. An' I know they are well able to carry out their vow of vengeance. Only a fool would stay here – ye will all die!' He turned and broke into a shambling run. Zerig snatched the spear from an ermine and flung it with swift accuracy. An easy target, Fargil now lay dead – his body slumped facedown with the spear's shaft protruding from between his shoulders.

In a great show of swaggering, Zerig pulled out the weapon, tossing it back to its owner. The fox captain's sword waved in an arc over the rest of the vermin. In a harsh and commanding voice, he ground out an ultimatum. 'Run now if ye want to join Fargil!'

The ermine and foxes stood motionless. Zerig pointed his blade at the Abbey and proclaimed boldly, 'When Lord Gulo arrives here, we will be sitting inside that place, eating the flesh of our enemies. I give ye my word on it!'

The vermin were scouring the woodlands for anything they could make a meal of, when Freeta came to where Zerig sat at the tree fringe. 'Well, Captain, will ye meet the hares on the flatlands at tomorrow's dawn?'

Zerig snorted. 'Do ye take me for an idiot? What beast would carry out his foe's orders?'

Freeta chewed on a grass blade. 'Thou art a bravebeast, Zerig, but thy sense often deserts thee.'

Zerig snatched the grass from her lips. 'How so?'

The vixen plucked another stalk, replacing it. 'Had I questioned Fargil, I would have asked him certain things: How many creatures did he see at the Abbey, what was the number of fighting beasts and who looked like the peaceable ones? Another thing, before he was captured, did Fargil see a way in – a loose gate, a wall that would be easy to climb, maybe a good spot where a tunnel might be dug? There was more I would have asked him. Did they have vittles an' drink aplenty in there, enough to withstand a siege? Now ye have slain Fargil, many questions still need answers.'

Zerig knew the sly vixen had the advantage of him. 'So, what do we do now, Freeta?'

She shook her head teasingly. 'Oh no, what do *you* do? I am not a Captain in command, that is thy decision.'

Zerig narrowed his eyes thoughtfully. 'What do ye want? Tell me!'

Freeta spat out the grass stalk. Her face hardened before she replied. 'Two things – revenge on Gulo for my mate, Shard, and half of everything we gain!'

Zerig smiled, realizing it was now his turn to tease. 'A tall order, but I fear Gulo, not you. He will come to this place, do not doubt it. So why should I cast my lot in with thine?'

The vixen played the captain like a fish on a line, drawing him in with her reasoning. 'That Abbey is the key to all, Zerig. Without the right plan, not even Gulo and ten times our number could conquer such a place. Gulo is blood, fur and bone, like anybeast. He cannot break through stone blocks with fang and claw. I am not returning to the lands of ice to fear Gulo and serve him. If we were inside that fortress, he could not harm us. Think of it, we could live in ease and plenty, as the creatures in there do now. You are in command, the others will follow you. But we need more brain than brawn. I have the brain!'

Zerig stared up at the south ramparts. 'And ye have a plan to get inside there?'

Freeta nodded decisively. 'I have an excellent plan!' She held out her paw. 'But it must be carried out by we two. If we work together, the victory will be ours!'

Zerig clasped her paw tightly. 'I am with ye!'

Friar Glisum and Brigadier Crumshaw were in the pantry, sampling some of last autumn's russet apples and discussing their merits over October Ale and mature cheese.

Kersey came dashing in, her words pouring forth at

breakneck pace. 'Beg pardon, sah, but our hawk reports three vermin outside the south wall. They're carryin' a flag o' truce. I think they want to parley, sah!'

Crumshaw wiped his lips fastidiously on a spotted kerchief. 'Oh, do they indeed! Well, lead on, young 'un, let's see what the scoundrels have t'say for themselves, wot wot!'

Sergeant Wonwill was at the bottom of the steps with three other hares, restraining the angry goshawk. He saluted smartly. 'Sah! This 'ere 'awk wanted to h'open the south wallgate an' slay the vermin. I 'ad to convince 'im that 'e couldn't do it to beasts under a flag o' truce, sah!'

The brigadier marched past Tergen, tapping his beak with the swagger stick. 'Know how y'feel, m'friend, but despatchin' the foe under a flag o' truce 'tis not done in the best o' circles, old chap. Bad form, doncha know, blinkin' bad form, wot wot!'

The goshawk squawked up the steps after him, 'Yaakaaaarrr! Kill all vermin, Wotwot – not talk . . . kill!'

Crumshaw polished his eyeglass and squinched his cheek around it. He sniffed, gazing in disgust at the trio of vermin with their stained and tattered scrap atop a spearpole.

Zerig called up to him, 'Be ye the one they call Brigadier?'

Crumshaw leaned on a battlement, his voice dripping disdain. 'At y'service. An' who pray am I addressin'?'

Zerig drew his sword and rapped his chest with the blade. 'I serve Gulo the Savage. I am Captain Zerig!'

The brigadier did not sound impressed. 'Are ye, indeed? Then some blighter ought to teach ye the rules o' war'n' combat, thickhead. Ye don't come to a parley under a flag of truce bearin' arms. Chuck that frogsticker away, or I won't bandy words with ye. Go on, sling it!'

The white fox captain shot Crumshaw a murderous glare, but he put the sword down upon the grass.

The brigadier snorted. 'Hmph, that's better, wot wot. Now state y'business, sah!'

Zerig tried to look as tough as he could under the

circumstances. He pointed skyward, announcing, 'At to-morrow's dawn, we will slay ye an' eat ye!'

This statement seemed to improve the brigadier's mood. He smiled. 'Well well well, good on ye, old scruff. Y'mean to say you actually accept our challenge, wot wot?'

Freeta, who was standing beside the ermine spearholder, smiled back at Crumshaw. 'You are old. We will have to roast ye a long time before ye are tender enough to eat.'

Crumshaw pulled a face of mock horror at the vixen. 'Atrocious table manners, marm. Still, I hope I taste as good as that poor wretch you made your flag of truce from!'

Zerig glanced at the grisly strip of Fargil's hide which served as the flag of truce. He bared his fangs. 'He was an enemy. The warriors of Gulo the Savage come from a land where enemies are eaten. When dawn comes, we will eat you!'

Crumshaw twirled his moustache casually. 'Listen, laddie vermin, my Long Patrol are a pretty tough lot t'chew. I've a feelin' they'll stick in your flippin' throat, wot! Tchah, enough of all this twaddle. Run along now an' take your last sleep. See you at dawn out on the west flats. Don't be late now – I can be jolly hard on latecomers. Off y'pop now, bye-bye!'

The brigadier suddenly dropped down behind the wall-top as four arrows zipped by overhead.

Wonwill came bounding up the steps. 'Are ye all right, sah? Dirty scum, firin' arrows over a flag of truce. Wait'll I gets me paws on 'em!'

Crumshaw marched briskly down the wallsteps. 'Wouldn't have expected anything else from those cads. I feel sorry for their mothers. Imagine havin' t'bring up bounders like that lot! Wot wot!'

Sister Armel and Ulba molemum were escorting some Dibbuns down to Brother Demple's vegetable patch. With the hares staying at the Abbey, there was a constant demand from Friar Glisum for more salad greens. They were startled by a mighty roar from the walltops. It was the Long Patrol's battle cry. 'Eulaliiiiaaaaaaa!'

Young Kersey came by, waving a javelin. For the first time since her brother's death, she was laughing. Brother Demple emerged from behind a berry hedge, dusting earth from his paws. He called out to Kersey, 'Are we being attacked, miss? Shall I get the little ones indoors?'

The young hare twirled her javelin in the air and caught it. 'Oh no, sir, it's the Patrol. We're goin' to do battle with the vermin, tomorrow dawn, out on the flatlands. Forward the buffs an' no surrender! Eulaliiiiaaaaaaa!'

Sister Armel was horrified at Kersey's obvious enjoyment. 'How can she laugh and cheer at such a thing?'

Ulba molemum shook her velvety head. 'Oi doant know, moi dearie. We'm peaceable creeturs whom knows nuthin' o' killin' an' slayin'!'

Brother Demple watched the hares leaping with joy on the walltops. 'Aye, 'tis a mystery sure enough, Sister. But we're simple Abbeybeasts, an' they're warriors, born to the art of war. Fightin' is in their blood, y'see.'

Mudge the molebabe struck up a boxing pose, as he had seen Sergeant Wonwill do. 'Oi bee's a gurt wurrier, zurr!'

Brother Demple could not help smiling at the little fellow. 'Oh I'm sure you are, Mudge, but you're too young, and us Redwallers know little of fightin'. Hmm, so I suppose we should be grateful for the hares.'

Armel shrugged. 'I suppose so, Brother, but why do creatures have to fight?'

Demple picked Mudge up and placed him on his shoulder. 'Because there's always good and bad in the land, and goodbeasts have to protect their friends an' families from evil ones who want nothing but to conquer an' destroy.'

The molebabe patted the gardener's head. 'You'm roight, zurr!'

25

It was still dark as a flotilla of logboats and rafts pulled into the bough-shaded bank. Rakkety Tam MacBurl, Doogy, Skipper, Ferdimond and Yoofus slipped ashore quietly. Guosim shrews held the other craft steady as the rest of the hares disembarked. Log a Log Togey joined them with his two scouts.

'Tam, this is Oneshrew an' Twoshrew, my best trackers. They know where Gulo an' his vermin are camped. They'll lead ye there. Do wot ye got to do, then get out fast, mate. My trackers'll take ye up to the pines where the black birds roost. The rest is up to you. Now when ye leave the pines, there'll be bushland an' a hill to the east. Beyond the hill is a fast-flowin' river – make for it. I'll be waitin' there with my logboats for ye. Be lucky an' don't hang around in the pines, or those birds will peck the eyes outta yore 'ead afore ye can wink at 'em!'

Tam shook the shrew chieftain's paw. 'My thanks to ye, Togey. Corporal Wopscutt, get your hares to follow us in skirmishin' order. Everybeast stick together. We can't hang about for stragglers.'

Doogy and Ferdimond were up at the front, with Yoofus between them. The water vole panted and puffed; he did not like keeping up the rapid pace through the still-dark woodlands. 'Ah sure, me ould limbs'll be entirely ruinated wid all this dashin' an' gallopin' about!'

Ferdimond lent a paw to pull him along. 'Save y'breath, old lad, an' let your paws do the runnin'.'

Doogy grabbed the thief's other paw. 'Och, ah'm fair grieved ye cannae stop tae sniff the daisies. Move yoreself, ye wee snail!'

Tam was at the head of the bunch with the shrews on either side of him. One of them beckoned him to slow down. 'The vermin camp's not far ahead. We best go careful now.'

The border warrior peered at the shrew in the grey haze which precedes dawn. 'Right y'are, mate. Which are you, Oneshrew or Twoshrew?'

The tracker scowled as a hare ran into her back. 'I'm Oneshrew. She's me sister, Twoshrew.'

Wilderry commented, 'Dashed funny names, wot?'

She was still scowling. 'No funnier'n yores, matey. We came from a big family, so me daddy called us all by number.'

Yoofus was regaining his breath, yet he managed to quip, 'An' how many brothers'n'sisters did ye have, a few hundred?'

Twoshrew glared at him. 'There was only twenny-six of us. Now shut yore face or the vermin'll hear us!'

Dawn was just breaking when a vermin sentry came stumbling into camp. Clutching a swollen ear, the ermine tripped as he skirted the fire embers, shouting, 'Mighty One! Quickly, sire!'

Gulo leapt up, brushing sparks from his fur. 'What is it fool? Speak!'

The ermine sentry pointed as he babbled. 'Over there, sire. 'Twas thy brother, I swear! There were others with him!'

Gulo grabbed the hapless sentry by the neck and swung him off the ground. The wolverine roared urgently, 'Askor, ye say? Where . . . What happened?'

'Gye goz gust . . . gluuurggg!'

Realizing that he was throttling the ermine, Gulo let go. The unfortunate vermin lay on the ground, nursing his throat with one paw and his ear with the other. 'Mighty One, I was standing guard when I heard a noise behind me. As I turned, a big cloaked beast banged my head against a tree, sire. The others trampled over me as they ran off!'

Gulo towered over the quaking sentry, whom he knew had been caught napping by the intruders. 'How did ye know 'twas my brother? Did ye see him clear?'

The ermine scrabbled backward as he explained. 'I did not see his face, Mighty One. But the size of him, it could have only been thy brother, sire. Aye, and when I saw the prints he left, they were the same as yours!'

Gulo thundered off in the direction the sentry had pointed. He spied the deep clawmarks with fur brushings at the edges and turned to bellow at his wakening followers. 'Leave everything save your weapons! Hurry, Askor must not escape! Move! Move!'

Dawn sunlight penetrated the woodland mists as Tam and his band dashed headlong through ferns and bushes. They made no attempt to disguise their tracks, shouting aloud as they ran, 'Askor! Askor! Askoooooor!'

Skipper lifted Yoofus from his broad shoulders, then kicked off the bulrush spikes attached to his footpaws. He ripped apart the two cloaks which had been sewn together, winking at Yoofus. 'Well, matey, d'ye reckon that did the trick, eh?'

The volethief grinned. 'Ah, 'twas a grand ould ruse, sir. But d'ye not think that a fine big beast like yerself could carry a poor, wornout water vole a bit further on those strong shoulders?'

The otterchief nodded readily. 'Good idea, cully. I'll carry ye 'til midday, then you carry me 'til sunset. Is it a bargain?'

Yoofus shook his head ruefully. 'Ah, yer a dreadful plank-tailed ould hooligan, so y'are. An' here's meself thinkin' ye were a kind friend!'

Vermin yells from not too far behind set them running pell-mell again. Doogy grabbed the volethief's paw. 'Ah wish't MacBurl'd think up some plans that are a wee bit slower. Come on, ye wee laggard, afore ye become vermin vittles!'

Tam urged everybeast onward. Then he took up the rear with Corporal Wopscutt and Ferdimond, allowing the Guosim trackers to lead everybeast to the pines.

Butty speeded up as the vermin howls behind them grew louder. He smiled wryly at Tam. 'Pretty desperate plan of yours, MacBurl. Let's hope the black birds haven't tootled off t'see their distant blinkin' cousins, wot?'

Tam dropped back a pace. 'No need to run so fast. We don't want to lose Gulo's mob, do we?'

Ferdimond slowed to match Tam's pace. 'You're right there, old sport. Bit risky, though, ain't it?'

The din from the vermin swelled louder through the trees; they were drawing closer. Tam laughed recklessly. 'All the best plans are a bit risky, Ferdy. Mind those tree roots now, there's a steep hill comin' up.'

Unfortunately, neither Doogy nor Yoofus was within hearing of Tam's remark. The water vole was gripping the Highlander's paw tight as he tripped over a mess of protruding hawthorn roots. They cartwheeled sideways and shot off to the side, rolling downhill together. Crashing through bushes but luckily avoiding several big trees, the pair thudded down into a dried-up ditch, deep with seasons of leaf loam.

Dizzy and bruised, Doogy managed to sit upright, so that his head stuck out above the loam. He spat out a few dried leaves. 'Ach, ye fiddle-pawed fool, why didn't ye leggo of mah paw?'

The head of Yoofus emerged, with a crown of rotten leaves wreathing it. 'Ah, give over, ye fur-tailed fibber. 'Twas yoreself that tripped, not me. Sure I only kept ahold of yore paw to try an' stop ye fallin'. An' that's all the thanks I get? You squirrels are mis'rable ould things, sure enough. Whups, duck yore head quick!'

He pulled Doogy beneath the leaves as the vermin thundered past, yelling and shouting. When the sounds receded, they both sat up again. Doogy spat out more leaves. 'Ah'm thinkin' we've been dropped from Tam's plan, eh?'

Yoofus sighed with relief. 'Ah well, thank goodness for that! There's an end to all that runnin' like a madbeast.'

Doogy stood up but immediately had to sit down again, groaning in pain. 'Agh! Ah think ah've broken mah footpaw!'

The water vole scrambled out of the ditch. He hauled his friend up and inspected the damaged limb. 'Sure that's never broken, 'tis only an ould pawsprain. An' ye've chipped a claw. I can fix that up for ye!'

The Highlander sat there, bemoaning his fate. 'Ah've mised a braw fight, an' we're lost, an' mah paw is achin' fit tae beat the band!'

Yoofus smeared the paw with mud, laid dockleaves on and bound it firmly with ivy vines. 'Will ye lissen to yoreself! Lost? I'm never lost in Mossflower. An' as for missin' any fightin', what good would ye be with a wounded paw? Give yore ould gob a rest, mate. We'll make out just fine!'

Doogy laughed mirthlessly. 'Doin' what?'

The thief wrinkled his nose mischievously. 'Did ye not notice? The vermin left their camp to chase after us in a grand ould hurry. 'Twill be unguarded now an' full of little gifts, just for me'n you, me ould tatercake!'

Doogy shook his head at the volethief's audacity. 'Och, ye don't miss a trick, do ye? I like the idea o' lootin' the vermin camp. Yer a canny wee rascal, Yoofus!'

The water vole danced a little jig, rubbing his paws at the prospect. 'Ah sure, there's nothin' grander than thievin' from thieves. Lend me yore big knife now, an' I'll cut ye a crutch to stump along on.'

Passing over his beloved claymore, Doogy warned Yoofus, 'Mind ye now, ah want that back!'

The thief's face was the picture of injured innocence. 'Ooh, pickle yore tongue, Doogy Plumm. Fancy sayin' somethin' like that to a friend like me!'

The Highlander watched Yoofus cutting a yew staff. 'Rakkety Tam MacBurl's the only true friend ah've ever had. Ah hope his plan's workin' out well for him right now.'

Tam noticed that the woodlands were not as dense and that the ground underpaw had become sandy. Oneshrew pointed through the thinning trees as they ran. 'Ye can see the pines up yonder, look.'

Beyond the trees, a stretch of heathland spread up to a gentle rise, atop of which was a sizable area of pine trees. Tam, however, could see no rooks or crows hovering about them. He mentioned this to his Guosim guides. 'I don't see any of the black birds around those pines.'

Twoshrew assured him, 'Don't let that fool ye, sir. The villains are there, sure enough.'

Oneshrew agreed with her sister. 'Aye, you just try enterin' the trees, an' you'll see 'em all right!'

Corporal Butty Wopscutt cast a backward glance. 'Birds or not, we'll have t'go forward pretty sharpish, old chap. The foebeasts'll be right on our tails in a few ticks. So what's the plan, eh?'

Tam drew the sword of Martin. 'We group together in a tight bunch. Everybeast with sword, spear or lance, hold your weapons point up. But only when I give the command, Up Arms! I want us to go in there like one giant hedgehog. Go slow across the heathland. I want Gulo an' his vermin to see us, so they'll speed up. The moment we're in the pines, we'll have to run twice as fast as the vermin. But remember, stay close together, keep your points up an' charge right through that pine grove like a bolt o' lightnin'. You shrews, stay out of the trees. Circle to the left, get to your Log a Log at the river an' tell him to make the boats ready, cos we'll be comin'.'

Wopscutt gripped his sword hilt as he gave the order. 'Long Patrol – blades, spears'n'javelins at the ready! Advance in close order at a jog . . .'

The younger hares were looking nervously over their shoulders. Behind them the roar of vermin was growing in volume. Catching sight of a white flash among the trees, Ferdimond knew that the foebeasts were not too far off. He was relieved to hear the corporal complete his command.

'Steady at the rear there! Long Patrol will advance!'

26

Gulo was making heavy going of the chase. Slowing down, he fell to the back of the pack, panting hoarsely.

A slender ermine runner with patched fur dropped back from the front to report, 'Mighty One, they are in sight!'

The wolverine wiped foaming slobber from his gaping mouth. 'We must catch them . . . Can ye see my brother Askor?'

The ermine moved sideways a pace, wisely out of Gulo's immediate reach. 'Sire, 'tis hard to tell. They are bunched up and the trees are in the way, but I am sure thy brother is with them. Methinks we have outrun them, sire. They have slowed down to little more than a trot.'

Wild hope surged through Gulo's huge muscular body as he bounded forward with a burst of renewed energy. 'Get them! Kill them! Kiiiiilll!'

Drawing curved swords, axes, spears and knives, the foxes and ermine dashed forward with their chieftain, howling as they broke out on to the heathland, 'Gulo! Gulo! Gulo! Kill! Kill!'

Harsh, raucous cries began echoing through the pines as great, dark shapes visibly flapped about amid the branches. Tam and the hares were mere paces away from the forbidding darkness of the groves. The vermin were roaring across the heath toward them.

Tam MacBurl's face was fixed in a tight, dangerous smile as he spoke calmly to the younger Patrol hares. 'Eyes front now, steady in the ranks. Don't run yet, nice steady pace now. That's the ticket! Don't look back.'

Ferdimond felt his fur rise like wire at Tam's shout.

'Up arms! Charge! Haway Braaaaaaaw!'

A sea of spear, sword and javelin points bristled upward. The hares charged into the pines, bellowing the Long Patrol war cry into the dim, green-cast gloom. 'Eulaliiiiiaaaaaaa!'

Then the air became thick with huge black birds – crows and rooks – winging down to attack the trespassers. A madness had fallen upon both birds and beasts. Weapons flashed upward as beaks and talons slashed downward. Tam took a big rook through its open beak as it dived to peck at his eyes. He swung it from his sword and parried at another with his dirk. Yelling out war cries like madbeasts, Ferdimond and Butty whipped away at the dark-feathered masses. Both warriors covered their eyes with a paw as they thundered ahead toward a glimmer of sunlight that pierced the dim grove. Alongside Tam, a hare stumbled, her ear half torn off by cruel, raking bird talons. By grabbing on to the hare's homespun tunic, Tam was able to drag her up and along with him. Then, thrusting his dirk into her weaponless grasp, the Borderer urged her on. 'Keep goin', me pretty. We're nearly there. Haway Braaaaaaaaw!'

The light from the outside grew brighter, dispersing the darkness and illuminating the flashing of steel. Paws pounded the thick floor of dead pine needles, scattering them broadcast. Ragged, dark shapes squawked; beaks pecked; and glistening talons ripped savagely at fur, eyes, paws – even at naked steel blades.

Then they were out!

The Long Patrol broke forth into the high, bright midday – sobbing, cheering, weeping, laughing and still shouting war cries.

Butty Wopscutt made sure the last hare was out. Never forgetting his duty, the gallant corporal rapped out orders to all and sundry. 'Straighten y'selves up now! Form ranks and keep those weapons drawn. Face to the trees – it ain't over yet, buckoes. Never mind y'wounds, stay on the alert!'

One or two crows almost came out beyond the grove but then wheeled and turned at the cries from within. Mad with bloodlust, they hurled themselves back to meet Gulo and the vermin headlong.

Ferdimond found Tam cleaning his blade on a tussock of grass. 'Tam, there's no sign of Doogy or Yoofus. I can't see 'em anywhere. What'll we do?'

The border warrior's jaw tightened. 'Not a thing if either of 'em went down among those birds. But somehow I can't see that happenin' to Doogy Plumm or that crafty vole. We've got to get away from here fast!'

Ferdy nodded curtly. 'Right y'are, Tam. We've lost three hares, an' there's a good number wounded. Gettin' back t'the river an' the shrewboats is the best plan. Then we can regroup an' plan ahead. By the way, was Doogy an' the volechap with you when we entered the pines?'

Tam shook his head. 'No! Weren't they with you, Wilderry?'

Lancejack sheathed his long rapier. 'No, I was bringin' up the rear. I never saw either of 'em. Come t'think of it, I didn't catch sight of 'em at the edge of the woods or whilst we were crossin' the heath. I hope those two are all right, wot!'

Tam accepted his dirk back from the young hare with the torn ear. 'Looks like they weren't with us for a while. Don't fret, I'll take my oath on it that those two rogues are safe an' well someplace.'

Wopscutt waggled a paw in his ear at the screeches and squawks which were emanating from deep in the pines. 'Good grief, let's get away from that racket. Patrol! Come to attention – smartly! About turn, lead off by the right an' head for that big hill yonder. Quick march!'

Going down the easy slope into a valley, the Patrol entered the trees and began marching uphill. Now that they had come through the ordeal of the pines and were temporarily free of the pursuing vermin, talk of the battle was bandied about. Weary but elated, the young hares chattered as they marched on.

'Wait'll we get back to Salamandastron and tell 'em about that, eh wot?'

'Rather, look at this scar I've got on me blinkin' cheek. Blighter who did that looked more like a bloomin' eagle than a crow! Huh, he won't be flyin' tonight though – no sir!'

'Hah, that's nothin'! There was one bird there the size of a flippin' feather mattress. Picked me up by me ear, would y'believe! I lost my sword, but I kicked him until the fiend let me go. Mister MacBurl loaned me his big knife, so I finished the villain off. Aye, an' two more like him . . .'

The speaker's voice trailed off as she noticed that Tam was within hearing range. The border warrior looked over at her and winked. 'That's right, I saw it myself. You were very brave, miss, an example to the Patrol.'

His remark set off a string of other tales, each one full of self-congratulation.

'Did y'see me, Mister MacBurl? I had two on the point of my javelin quick as a flash!'

'One was swoopin' down on me, an' I remembered Sarge Wonwill's boxin' lessons. I hit him such a punch that the blighter shot to one side an' buried his beak in an oak. Hoho, you should've seen him strugglin' t'get loose, flappin' an' scratchin' like I don't know what, wot!'

'Hold on, buried his beak in an oak? That was a pine grove! Wasn't a flamin' oak in sight, old lad!'

'Oh, er, haha, did I say oak? I meant a pine, yes, a pine!'

The boasts went back and forth until Wopscutt whispered to Tam, 'Did I tell you about how I slew a score of rooks an' carried four wounded out on my back?'

Tam stifled a laugh as he replied, 'Don't be too hard on

the young 'uns, it was prob'ly their first real battle. Can you remember how you boasted after your first encounter, mate? I can – it took them a full season to shut me up, the way I bragged about it.'

Butty chuckled. 'I recall it well, Tam. I was very young then, but to hear me tell the tale o' that battle, 'twas a waste o' time attendin' it for the Long Patrol. Accordin' to me, I won it single-pawed. Let 'em carry on with their tall tales, wot. They're not doin' harm to anybeast by boastin'. After a few days the excitement'll wear off. Then one night they'll cry themselves t'sleep, rememberin' the pals they lost back there.'

Tam nodded slowly. 'Aye, I can remember doin' that myself.'

When they reached the hilltop, the Patrol could see the river far below through the trees. Oneshrew and Twoshrew were waiting to meet Tam at the hilltop.

Oneshrew shook his paw. 'Well, sir, ye came out of it alive. Did yore plan work?'

The border warrior glanced back at the pine grove on the far hillcrest. 'I think so, at least Gulo isn't out of there yet. Though I can't imagine a monster like him t'be defeated by any number o' black birds. Can you?'

Twoshrew shrugged eloquently. 'Maybe, maybe not. We've been sent here to watch the land, an' get word back if he shows by tomorrow's dawn. Our Log a Log is waitin' down there for ye, he's got a feed laid on.'

Tam tweaked Ferdimond's ear. 'Did ye hear that? The Guosim have got vittles ready for us.'

Without further ado, Ferdimond set off briskly downhill. 'I say, jolly decent of the old shrewtypes, wot. They certainly know how to sling a salad an' present a pastie. Haw haw haw! Fightin' by mornin' an' feastin' by night, eh? Just show me that bloomin' grub!'

Tam nodded to Butty. 'Hear that? He's almost forgotten the fight, the moment food was mentioned!'

The corporal marched off smartly in Ferdimond's wake. 'Well, wot can one expect? The chap's young – he's got an appetite an' he's a hare. Stands t'reason, don't it?'

Tam kept pace downhill with Butty, listening to a little ditty he was singing.

'I wake up in the mornin', so glad the night is past,
it's straight down to the table, to break my flippin' fast.
O Breakfast! Breakfast! Us chaps must have some break-
    fast,
there's oatmeal honey toast an' tea, an' seconds just for
    me!

When I finish brekkers, I hang around the kitchen,
the smell of vittles cookin' is gettin' quite bewitchin'.
Luncheon! Luncheon! That's wot I'll soon be munchin',
on soup'n'salad chomp an' chew, I think I should eat
    two!

The afternoon's a desert, I wait impatiently,
until I hear the cook call, he's servin' noontime tea.
O Teatime! Teatime! An utterly sublime time,
each dainty cake an' homely scone, I'm first in line for
    one!

When chaps race to the table, it's always me the winner,
I'm fairly famished as a frog, when I run in to dinner.
O Dinner! Dinner! My figure ain't much thinner,
I lick at both my plate an' paw, then I yell out for more!

I'm starvin' flippin' hungry, oh isn't it a crime,
that interval from dinner, to good old suppertime.
Supper! Supper! How super, serve 'er up, sir,
then pack some scoff up good'n'tight, to take to bed
    tonight!'

The Guosim cooks had dug a baking pit on the riverbank with a fire to one side of it.

Log a Log Togey greeted Tam and Butty warmly. 'It does

233

me heart good to see ye again, mates. Well then, how did yore plan work out? Is everybeast back in one piece?'

Tam returned the Guosim chieftain's hearty pawshake. 'We left Gulo an' his vermin to argue it out with the black birds. I'm still waitin' on the outcome of it. There's six or seven hares wounded, but not too badly. We lost three to the crows'n'rooks – I didn't imagine there'd be so many birds roostin' in those pines. Doogy an' Yoofus have gone missin', but I'm sure those two rogues are still on the loose someplace. So, how goes it with you an' yore Guosim, friend?'

Togey pointed to the pit and the fire. 'Whilst we was waitin', the cooks spotted a shoal o' trout swimmin' upriver, so we snared a few. They've got a troutbake goin'. It'll be ready afore evenin'. I've posted two lookouts to watch the pines for ye. My healers will tend to yore wounded. Come aboard for some snacks an' a drink. There's somethin' that's been botherin' me, I want to talk with ye about it.'

Tam, Butty and Ferdimond sat beneath an awning on Togey's big logboat, drinking rosehip cordial and nibbling at a tray of preserved fruits. With the late noon sunlight shimmering off the gently flowing water, Tam and the hares sat back and relaxed for the first time that day.

Butty called to the young hares on the bank who were shouting and gesticulating as they told the Guosim of their heroic exploits. 'I say, you chaps, please keep it down to a dull roar!' He turned to the shrew chieftain. 'Now then, old lad, what's on y'mind, eh?'

Togey scratched his beard. 'It's somethin' ye said back at the water meadows, Tam. When ye joined up with the Long Patrol hares, how many vermin were ye trackin'?'

The border warrior pursed his lips. 'Oh, about fivescore, I figured – an' Gulo, of course. But no more'n that.'

Togey nodded. 'I thought that's wot ye said. But when I sent Oneshrew an' Twoshrew out to find where the vermin were camped last evenin', they reported back that there was only slightly more'n twoscore of 'em!'

Ferdimond glanced from one to the other. 'Oh corks! That leaves half o' the blinkin' villains unaccounted for, wot?'

Butty bit his lip. 'Y'know what that means, Tam?'

Tam stood up, fired by a sense of urgency. 'The other half'll be attackin' the Abbey. We'd best get the Patrol on the move back to Redwall!'

Log a Log Togey gestured the squirrel back to his seat. 'I've lived a few seasons more'n you beasts. Runnin' off with half a scheme is a sure route to failure. Let's take time to figure things out properlike. I've got one or two ideas I'd like to put to ye.'

Tam sat down. 'I'm always ready to listen an' heed a Chieftain of your experience, Togey. Carry on, mate.'

The Guosim leader explained his scheme. 'If'n you could get through those birds in the pines, then Gulo could, though I don't know wot shape his number o' vermin'll be when he does. Rest assured, though, he'll be comin' after ye, so we can't afford to ignore him. Yore first plan was to draw the vermin away from Redwall an' pick 'em off until they were finished, but that plan won't hold water any more, Tam. I think we should stay put by this river. When Gulo comes out o' the pines an' picks up the trail again, then we move. We'll wait 'til the last moment, then leave a clear trail for him t'follow. My Guosim can get ye back to Redwall, by one waterway an' another, until we're not far from the Abbey. I'll have scouts sent out to otherbeasts who'll help us. I know lots o' creatures who are friendly to the Redwallers. They'll help without question.'

Tam winked at the wise old shrew. 'Right, Togey, a great plan! What d'you think, Butty?'

Corporal Wopscutt smiled his approval. 'Capital tactic, wot! Right, what's the next move, chaps?'

Tam quaffed the last of his drink and rose once more. 'Get out there on the riverbank, make lots o' noise an' keep a good fire goin'. Then Gulo an' his vermin can see where we are an' come after us again, eh, Togey?'

The Guosim chieftain was in complete agreement. 'Don't want to lose 'em, do we?'

It was dark by the time the troutbake was ready. By the light of three good fires, the Guosim cooks raked away the glowing embers on top of their pit. Uncovering a layer of earth and steaming damp foliage, they scooped out the apples, celery, onions and watercress lying on top of the baked trout. The fish, which had been placed on a bed of hot stones at the bottom of the pit, were cooked to perfection. Hares and shrews sat together on the riverbank, drinking old shrewbeer and doing justice to the delicious meal. Four young Long Patrol members entertained everybeast with a barracks room ditty which was an old favourite from the sergeants' mess at Salamandastron. Some of their harmonies were a bit off-key, but what they lacked in melodic content they made up for in volume. All the others knew the 'walla walla' chorus and taught it to the shrews as they sang along raucously.

'A gallant young warrior lay weary,
on a battlefield far from his home.
He tried to sit up and sound cheery,
an' these were the words he did moan. Oooooooohhh
Walla walla wimbo, bing bang bimbo,
wullyah wullyah wullyah whoo!
Wot I wouldn't give for a basinful
of me grandma's hard-baked stew!

Give this pudden back to me dear mother,
an' tell her I slew ten vermin with it.
Say I don't wish to cause any bother,
but the Sergeant's a silly great twit! Oooooooooohhhhh
Walla walla wimbo, bing bang bimbo,
wullyah wullyah wullyah whoop!
I must complain I've got a pain, _
an' the cook makes poison soup!

Tell my fat little sister I love her,
an' give her this flea-ridden coat.
Say it comes from her handsome young brother,
it was swiped off a greasy old stoat. Oooooooohhhhh
Walla walla wimbo, bing bang bimbo,
wullyah wullyah wullyah whoo!
Me ears are green an' me bottom's red,
an' me nose is turnin' blue!

Now the foebeasts are nearly upon me,
I'm eatin' a raw onion pie.
I'll remember me auntie quite fondly,
but it's so jolly hard not to cry. Ooooooohhhhhh
Walla walla wimbo, bing bang bimbo,
wullyah wullyah wullyah yaah!
I've finished me scoff so I'll be off,
I'll be home by teatime, Ma!'

Log a Log Togey, having learned the 'walla walla' bit quickly, sat tapping both footpaws and singing rowdily throughout the proceedings. When the song was over, he smoothed his beard and sat up straight, remarking to Tam, 'Silly pointless song, huh? The things these young hares sing! Y'wouldn't catch a Guosim warblin' rubbish like that!'

Just then Threeshrew, another one of the sisters, and Fourshrew, her brother, leapt up. They cavorted around the bank, holding paws and splashing in and out of the shallows as they performed a lively rendition of a Guosim favourite. Tam had trouble keeping a straight face in Togey's presence as he listened to the words.

'Splish splash bumpitty crash!
all in and out the water.
Amid the cascade, bow to the maid,
an' kiss the cook's young daughter!

How happy we'll be, just you'n me,
we'll have a good ole wash.

Yore mother'll say "O lack a day,"
Splish splash splosh!

Splish splash bumpitty crash!
The little maid she said, "Sir,
Just look at the mess o' my fine dress,
I'll blame it on the weather!"

And as for you, I'll tell you true,
my daddy'll yell, "Good gosh!"
He'll tan yore tail an' make you wail,
Splish splash splosh!'

Tam glanced sideways at Togey. 'Splish splash splosh?'

The Guosim chieftain glared challengingly at him. 'Aye, a fine old song, part of our shrew tradition. A bathtime ditty, as I recall. Mothers sing it to their babes whilst they scrub 'em in the tub. Anythin' wrong with that, Mister MacBurl?'

The border warrior hastily reassured the old patriarch, 'Oh no, sir, a traditional Guosim song, just as y'say!'

One of the young shrews seated nearby called out to Threeshrew and Fourshrew, 'Sing us another, mates! How about Wully Wolly Whoppo or Groggity Groo Mallog?'

Log a Log Togey tweaked the young one's ear, murmuring quietly to him, 'Enough of that, 'tis past yore bedtime.'

He turned to Ferdimond, changing the subject quickly. 'So then, wot did ye think o' Guosim vittles, eh?'

The hare was mopping his platter with a crust, watching the cooks eagerly for a third helping. 'Oh, absolutely tophole, sah! If this is the standard of Guosim grub, I might join up with your flippin' crew an' become a jolly old shrew, wot?'

One of the cooks was heard to groan. 'Fates forbid the day. I'd sooner run off an' be a vermin than have t'feed that famish-faced glutton for a season!'

Night wore steadily on, the fires burning down to scarlet embers, tingeing the broad, calm river with their glow.

Gulo the Savage and his vermin had emerged from the pine thickets just before sundown. They had fought their way out to a point south of the hares' exit place. The wolverine's losses were severe, his followers now numbering only thirty – all due to Gulo's insane love of killing and fighting. He had revelled in the combat against the birds. Forgetting all else, he had stayed within the pines to inflict mighty slaughter upon the rooks and crows who had dared to attack him. The deep-carpeted pine needle floor was littered with winged carcasses.

Unwittingly, Gulo had done the shrews a great service. Never again would the predatory birds roost in sufficient numbers to harass the Guosim in their water meadows. This, however, did not concern the wolverine as his mind settled back to more urgent matters – the capture of the Walking Stone and deadly revenge upon his brother. He ignored the raking scratches, wounds and dried blood upon his powerful frame, tearing feathers from a slain rook and sinking his fangs into it.

The surviving vermin had lit a fire out on the open hillside. Crouched about it, they licked scratches, tended injuries and roasted the bodies of their dead enemies. Gulo watched them closely, gauging their mood, which he knew to be less than willing. It did not matter to him how they felt: a beast such as Gulo the Savage was concerned only with his own desires.

A badly wounded ermine gave a whimper of pain. Tossing aside a half-eaten crow, he lay back, exhausted and dispirited. Unaware that his leader's keen senses were focussed on him, the ermine moaned softly to his comrades, 'I lost an eye to those black birds. They tore such a rip in my guts that I can't hold vittles down. Ohhhhh! Methinks I need to rest for a long while.'

Gulo padded over to the wounded vermin. He leaned over him, enquiring in an unusually gentle voice, 'Thy injuries are bad. Do ye crave sleep, friend?'

The ermine was both pleased and relieved at his master's concern for his welfare. 'Aye, Lord.'

A single brutal blow from the wolverine's paw broke the vermin's neck. Kicking the lifeless beast to one side, Gulo straightened up, the campfire flames reflecting in his insane eyes as he growled out a harsh warning. 'Who wants to join this whining coward?'

The remaining ermine and foxes averted their eyes and held their breath as his wild stare swept over them. Gulo grabbed a charred crow from the fire, crunching his fangs into it. After devouring the bird, he sat down, gazing into the flames while snarling out his commands. 'Two of ye, go and scout out where my brother and his band are at. The rest of ye, eat! Fill your mouths on the flesh of our foes. Mayhaps 'twill put some fire into your bellies, some iron into your spines!'

Nearly every vermin stood up – all wanted to go scouting, fearing to stay in their wild leader's company.

Gulo's voice stopped them in their tracks. He pointed with the dead crow's taloned leg. 'I said two, you an' you. The rest of ye, stay with me. Let me hear a chant of war to show me ye are ready to serve Gulo the Savage.'

His creatures knew better than to refuse. They stood around the fire, stamping their footpaws and waving blades as they roared out one of their battle rousers from the lands of ice beyond the great sea.

'What is fear, I know it not!
What is death, the foebeast's lot!
Gulo! Gulo! Gulo!
Blood is what my blade drinks,
slaughter what my mind thinks.
Kill! Kill! Kill!
Lead us on, O Mighty One!
O'er the bodies of the slain.
Gulo! Gulo! Gulo!
Blood will swell into a lake,

smoking fires blaze in thy wake.
Kill! Kill! Kill!
Eat the flesh of those who fall!
Let them tremble when we call.
Gulo! Gulo! Gulo!

In the pinetops, a bedraggled crow perched on its empty nest, awaiting a mate who would never return. It raised its head, squawking mournfully at the calm golden dawn which creamed the eastern cloudbanks to the hue of newly churned butter.

The white fox who had been sent scouting, in company with an ermine, made his report to Gulo. 'Mighty One, they are camped by a broad river, beyond yonder wooded hill to the east. They have boats.'

The wolverine's hooded eyes bored into the fox searchingly. 'Askor, my brother, what news of him? Did ye see him?'

The scout's limbs trembled, but he answered truthfully. 'Nay, sire, neither of us saw him – only a treemouse, a riverdog, tall rabbits and otherbeasts, small ones who know the ways of rivercraft. They were all we saw, Mighty One.'

Gulo the Savage rose, shaking his huge barbaric head. 'I know Askor is with them. Get in front of me, all of ye. We go to the river with all speed!'

27

Dawn had not yet broken over the west flatlands outside Redwall. Brigadier Crumshaw stood on the Abbey walltop above the main gates, accompanied by Sergeant Wonwill, Captain Fortindom, Abbot Humble and Burlop Cellarhog.

The brigadier jammed his monocle into position as he polished it. Peering out impatiently over the darkened plain, he muttered aloud, 'Confound the rotters! Y'know, it wouldn't surprise me at all if their bally nerve failed 'em an' they didn't turn up – eh, Sergeant? Wot wot!'

Wonwill screwed his eyes up, trying to catch a glimpse of the foe. 'Might be as y'say, sah, h'I can't see a blinkin' sign of 'em. Huh, but me ole sight ain't wot it used t'be, sah.'

Tergen came hobbling up the wallsteps, still munching on a breakfast oatcake. 'Haraaaark! This bird will see what you cannot!' With a hop and a skip, he leapt into a space between the battlements. His keen gaze swept the area, then he nodded knowingly. 'Yahaaar! This bird has sighted vermin!'

Crumshaw glared at the goshawk. 'Where away, friend?'

Tergen indicated with a talon. 'Kaaaarrr! See, Wotwot, two arrow flights to the north. The vermin make fire over yonder, look!'

Burlop turned his attention to the pale flicker which

showed to the northwest. 'I can make 'em out, sure enough, all gathered round the fire in their cloaks. Well, it looks like we're going to get our battle today, Brigadier.'

Crumshaw stared askance at the solid young hedgehog. 'We, sirrah! D'ye mean you'll be joinin' us out there?'

Burlop held up the stave axe and the coopering mallet he had brought along. 'Never fear, I'll be right there! I live at Redwall, so I'm fit an' able to defend my Abbey.'

Derron Fortindom posed elegantly, paw on sabre hilt. He gave Burlop an admiring glance. 'Well said that, chap, wot! Pity you won't be takin' the field t'day, Brigadier. But never fret, sah, I'll put a few vermin on the account under your name.'

The monocle fell from Crumshaw's eye in astonishment. 'What the dickens d'ye mean, Captain? Who says I won't be joinin' the skirmish, eh?'

Abbot Humble summoned up his courage and faced the angry old hare. 'Er, begging your pardon, friend, but I for one must say it. You can hardly fight with one paw in a sling and a hole through your shoulder that isn't healed.'

The brigadier's moustache bristled with indignation. 'Pish tush, Father! 'Tis me duty, I've got to go, wot wot!'

Tergen attempted to flap his bandaged and splinted wing. 'Akkaawww! Wotwot, you like this bird, hurted. You, me, we cannot go. Be inna way of fightin' beasts. We stay!'

The brigadier raised his swagger stick as if he were about to strike somebeast. He vented his fury on them. 'Never! I say never, d'ye hear? My orders are orders around here. I say I go, an' by the cringe I shall go!'

Wonwill attempted to placate him. 'Beggin' y'pardon, sah, but you'll be far better off up 'ere with the Father H'Abbot. You ain't in no fit state to fight, sah, if'n ye'll forgive me sayin'.'

Crumshaw rounded on him. 'No, I will not forgive ye sayin', Sergeant. One more word from ye an' I'll slap ye on a flamin' charge!'

Wonwill turned away, shrugging his shoulders. 'Is that yore last word, Brigadier sah?'

Crumshaw stuck his chin out defiantly. 'Indeed it is! The very idea, not leadin' me own hares out t'fight the enemy. Unthinkable, Sergeant, unheard of . . . !'

He got no further because Wonwill spun on his paws and shot a neat, powerful left hook to his brigadier's chin. Before Crumshaw's unconscious body collapsed to the walkway, Wonwill had him tightly, supporting him.

'Mister Derron, take the h'officer's footpaws an' 'elp me get the ole boy downstairs. Father, is there any place we can make 'im comf'table?'

Burlop stepped in and relieved Wonwill of his burden. Lifting Crumshaw easily, the strong young Cellarhog strode down the wallsteps with no apparent effort. 'Brother Gordale will be in the kitchens for breakfast. I'll put the Brigadier in the gatehouse bed. 'Tis a big, soft 'un.'

The Long Patrol were forming up on the front lawn by the gatehouse. The young hares broke ranks to gape at the curious sight.

'I say, has the old chap dozed off?'

'Haw haw, now there's a cool head on the mornin' of a blinkin' battle, eh wot?'

Wonwill came marching down the wallsteps. 'Nah then, wot's all this then? Back in y'ranks, eyes front, stan' to attention. That means you, too, Miss Folderon!'

The hares fell into formation as Derron Fortindom came on to parade with an announcement to make. 'Right, listen up, you chaps. My goodself an' the Sergeant will be leading the attack today. Make sure blades an' lances are at the ready. Don't want t'see anybeast trippin' up or stumblin' over a weapon. Slingers, check your stone pouches. Archers, I hope those bowstrings are unfrayed an' quivers are full. Any questions?'

Flummerty piped up. 'Is the Brigadier ill, sah?'

The captain thought up an answer quickly. 'Er, no. Actually his wound was botherin' him. He had a bad night, so he's gone off to catch a little sleep.'

The haremaid fluttered her long, dark eyelashes. 'I had a bad night, too, Captain. That Folderon, she was snoring like a bucket o' frogs, kept me jolly well awake. Can I nip back to the dormitory an' catch a little sleep too?'

Captain Fortindom, often tongue-tied in the presence of pretty young maids, was temporarily lost for an answer. Wonwill, however, was made of sterner stuff when it came to fluttering lashes and coy glances.

He tweaked Flummerty's ear. 'Nah then, me blushin' beauty, ye can sleep when you've battered a few o' those vermin flat with those eyelashes, but if ye pout any more you'll 'ave 'em dancin' on that rosy red bottom lip o' yores. Straighten yore face, miss!'

Daybreak was soon upon them. With the rising sun warming their backs, the warriors came out of the front gates, marching in double file.

Burlop halted out on the path. Turning, he waved to Humble up on the ramparts. 'See the gates are shut tight, Father, an' keep everybeast indoors until this is over. We don't want 'em straying out on to the wall an' riskin' any harm.'

The Abbot smiled down at his young protégé. 'I will, Brother Burlop. You watch yourself out there. Pay heed to the officers' orders. Go safely, my son!'

The young Cellarhog waved his mallet and hurried off to join the rear. Humble's emotions were mixed as he watched him go: though very proud of Burlop, he was also very sad to see a normally peaceful young Redwaller going out to battle. The old hedgehog wiped away a tear, murmuring aloud to himself, 'If I'd had a son, he could not be dearer to me than you are, young Burlop.'

Fortindom strung his hares out on the flatlands in skirmish order after they had entered the plain to the south. The

Patrol stood facing the vermin, both sides just out of arrowshot of each other.

The sergeant squinted forward at the enemy. 'Cap'n, they've got about twoscore comin' at us. The rest look t'be layin' in reserve around that fire. Wot do ye think, sah, a pincer movement may'aps?'

Fortindom drew his sabre as he weighed the situation up. 'Hmm . . . I think not, Sergeant. When the points of our pincer meet, that'd leave the vermin reserves to strike at our centre. I think we'll take a straight runnin' fight to 'em. Not just a charge, mind – leave lots of halts for arrows an' slingstones but keep pressin' forward, eh?'

Wonwill liked the idea. 'Aye, then if'n those scum find the guts, they might try to charge us. Hah, 'twill be bad luck to the vermin, Cap'n. Our Long Patrol's never been beaten in a charge, 'tis wot we do best.'

Fortindom clipped a buttercup with an artful cut of his blade. He pinned the flower in his buttonhole. 'Have 'em advance five paces behind me, Sergeant. Right, let's open the ball, eh wot!'

The gallant captain strode forward a certain number of paces, then halted. A deadly hush lay over the ground from both sides. He raised his sabre elegantly, kissing the blade as he did. 'A fine mornin' for filthy flesh eaters t'die, wot?'

The hares held their breath as a dozen arrows whipped through the air from the vermin ranks toward the lone hare standing out front. But Fortindom, an excellent judge of distance, did not back down. As the arrows thudded into the earth, a mere pace short of his footpaws, he rapped out sharply, 'Longbows . . . fire! Slingers . . . stand ready!'

The Long Patrol used much larger bows than the vermin archers. Ten hares had been waiting with long ashwood shafts fitted to their tall yew bows. They let fly, angling the bows slightly upward. The arrows buzzed through the sunlit morn like angry bees as the air played through their grey gull feather flights. The vermin archers fell back fast, but four of their number were not fast enough, and the shafts found them.

Then the battle began in earnest. Whirling their slings, the hare throwers ran out beyond the archers. They cast off their stones as the war cries thundered forth. 'Eulaliiiiii-aaaaaa! Give 'em blood'n'vinegaaaaaar!'

The vermin archers regrouped and fired. Two hares went down. 'Gulo! Gulo! Kill kill kiiiiiillll!'

The vermin slingers came forward slowly, with the spear, sword and axe carriers following as the slingers cast their stones. The hare archers began firing on the run, the slingers advancing too.

Still out front, Fortindom levelled his fearsome sabre blade straight at the foe, shouting, 'Forward the Patrol! Chaaaaaarge!'

Burlop Cellarhog found himself plunging forward with the Long Patrol warriors. Brandishing both axe and mallet, he roared out bloodcurdling war cries with the best of his comrades. Filled with an exultation he had never known, the young Cellarhog covered the ground just as swiftly as the fleet-pawed hares.

But there was no crash of conflict as both sides met. Splitting into two groups, the vermin veered off in two directions. Burlop was level with Captain Fortindom as they sped forward, heading straight for the smaller group of reserve fighters around the fire. Two unsuspecting ermine were facing the frontrunners. Fortindom's sabre flashed like summer lightning, decapitating one. The other dithered for a brief moment, his eyes searching out any avenue of escape before meeting those of Burlop in a fleeting glance. Then the Cellarhog's heavy coopering mallet cracked down on the ermine's skull, slaying him instantly. Fortindom whirled, slashing with his lethal blade at the cloaked figures around the fire. He ground to a halt as the vermin crumpled and collapsed around him. The captain's sabre sliced through another spearhaft, which was propped upright beneath a cloak.

He howled furiously, 'Decoys! They were only decoys, set up to fool us, with a couple o' real ones to bait the trap!'

Hurtling across to where Burlop was sitting next to the ermine he had despatched, Fortindom cursed, 'Hell's teeth of blood'n'fire! Decoys!' Then he shouted to the hares who were pursuing the fleeing vermin, 'Run 'em down, me buckoes! No surrender an' no quarter! Run the scum into the ground. Take no prisoners!'

With dust spurting from his footpaws and bloodlight shining in his eyes, Fortindom thundered off in search of prey.

Burlop was in no state to heed the fray. He sat, motionless at first, staring at the creature he had slain. Then he began to rock back and forth, tears streaming down his homely face as the awful realization hit him. He sobbed brokenly. 'I'm sorry, I never meant to kill you. I'm only the Cellarhog from the Abbey. Please, please forgive me. I've never done this before, I'm not a warrior!'

But the sightless eyes of the dead ermine were turned up to the high bright sun, as if ignoring his killer's pleas. Axe and mallet fell unheeded from Burlop's paws. He rose slowly, staggering back towards Redwall like a creature in a walking dream, his tears watering the small flowers of the flatlands as he stumbled back home to the Abbey.

Throughout all the commotion, a pair of grappling hooks clanged over the battlements at the east wall. They grated upon the red sandstone, taking the strain as eight white foxes scaled the rope ladder which was attached to the grapnels.

Freeta the vixen was first over the walltop. She helped the others up, reminding them of their mission. 'Rogel, Farn, get down below and open that little wallgate. Ye know what ye must do?'

Rogel drew his curved sword. 'Aye, we hold it until Captain Zerig and the others get here. After we let them in, we lock the gate an' check all other entrances are tight shut. Then the tall rabbit warriors will be locked outside the Abbey.'

Gazing from the walltop at the deserted grounds inside the outer wall, Freeta squirmed with delight. 'Who but a vixen could think of such a plan? Look ye at this place – 'tis a paradise!'

Farn strung an arrow to his bow, grinning wolfishly. 'Aye, an' peaceful too. All the creatures who are not warriors must be hiding inside the big house.'

A tall, gaunt fox gazed hungrily at the Abbey building. 'Methinks 'tis like a great meatstore!'

Freeta pointed her blade at him meaningly. 'Thy life will be short if ye touch them before Zerig arrives an' this place is secure. We will need captives to show us about this wondrous place. They can tell us where all their treasures are hidden. We will make them talk.' She licked her blade before adding, 'One way or another. Follow me an' heed my orders. We will find a way into the big house.'

In the second-floor dormitories, Redwallers crowded the west windows, watching the fight out on the flatlands.

The ottermaid Brooky shaded her eyes. 'It's a bit far out to see 'em properly, Armel. Oh, what a shame, I was enjoying seein' those horrors gettin' their comeuppance. Where are they now – can anybeast see?'

The goshawk stood on a sill, his keen eyes missing little. 'Harraaaggg! They scatter like flies, but our warriors are after them. Now the vermin run back to the woodland.'

Foremole Bruffy smote the sill with a heavy digging claw. 'You'm cowurds! Oi 'opes ee 'arebeasts h'appre'nds they'm villyuns afore they'm gets 'idden in ee trees!'

Sister Armel had lost any great interest in the battle once she had witnessed the vermin being routed. Her immediate concern was to prevent any of the Dibbuns from falling out of the dormitory windows. She grabbed the tail of Mimsie the mousebabe, not a moment too soon.

'Back in here, missy, right now! Down you go on to the floor. Tergen, please don't lean against the shutters on that injured wing like that, it'll never heal properly. Mudge, don't lean out so far, you'll fall. Oh come in, you rascal, there's nothing to see any more!'

Abbot Humble took hold of the molebabe, but the little one clung to the sill, resisting any attempt to pull him back into the safety of the dormitory.

Mudge protested. 'Burr leggo, H'Abbot zurr. Oi'm watchin' ee foskers down thurr on ee steps!'

Humble drew Mudge inside, looking over the sill as he did. 'There's no foxes down there, you little fibber . . .' Then he caught sight of Freeta and her crew, who had stepped back from the Abbey door and were looking upward.

Humble pulled back hastily. 'Tergen, come in off that sill! Jem, Walt, close the shutters. Be still and quiet, everybeast, please!'

Sister Screeve glimpsed the Abbot's shocked face. 'Father, what's the matter?'

Humble pointed to the window, his voice a hushed whisper. 'Foxes at our Abbey door. How did they get into Redwall?'

'Search me, I never asked 'em. Sneaky villains, hahaha!' Everybeast turned to glare at the ottermaid.

Armel silenced her sharply. 'It's no laughing matter, Brooky!'

Brooky looked around sheepishly. 'Sorry!'

Brother Gordale turned to Humble. 'What shall we do, Father?'

The Abbot sat down on a bed. 'Er, er . . . give me a moment will you, friend? Let me think.'

The strong young ottermaid grabbed two long window poles, tossing one to Armel. 'Let's get down there. The rest

250

of you, find something to use as a weapon and follow us quietly!'

Freeta banged on the Abbey door with her sword hilt. Another fox placed his mouth to the crack of the doorjamb and called aloud, 'We have seen ye. Open this door or 'twill go badly with ye!'

There was no answer. Freeta instructed two other foxes, 'Climb up one of those ledges to the right. Have a look through those long, coloured windows an' tell me what ye see.'

The one fox, by climbing on to the shoulders of the other, was able to reach the sill, then easily scrabble up over the smooth stone. He spat on the windowpane, then began rubbing at it with his paw.

Armel and Brooky were crossing Great Hall when the ottermaid, detecting a squeaking noise from the windows, spotted the fox peering in through a section of amber-coloured glass.

Holding the brass-hooked window pole low, she whispered to her friend, 'Go and see what he wants. Don't look at me . . . Go!'

Once she reached the window, Armel mouthed a question to the fox on the other side of the glass. 'What do you want?'

She had to repeat the question before the intruder understood. Pointing to his open mouth and grinning wickedly, he pantomimed an eating gesture, clearly indicating Armel as his desired meal. She smiled back at him, mouthing a reply. 'You want to eat me?!'

The white fox nodded. Walking out of his view, Brooky stole along the wall beneath the window until she reached a bench nearby. The fox was still mimicking the act of eating, licking his lips and showing his teeth, when Brooky jumped up on the bench. The large, solid ottermaid slammed the window pole hard at the stained-glass section, smashing it through the window – and the fox's fangs at the same time. He fell backward with a gurgling scream.

Freeta and the others came running. She grabbed hold of the injured one, heaving him upright and shaking him as she grated angrily, 'What happened . . . Who did this? Speak, fool!'

The fox tried to mumble something, but his mouth was too badly injured. Blood spattered the vixen's face.

Repulsed, she pushed him away before turning upon his companion. 'Why weren't you up there, too, mudbrain?'

He protested. 'There was no room for two. I was holding his paws lest he fell . . . Duuuunnnhhhh!'

Freeta ducked sideways, narrowly missing two window poles which, instead, thudded down so hard on the fox's head that he collapsed to the ground – unconscious. The vixen managed to grab the end of one pole. Tugging it, she yelled at the other foxes, 'Do something! Shoot arrows through that broken window!'

'Eulaliiiiaaaaaa!'

The vermin whirled about, just in time to see Brigadier Crumshaw emerging from the gatehouse, making a lone charge across the lawns towards them. The old hare was waving his swagger stick, running right for the foxes.

Freeta snapped an order at the three vermin who had already notched shafts to their bowstrings. 'Stop him! Fire!'

One arrow went wide of its mark, but the other two struck Crumshaw. Amazingly, he carried on with his headlong charge, still waving his stick and roaring, 'Give 'em blood'n'vinegar! Eulaliiiiiaaaa!'

Freeta was backed up against the Abbey wall as the brigadier bulled his way through to her. She slashed at his face with her sickle-curved sword. Crumshaw was injured a second time, but he was unstoppable. Struggling to gain control of the weapon, he had seized the sword by the blade, which resulted in deep cuts to his paws. Despite the brigadier's pain, in one last desperate effort he turned the blade until its point was against the vixen's neck, hurling his full weight on to it. They fell to the ground together, locked in a death hold. Freeta stared at him disbelievingly and gave a dying gurgle.

The brigadier slumped forward, his mouth against the dead fox's ear as he gasped his last words, 'Forward the Buffs . . . wot . . . Eulayyyyy.'

28

The Abbey doors were flung open wide. Redwallers charged forth, armed with anything that would stop vermin – window poles, ladles, kitchen knives, garden shears and digging forks. The white foxes scattered; these Abbey-dwellers looked anything but peaceable. Mice, moles, squirrels and hedgehogs were all bellowing and shouting, 'Redwaaaaaaallllll!'

Everybeast joined in. Abbot Humble and a crowd of Dibbuns raced up the belltower stairs and threw themselves on to the bellropes of the twin bells. *Boom! Clang! Bong-boomclang! Clang! Bong! Kabooommm!*

What they lacked in expertise they made up for in enthusiasm. Deep, brazen belltones tolled out their message over woodland, Abbey and plain. Armel and Brooky dashed to the big western wallgates. Throwing them wide open, the ottermaid stood out on the path, waving a flower-embroidered bedspread, which was attached to her long window pole. Sister Armel guarded the gates for her.

The Long Patrol were split to the north and south of the flatlands, pursuing the retreating vermin, arcing back towards the woodlands after them. Captain Fortindom was at the north end, close to the path, when he heard the bells and saw Brooky waving her flag outside the main gates. Sergeant Wonwill, heading the south contingent, also heeded the alarm.

Calling off the chase, both hares directed their forces to the main gate. A brief word with Armel and Brooky was all the two officers needed before issuing the go-ahead: soon the Long Patrol flooded into the Abbey grounds. Fortindom and Wonwill intercepted Sister Screeve and Foremole Bruffy coming up from the pond.

The hare captain wielded his sabre in a businesslike manner. 'Marm, sah, how many vermin are on the grounds?'

The mole leader wrinkled his snout. 'Thurr bee's none naow, zurr. Ee Sister'n'oi just slayed th' larst wun. Gurt big fosker ee wurr!'

Sister Screeve prodded the air with a garden rake. 'Aye, but he couldn't swim! Nasty beasts, foxes. We'll have to haul his carcass out of the pond later.'

The sergeant saluted the little mouse Recorder. 'Go easy with that rake, marm. We're on yore side!'

The Sister shouldered it like a pike. 'Oh look, there's young Burlop! He doesn't appear too happy. I'll go and see what ails him. Bruffy, you can tell the Father Abbot and those Dibbuns to stop tolling the bells now. I can't hear myself thinking with that din.'

Fortindom ducked, avoiding a swing of the rake as Sister Screeve turned to indicate the east wall. 'Hitheryon Jem says the foxes came in by the wicker gate in that wall. Fat lot he knows! They climbed over the wall using a double grapnel attached to a rope ladder.'

Wonwill set off for the east wall. 'We'd best go an' h'investigate, sah!'

Hitheryon Jem and Wandering Walt were securing the small wicker gate as the hares marched up.

Jem pointed to the crumpled form of a white fox in the bushes nearby. 'There was two of 'em – one escaped, but me'n ole Walt put paid t'this 'un. Those two foxes wasn't chasin' about like the other vermin. They was just standin' 'ere, mindin' the open gate like sentries. Bit odd that, eh?'

The captain and the sergeant stared at each other as the realization of the vermin plan became clear to them.

Fortindom twitched his long ears. 'Good grief, the crafty scum! So that's why they turned an' ran from us, wot!'

Wonwill's hooded eyes widened. 'Aye, a clever scheme, sah. They was doublin' back to come through this liddle gate an' lock us out o' the h'Abbey. That would've put us in a fix, if'n ye'll pardon me sayin', sah.'

Fortindom began unlocking the bolts and reopening the wicker gate. 'Indeed, Sergeant. With a bit o' luck we'll jolly well let 'em do just that. Gather the Patrol. Then get the Redwallers back into their Abbey an' tell 'em to stay inside. This is our bloomin' party. Make sure the other gates are all secured an' guarded. We'll have to look lively, Wonwill. If the vermin are bent on carryin' out their idea, the blighters should be here quite soon now. Keep the Patrol well hidden until the vermin are all inside. I'll lay low nearby here an' lock 'em in.'

Zerig met up with the rest of his vermin in the woodlands behind Redwall. The white fox captain took stock of his warriors, their number considerably thinned down since he had arrived at Redwall. Zerig, however, was still confident that he could pull off the audacious scheme. Continuing to size things up, he spotted Rogel, who was trying to blend in unnoticed with the other vermin.

Zerig questioned the fox. 'Rogel, weren't ye supposed to be with Freeta?'

'Aye, Captain, that I was, but I had to run for my life.'

Zerig stared hard at him. 'How so?'

Rogel explained. 'We gained entry well enough. Freeta opened the gate an' left me an' Farn to guard it until you came. She went off with the others to gain entrance to the big house. Suddenly the bells began ringing, an' a horde of beasts, all armed with broomsticks an' other things, came charging out at us . . .'

Zerig interrupted Rogel. 'A horde of beasts?'

The fox nodded. 'Aye, sir – mice and others from within the big house. We were going to be attacked. I had to run, I had to! They would have slain me, Captain!'

Zerig shook his head in disbelief. 'An' where, pray tell, are Freeta and the others?'

Rogel shuffled awkwardly. 'I know not, Captain.'

Zerig's voice dripped scorn and sarcasm. 'Ye ran away from mice armed with broomsticks! Were there no tall rabbits with javelins an' swords there?'

Rogel stared at the ground. 'I saw none, Captain.'

Zerig turned to the rest of his warriors, as if appealing to them for an answer. 'No hares were there, like those we fought, but this bold creature ran away from mice with broomsticks . . . Did ye fear that they would sweep ye up, wormbrain?'

Sniggering broke out among the remaining ermine and foxes. Zerig caught Rogel by an ear, as though he were a naughty young one, twisting it so hard that he raised his subordinate tippawed. 'Now we will go to the small gate, my brave Rogel. If it be still open, we will show thee how the warriors of Gulo the Savage deal with mice waving broomsticks. But if the door is locked, I will show thee how to skin a coward an' roast him alive before we eat him. March!'

Sergeant Wonwill and the Patrol hares crouched behind a border of rhododendron and hydrangea bushes which separated the east end of Brother Demple's vegetable drills from the back lawns. Somebeast sniffed aloud and began sobbing. The sergeant looked around until he found the culprit, Flummerty.

The tough Wonwill gave an exasperated sigh. 'Now then, missy, you ain't gettin' sulky cos ye want to go t'bed, are ye? Stop those waterworks h'immediately!'

The haremaid continued to weep loudly. 'S . . . s . . . sorry, sah, I can't help it.'

The sergeant turned his eyes skyward distractedly. 'I said stop snifflin'. That h'aint a request, it's a h'order! Cartwill, lend 'er yore kerchief, will ye?'

The young hare passed Flummerty his kerchief, but she continued to sob piteously. Crawling along to where she was crouched, Wonwill patted her ears gently. 'Nah then, me beauty. Yore goin' to soak all the curl out o' those pretty eyelashes. Wot is it, me little maid? Why all the snuffles n'tears?'

Flummerty wiped her eyes hard, struggling to regain her composure. She explained the reason for her sorrow haltingly. 'It's . . . it's the Brigadier. I found him in a corner by those long windows. They killed him!'

Wonwill's eyes glazed over as he seized the haremaid by her shoulders. 'Y'mean our Brigadier . . . Crumshaw . . . dead?'

She nodded, her hot tears splashing on his chest. 'He must've charged the foxes single-pawed. There were two broken arrows in his chest, and a sword had cut his face from ears to jaw. The Brigadier was lying beside the fox that did it, sah. He must've killed the brute with his last breath. He . . . he died all alone, sah!'

Wonwill gazed around at the stricken faces of the other hares. He blinked hard, then smiled through the tears that hung unshed in his eyes. 'Forward the Buffs, eh! The ole battlebeast, I never h'imagined Brigadier Crumshaw dyin' in bed of long seasons, surrounded by medicines an' such. Dry yore eyes, missy, an' the rest of ye. D'ye think yore h'officer'd want ye lookin' like this?'

Young Flunkworthy took a deep breath and mastered his grief. Squinching up one eye as though it held a monocle, he did an amazing impression of the brigadier. 'By the left, next one I catch blubbin', I'll put him on a flippin' fizzer, wot wot! Not the done thing, y'know. Can't abide any bloomin' beast mopin' about like a dratted duck at a drownin', eh wot!'

That did the trick. Though there was still a bit of sniffing and paws being rubbed across eyes, the young hares were much better.

Wonwill winked at Flunkworthy. 'That's the ticket, young Flunk. We'll mourn the Brigadier later. But for now, let's see if'n we can't face up t'the scummy villains who started all this.'

Kersey ground her teeth audibly. 'Blood'n'vinegar an' guts'n'gore, that's what those murderers are in for when I meet up with 'em!'

Wonwill forestalled further threats by reverting to his old parade-ground-sergeant manner. 'Silence in the ranks there, young sahs an' marms. Keep your 'eads down, weapons ready, an' wait on my command!'

Captain Zerig gave a grunt of triumph when he saw the small east wallgate still lying ajar. Releasing Rogel's ear, he strode cautiously into the Abbey grounds and stared all around.

Motioning the vermin in, he remarked to an ermine alongside him, 'Mice with broomsticks! There isn't a mouse in sight anywhere. 'Tis so peaceful an' quiet ye could lay down an' take a nap. Hark, Rogel, where are the hordes of mice with broomsticks, eh?'

As the last vermin came through the doorway, Derron Fortindom kicked him in the back, laying him out flat. He slammed the door, shot the bolts and drew his long sabre in one fluid movement. 'Apologies for the mice. I sent them indoors. Are hares more t'your likin', sirrah?'

Zerig saw his fate written plain in the perilous eyes of the sabre-fighting captain. Both he and the vermin who served under him turned to run and seek some means of escape, but none existed: Their way was barred by the swords and javelins of the Long Patrol.

Inside the Abbey, Foremole Bruffy, Sister Armel, Brooky and Burlop Cellarhog, whom they had found wandering in the grounds, had their paws full. At the first shouts of battle, Tergen had tried to get out into the thick of the fray. Clashing his beak and flexing his talons, the maddened goshawk screeched, 'Haayaaakah! Stand aside . . . this bird will kill vermin!'

To curtail Tergen's wild desires, Brooky the ottermaid dropped a huge woven wall hanging over him. The whole thing began leaping about as though it were alive.

Brooky shouted as she tried to hold the covered hawk still, 'Somebeast help me before I'm dragged outside!'

Sister Armel, Foremole and Burlop added their weight by sitting on the wall hanging, holding on to the big bump at its centre which jolted up and down. Though Tergen tried to break free, the four Redwallers managed to restrain him.

The roars and bellows from out near the east wall, mingled with the bloodcurdling battle cries of the hares, grew to a crescendo.

Friar Glisum clapped both paws over his ears. 'Oh, the dreadful din! What's happening out there?'

Sister Screeve began climbing on a table to look out of the windows. Her voice had a hysterical ring to it. 'It's slaughter, that's what it is. Slaughter!'

Surprisingly, it was Abbot Humble who pulled her down. He shook the Recorder mouse, shouting at her, 'You were out there a short while back, Sister, killing the vermin with other Redwallers. Of course it's slaughter – goodbeasts slaughtering evil ones!'

Wandering Walt sat Screeve down, calming her. 'Thurr naow, doan't ee fret yurrself o'er yon vurmint villyuns. They'm h'only gettin' wot bee's due to 'em.'

Brother Demple viewed the situation logically. 'Sister Screeve, would you sooner have the vermin in here, slaughtering us? I for one would not.'

The two Dibbuns, Mudge and Perkle, had been dashing

hither and thither, their voices shrill with excitement. 'Bludd'n'vin'ger! Yooleehayleeee!'

Ulba the molemum collared both the babes. 'Coom yurr, likkle scallawaggers, sitt still noaw, or oi'll chase ee both up to you'm beds!'

A sudden silence fell outside. In the eerie quiet which followed, Brooky began laughing. 'Hahaha! It's like hitting yourself over the head with a saucepan, cos it's nice when you stop. Hahahaha!' Her merriment was halted by somebeast banging on the Abbey door.

Abbot Humble called out, 'Who is it?'

Wonwill could be heard outside. ' 'Tis us, Father. You can h'open up, sah!'

The Redwallers set up a rousing cheer as the hares marched into Great Hall, but it died upon the lips of everybeast when they saw what the slow-marching Patrol bore between their ranks. Laid out upon a trestle taken from the orchard was the still form of Brigadier Crumshaw. In one paw, the old warrior still held his swagger stick. The broken arrows in his chest and the awful wound across his face could be seen by all. Crumshaw's monocle dangled from his bloodstained tunic by its cord.

Captain Fortindom saluted Humble with his sabre, nodding toward the makeshift bier. 'Father, may we request someplace to lay him until the evenin'? The burial will take place at sundown, in the Abbey grounds, with your permission, sah.'

Humble, who had become firm friends with the feisty old officer, led Fortindom and the bearers over to the great tapestry. Then he addressed the group. 'I think the best way we can honour your Brigadier is to lay him there, beneath the likeness of our warrior, Martin.'

Wonwill smiled up at the brave mouse's picture. 'A warrior watched over by a warrior. Father h'Abbot, I think the Brigadier would've liked that. Thank ye kindly!'

BOOK THREE

'The Walking Stone'

Rakkety Rakkety Rakkety Tam,
the drums are beatin' braw.
Rakkety Rakkety Rakkety Tam,
Are ye marchin' off tae war?

That savage from the lands of ice,
he's no' like any other.
He's sworn tae get the Walkin' Stone,
an' murder his own brother!

'Tis braw tae woo a bonny maid,
for love is aye sae sweet.
Yet who'll be left tae tell the tale,
when steel an' fang must meet?

29

To say that Wild Doogy Plumm and Yoofus Lightpaw looted the vermin camp would have been a gross under-statement. Between them, the Highlander and the volethief left the place stripped bare to the earth. The happy pair came away decked from ear to tail, and from pawtip to snout end, with ornaments the vermin had left behind in their haste. Earrings, tailrings, pawrings, bracelets, neck-lets, belts and sashes were all donned as the two victors criticized and complimented each other.

'Och, yer no' goin' tae wear yon great daft medallion hangin' from yore tail, are ye?'

'Sure, an' why not, pray? I think it makes me look like a grand ould savage, so it does!'

Doogy scoffed. 'More like a broody duck wi' a half-laid egg hangin' from its tail. Here, ah'll swap ye for this braw gold an' purple sash. Ye can bind it aroond yore brow.'

They exchanged the plunder, with Yoofus winding the sash several times about his middle. He began thrusting knives, hatchets and curved swords through it, until he could hardly bend to pick up another blade from the stack of arms they had found. Bristling with weaponry, they surveyed one another.

Yoofus grinned proudly. 'Y'know, if I had six extra sets o'

paws, I could charge an army with this liddle lot. I'd put that axe in the front of me belt if'n I was you, mate, cos if ye fell backwards ye'd chop yore tail off!'

Doogy took his friend's advice. 'Och, mayhaps yore right. That's a fine wee dagger ye've got stowed in yore belt. D'ye want tae trade it for this axe o' mine?'

The volethief wasted no time in responding, 'Sure 'tis a pretty blade, all right. Tell ye wot, I'll exchange it for that big ould knife o' yours, Doogy.'

The Highlander's paw shot to his dirk hilt. 'Ye'll do nae such thing, ye rascal. That was mah father's dirk, an' his father afore him. Huh, 'tis a pity the vermin never left any vittles layin' about – ah'm peckish!'

Yoofus wrinkled his nose in disgust. 'I'm famished meself, but I wouldn't be found dead eatin' all that tripe an' offal those hooligans feed on. Come on, mate, let's go an' see if'n we can't search out a gobful o' some decent rations. Here, lend a paw with me drum, will ye? 'Tis too big for one beast t'be draggin' round.'

Doogy was swift to point out the error of his companion's ways. 'Whoa now, hauld on a tick, thief. That's no' yore drum. By rights that drum belongs tae the beasties o' Redwall Abbey. The hares were bringin' it as a gift tae them!'

The water vole shot out his chin defiantly. 'Finders keepers, losers weepers! That's wot my ould mammy always said!'

Doogy was just as truculent as Yoofus in his reply. 'Did she now! Well, yore auld mammy must've been a worse robber than ye are, mah friend!'

Spitting on his paws, Yoofus performed a little dance. 'Now lissen t'me, ye ould branch bouncer. Don't you dare talk about me darlin' mammy like that, or I'll lay ye out flat as a fluke!'

The Highlander adopted a boxing stance. 'Oh will ye now? Come on, ye fat, tatty-furred water walloper, let's see ye try it. Ah'll knock yer block off!'

Yoofus darted towards Doogy, but, owing to all the armament he was carrying, he stumbled and fell forward, striking his nose on the Highlander's clenched paw. Yoofus sat down hard but instantly shot upright, holding his nose and rear end at the same time.

Immediately, Doogy was concerned for him. 'Ah'm sorry, mate, 'twas an accident. Are ye all right?'

Far from being all right, Yoofus was the picture of outraged dignity, and he wasted no time letting the squirrel know about it. 'Ooh, ye mizrubble brush-tailed slybeast! Strikin' a defenceless beast like that! An' here's me thinkin' we were friends. Ye durty ould turncoat!'

Doogy could not help laughing. 'Defenceless? Yore carryin' enough weapons tae outfit a regiment! Och, come on now, matey, yer no' that bad hurt.'

Yoofus knew the squirrel was right, but he had a good sulk nevertheless. 'Lookit me, will ye? Me nose is swellin' like a summer sunset. Ye've ruined an' destroyed me han'some young face, an' me nether regions are slashed t'blazes!'

Doogy inspected his comrade's supposed wounds. 'Nae sich thing, laddie. There's nought wrong with yore snout. An' as for yore bottom, ye nicked it on that curved sword at the back of yer sash. Ach, 'tis only a wee scratch, ye'll live. Let's shake paws an' be friends!'

Yoofus half stretched his paw towards Doogy. 'Then ye'll help me with me drum?'

Doogy withdrew his paw. 'Ah'll no' help a robbin' thief tae carry off stolen property. 'Tis agin mah principles!'

'D'drum be our prop'ty now, fancybeasts. Yarrrr!'

They both turned to see six creatures had been watching them: two ferrets, a weasel and three rats. They were an unsavoury-looking gang, garbed in an assortment of rags and pieces of foliage. Each one was armed with a club and a long, flint-tipped spear.

Their leader, the weasel, prodded Yoofus with his spearpoint, grinning wickedly through snaggled, yellow teeth. 'T'row down dose nice fancy weppins, or we killyer!'

Doogy winked at Yoofus as they unbuckled their arms. 'Och, let's play along wi' yon scruffy frog frightener for a wee while. Mebbe we'll get fed, eh?'

Unable to understand the Highlander's thick northern brogue, the weasel snarled at Yoofus, 'Wotta 'e bee's talkabout?'

Before replying, Yoofus murmured to Doogy, 'Aye, an' they might have some loot stowed back at their den. Let's play along with this ould eejit, mate.'

The water vole turned to the weasel, pretending to be terrified. 'Ah now, y'won't hurt us, sir. We're just pore travellers, harmless as a pair o' butterflies, that's us. So go easy.'

The weasel took Yoofus's new sash, cackling to his cronies, 'Go easy, eh? Ho yarrrr, we go easy, sure nuff!'

The others dived on Yoofus and Doogy's loot, fighting and scrabbling. The weasel kicked and bit at them, loading most of their gear on to two of the rats. 'Carry diss, me say who gets wot. Bring fancybeasts along!'

The pair allowed themselves to be prodded and pushed through the undergrowth by the vermin. Doogy tried to keep his volatile temper in check, whispering to Yoofus, 'If yon wee rat keeps ticklin' mah tail with his spear, he'll be wearin' it as a nose ornament afore he's much older. Where in the name o' fur are they takin' us?'

Yoofus noted the direction in which they were travelling. 'Ah, never fret, me ould tater, I think we're bound to my ould neighbourhood. If I gets the chance, I'll take ye to my neat liddle home, an' ye can visit with me darlin' wife, Didjety. Ouch! Will ye be careful with that ould spear, sir! Me backside's smartin' enough as it is!'

They were over half a day marching through wood and fenland, until they began following a streambank to the southwest.

Yoofus smiled. 'Ah sure, an' wasn't I only right, Doogy

Plumm? We're almost back on me ould patch. Seasons be praised for those fine vermin, carryin' all our stuff an' totin' that big heavy drum o' mine for us. Aren't the thick-'eaded duffers a grand ould crew?'

The weasel snarled at the water vole, 'Yew shurrup ya mouth 'an go disaway!'

He led them to a hole at the base of an elm. It sloped down into a big roomy cave, whose walls and ceiling were part of the tree's root complex. Four vermin were inside – two ferrets and two more rats. There was also a family of dormice – two adults and five little ones. The cave had once been their tidy home, though now it was in a mess, owing to the vermin occupation.

The male dormouse recognized Yoofus straightaway. 'Mister Lightpaw, what are ye doin' here?'

The water vole winked at him. 'Hush now, Mister Muskar, don't ye go crackin' on that ye know me!'

The weasel glared at Yoofus. 'Youse two knows each odder, yarr?'

The volethief shook his head vigourously. 'Who, me, sir? Sure I never met the feller in me life. Ask his good missus, she'll tell ye. Ain't that right, marm?'

Mr Muskar's wife, Lupinia, was stirring a cauldron of stew over the fire. She winked at Yoofus, showing she was far quicker on the uptake than her husband. 'Oh, er, no, we've never had the pleasure. Pleased t'meet you, I'm sure. I'm Lupinia Muskar. That's my husband, Muskar Muskar, and these are our young 'uns – Pippat, Gretty, Wortle, Berrin and Bappik. Say hello to the nice gentlebeast who we've never met, m'dears!'

The young dormice caught their mother's look and called out as one, 'Hello, Yoofus!'

Doogy watched Lupinia pull bread and a batch of scones from the oven by the fire. He sniffed the stew appreciatively. 'Ah must say, that smells very good, marm!'

The rat who had been prodding Doogy sniggered. 'Dat's not fer yew, fancybeast!'

He poked the Highlander's tail again with the stone-tipped pole. Doogy looked pointedly at the water vole. 'Dearie me, ah reckon ah've took enough o' this nonsense!'

Yoofus smiled politely at the dormouse couple. 'Would ye not like to take the babbies outside to play for a while?'

As is typical of many father dormice, Mr Muskar was fairly dim-witted. Clearly not having caught on, he blinked and scratched his stomach as he replied, 'Er, it'll be their bedtime soon.'

His wife gathered the young ones together. 'Do as the goodbeast says, dear. Let's take them outside into the fresh air for a bit.'

A sly kick to her husband's paw set things right. 'Oh, er, outside, yes, why not? Still some daylight left.'

The weasel nodded towards the food. 'Worrabout dose vikkles, eh?'

Yoofus reassured him fawningly, 'Ah, don't get yore tail in a knot, sir. Sure we'll serve ye. Won't we, mate?'

Doogy grinned widely. 'Och, ye can wager yore bad teeth on that, mah friend. We'll serve ye, sure enough!'

The weasel pointed at Doogy. 'Wot 'e says?'

The water vole chuckled. 'He says he's highly delighted t'be servin' ye, sir. 'Twill be a meal like ye've never had before. So sit yoreselves down now.'

Lupinia and her husband sat watching their young ones by the streambank. The young dormice were making small twigboats with leaves for sails and floating them on the water.

Mr Muskar expressed his confusion and unhappiness with everything. 'Huh, 'tis bad enough being threatened an' overrun by vermin, but when we're put out of our own home to play with the young ones, well that really is the limit! By the time we're allowed back inside, those vermin brutes will have eaten all the food. There's little enough left as it is. To cap it all, that rascal Lightpaw invites himself and a friend around for dinner. But we've got a family to

270

think of, so I've got to put up with it all. What are we to do, Lupinia?'

His wife replied soothingly, 'Don't worry, dear. I'm sure everything will work out all right.'

The conversation was interrupted by the sounds of uproar from within their home. Muskar leapt up with alarm. 'Oh good gracious, what's all this about?'

The body of a rat came sailing out of the dormouse's home, landing in a heap across Muskar's footpaws. He recoiled from the carcass as the din from indoors increased.

'Haway Braaaaaw! Come on, ye villains. Ah'm no' a dormousie, ah'm Wild Doogy Plumm! Haway Braaaaaaaw!'

Footpaws pounded madly about, mingled with vermin screams.

'Aaaagh, leggo a me!'

'Getta spear . . . Ooooffff!'

'Ah, come here, me scruffy ould beauty, I'll teach ye to bully my neighbours, so I will!'

'Get be'ind der fancybeast. Use yer spear!'

'Och, ye'll prod no more creatures wi' that thing, mah bonny vermin. Here, taste a claymore blade!'

A ferret staggered out. Clutching his stomach, he gurgled horribly before collapsing.

Muskar stared at his wife in amazement. 'It's Lightpaw and the squirrel. They're fighting the vermin, but how . . . ?'

His wife called to her young ones, 'Play further up the bank, but don't wander too far away.'

She turned to her husband. 'I told you not to worry, dear. Mister Lightpaw and his friend are warriors. Trust me, they'll take care of those dreadful vermin.'

Muskar grabbed the club from the paws of a dead rat. 'Go and look after our young 'uns, Lupinia. I've been longing for a chance to have a crack at those vermin!'

He rushed indoors, waving the club and roaring, 'Invade my home an' steal my food, would you? Ye bottle-nosed, snaggletoothed, tat-furred bullies! Take that, an' that . . . an' have some o' this too!'

When the atmosphere became calmer, the dormouse mother brought her brood back to the cave. Muskar was helping Doogy and Yoofus to throw the slain vermin into the stream.

Yoofus bowed politely to her. 'Ye'd best take the babbies inside, missus. Sure they don't want to be seein' this lot departin'!'

Doogy doffed his cap. 'Aye, marm, we kept 'em well away from the vittles. Go on in now, the bairns will be wantin' tae eat yore fine cookin'.'

Lupinia curtsied prettily to her saviours. 'My thanks to you, goodbeasts. Will you join us for supper?'

Yoofus nodded to Doogy and Muskar. 'You two go on. I'll finish up here an' join ye later!'

With stew, new-baked bread and some honey and preserved fruit, they dined thankfully.

Mr Muskar produced a gourd of his special bilberry and apple cordial. 'I was hiding this from the scum.'

After a while, Yoofus strolled in, washing his paws off with streamwater. He accepted his platter gratefully. 'Ah well, that's that! Er, ye don't mind me sayin', mate, but ye've got me pretty little dagger stowed in yore belt. I'll thank ye to return it.'

Deftly catching the blade which Doogy tossed to him, Yoofus eyed a small stringed instrument hanging on the wall. 'Is that a manjaleero, sir? Faith, 'tis long seasons since I saw one of those. Could I try it, sir?'

Mr Muskar took it down. 'Be my guest.'

The water vole twiddled the tiny carved pegs, tuning it until he was satisfied at the tone. He winked at the young Muskars. 'Shall I give ye a bit of an ould song?'

The little dormice nodded eagerly. Yoofus took a swig of Muskar's special cordial and strummed a chord. 'Right then, this is an ould ditty me grandma used to sing. I wrote it meself this mornin'.'

He launched straight into the lively air.

'There's some likes the sportin' an' throwin' the ball,
but I love the howlin' an' fightin' an' all.
So if yore in a ruction just give a loud call,
an' meself will come chargin' to aid yeh!

I've walloped a weasel an' stiffened a stoat,
I can beat any durty ould vermin afloat.
An' if I grab a lizard or newt by his throat,
sure he'll wish he'd stayed home with his mammy!

I've fought with a ferret an' rousted a rat,
I biffed a big fox, aye, an' laid him out flat.
I'm as tough an' ferocious as any wildcat,
mind yer manners when Yoofus comes callin'!

One mornin' I strolled all alone by the lake,
an' spied a great serpent whose name was MacSnake.
I seized hold of his tail an' gave him such a shake,
that the adder became a subtracter!

If there's ever a chance for a row or a fight,
I'll battle all day an' long into the night,
an' put all those baggy-nosed vermin to flight,
that's providin' I'm home for me dinner!

I got home last night an' me mammy did say,
'Have you been out scrappin' the whole livelong day?'
She spanked me young tail in her ould-fashioned way,
an' sent me off to bed with no supper!'

30

The fire had burned low, and the young dormice were asleep. Lupinia Muskar picked up her broom, then sighed and cast it aside. 'I'll make a start on the cleaning tomorrow. Oh, for a peaceful night's rest without vermin belching and snoring all around us! Thank you both, I don't know what we'd have done without your help. If there's ever anything me or my family can do for you, then just ask.'

Doogy rolled himself in his plaid cloak by the embers. 'Mayhaps ye could tell me the way tae Redwall Abbey, marm. We'll be headin' for there after we've visited Yoofus's wife at their home on the morrow.'

Mr Muskar pointed. 'It's two days' journey downstream. There's a raft just upstream that belonged to the vermin. You can take it and sail most of the way. When you see the rapids at the big east bend, leave the raft and walk west into the woodlands. You'll sight Redwall after a while.'

Yoofus had settled down in a comfy old armchair. 'A raft, ye say? That'll be grand, I like rafts.'

Doogy was about to drop off when something occurred to him. 'By the bye, Yoofus, have ye seen the big drum around? Ah'd almost forgotten about it.'

The water vole yawned. 'Oh, that ould thing. The vermin left it outside on the streambank cos there was no room in here. Don't ye fret, Doogy mate, 'twill still be there in the mornin'. Sleep tight now.'

No longer held hostage by the vermin, they all slumbered peacefully in the calm, homely warmth.

Shortly before dawn, Doogy was wakened by one of the young dormice. 'Sir, where's your friend, Mister Lightpaw? He's not here.'

The Highlander sat up, rubbing his eyes. 'Not here, laddie? Then where's the rascal gone, eh?'

The young dormouse had no idea, so Doogy arose and went out to the streambank to look. He was back inside immediately, girding on his numerous weapons.

Lupinia Muskar was rekindling the fire to cook breakfast. She noted the concern on Doogy's face. 'Mister Plumm, what is it? Is something the matter?'

The Highlander clapped a paw to his belt. 'Mah travellin' companion's decamped, marm. Aye, an' he's taken the big drum an' mah dirk too!'

She roused her husband. 'Muskar, go with Mister Plumm. See if you can find his friend. Hurry, dear!'

The dormouse blinked sleep from his eyes. 'Come on, sir, we'll find him. He can't have gone far.'

But Muskar's opinion proved incorrect when he drew back a screen of bushes upstream. 'Oh dear, it looks like Mister Lightpaw has sailed off on the raft. He's probably heading home.'

Doogy set his jaw grimly. 'D'ye know where he lives, sir?'

Muskar nodded upstream. 'Mister Lightpaw has a home up that way, on the edge of a pond. I've been there before.'

In no mood for chitchat, Doogy grabbed the dormouse's paw. 'Aye, well ye can show me the way. Come on, Muskar. Ah'm wantin' tae have a wee chat wi' that saucy robber!'

'Robber!' Muskar echoed in shocked tones. 'Do you mean to tell me that Mister Lightpaw's a robber?'

The Highlander yanked the dormouse energetically

along the streambank, muttering fiercely, 'Aye, a robber, thief, pilferer, purloiner, looter! Call him what ye will. Yoofus steals anythin' that comes tae paw. He'd have the eyes oot o' yer head if'n ye weren't watchin' him!'

Muskar Muskar looked bewildered. 'Good grief, who'd have thought it! Mister Lightpaw, a thief. And he seemed such a nice and jolly sort.'

Doogy smiled in spite of himself. 'Och, it just goes tae show, ye never know who's livin' in the area nowadays, eh?'

They followed the streambank, then cut off west. As soon as Doogy and Muskar came in sight of the lake, they immediately spotted Yoofus outside his dwelling, busily polishing the sides of the big drum. Every now and then he would strike the drum a few taps with a stick he had gripped in his thick little tail.

His wife, Didjety, came out to complain. 'Will ye stop beltin' that great thing, it's drivin' me scatty! Yore like a babby with a new toy, so y'are.'

Yoofus gave the drum a few more raps. 'Ah sure, ye've got no ear for music at all, me little sugar plum. Will ye just hark t'that grand boom!'

He was striking the drum again as his visitors walked up. The volethief showed neither apprehension nor surprise at the sight of Doogy. 'Faith, an' wasn't I just sayin' to meself that me good mate Doogy Plumm'd be along soon. I'd an idea that ould Muskar knew the way, so I was sure he'd bring ye. Will ye not listen t'the great boom o' this drum. 'Tis a sound for heroes an' warriors, so 'tis!'

Didjety greeted Muskar before questioning her husband. 'Who's that serious-lookin' squirrel, a friend of yores?'

Yoofus gave the drum a resounding roll with his stick. 'That he is, me darlin', a true blue pal in all weathers. Why don't ye take Mister Muskar inside an' put the kettle on for some nice mint tea? Meself an' Mister Plumm have business t'talk. We'll join ye in a tick.'

The moment they were alone, Doogy spoke in a flat, dangerous voice. 'Where's mah dirk?'

Yoofus smiled disarmingly. 'Dirk? Isn't that the funny ould long dagger ye carry? Sure ye must've mislaid it, matey.'

The Highlander shook his head. 'Don't matey me, ye rogue!' The claymore flashed out, its point pricking the vole's throat. Doogy meant business. 'Hear me, thief. If ah don't have mah dirk by the time ah've counted tae three, ye'll no' be drinkin' tea any more. One . . . Two . . . !'

The bladetip moved up and down as Yoofus gulped. 'Ah wait, wait now, let me think! The dirk, the dirk, now let me see . . . Oh, I remember now, 'tis hangin' from the back o' the door inside. I was takin' care of it for ye!'

Doogy used his claymore to motion the volethief inside. 'It better had be, Yoofus, or that bonny wee wifey o' yores will make a bonny wee widow. Go on, you first.'

Just as the Highlander was retrieving his weapon from the hook behind the front door, Didjety placed a tray of pasties and some long, fat objects on the table alongside her tea service.

'Mister Plumm, sit yoreself down an' take a sup'n'bite with us. The pasties are filled with wild cherry an' rhubarb. But if ye fancy somethin' savoury, then try me sausages. They're straight out the oven, y'know.'

Doogy enquired, 'Sausages, marm? What are sausages?'

The volewife explained. 'I invented them meself, sir. I make a mixture of fine ground barley, oats, carrot and mushroom. Then I wrap them in onion skin and bake them slow overnight. Everybeast likes me sausages, have one. Ah no, don't sit there, Mister Plumm. He doesn't like bein' sat upon, do ye, Rockbottom?'

Doogy stood to one side, staring at what he thought had been some kind of stone seat. It looked like stone, though it was covered with a curious square pattern. Yoofus rapped gently on the object. Doogy could not believe what he was seeing. A head emerged slowly from one end of the thing.

It resembled a serpent's head, but it had a much friendlier expression, with a mouth more like a beak. The creature, its neck wrinkled and scaled, looked as if it were from another world.

Didjety stood a short distance from it, holding out a piece of sausage. She spoke to it coaxingly. 'Come on then, me beauty. Here's some of yore mammy's sausage for ye, me lovely ould Rockbottom.'

Doogy's eyes grew wider as four scaly little limbs emerged from the beast. Opening its small, pink-tongued mouth, it trundled towards the food in the volewife's paw.

Totally flabbergasted, Doogy scratched his tail in bewilderment. 'Where in the name o' moles'n'mountains did ye get that beastie? What manner o' creature is it?'

Didjety fed her small friend fondly. 'Ah sure, Yoofus gave it t'me as a gift to keep me company while he's out rovin' goodness knows where.'

Doogy grabbed the volethief's whiskers and tweaked hard. 'Where did ye steal it? An' I want tae know the truth!'

Yoofus came up on tippaw as Doogy tweaked harder. 'Owowow! Leggo, ye great murderin' hooligan. I never stole it – on me honour as a thief, I didn't. Yowch gerroff!'

Doogy released him, listening whilst the vole related his story. ' 'Twas a curious thing but true, as ye'll hear. One mornin' I was sittin' fishin' by the lake, with me back up against a sycamore tree. Well, there's me, tryin' to catch a sly ould perch I've been after all season, when right beside me the earth starts t'move! Hoho, sez I to meself, here comes a mole who's lost his way. But it wasn't any mole at all. Somebeast must've filled in a hole near the tree with a pile o' moss an' dead leaves, cos all of a sudden up comes ould Rockbottom, calm as ye like. Then he tumbles over on to the back of his shell, with the effort of climbin' out, d'ye see. So there's him, layin' an' lookin' at me, an' there's me, sittin' an' lookin' at him. I sez good day, an' how d'ye do, but the beast doesn't say a thing back t'me. So I turned him over an' set him back on his liddle legs. Then, d'ye know what he did? He follered me back home, without a word or a by yore leave. Didjety took to the liddle feller right away, so she did. We named him Rockbottom, an' he's been with us ever since. An' grand ould company he is too. Aren't ye, Rockbottom, me ould tatercake?'

With eyes twinkling, the creature nodded its head as Didjety stroked it lovingly. 'Sure he's neither beetle, crab nor newt, but I wouldn't be without me darlin' pet, not for anythin'!'

The truth hit Doogy like a bolt of lightning. 'That beast is a Walkin' Stone. It's the thing that auld Gulo the Savage wants tae get his paws on!'

At the mention of Gulo, the little creature shot its head back into its shell.

Didjety scowled. 'Well, I don't give a mouldy acorn who this Gulo is, but he's not gettin' me Rockbottom!'

The Highlander nodded decisively. 'No, he ain't, marm, cos Rockbottom's comin' back tae Redwall Abbey wi' me!'

Yoofus stood up, placing his paw aggressively on his dagger hilt. 'My Didjety's liddle pet leaves this place over me dead body. So what d'ye say t'that, me bold squirrel?'

Quick as a flash, Doogy drew his dirk, rapping the volethief's paw sharply. Then he laid the blade on Yoofus's nose. 'That can be easily arranged, mah wee saucy vole!'

Mr Muskar, who had sat silently downing sausages during the dispute, protested, 'But you can't just march in here and take that creature away from the Lightpaws. That makes you as big a thief as Yoofus, if you'll pardon my saying, Mister Lightpaw.'

Doogy thrust another sausage into the dormouse's mouth. 'Ah'll thank ye t'stay out o' this, sir. Rockbottom is goin' tae Redwall, an' so is the drum. Yore comin', too, Yoofus. But before we get tae the Abbey, yore goin' tae take us tae yon hole in the streambank. D'ye recall it? Ah think that's where ye hid Rakkety Tam MacBurl's claymore an' the banner ye stole when ye escaped from the Abbey.'

Yoofus pushed the blade away from his nose and nodded. 'Faith, you ain't as thick as ye look, Mister Plumm. You've had yore eye on me closely. I thought ye'd forgotten the sword an' the flag. All right, friend, you win. I'll go with ye!'

Now it was Didjety's turn to protest. 'Hold fast there! Ye ain't traipsin' off an' leavin' me here all alone.'

Doogy shrugged. 'Then ye'd best come with us, marm.'

The volewife looked around at her neat home. 'But who's goin' to take care of this place?'

Mr Muskar volunteered. 'Myself and my good wife Lupinia will do that, Mrs Lightpaw. That's if you'd be good enough to leave us a supply of your delicious sausages?'

Yoofus suddenly took a shine to the idea. 'Sure, we'll take the raft, it'll be a nice little trip downstream. Ah, ye'll love Redwall, Didjety me darlin', 'tis a grand ould place. Right then, let's get packed!'

Doogy sat down and began loading up a plate. 'Not before ah've helped mahself tae these vittles!'

He immediately pronounced Didjety's sausages excellent. 'Och, ah never met a sausage until taeday, but ah could happily live on 'em for the rest o' mah life, marm!'

The vermin must have stolen the raft from some otherbeasts, because it was a stout, well-built craft, and it rode the stream smoothly. Mr Muskar leapt ashore as they passed his dwelling. The dormouse family came out to wave farewell as they drifted off downstream, with Yoofus and Doogy plying the long paddling poles.

The highland squirrel watched the deep quiet stream running silently by, murmuring to himself as he wielded his paddle, 'Ah hope Tam's lookin' after himself an' no' frettin' about me too much.'

31

Gulo the Savage and his twenty-nine vermin arrived at the broad stream too late. Tam and the hares had gone with the Guosim, sailing two hours or more downstream. The wolverine sat down upon the bank, wearied after his ordeal in the pines and the subsequent race to catch up with his foes. He knew his warriors were exhausted too. Gulo, however, would permit no signs of fatigue – neither his own nor those of his vermin.

Watching the foxes and ermine flopping down, sorely in need of rest, the tyrant scorned them harshly. 'Hah, even as a babe I could fight all day an' run beasts like ye into the ground. Rest, then, drink the waters an' cool your paws, for 'twill be woe unto the beast who lags behind when we get going!'

He called Eissaye, an ermine tracker, to his side. 'Our enemies do not travel without purpose, methinks. Whither would they be bound to on this water?'

Eissaye shrugged. 'Who knows, Lord?'

He squeaked with pain as the wolverine's claw pierced the lobe of his ear. Gulo dragged him forward until they were face-to-face. His voice brooked no argument. 'Thou art a tracker an' a scout. Who would know better than thee?

Now use thy brains before I spill them on to this bank, fool! Tell me, where are they bound?'

With his face screwed to one side, Eissaye gasped out an explanation based on what he had learned of the territory thus far. 'Unless the watermice have some secret hiding place downstream, 'tis likely they are going north again, Mighty One. If this water does not go straight to the red-stone fortress, it must pass by it someplace that is but a short march from the water. That is where they will go, Lord.'

Gulo released him and sat pensively, licking the blood from his claw. 'Well said. The Redwall place would be a wise refuge for my brother and his creatures.'

Eissaye was certain that Askor was not with those they were tracking, but he was not prepared to doubt Gulo's supposition. 'Aye, 'twill be as thou sayest, sire.'

Rakkety Tam stood watch at the stern of Log a Log Togey's big logboat, gazing back upstream. Skipper joined him. 'No sign of 'em followin' yet, mate?'

Tam eyed the point of the bend they had just negotiated. 'No, Skip, but ye can rest assured they'll be on our trail soon enough. But we've got an advantage – we're afloat on a pretty fast current, an' they don't have boats. This is the way to travel, eh?'

The otter chieftain nodded. 'Aye, Tam, so 'tis. Those vermin'll have the paws run offa theirselves, tryin' to follow the bankside. We could do with sailin' a bit slower, if'n we want to keep 'em on our tails.'

A shout from Togey in the bow interrupted them. 'Ho there, back-water, Guosim, tree ahead!'

Tam grinned wryly. 'Well, that'll slow us down if anything does. Let's go an' see this tree!'

The other Guosim craft had pulled into the bank shallows. Aboard the big boat, shrews back-watered energetically with their long paddles, fighting the swift current. A massive old willow had collapsed across the stream, blocking it completely. Heeling about until it was broadside on, the big logboat slowed down, coming to rest against the willow trunk with a gentle bump amidships.

The Guosim chieftain turned to Skipper and Tam, sighing irately. 'Well, this is a nice liddle mess we've run into. I'll have t'see wot can be done.'

A young shrew called out from the shallows, 'Looks like we'll 'ave to portage the boats, Chief!'

Log a Log Togey eyed him sceptically. 'Portage, y'say? Ten tribes o' badgers couldn't lift this craft o' mine to carry it over that ole monster!'

Lancejack Wilderry leaned against the protruding willow trunk. 'Well, what the dickens d'you suggest, sah?'

Togey laughed humourlessly. 'I dunno, sah. Ye got any bright ideas yoreself?'

Corporal Butty Wopscutt emerged from under the awning where he had been assisting the Guosim cooks. 'Bloomin' great log, ain't it, chaps? Can't go under it or bally well over it, wot!'

Togey glared at him. 'Is that all the help ye can offer, matey?'

Wopscutt dusted flour from his paws, grinning from ear to ear. 'Oh, sorry, sah. Were y'lookin' for suggestions? Well, how's about the old fulcrum'n'lever, wot?'

The one called Fiveshrew clapped the hare's back soundly. 'That's it, fulcrum'n'lever! Ye could shift anythin' that way!'

Shrews like nothing better than a good argument, and the Guosim crew were no exception. One shrewmate after another exchanged comments vociferously.

'Fulcrum'n'lever . . . rubbish! There's no movin' that thing!'

'Ah, who asked you? Get me a fulcrum'n'lever an' I'll move it!'

'Huh, you an' whose army? Ye'd never find a lever long enough t'shift that trunk. Don't talk twoddle!'

'Ahoy, big gob, I'll twoddle you if'n I comes over there. I'll tell ye how t'do it!'

'Oh ye will, will ye? Go on then, clever clogs!'

'S'easy, ye use two o' the smaller logboats. One fer a fulcrum, the other fer a lever. Ain't that right, Eightshrew?'

'Oh aye, but while yore leverin' one end, ye'll have to get the other end movin' too.'

'Move the other end . . . why's that?'

'Don't ye know nothin', thicktail? So as the log'll lie straight in the water an' get washed downstream outta our way. That's why!'

Soon everybeast was shouting, with clenched paws raised and snouts butted together truculently.

Log a Log Togey broke up the argument, bellowing, 'Rifto, get yore boat over 'ere, that'll be the fulcrum. Streambob, yore craft'll do as a lever. Use both of yore crews t'do it. The rest of ye, start shovin' wid paddles agin the root end o' that trunk. Come on, Guosim, get an ole heavie ho goin'!'

The shrews leapt into action as Log a Log murmured to Tam, 'See that? That's the way to solve a problem Guosim fashion – by democratic an' sensible debate!'

Skipper stifled a chuckle, whispering to the Borderer, 'It looked so democratic an' sensible there fer a moment, I thought they was all goin' to knock one another out flat!'

As the shrews went about the business of moving the fallen tree, Tam took Skipper and the hares back up the bank to watch out for signs of Gulo and his vermin pursuing them. As they moved cautiously along, using the trees close to the water as cover, Tam shook his ears in vexation. 'Listen to those shrewbeasts singin' their heads off. The vermin are sure t'hear 'em if they're in the area!'

Skipper took a more philosophical view. 'Well, it ain't as if ole Gulo don't know we're up this way, mate. The Guosim are only singin' to 'elp the job get done.'

Corporal Butty wrinkled his nose. 'I say, catchy little tune, ain't it, wot?'

Tam set his jaw, trying to ignore the heaving song.

'Shove an' push! Heave an' ho!
Bend yore backs, each mother's son.
Lean down haul! One an' all!
'Tis the only way the job gets done.

Shove an' push! Heave an' ho!
Do yore best, 'tis all I ask.
Lean down haul! One an' all!
Git yore paws into this task.

Shove an' push! Heave an' ho!
Guosim don't ye slack about.
Lean down haul! One an' all!
Bring 'er round an' drag 'er out!'

Since young Eissaye had the best sight and the sharpest ears of all the vermin, Gulo had despatched him to scout ahead. The wolverine was still weary, but reluctant to give up and rest. In high bad temper, he followed up the rear of his command as a threat to any who would dare to stop or drop out.

After a long and arduous march along the streambank, squelching through mud and sliding over wet rocks, Eissaye came hurrying back to report, 'Lord, I heard singing ahead!'

Gulo called his band to a halt. One look from him warned them to be silent. He strode several paces ahead of where the rest stood, bringing Eissaye along with him. 'Singing . . . where? I hear no singing.'

Eissaye could hear it, but he knew better than to contradict the wolverine. Cupping a paw around one ear, Gulo continued his interrogation. 'No, I cannot hear it! What was the singing about?'

All the ermine could do was to explain and suffer the

285

consequences. 'Mighty One, I could not hear the words, but my ears are keen. I heard the sound of singing.'

His answer did little to improve Gulo's mood. The wolverine's paws shot out, buffeting Eissaye so heavily about both his ears that the force knocked him down.

Gulo stood over him, snarling, 'Now I'll wager thy ears are singing aloud. Idiot, we are wasting time here. Get up and fetch the others!'

Moving the willow trunk by fulcrum and lever was not as easy as the shrews had figured. The mere size of the huge, ancient tree was a daunting sight. Long, thick limbs, branches, boughs, twigs and foliage covered the fallen giant's crown. A mass of twisted and tangled roots, some half as thick as the actual trunk, formed the base, protruding in all directions above and below the waters of the broadstream. The Guosim laid one of their logboats sideways at the top of the trunk; the second, lifted clear of the water, was placed across the middle of the first craft amidships, forming a type of seesaw. At the rooted end of the willow, shrews crowded the shallows – some ready to push, whilst others attached ropes at the other side, ready to pull. The principle of the scheme was to move the tree until it floated in the water, parallel to both banks, enabling the entire thing to drift off downstream, clearing the navigable waterway.

But theory and practice were strange bedfellows to the argumentative Guosim. Log a Log Togey stood on the centre of the mighty trunk, roaring orders, whilst his shrews squabbled and disputed furiously.

'Take the strain on those ropes, Guosim! Right, now dip the for'ard bow of the top boat down, underneath the tree. Puddenhead! I said the for'ard end, not the stern!'

'Ahoy, Chief! When we pull on these ropes, we might drag the tree over on top of us!'

'No ye won't, dulltail. You just pull an' we'll push!'

286

'Huh, that's easy fer yew t'say, rumblegut. Yore over on the safe side!'

Togey did a dance of rage. 'Shuddup, all of ye! Ready, now all at once. Puuuuush! . . . Shoooove!'

Within moments, the crossfire of shrew comments began anew.

'Waaaah! The bottom boat's sinkin'!'

'Well, geroutofit, mothbrain! Yore not s'posed t'be in it!'

'Whoa . . . 'elp! I'm swingin' in the air, hangin' on to the stern of this boat 'ere!'

Togey ran up and down the trunk like a madbeast. 'Ye bottle-nosed beetlebrains! Lend 'im a paw on the stern there! Take the strain on those ropes! Gerroff yore bottoms an' push that root end. Move! Push! Pull! More of ye down t'the stern, get yore weight on to it! Heeeeeaaaaave!'

Gulo and Eissaye crept forward with the rest of the vermin behind them. The distant squabbling and roaring of orders reached Gulo's ears.

Just as he halted, preparing to speak, one of the white foxes whispered to him, 'Lord, there are the foebeast, yonder! See?'

Gulo drew back behind an elm as he glimpsed the lanky figure of a hare dead ahead, no more than half a stone's throw. He spotted more hares, a squirrel and an otter, coming slowly along the streambank.

Gesturing in a semi-circular movement towards the woodlands, the wolverine gave murmured orders. 'Scouts, eh? We will get around the back of them and cut them off from the watermice and their boats. Follow me quietly if ye want fresh meat!'

Drawing their weapons, the ermine and foxes stole off to the left, following Gulo in a long arc.

Skipper shouldered his lance. Turning away from the up-stream bank, he addressed Tam. 'No sign o' the vermin, mate. They must be limpin' along after their scrap wid those black birds.'

Tam put up his sword. 'Aye, let's get back to the Guosim. Mayhaps we can lend 'em a paw to shift that tree.'

As the company turned, an arrow whipped out, catching Skipper through the side.

Corporal Wopscutt, who had been bringing up the rear, yelled, 'Ambush! It's the vermin!'

Two hares went down, felled by arrows and a spear. Then Gulo dashed out at the head of his vermin, roaring, 'Gulo! Gulo! Killkillkill!'

Completely taken by surprise, Tam called to the Patrol hares, 'Into the water! Get downstream!'

Arrows, axes and spears pelted at them. Tam grabbed Skipper, hauling him into the water and thrusting him out into the current. 'Get back to the Guosim, quick!'

Rushing back ashore, he drew the sword of Martin. After striking down a fox that was about to spear Lancejack Wilderry, Tam hurled himself at the advancing vermin, still yelling for the hares to get in the stream, where they would stand a chance of being saved by the swift current. Five hares were down, but the rest broke free, retreating into the broadstream.

Corporal Butty Wopscutt was harassed to the front and left by vermin. Tam had run no more than a few paces in the direction of his beleaguered comrade before he was stopped in his tracks by Gulo the Savage, who suddenly bounded out at him. The border warrior slashed out blindly with his sword. Gulo screeched as the blade lopped off his right ear. Blood was flowing freely from the wound as the wolverine clapped a paw to it. Tam ran by him, finally reaching the besieged Butty, who was gallantly holding off the main charge with his long rapier.

Together the two warriors fought, side by side, their backs to the stream, stifling the advancment of the vermin. Though vastly outnumbered, Tam and Butty, each with his blade slashing like a windmill in a gale, fought so furiously that their foe could not overcome them.

Gulo was screaming in the background, urging his vermin on. 'Kill! Kill! Charge and bring them down!'

Ashen-faced and tight-jawed, Butty muttered to Tam as they battled on, 'Into the water, friend. Save yourself.'

Tam's blade thrust at a leering face. 'Not while you're by my side, mate. We go in together!'

The hare caught Tam's eye as he repelled an axe swing. 'We'd be slain in the shallows! There's too many of the scum. I order you, go now, sirrah!'

Tam feinted a spearthrust. 'Not without you, Corporal!'

Butty almost doubled up but recovered himself. 'Gulo got me in the back with his fangs an' claws. You must go before he gets you. Go, Tam, I'm already a deadbeast!'

The border warrior chanced a quick glimpse over his friend's shoulder. He gasped in horror at the long, ripping wounds, Butty's blood now mingling with the water in the shallows. 'Matey, come with me. We'll make it together!'

Butty shook his head resolutely. 'No, sah, my string's run out. I've only got moments. Go while I still have strength to cover your back, friend. If y'get a chance another day, then slay Gulo for me, wot!'

Without waiting for an answer, the hare charged straight at the press of vermin, roaring out his last war cry, 'Eulaliiiiiaaaaaaa!'

Tam turned and dived into the current. He was caught in the downstream swirl and whipped away. Water filled his mouth and nostrils as he vowed silently to fulfill the task the hare had put on him.

Fortunately, Rakkety Tam was out of sight before his friend was slain. He had not died easily. Pierced by a forest of weaponry, the gallant hare broke his rapier blade in two and flung it at the enemy. He had no time for another war cry, because his teeth were set in the throat of a screaming ermine. Thus died Corporal Butty Wopscutt of the Long Patrol, a fighter to the bitter end.

Log a Log Togey and his shrews finally moved the fallen tree, but not as planned. Several Guosim were lost, crushed beneath the heavy, rooted base as it shifted back on them. The tree did not move free in one go: first the top half budged under the pressure of fulcrum and leverage, but the base end remained put. Then, aided by the current, the willow swept side on over the water in a single mighty rush. Instead of landing midstream, the tree had positioned against the far bank, rolling backwards through the shallows and killing the shrews who had been pushing at the rooted end. The haulers had been forced to wade for their lives without benefit of the ropes, which had been swept underwater but now lay tangled beneath the trunk. The waterway, however, had been cleared. Under Togey's frantic orders, the crew righted the longboats and brought them into the bank.

Before they even had time to recover the bodies of their dead comrades, Skipper came wallowing downstream, gasping, 'Lend us a paw, mates, an' make ready t'sail!'

Once the otter had been pulled out of the water by the long Guosim rowing poles, it was clear that, somehow, he had been injured. Log a Log Togey enquired, as he slapped bankmud on the wound to the otter chieftain's side, 'Wot 'appened, Skip?'

The otter spat out a jet of water. 'Ambushed by the vermin. No time fer chitchat, mate, 'ere come the others. Pull 'er out an' git under way. Y'best put a move on, Togey. Gulo an' the vermin are on our tails!'

Groups of Long Patrol hares were hauled from the racing current on to the logboats. The bloodcurdling yells of Gulo's band could be heard drawing closer as the hares were pulled aboard and the small flotilla of logboats shot out into midstream.

Skipper grabbed a shrew. 'It's Tam! See, there he is. Pass 'im an oar, quick!'

Exhausted, the warrior squirrel was trying to keep his head above the surface as he was rushed downstream. Behind him, vermin were running along the bank, shooting arrows at him. Tam had never let go of Martin's sword since the start of the ambush. He saw the thick ash paddle splash into the stream ahead of him. With his last ounce of strength, he swung the blade, bedding it in the paddle and hanging on tight to the sword with both paws. The Guosim crew heaved him aboard just in time.

The banks had become rocky, rising higher, funnelling the already fast water into a roaring, boiling tunnel. Gulo's archers vanished from view as the boats swept away on the wild torrent. Everybeast threw themselves flat to the decks of the logboats, which were well out of control as they hurtled through a chain of rapids. High, white-crested masses of water shot by madly as the logboats bumped against one another and scraped over protruding rocks.

The returning archers found Gulo the Savage sitting on the fallen willow at the bankside, slapping pawfuls of bankmud on his severed earstump to stem the bleeding.

Eissaye pointed with his bow. 'Mighty One, they escaped downstream. The flow was too fast, and the banks high with rock. We could not keep up with the speed of their craft, Lord.'

Gulo was off the trunk with a bound and on to the bank. 'My brother Askor, and the Walking Stone – did ye sight them?'

Eissaye wisely backed out of range. 'Nay, sire . . .'

Gulo, his eyes gleaming madly, seemed to ignore the scout. 'Hah, hiding in the boats, that's where they'll be! But never fear, I'll get them. You there, and you . . . all of ye! We have our own craft, use your spears. Roll this tree into the water! We will travel as fast as they do. I will have them before they reach the Redwall place. Cut those ropes 'an make haste!'

Eissaye wanted to tell Gulo about the rapids, but he held his silence. There was no talking to the wolverine in his present mood.

Within moments, the huge willow trunk was crashing downstream with the vermin clinging to it for their lives. Oblivious to the blood that streamed from his wounded ear, Gulo stood upright, filled with exhilaration at his first taste of riding rough waters. An insane light shone in his glittering eyes. He kicked at the nearest vermin, shouting at them above the thundering current, 'Paddle! Use thy spears an' paddle! Fast! Fast!'

32

Yoofus the volethief had made a lead of woven linen strapping for his wife's pet, Rockbottom. Neatly plaited in red, green and white, with a loop that fitted securely round the little reptile's shell, the leash came in handy when Didjety took Rockbottom for walks around the deck of the raft.

Doogy sat at the tiller, remarking to Yoofus as he watched Rockbottom's slow progress about the craft, 'Och, ah wonder if'n yon beast ever breaks intae a gallop. He's certainly in no hurry tae go anywhere.'

Yoofus patted Rockbottom's head as he slowly ambled by. 'Ah sure, he's the slow'n'steady one all right. Look there . . . further up the bank on the left. That's the cut-off leadin' to the stream where I hid yer friend Tam's sword an' flag. Here, give me the tiller, I'll take her round.'

Doogy allowed the water vole to manoeuvre the tiller, leaving the small Highlander free to perch upon the drum. Watching the sidewater loom up, he expressed his doubts. 'Are ye sure this is the right stream? Ye've already took us up two dead ends!'

Yoofus winked confidently at him. 'Sure I'm sure! Don't I know these woodlands like me own darlin' wife's dear face?'

Doogy stood in front of him, blocking Yoofus's view of

Didjety. 'Oh ye do, do ye? Well, what colour are yore wife's eyes?'

The cocky thief made several guesses. 'Er, blue . . . no, green . . . er, grey. A sort of a bluey greenish grey, I'm sure of it!'

Didjety wagged an indignant paw at her husband. 'Aren't you the great ould fibber, Yoofus Lightpaw! Me eyes are dark brown wid hazel flecks, so there!'

Yoofus rounded the bend into the slipstream, chuckling. 'So they are, me liddle sugarplum, but they enchant me so much that I ferget when I'm gazin' into 'em!'

Didjety stood glaring at him, paws akimbo. 'Get away, ye fat, silver-tongued rogue! I'm thinkin' I might just make dinner for me'n Mister Plumm, an' ferget about you!'

The slipstream was narrower than the broadstream they had come down. Trees hung thick over it, and the water was sluggish, with a coating of green algae when they got further along.

Doogy watched Rockbottom whilst the shrew wife prepared dinner. The Highlander kept shaking his head doubtfully. 'Ach, ah dinna think this is the right way. What have ye tae say about all this, mah friend?'

Rockbottom closed his eyes and withdrew his head into his shell.

Doogy sighed. 'Ah get the message, mate!' He tied Rockbottom's lead to the drum and went beneath the raft's awning to join Yoofus and Didjety for dinner.

As Doogy had hoped, the volewife had brought along some of her sausages. These she had encased in pastry. Doogy watched as she heated them up on a small fire which Yoofus had kindled atop of some flat stones.

The volethief winked at him. 'These are called sausage rolls. Me darlin' Didjety makes the best sausage rolls anywhere. D'ya know how to make a sausage roll, Doogy?'

The Highlander bit into one, finding the sausages

294

delicious indeed. 'No, ah'm afraid ah don't know how tae make a sausage roll.'

Yoofus answered, 'Ye just push it down a hill, that's how ye make a sausage roll!'

Doogy did not find it funny, but both voles hooted and giggled. 'Push it down a hill! Hahaha heeheeheehee!'

Doogy took another sausage roll. Then, glaring at Yoofus, he spoke firmly. 'If you've got us lost, mah friend, ah won't push ye down a hill, ah'll fling ye over a cliff!'

Didjety pressed more sausage rolls upon Doogy. 'Ah sure, don't be frettin' yerself, Mister Plumm. My Yoofus will get us there. Here now, I'll sing ye a song t'cheer ye up!'

The volewife, with her sweet little voice, launched straight into song.

'Ould Roderick vole had a grand appetite,
sure he'd lived with it all of his life,
an' when he got home to his cottage one night,
he called out to his own darlin' wife,
'O bring me some stew, a big bucket or two,
an' ten of yore ould apple pies,
a cheese from the shelf as big as yoreself,
an' a trifle just as a surprise!
Now me stummick is slack, for me health to come back,
then ye must keep me nourished an' fed,
I'll be happy all right an' well rested tonight,
when I toddle off to me ould bed.
So bring out the cake for a dear husband's sake,
an' a bathtub o' soup nice an' warm,
six loaves for to dunk, sure an' when 'tis all drunk,
then I'll sleep like a babe 'til the morn.
Providin' 'tis clear there's a barrel o' beer,
for to save me ould teeth from the drought,
some cordial an' tea sure I'll sup happily,
get a move on before I pass out!'
Well his wife did no more than fling him out the door,

hit him squarely wid all the ten pies.
She poured all the stew o'er his head, an' it's true,
that the trifle came as a surprise!
She loosened his teeth with the cheese if y'please,
stuffed the loaves down his ears gleefully.
Then both him an' the cake she slung into the lake,
Shoutin', "Come back tomorrow for tea!"'

Doogy smiled and applauded the song, but he was still far from being cheered up. 'Very entertainin', marm, but jokes an' comic ditties won't find the banner an' the claymore yore husband thieved. Aye, an' ah'm thinkin' they won't get us any closer tae Redwall Abbey.'

Yoofus began poling the raft up the narrow stream as if he had not a care in the world. 'Ah, sure yore a proper ould worry wart, Mister Plumm. Do ye not think I know me own way around Mossflower? Don't get yore tail in an uproar now. I'll wager we find yore gear soon enough. I recognize this stream.'

But the day wore on without success; in fact, their position worsened. By early evening the stream had narrowed. Trees and bank foliage pressed in on them, and the water became murky and stagnant. Doogy's mood darkened as he assisted the water vole to pole the craft along, constantly having to slash at the encroaching vegetation with his claymore blade.

Didjety swiped at a cloud of annoying insects with her pinafore. 'Be off, ye pesky mites, before I'm eaten alive! Yoofus, are you certain sure this is the right stream?'

The volethief brushed a hairy caterpillar off his paw. 'Er, I think so, me dear.'

Doogy spat at a gnat which was trying to get in his mouth. 'Ye *think* so? Ach, ye great fat-tailed fibber, ah've a good mind tae boot yer lyin' bottom intae that water!'

Yoofus tried a weak smile, which faded on his lips. Even Rockbottom shook his head in disgust.

The raft had been slowly drifting forward, but now it

ground to a halt with a bump. A huge, rotted beech trunk blocked their way; beyond it the stream was a mere trickle. Doogy flung his pole into the water, wrinkling his nose at the odour which arose from it.

Didjety began to weep, throwing her pinafore over her face. 'Oh, Yoofus, how could ye do this to us?'

Doogy rolled the drum on to the solid bank ground and placed the tortoise upon it decisively. 'Dry yer tears, marm, an' come ashore with me. Ah'll try tae find us a way out o' this without that lyin' buffoon ye call a husband!'

He lifted the volewife on to the bank, passing the supplies to her and glaring at Yoofus. 'An' as for ye, mah foolish friend, y'can shift for yerself. Ah can stan' yore thievin' an' lyin' no longer!'

As darkness fell over the woodland depths, a small fire made an island of light in the gloom. Doogy, Didjety and Rockbottom gathered around the flames, roasting sausages on sticks and drinking beakers of the volewife's plum-and-gooseberry cordial.

Didjety glanced anxiously at the Highlander. 'I wonder where Yoofus has got to. D'ye suppose he's all right, Mister Plumm?'

Doogy jiggled a hot sausage from paw to paw, breaking off a piece and tossing it to Rockbottom. 'Och, ah wouldnae bother mah head about him, marm. Ah can hear him out there watchin' us. He'll come tae no harm, an' mebbe he'll learn a lesson or two, eh?'

The volethief's voice came through the trees to them. He sounded lonely and forlorn. 'Ah, 'tis a sad thing t'be left to die alone in this ould forest, an' all because of one liddle mistake. Sure, an' it must be grand for some I know – sittin' round a nice warm fire an' feedin' their gobs on sausages an' cordial while the likes of meself is cast out into the wilderness to be et by flies an' die of the hunger an' drought. I must've led a wicked life to come to this!'

He sounded so pitiful that Didjety had to wipe a tear from her little tortoise's eye.

Doogy heaved a sigh. 'Och, ye may as well call the roguey in, marm.'

Before the volewife could say anything, Yoofus dropped out of a tree to sit beside her, grinning from ear to ear. 'Top o' the evenin' to ye, mates! Pass me a sausage, will ye, me ould darlin' daisy? I'm dyin' fer the lack o' vittles. Doogy, me luvly friend, how are ye?'

The Highlander passed him a beaker of cordial before responding. 'None the better for yore askin', thief. Now understand this! Ah'm leadin' the way from now on, ye've got no say in it. If'n ah want tae get lost, ah can do it without yore help. You just roll that drum along an' follow me!'

Yoofus saluted several times, nodding in agreement. 'Ah, sure yore right, sir. Orders are orders, an' 'tis me faithful self who'll be carryin' 'em out. Isn't he right, Didjety, me liddle rosebud?'

The volewife slammed a hot sausage into her husband's smiling mouth, leaving him spluttering. 'Oh, Mister Plumm's right, sure enough. One more word from yore fibbin' lips, Yoofus Lightpaw, an' ye don't get another bite to eat or drink from me. Is that clear now?'

Yoofus patted Rockbottom's head and fed him the sausage. 'Hoho, me liddle pal, that one's not a creature to argue with. Ah, cheer up now an' I'll sing ye all a grand ould song about a pore mouse who had a shrewish wife.'

Doogy's paw strayed dangerously close to his sword hilt. 'No ye won't. Ye'll eat that supper an' go tae sleep!'

Yoofus collapsed backwards, saluting as he did. 'Go t'sleep, sir. Orders is orders, right y'are!'

Like a broken silver coin, a half-moon shone down on the small group sleeping around the glowing embers of the fire. Doogy lay wrapped in his plaid, wondering if he would ever again see his friend Tam, or walk through the welcoming gates of Redwall Abbey.

33

The broadstream was running so furiously that there was little need of oars, though the Guosim held them ready to fend off their vessels from rocks and to keep the logboats in midstream.

Tam sat in the stern of Togey's big boat, his paws clenched tight to the gunnels. He gazed about in awe: to his right, high limestone cliffs towered over the waters; to his left, rocks were broken into large chunks, overgrown by trees and vines. He realized they were speeding down an ever-narrowing slope, which concentrated the stream so greatly that little could be heard but the roaring of water. A fine spray enveloped everybeast.

Log a Log Togey sat beside Tam, his eyes narrowing against the rushing spray. The shrew chieftain manoeuvred the tiller skilfully with one paw whilst signalling directions to the other logboats in his wake. They were travelling ahead of the other boats.

Tam glanced back upstream, shouting to Togey, 'No sign of Gulo an' the vermin, mate!'

Togey called back, 'Keep yore eyes peeled on that left bank. That's the route they'll be followin'.'

Skipper was in the last logboat. He balanced upright, steadying himself on his broad rudder as he peered back upstream. His keen eyes caught movement. Pointing, he roared at the top of his voice, 'They're on the river, comin' fast this way!'

Tam and Log a Log both turned to look. In their wake, the broad stream resembled a single long and narrowing avenue. In the distance, the big willow trunk was thundering downstream, loaded with vermin. Gulo could be seen standing high amid the roots which formed the prow. The wolverine was gesturing madly as he exhorted his crew to paddle with branches and spears. Tam's first reaction was one of alarm. The huge tree seemed to be gaining on them, travelling at a very fast pace indeed. Log a Log Togey nudged a nearby shrew. Together they studied the unusual craft racing along in their wake. Then they held a hasty whispered conference, both smiling and nodding.

The Borderer looked enquiringly at the Guosim chieftain. 'What's so funny, mate?'

Togey pointed ahead. There was a turn coming up in the distance where a massive rocky outcrop poked out into the water. He put his mouth close to Tam's ear. 'Wait'll we round that curve, an' you'll see!'

He waved to the other logboats, pointing to the curve and nodding off to the left. They signalled back that they had understood the order. Immediately all the Guosim crews dipped their oars and began paddling strongly with the headlong current. All the logboats shot forward.

Lancejack Wilderry was seated in the prow of the big front boat. He became so exhilarated by the sudden turn of speed on the wild waters that he rose up, roaring, 'Eulaliii-iiaaaaa! Let 'er go, chaps!'

A stern old shrew shoved the young hare down, clambering over him to crouch in the very peak of the prow. 'Keep yer 'ead down, matey. I gotta watch out fer the Chief's signals. Stay out o' me way now!'

The hares in all the boats had drawn their weapons at first, thinking that Gulo and his vermin might overtake them. But when it became obvious that he would not, they put up their arms and clung tight to the gunnels, their ears blowing out straight behind them as the logboats skimmed over the boiling waters. The shrews in the prows of other boats began uncoiling stout ropes with grappling hooks attached. Log a Log and Tam watched as the foebeasts tried to put on more speed. Gulo, lashing about with a long, whippy willow bough, exhorted them to greater efforts.

Togey shouted to Tam above the watery din, 'Grab this tiller with me. Now when I call starboard, you push it t'the right with all your might. Got that?'

Tam nodded, repeating the instruction. 'Starboard, push to the right!' He set both paws on the tiller, gripping it fiercely.

Suddenly the bend was upon them. Tam felt Log a Log Togey tense. Then the shrew warrior bellowed out his commands, 'Starboard! Starboard! Push for yore life!'

Bracing his footpaws against the port bulkhead, Tam pushed until veins stood out upon his neck. Water was dashing into the logboats as shrews in the prows whirled ropes with grapnelled ends and cast them.

A hidden inlet, diguised by overhanging trees, was right around the bend. Tam felt the big logboat shudder as it turned sideways in the melee of water. He caught but a brief glimpse of the rocks on the right, looming up at the stern, before a powerful shock knocked him almost flat.

The shrew in the prow had thrown his rope, its grapnels thunking into the body of an ancient pine. Guosim shrews threw themselves upon the ropes, hauling madly. Logboats heeled almost on to their sides as the bounding current pounded them. Then they righted. Ropes thrummed tautly, and the boats were hauled swiftly into the tree-covered inlet.

Tam found himself soaked to the fur and gasping for breath, still gripping the tiller.

Log a Log Togey patted the warrior squirrel's back,

complimenting him. 'We'll make a streambeast of ye yet, Tam. Well done, mate!'

Then the Guosim leader turned his attention to the other boats. 'All craft in now? Oars shipped an' boats well hid?'

Skipper, whose logboat was the last to be hauled in, gave Togey a wave. 'All craft in an' tied up tight, Chief!'

One of the hares whispered to Threeshrew, 'Rather neat, wot! D'you chaps do this often?'

Looking grim, she responded, 'Nobeast ever tried it afore, we're the first to do it. I thought we was all deadbeasts for a while back there.'

The young hare's ears stood up rigid. 'Good grief, y'might have told us 'twas your first time!'

Tam could not help but smile. 'Would it have made any difference?'

Skipper murmured to Togey, 'They should be here soon. Wot if'n they sees us as they pass by?'

The shrew chieftain shrugged. 'Wouldn't make any difference if we stuck our tongues out at 'em an' sang rude songs, mate. They wouldn't be able to stop. That tree's headed for a waterfall so steep you can 'ardly see the bottom. Though if'n ye did, ye wouldn't like it – the bottom of those falls is nothin' but a big heap o' rocks stickin' up. Mark my words, Skip – Gulo an' his scummy crew are all deadbeasts!'

As it happened, Gulo did not spot the hidden cove as the big willow trunk shot by. He was too busy lashing about at his vermin and yelling out over the din of wild water, 'Faster! More speed! Keep going, ye idle fools!'

With nobeast to steer or otherwise control it, the huge bulk of the fallen tree continued to hurtle through the water as it went with the currents. Veering in to the right, the massive treetrunk eventually struck the enormous outcrop of rock, directly on the bend. Were it not for his powerful claws, which he had latched into the trunk after releasing his willow whip, Gulo would have died on impact.

Then disaster struck the tree, the shock of the collision turning it end to end. And it carried on – turning and turning and turning . . . The wolverine and his terrified crew clung to the log, lost in a whirling chaos of water and rock, the sky revolving above them.

When Tam and Togey last caught sight of them, the vermin were gripping tight aboard the spinning log, screaming and yelling as it swept out of sight around the bend.

Log a Log Togey relaxed his hold on the tiller. 'There's about six more bends afore they reach the big waterfall. When they hit the bottom, there won't be enough left of 'em to scrape up in a basket!'

Tam looked stunned, but he responded to the shrew's remark. 'Good riddance to bad rubbish, mate!'

Leaving the logboats securely moored to trees, they clambered ashore over the rocks. Guosim cooks found a convenient spot among the conifers to set up camp. There a fire was built, water fetched from the stream and wet garments set out to dry. Everybeast took their ease, weary after their ordeal on the wild waters, which could still be heard thundering along in the background.

Tam sat with Skipper and Togey, watching the westering sun setting distant trees into silhouettes tinged with purple and gold. The trio were silent, each with his own thoughts, until the shrew chieftain stroked his beard reflectively.

'Well, mates, a good end to a long, hard day, eh?'

Tam began slowly honing the blade of his dirk against a rock. 'Aye, 'twas that, though I'll wager Gulo the Savage had an even harder day on his journey to Hellgates. I never kept my vow to slay him, though.'

Skipper flicked drops of water from his rudder. 'Ye ought to bless fate for that, Tam. We should thank Mother Nature for takin' care o' that one. I don't think any ten beasts could've faced a monster like Gulo in combat. That 'un was a mad slayer an' a flesh eater. Yore a warrior, Tam, but I don't think you'd have stood a chance agin a beast like Gulo the Savage.'

The Borderer tested the edge of his blade. 'We'll never know now, will we?'

Sensing the challenge in Tam's voice, Log a Log Togey changed the direction of the conversation. 'Makes no difference now, mates. Ole Gulo's out the way, an' yore headed back to Redwall.'

Tam nodded. 'First thing in the morning, an' we'll have to step out sharp. The Abbey's probably under attack by half a hundred vermin – remember, Gulo split his forces.'

Skipper looked grim. 'Yore right there. I 'ope our friends aren't in any difficulties, I'd hate to think ole Humble or my young Brookflow was in any trouble. I expect you feel the same way about Sister Armel. Eh, Tam?'

The warrior looked surprised. 'I hope they're all safe an' well, Skip. Why should I be particularly worried about the Sister?'

The otter chieftain chuckled. 'Hah, you ain't foolin' anybeast, Rakkety Tam MacBurl. Everybeast noticed the way you two was gazin' at each other an' whisperin' together!'

Suddenly Tam was lost for words. He was saved by the arrival of Lancejack Wilderry. 'I say, you chaps, are you goin' to sit there chunnerin' away all blinkin' evenin', or d'you want some scoff?'

It was Guosim tradition that, whilst on campaign, the Log a Log was served first. Out of deference to the shrews, the Long Patrol hares observed this rule. Gathered around the spread the cooks had set out for them, both groups eagerly awaited Togey's arrival, which would signal that it was time to dig into the feast. Upon his appearance, however, the shrew chieftain first had a few words to say.

'Comrades, this is a fine meal laid out for us. I want ye to enjoy it an' give thanks for livin' through today. Not just us

Guosim, but you hares too. We lost some fine friends today, good shrews an' gallant hares. Our victory was gained, but at a price. So I want ye to give a moment's silence an' think of the ones who ain't with us t'share these good vittles.'

In the silence that followed, the Guosim thought of their mates who had been lost whilst freeing the broadstream of the fallen willow. Many wept openly. The Long Patrol hares kept a stiff upper lip, but it was hard: they all had memories of gallant Corporal Butty Wopscutt, who had given his life for his friends. Tam thought of Butty too; he had been very fond of the jolly corporal. At the same time, he could not help thinking of Doogy. Where was the little Highlander? Was he safe and well? Then his mind wandered to other things. His feelings for Sister Armel were just as Skipper had expressed them. Tam smiled to himself as he reflected on what an unlikely match they made – the warrior and the gentle healer!

The reverie was broken when a shrewcook held out a plate of stew, some rough bread and a beaker of shrewbeer to Tam. 'Here y'are, matey. Get that lot inside o' ye!'

As night fell over the waters and the woodlands, they did what warriors always did after a long hard day – ate well, drank heartily, told tales and, especially popular with the young hares of the Long Patrol, sang songs. One Merriscut Fieldbud, a haremaid with a trilling voice, entertained them with a barracks room monologue.

'Well pish an' tush an' 'pon my word,
I am the Primrose Warrior.
The day I joined the Long Patrol,
no maid was ever sorrier.

They woke me up at break o' dawn,
and sent me off to war,
before I'd had a chance to bathe,
or dust each dainty paw.

I went away to fight the foe,
with comrades rude an' rough.
They'd never seen a perfume spray,
much less a powder puff.

With not a drop of daisy balm,
or any rosehip lotion,
I marched along, a dreadful sight,
my ears shook with emotion.

Then soon we faced the enemy,
an' it was my firm belief,
between that awful scruffy lot,
was not one handkerchief!

What were their mothers thinking of?
Not one had washed his face.
I mentioned to my Officer,
they looked a real disgrace!

All filled with indignation then,
I charged them single-pawed,
with boudoir mirror for a shield,
and parasol for sword.

I curled their ears and brushed their teeth,
and wiped their runny noses,
then sprayed on toilet water,
until they smelt like roses.

They ran away in swift retreat,
that rabble so unseemly.
My General then promoted me,
for beating them so cleanly.

So when you see me on parade,
you chaps must all salute.
I'm called the Primrose Major now, and
Isn't that a hoot?'

Everybeast laughed and applauded, especially the shrews.

Log a Log Togey remarked to the lancejack, 'Hohoho, that 'un's a pretty liddle maid, ain't she?'

Wilderry nodded. 'She is indeed, sah, but don't be fooled. Merriscut is hard as steel, an' death with a lance. She's what y'd call a perilous beauty, wot!'

Togey observed drily, 'All these young 'uns are perilous, both shrews an' hares. 'Tis the life we chose.' He turned to Skipper. 'Well, matey, wot d'ye reckon to Guosim stew, eh?'

The burly otter was into his third bowl. 'Ho, very tasty, very nice! But ain't you buckoes never 'eard of hotroot pepper?'

Togey pulled a wry face. 'Aye, but that stuff's a bit too warm for Guosim stummicks. No doubt ye'll soon be slurpin' it down when ye get t'the Abbey. They prob'ly got lots of hotroot pepper there.'

The otter chieftain gazed fondly into the fire. 'They do indeed, mate. Good ole Redwall, I can't wait for dawn when we begin the march to my Abbey!'

Dawn came soon enough, sooner than some expected, who were looking forward to a late sleep. The camp came abustle with hastily taken breakfast.

Log a Log Togey briefed Tam and Skipper. 'I'm takin' my crews back off t'the logboats. Got some business t'see to, mates. Redwall's about a couple o' days good marchin' from here. I'll leave ye Oneshrew an' Twoshrew. They'll guide ye back to the Abbey.'

After they had said their goodbyes, Tam found that, in the absence of Corporal Butty Wopscutt, he was left to give the orders. The Borderer did so with practised ease. Soon his bark was echoing round the camp.

'Come on now, me lucky lads'n'lassies, time to march for Redwall! Fall in the Long Patrol. Lancejack an' Fieldbud, front'n'centre! Right markers, fall in! Tenshun! Look to your dressin', yew sloppy lot of fiddle-pawed, wobble-lugged excuses for hares! Silence in the ranks there! By the left! Quick march! Hup two, hup two, hup two . . .' The column strode off briskly through the morning woodlands.

One of the young hares murmured to his companion, 'Strewth! Did ye hear Mister MacBurl then? I thought it was ole Sarge Wonwill for a blinkin' moment!'

His friend replied, 'Sounded jolly well like him, wot! Nearly brought a tear to me flippin' eye, thinkin' about Sarge Wonwill, grumpy ole gravel-gutted beast. I miss him.'

'I'll bring a tear to yore eye, laddie buck!' The young hare cut his eyes sideways to see Tam marching on the other side of him. The Borderer looked every inch the sergeant major, with his dirk tucked horizontally like a swagger stick.

He scowled ferociously at the talkers. 'I'll bring so many tears to both your eyes you'll think yore marchin' underwater! Now straighten those shoulders, move those paws an' shut those mouths! No gossipin' in the ranks, d'ye hear me?'

Both hares tucked their chins in and bawled simultaneously, 'Yes, sah! No gossipin' in the ranks, sah!'

Tam fell back a pace or two, smiling to himself. Skipper caught up with him, nodding his admiration. 'That sounded good, mate! Where'd ye learn to give orders like that? 'Twas just like a proper roughneck officer.'

Tam shrugged. 'Oh, here'n there . . . y'know, Skip. For the past few seasons, I've been in the service of a fool Squirrelking. You sort of pick it up as y'go along.'

Midafternoon, the shrewscouts reported back. Oneshrew and her sister had nothing urgent to convey – the route was clear, and they had picked out a spot for an early evening stopover.

Tam dismissed them, then called out to his hares, 'Listen up now, you bedraggled, bewildered beauties! Our scouts have found an early evenin' layover spot. D'ye want to stop there, or march on until dark an' see if we can make Redwall Abbey in record time?'

A roar of well-drilled voices came back at him. 'March on, sah, march on!'

Skipper surprised Tam by bellowing out, 'March on it is, ye lollopin' lilies! Keep up the pace there! I want to get to Redwall afore I grow old an' need a stick. Step lively there!'

The otter chieftain winked at Tam. 'How d'ye think I did?'

Tam saluted his friend. 'Well done, Skip. Yore a born Sergeant Major! We'll share the commands from here to Redwall.'

Skipper beamed like a morning sunrise. 'Righto, Sergeant!' They camped that night at another spot the shrewscouts had chosen further on. It was dark, and the marchers were weary. Tam and his company bathed their paws in a small brook. After a short snack of haversack rations, they curled up in a shaded glade and fell asleep immediately.

Skipper was awake shortly after daybreak. He roused the hares like a true regimental sergeant. 'Come on, my liddle beauties, up on yore dainty paws now! Right, who'd like a luvverly brekkist o' fresh salad, 'ot scones an' some blackberry tarts?'

A gullible young hare stretched and yawned. 'Oh, I say, sah, that'd just fit the bill nicely!'

The otter chieftain gave him a jaundiced eye, roaring at the unfortunate in a voice like thunder, 'Well, you ain't goin' t'get nothin' like that 'ere, laddie buck! Grab an apple an' some water, then up on yore hunkers an' get fell in for marchin'! Yew lollop-eared, bottle-nosed, misbegotten muddlers! Move, or I'll 'ave yore guts for garters an' yore tails for tea!'

Tam winked at the otter's verbosity. 'I like that one, Skip! Misbegotten muddlers . . . I must remember that. How far to the Abbey now, I wonder?'

Skipper studied the woodlands ahead. 'Not too far now, mate. I'm startin' to recognize a few landmarks. Oneshrew an' Twoshrew are good liddle maids, they're trackin' well.

If'n we make fast time, I reckon we'll reach the Abbey early tomorrow morn.'

They marched on through the day, making only one brief halt in the early noontide. Just before dusk they stopped at a place the two Guosim sisters had chosen for the night's rest. It was situated on a streambank.

Skipper nodded with satisfaction. 'Well, root me rudder, mate! D'ye reckernize this place?'

Tam dabbled his paws in the cooling waters. 'Everywhere's beginnin' to look the same t'me, Skip. I'm a Borderer, not a Woodlander. Where are we?'

The otter pointed slightly downstream. 'Round about there, that's where wotsisname, the pesky liddle vole robber, hid yore sword an' the flag. Let's see!' He dived like an arrow into the water and streaked away beneath the surface.

Not having heard Skipper's conversation with Tam, the hares watched him in awe. Two of the most opinionated in the group exchanged comments.

'Strewth! Must have some blinkin' energy, wot? Marchin' since dawn, then goin' off for a jolly old swim like that!'

'Indeed, you wouldn't catch me doin' that, old lad. Dabble the paws a bit, that's my style. Where's the Skipper gone, sah?'

Tam lay back on the bank, closing his eyes. 'Wait an' see.'

They had not long to wait. Shortly thereafter, Skipper bounded up on to the bank and tossed a long, wrapped bundle to Tam. 'Found these in a hole on the other bank, right where that rascal stowed 'em awhile back!'

Tam unwrapped the wet banner of Squirrelking Araltum from about his claymore. He wielded the blade fondly. 'My thanks to ye, Skip. You've done me a great favour!'

Skipper shook himself like a dog, spraying some young hares with water. 'My pleasure, Tam. The sun'll dry yore flag out tomorrow. Ye can polish yore sword up, an' the followin morn y'can march into the Abbey – double-bladed, wavin' the flag an' singin' yore 'ead off!'

Tam looked thoughtful. 'Maybe, Skip. That's if Redwall hasn't been taken by the vermin!'

34

Abbot Humble was halfway between sleep and wakefulness in the grey dawn when he realized that somebeast was
pounding on the wine cellar door. Rising in his bed slowly,
the old hedgehog called out hoarsely, 'Who in the name of
seasons is banging like that?'

The sounds had roused young Burlop. He hastened to
the door, assuring the Abbot, 'I'll see who it is, Father. Don't
disturb yourself!'

Humble sat up in his little truckle bed, rubbing his eyes
and yawning. He looked up and found himself confronted
by Sister Armel. 'What is it, Sister? Has somebeast been
taken ill? Do you need my help at the Infirmary?'

Armel sat down on the side of the bed. 'Nothing like that,
Father, but I must speak with you.'

Blinking dozily, Humble held up a paw to silence her.
'Wait, don't tell me! You've had a dream . . . Martin the
Warrior spoke to you. Am I right?'

Astonishment was evident on the Sister's pretty face. 'But
. . . But . . . How did you know?'

The old hedgehog smiled indulgently at his young friend.
'Because I've had one too. It all came back to me the moment I looked up and saw you standing here.'

Armel's big brown eyes went wide. 'Martin sent me a message in verse. Listen to this . . .'

Before she could speak further, Humble was repeating the words, line by line.

'Behold two swords and a banner,
watch out for the Walking Stone.
The brother is gone, 'tis the warrior
who must face the Savage alone.'

Sister Armel grasped the Abbot's paw. 'Those were Martin's very words, Father. What does he mean?'

Humble shook his head. 'If I knew that, Armel, I would be wiser than any beast who ever ruled Redwall as Abbot.'

Brother Burlop arrived with two pottery beakers of freshly brewed mint-and-comfrey tea. 'Just a liddle somethin' I made on the forge fire for ye. Be careful, Sister, it's hot. You'n the Father sip that. 'Twill wake ye up while you talk. Don't mind me, I'll just go about my chores.'

They thanked Burlop. Armel watched him strapping on his heavy coopering apron and trundling off with an empty cask. 'He's such a kind and caring creature! Isn't he, Father?'

Humble blew steam from his beaker and sipped gratefully. 'The best! Young Burlop's the son I never had. Now, what about our dream, Sister?'

They were interrupted by a thump against the door and muffled squeaks from the stairs outside. After another thump, the frowzy little head of Mimsie the mousebabe appeared around the door.

'Sitter H'Armil, that naughty Mudge bee's pullin' me tail!'

Mudge the molebabe could be heard behind her. 'Ho no, oi b'ain't! You'm a-tellin' tales abowt yurr tail, jus' to get oi in trubble!'

The door creaked open to reveal both Dibbuns, still in nightshirts, wrestling.

313

'Hoo! You'm pullen' moi nose! Lookit, marm, she'm turmentin' oi gurtly!'

Mimsie let out a piteous wail. 'Waaaaah! Mudge jus' stampid on me paw!'

Armel smiled apologetically at the Abbot. 'Sorry, Father. Our talk will have to wait until later.'

She hurried to the stairs and separated the tiny pair. 'Be still, both of you! What are you doing out of bed? It's nowhere near breakfast time yet! The morning bell hasn't even sounded and you're running around down here in your nighties. I can't abide naughty Dibbuns, nor can the Father Abbot!'

Tearfully, Mimsie pointed an accusing paw at Mudge. 'He woked me up an' hitted me wiv a pillow!'

The molebabe stuck out his small, fat stomach truculently. 'No oi diddent! You'm a gurt mowsey fibber!'

'Yis y'did!'

'No oi diddent!'

'Did!'

'Diddent!'

Armel raised her voice. 'Silence, both of you! Mudge, what did I tell you only yesterday about fighting with your friends?'

The molebabe growled out indignantly, 'You'm only telled oi not to foight wi' Perkle, marm. Ee diddent say ought about foightin' Mimsie!'

Armel wagged a paw severely at him. 'I meant all Dibbuns, not just Perkle.'

Mudge stared at the Sister pityingly, then threw up his paws. 'Then you'm should've said h'all. 'Ow bee's oi apposed t'know?'

The Abbot appeared, fully dressed. A broad smile was growing over his face as he grabbed both Dibbuns by their paws. 'Sister Armel, what do you say we take these two rogues up to breakfast? I'm sure Friar Glisum is up and about now. But we'll have to ask him nicely, because I don't think he serves early breakfast to naughty Dibbuns. Come on.'

All four retreated upstairs, chattering animatedly.

'Does h'Abbots bee's naughty, too, Sitter H'Armil?'

'Certainly not, Mimsie. You have to be good if you want to be Abbot. Isn't that right, Father?'

'It certainly is, Sister Armel. I was a good little Dibbun.'

'Hurr, no you'm wurrn't, zurr. Wunderin' Walt sayed you'm wurr a likkle villyun.'

'Oh, did he indeed? I'll have to have a word with Wandering Walt!'

'Oi'm goin' t'be naughty when oi'm h'Abbot!'

'Hmph, when you grow up we'll probably make you Abbey villain!'

'Hurrhurr, h'Abbey villyun. Oi loikes that gurtly, marm!'

Morning brought with it soft, grey skies and a fine drizzle of warm rain, which many Redwallers predicted would last through midnoon. There was plenty to do inside the Abbey; everybeast busied themselves with a multitude of chores. Sister Armel sat in the Infirmary with the Abbot and Sister Screeve, trying to figure out the meaning of Martin's cryptic message. Outside, Brother Demple tended to his vegetable patch and orchard. A true son of the soil, Demple was never bothered by rain. The stolid mouse made a hood, which went over his head and shoulders, from an old sack. He worked on alone, weeding between the drills of his salad crop.

The Abbey Gardener was totally unaware of any activity on top of the east wall. Rakkety Tam MacBurl had scaled a high elm, close to the wall in the outside woodlands. He raced along a broad branch which quivered up and down as he bounced upon it. With a tremendous bound he flung himself out into space. No other beast but Tam could have accomplished such a daring feat. His paws latched on to a battlement; there he clung a moment before leaping up and over, landing silently on the walkway. Drawing the small Sghian Dhu from his hat, the squirrel warrior cautiously descended the east wallsteps and quietly opened the wallgate. Leaving Skipper and the Long Patrol hares to follow him, Tam raced through the deserted, drizzle-cloaked grounds, heading for the hooded figure he had espied.

Hit from behind, Brother Demple went down like a sack of cabbages. The Borderer spun him over swiftly. Clamping a paw across Demple's mouth, he whispered urgently, 'Brother, I don't have time for idle chitchat, understand?'

Demple nodded, and Tam continued. 'Has the Abbey been attacked by vermin?' Eager for an answer, Tam released his paw from Demple's mouth.

The gardener licked his lips nervously. 'Aye, they actually got inside the grounds.'

The border squirrel's jaw tightened. 'Where are they now, inside?'

Brother Demple sat up. 'No, they were all slain. We buried them out on the flatlands.'

Skipper and the hares gathered around him.

'I say, good show, wot!'

'Indeed, old lad, at least the chaps we left behind didn't spend all their time jolly well feastin' an' nappin' whilst we were dashin' round the blinkin' woodlands.'

Brother Demple wiped drizzle from his eyes. 'We helped the hares. In fact, we Redwallers actually took out quite a few of the vermin. How did you lot get on?'

Skipper helped Demple up. 'Oh, we did our bit, mate, but let's get in out of this rain. We can swap yarns over a good meal. Yore dealin' with 'ungry beasts here!'

Everybeast came rushing into Great Hall to meet the returning creatures. Friar Glisum threw up his paws in alarm, squeaking at his helpers.

'Stoke up the oven fires, load up the ovens! We need lots of fresh bread! Extra salad, cheeses, pasties, mushroom an' cauliflower soup, a crumble – no, six large rhubarb'-n'blackberry crumbles, with sweet arrowroot sauce! Er, er, scones, extra batches of hot scones, with plum'n'damson preserve! Hurry 'em along, Murly. These famine-faced hares need feeding!'

The mole hitched up her pinafore. 'Gurt seasons, get ee frum under moi paws, you'm Dibbuns. We'm got lots o' vikklin' t'be dun!'

Abbot Humble embraced Tam fondly. 'Welcome back to Redwall Abbey, my friend. Welcome!'

'Mister MacBurl, thank goodness you're safe and well!' Tam found himself gazing over the Abbot's shoulder into the Sister's gentle brown eyes.

He winked at her roguishly. 'I would've torn down the Abbey walls t'be back here with you, Sister!'

She cast her eyes down, smiling. 'Is that a compliment or a threat, Tam?'

Releasing himself from Humble's grip, Tam bowed gallantly. 'Beauty is to be complimented, not threatened, Armel. See, I kept my promise – I brought back the sword.'

She stayed his paw as he grasped Martin's blade. 'Please, keep it by you, Tam. I'll explain later, but the Abbot and I think you'll have need of it.'

The border warrior looked puzzled. 'But why?'

Skipper was whirling his niece, Brookflow, round the floor. They both collided with Tam and Armel, almost knocking them over.

The ottermaid hooted with laughter. 'Whoohoohoooo! Never mind that now. Give the pretty Sister a kiss. She's done nothin' but mope since you went away!'

Armel glared reprovingly at her friend. 'Really, Brooky!'

The hares had begun ragging their comrades good-naturedly. The ones who had remained at Redwall were singing.

'I can't believe me eyes, what a horrible surprise,
yore as welcome as a famine at the door.
Look what the wind blew in, all bedraggled, wet'n'thin,
an' look at the mess yore makin' on the floor!

Come sit down by the fire, if eatin's your desire,
there's not a bit o' scoff nowhere about.
You missed breakfast, lunch'n'tea, an' I'll tell ye can-
didly,
you'll have to call again when we are out!'

Sergeant Wonwill's voice cut across the banter. 'Nah then, you dreadful lot, fall in line an' get down to Cavern 'ole. Clean up an' get out o' those rags! Cartwill, Folderon, Flummerty . . . issue 'em with their proper regimental tunics. On the double now!'

Owing to the efficiency of Redwall's kitchens, lunch was prepared and laid out before midday. Lancejack Wilderry had brought Captain Fortindom up-to-date on the losses they had sustained, whilst the sergeant broke the news about Brigadier Crumshaw to the returning hares. But nobeast could give Tam any information about the whereabouts of his friend Doogy.

Normally Tam never worried too much about his Highland friend. He and Doogy had been separated many times in the past. However, he could not help feeling a growing anxiety about Doogy. This was confirmed as he sat down at table with Armel. She recited Martin's words to him.

'Behold two swords and a banner,
watch out for the Walking Stone.
The brother is gone, 'tis the warrior
who must face the Savage alone.'

The Borderer looked grim. 'So, is that why you told me to hold on to Martin's sword?'

He turned to Skipper. 'Do you think that Gulo is still alive, Skip? Maybe the waterfall didn't kill him.'

The otter chieftain looked up from a bowl of shrimp'-n'hotroot soup, which Friar Glisum had made specially for him. 'Well, accordin' to ole Log a Log Togey, nobeast could ride over those falls on a log an' live. A Log a Log of the

318

Guosim knows wot he's talkin' about when it comes to rivers'n'streams, mate. But who can tell? That Gulo ain't nobeast like we've ever seen!'

The homecoming meal was not the jolly event Abbot Humble had hoped it would be. There was an undercurrent of sadness over lost comrades; even the Long Patrol hares seemed to lack their usual gaiety, though Hitheryon Jem noted they had lost none of their ravenous appetites.

'Hmm, they ain't jokin' an' singin' much, but those buckoes can certainly tuck the rations away. Eh, Tam?'

The warrior chuckled. ' Aye, I'm a wee bit peckish myself.'

Sister Armel passed him a hot leek and mushroom pastie. 'No doubt you've been missing our cooking.'

Tam tackled the pastie appreciatively. 'I wonder some of you Redwallers aren't as fat as barrels, eating food as delicious as this. By the way, Armel, I don't see our goshawk Tergen around. Is he still with you?'

Armel topped up a tankard with October Ale for Tam. 'Don't mention that bird to me. He's become very sulky and bad-tempered because his wing hasn't healed yet. I think he also misses the Brigadier a lot, they were such close friends. I worry about Tergen, he's taken to living in the attics above the dormitories, and he won't talk to anybeast. We never see him at meals – I think he eats very little. He never comes to the infirmary. I think Tergen is feeling forlorn.'

Wandering Walt dug his spoon into a crumble and served himself a hefty portion. 'Hurr, that ain't apprisin', missy. Ee burd were used to flyen' an' huntin' all 'is loife, b'aint gudd t'be ee hawk wi' a broked wing – no, marm!'

Desultory talk went back and forth over the lunch. Outside the drizzling rain continued for longer than the Redwallers had predicted. After eating, some of the hares retired to the dormitories, while others went down to Cavern Hole to nap the dull noontide away.

Whilst Sister Armel tended to the Dibbuns, Tam went outside. He roamed the walltops, peering into the misty veils of drizzle in the hope that he would spy the short, sturdy figure of Doogy Plumm returning to Redwall Abbey. But there was no sign of his Highland friend.

35

Fortune, they say, favours the valiant – though not always, for Dame Fortune is a fickle lady. Sometimes she is quite impartial to the goings-on of those in her charge and gives her favours to evil creatures.

Gulo the Savage was alive!

When the huge fallen willow tree shot off wildly down the rapids with its cargo of vermin, it was spinning about from roots to foliage, whirling uncontrollably on the racing current. On and on it careered, revolving crazily. The vermin clung on with fang, tail and claw, their screeches and screams drowned out by the ever-increasing roar of the approaching waterfall. Gulo lodged himself between the roots, enveloped in boiling white spume as he grasped the limber taproots fiercely. Just ahead of them he spied the dead end of the rapids, where the maddened waters were transformed into a cataclysmic torrent. A fearful howl ripped from his mouth as the tree went round and round like a top, headed for destruction.

Whuuuump! Suddenly he was almost dislodged from his perch. The treetrunk had temporarily stuck lengthways across the towering rocks, right on the brink of the cascading deluge! Gulo swayed perilously but held on to the roots, whilst all along the length of the trunk vermin were knocked loose by the shock of the collision.

Yeeeeeaaaaaarrrgh! Ermine and white foxes hurtled off into mid-air. Down, down, down they plunged into the seething curtain of waterspray. Gulo gritted his fangs, seeking a firmer pawhold. The willow creaked and groaned as it moved, the crashing torrent slowly pushing it forward. An ermine close to the wolverine stretched out his paw for help. He vanished with a wail of despair as he grasped his leader's footpaw, only to have Gulo kick him off angrily.

Self-preservation was uppermost in Gulo's mind – he had to act swiftly or die. With a mighty bound he flung himself from the spreading roots, landing awkwardly on a crag that protruded from the left bank. Sliding over on to a slippery ledge, the beast watched the willow being swept further ahead.

Gulo bellowed at the small group of vermin closest to the roots, 'Jump, fools! Jump or be killed, now!'

In a blind panic, the vermin released their holds on the log and came leaping and stumbling along it. Only eight made the rocks. The others, who had still been nerving themselves for the leap, met their demise when the furious current pushed the willow over the brink and off into the awful void. The survivors lay on the wet, moss-covered ledge, wide-eyed with shock and speechless with terror.

Gulo broke through their fear with a harsh command. 'Follow me, or I'll see ye follow them!'

Knowing that the wolverine never made empty threats, they scrabbled along the slippery ledge in his wake.

By early evening they made the top of the rocky canyon and tumbled exhausted on to firm ground. There Gulo the Savage, and what was left of his army, fell dripping to the woodland floor amid a welter of streamwater and slathering sweat. No fires were lighted, no food searched for. Sobbing with weariness, they collapsed into deep sleep, punctuated throughout the night by whimpers and wails as they dreamt of being hurled into endless depths and smashed to pieces on the rocks below. The thunderous boom of the mighty falls echoed up through the rocky canyon to reinforce the stark terror of their nightmares.

The morning was half gone when Gulo blinked his eyes and stirred. Rising, he kicked his small band into wakefulness, ordering two to kindle fire and four others to forage for food. The two remaining – a scrawny female ermine called Duge, and a male white fox named Herag – stood frozen, awaiting Gulo's commands.

He nodded to the ermine. 'Climb yon tall fir tree and tell me what ye can see.'

The wolverine stared at the fox, who shifted uncomfortably. 'Thou art my Captain now. Have ye a name?'

The fox gulped out, 'Herag, Mighty One.'

Gulo spoke almost to himself as Herag stood to stiff attention. 'We will go to the Redwall place when we have eaten.'

Leaving the new captain staring after him, Gulo wandered off amid the trees, talking to himself aloud. 'It does not finish here. Askor, my brother, I will find thee. Mayhap my captains already have. Doubtless they have conquered the Redwall place an' have thee bound in some cellar, awaiting my arrival. Hahaha, 'twill be so, I know!'

A white fox came into the camp carrying firewood. He began stacking it and setting steel to tinder over some dry moss.

Herag crouched down beside him, whispering, 'Listen, can ye hear Gulo? Methinks his brain has snapped! He talks with himself and laughs like a madbeast!'

The other fox, far older than Herag, murmured flatly, 'Have ye only just realized that? I served under both brothers, aye, and the father. They were all three crazed, though methinks Gulo is the maddest of the lot, an' the most dangerous. Keep thy mouth shut and avoid his eyes, ye might live longer that way. Now leave me to my work.'

Herag stayed crouching beside the elder. 'This is a fine

warm land of plenty Gulo has brought us to, though we have had nought but strife an' hardship whilst we've been here. Methinks the bodies of our comrades are scattered all across these fair lands.'

The old fox could sense which way Herag's conversation was going. He watched the spiral of blue smoke transformed into a pale tongue of flame as he breathed on it gently. He looked around, checking that Gulo was not within earshot.

'Heed me now, young 'un. What I say may save thee from an awful death. We are bound to Gulo the Savage, for better or worse. We serve him, not through love or loyalty, but through fear. Put any thoughts from thy mind about deserting. Gulo would find ye, an' ye would scream for death ere he was done with ye. Now begone, an' speak no more to me of foolish ideas.'

The ermine Duge climbed down from her perch in the tall fir. She approached Gulo, who appeared to be in conversation with a bed of ferns. He was smiling slyly and nodding his head.

'Go tell thy master that I, too, am a son of Dramz. But 'tis I who rules the lands of ice and snow. I, Gulo the Savage, the one who slew the Great Dramz. Say to Askor my brother that I am coming, an' I will devour his heart!'

He whirled suddenly, glaring at Duge. 'Did Askor send ye to spy on me?'

The ermine backed off, avoiding her master's insane glare. 'Mighty One, ye told me to climb a tree an' scout the land.'

Gulo looked at her as if suddenly seeing her anew. 'I told ye to do that?'

Duge nodded. 'Aye, sire, I have come to report what I saw.'

Gulo placed a claw to his lips, his mad eyes darting furtively to and fro. 'Ssshhh! Not here, they will hear ye. Come.'

The fire was burning well. Beside it lay a woodcock,

which the foragers had slain with stones as it sat on its nest. There was a clutch of eggs from the nest, plus some edible roots, a small heap of half-ripe pears and a few berries they had gathered. Everybeast stood back as Gulo led Duge to the fire. He crouched by the flames, pulling the ermine down close to him.

Seemingly oblivious of the others, the wolverine whispered to Duge, 'Now speak softly. What did ye see?'

Absentmindedly, Gulo grabbed the dead bird and began eating it raw, spitting out feathers as he placed his ear close to the ermine's mouth. Feathers landed on Duge's nose as Gulo's fearsome mouth, a hair'sbreadth from her own, crunched through flesh and bone.

The terrified ermine tried to control her voice. 'Mighty One, over to the north I saw a broadstream. It flowed down this way to join the waters we travelled yesterday. It flows down from the northeast through the woodlands.'

She fell silent, watching Gulo apprehensively as he dug a feather from between his fangs before responding. 'Is that all there was?'

Duge nodded, her head bobbing nervously. Gulo ripped another mouthful from the bird. Ignoring the ermine, he stood up, dropping the remnants of the woodcock carelessly into the fire as he strode off, his eyes darting hither and thither at the trees in front of him.

'Tell my Captain to bring the others. We go to the Redwall place.'

Herag watched as he walked off into the woodlands. Duge looked perplexed. 'Does he mean we go now?'

Herag shook his head. 'But we have not yet eaten.'

The older fox pulled the remnants of the bird from the fire and extinguished the burning feathers. He grabbed a pear and set off hastily after Gulo, cautioning the others, 'If Gulo says go, then we go. I'll do my eating on the march!'

The other vermin knew it was useless to protest. Shoving against one another, they seized the remaining food and hurried after the old fox.

Morning had ended when they reached the banks of the broadstream. The pace had been furious, and the vermin were panting for breath. Sometimes they had to run to keep up with Gulo; other times they went at a swift jog as he trotted in front of them, wagging his paw at rocky outcrops and speaking to them as though they were living creatures.

'Tell him he cannot hide from me, the Walking Stone is mine by right. Thy days are numbered, brother!'

Without warning, Gulo halted on the streambank and smiled. ' 'Tis pleasant here, do ye not think?'

The old fox nodded. 'Aye, pleasant, Lord.'

The wolverine lay down amid the moss on the sunny bank where he curled up and promptly went to sleep.

The others watched him in puzzlement. The old fox shrugged, his face expressively silent as he beckoned them to follow their leader's example. With a collective sigh of relief, the weary vermin settled down to sleep.

Serene summer afternoon pervaded the area – it was, as Gulo had remarked, pleasant. Over the smooth-running broadstream, dragonflies patrolled on iridescent wings. Mayflies basked on rush stalks, whilst yellow brimstone and swallowtail moths grazed among the late-flowering hawthorns. Osiers spread their variegated shade over the bankmoss, creating dappled patterns when stirred by the warm, gentle breeze. A kingfisher swooped over the water, glinting like a bejewelled brooch. The cooing of distant woodpigeons blended with small birdsong in the background. The old fox slept on, dismissing the thought of Gulo actually having described the scene as pleasant. The wolverine had never commented on nature's beauties, but his mind was crazed, so the old fox absolved him from this temporary lapse.

Noon shadows were lengthening when the vermin arose. Gulo was already awake and seemed in good humour. He sat watching the head of Herag drifting away on the broad-stream current.

Without turning, the wolverine spoke to his remaining followers, the usual shouting and snarling absent in his tone. 'I knew that one was going to run, so I stayed awake and watched him until he made one foolish move.'

He turned to Duge, explaining almost apologetically, 'Gulo has to make examples for his warriors to follow, do ye not think?'

Totally robbed of words, the ermine could only nod.

As Gulo surveyed his remaining seven followers, his eyes glittered evilly. He rose and continued the march, calling to them, 'Now that we are rested, we will carry on through the night until dawn. Methinks we will soon sight the Redwall place.'

Behind them the broadstream placidly flowed on into evening, the bank where they had camped restored to its former serenity, as though murder had never occurred there. A pleasant place.

The old fox tramped on through the long night hours. Like the rest, he was afraid not to keep up or to fall behind through tiredness. Truly Gulo was mad! Who in his right mind would slay a warrior from a force so severely diminished? But now nobeast would even think of deserting. The old fox bit down hard on his lip to keep himself awake as he stumbled onward, reflecting. It was a salutary lesson, enforced by a beast made cunning by madness.

36

It was late afternoon on the day following the continuous drizzle. During the night, the rain had ceased altogether. Dawn rose brilliantly over a small camp in southeast Mossflower. Doogy Plumm, Yoofus Lightpaw and his wife, Didjety, together with the little tortoise Rockbottom, had spent a passably comfortable night. In a worn old sandstone formation they had come across amidst the trees, they had made a small shelter by laying boughs and ferns over an undercut ledge. Bright sunlight reflected in each dewdrop hanging from bush and bough. Somewhere nearby, two finches were cheeping, and a mistle thrush warbling. Rising sunrays shafted through the foliage.

But it was not the plop of dewdrops or the charming birdsong which wakened the sturdy Highlander – it was Yoofus. Unable to sleep, and in an effort to stir his wife into providing breakfast from the sack which now served as her pillow, the water vole began singing and tapping a footpaw against the great drum. *Boom baboom babumpitty bumpetty boom!*

'Sure there was an ould vole called Dumplety Tim,
now wasn't he just the grand feller.
He wore britches of scarlet, a scarf snowy white,

an' a tailcoat with buttons of yeller.
He could dance a fine jig in his high-buckled boots,
he could quaff off a flagon of scrumpy,
he wore a great feather of green in his hat,
an' his stummick was round, fat an' lumpy.

Ah rumplety bumplety Dumplety Tim,
he could charm all the ladies around.
He was merry'n'cheery an' never grew weary,
the smile on his face never frowned.
Such a nice darlin' creature in every fine feature,
you'd hear any ould biddy remark,
'He's oh so polite an' from mornin' 'til night,
he can sing like a silver-tongued lark.'

Ah rumplety bumplety dumplety . . . Yowwwccch!'

Yoofus was knocked sideways as the loaded foodsack
clouted him over the head. Didjety, who had thrown it,
stood over him, paws akimbo.

'Now will ye hush that rambunctious din! Yore fright-
enin' all the frogs in the neighbourhood with that racket!'

Yoofus massaged his ear ruefully. 'But I thought ye were
fond of me singin'!'

Doogy unwrapped the cloak from around his head.
'Singin' ye call it? Och, 'tis more like somebeast killin' a
duck with a mallet! Thief is the right title for ye. Ah've
been robbed o' mah sleep with all that drumbangin' an'
caterwaulin'!'

The incorrigible Yoofus gave him a wink and a grin. He
began rummaging in the foodsack. 'Ah, but Mister Plumm,
me ould darlin', ye wouldn't want to be sleepin' such a
sunny mornin' away now, would ye? Sure a day like this
gives a beastie like meself a roarin' appetite. Let's see wot
we've got fer brekkist.'

Didjety snatched the foodsack from him. 'I'm in charge of
the rations around here! Stir yore stumps now, an' find me
some firewood.'

Thrusting her head into the sack, the volewife investigated its contents, then called to her husband, 'Don't bother yoreself with the firewood. There's nothin' in here but a few crusts an' me cookin' pan an' kettle.'

The volethief's jaw dropped. 'Ye mean t'tell me we're out o' vittles?'

Didjety's paws poked through a big hole in the bottom of the sack. 'Indeed we are, an' here's the reason why!'

Her husband's normally cheerful face was the picture of misery. 'We'll starve t'death completely, so we will!'

The volewife glared at Doogy and Yoofus. 'All the more reason for you two witless wanderers to find the Abbey o' Redwall then, isn't it?'

Yoofus pointed the paw at Doogy. ' 'Twas him that got us lost, not me!'

The Highlander defended himself indignantly. 'Och, ye wee fibber! Who was it wanted us tae turn left at that three-topped oak last night, instead o' right as I suggested, eh?'

Yoofus looked shocked. 'Startin' that, are we? Then who suggested we turn west by the stream yesterday mornin'? Tell me that, ye great fluffy-tailed fraud!'

He dodged behind the drum as Doogy came after him angrily. 'Ah never said west. Ah was all for carryin' on north!'

Yoofus hooted. 'North? Sure ye wouldn't know north from the nutnose on yore face. I was the one who said to go north. I may be a thief, but I ain't a liar like some I could mention!'

Doogy was outraged. 'Who are ye callin' a liar? Ah'll punch yore fat head intae the middle o' next season – aye, an' send yore fat wee bottom after it!'

Booooooommmm! Didjety struck the drum hard with her cooking pan. 'Silence, the pair of ye! This is gettin' us nowhere. Any more arguin' an' I'll settle it with this pan over both yore thick skulls, d'ye hear me?'

They both sulked about like two Dibbuns being sent to bed.

330

'Och, 'twas yore husband that started it, marm!'

'Ooh, did ye hear that, Didjety? He's tryin t'put the blame on me now!'

'Aye, well that's where the blame belongs, mah friend.'

'Oh no it doesn't!'

'Och yes it does!'

Bonk! Bonk! Didjety once again wielded the pan as Yoofus and Doogy both stood, rubbing their heads. 'I warned ye! Now let's pack up an' get goin'. I'll lead the way. You two follow, I'll find Redwall for ye.'

Yoofus touched his head gingerly. 'But, me luv, ye've never been to Redwall Abbey afore!'

The volewife squared her shoulders decisively. 'Maybe not, but I can't make much more of a mess findin' it than you two bright sparks. Come on, quick march!'

They crawled out of the little shelter, and Doogy shrugged. 'Quick march sure enough, marm, but which way?'

Didjety placed her pan on the ground and spun it. She nodded at the direction the panhandle was pointing. 'This way!'

Then she looked at Rockbottom. The little tortoise nodded his agreement.

Though they had to ford a shallow stream and skirt some patches of marshland, the going was fairly smooth. Wherever possible, the volewife kept to what looked like obvious paths betwixt the tall trees. Doogy followed behind her, rolling the great drum along, whilst Yoofus trudged in the rear.

The volethief began grumbling and muttering to the tortoise, who was strapped to his back. 'Sure I thought you'd have taken my side o' things back there agin those two, but ye never supported me cause by a nod or a wink, did ye? Now look where it's got us! We'll wind up at the back of noplace like this. I'm tellin' ye, me liddle stony friend, my Didjety's a darlin' creature, but she couldn't

331

find the floor if she fell on it. See, I told ye, she's had to halt.'

Yoofus approached his wife triumphantly, nodding and smirking. 'Sure, an' why've ye stopped, me ould duckodill? Lost, are ye?'

Didjety looked up from the watercress she was gathering from the side of a tiny brook. 'Does it look like I'm lost, ye great omardorm? Go an' gather some firewood an' I'll make us somethin' to eat. Mister Plumm, will you gather those wild mushrooms an' pick some of that ransom? Not too much, though, it can taste a bit strong in a soup.'

Upon the mention of food, Yoofus hurriedly began gathering dead twigs and dried grass. 'Soup! Will ye lissen to her? Mister Plumm, sir, don't ye wish ye had a grand liddle wife like me?'

When it came to cooking, the volewife certainly knew what she was doing. Toasting the crusts of oatcake over the fire, she crumbled them into her cooking pan, which she had filled half full with brookwater. Borrowing Doogy's dirk, she chopped her ingredients into the pan – a touch of the wild garlic known as ransom, a few dozen of the white mushrooms, lots of watercress, some dandelion roots, charlock pods, wild radish, hedge mustard, sweet woodruff petals and a good pinch of the rock salt which she always carried in her apron pocket. Yoofus and Doogy sat by the brook, sniffing appreciatively at the savoury aroma emanating from the bubbling pan over the fire.

The Highlander winked at the volethief as he fashioned some scoops from a piece of bark. 'Yore a braw lucky beast, mah friend, havin' a wee wifey who can make a meal out o' nothin'. That soup smells bonny!'

Yoofus smiled. 'An' she can sing too. Lissen!'

The Highlander pushed him playfully. 'Aye, an' ah ken she sings far better than ye do!'

Didjety stirred away at the thickening soup, singing in a clear, sweet tone.

'Now me mammy once said, don't ye live all alone,
keep yore bits an' small pieces together,
for one day you'll need them to furnish yore home,
'neath a roof warm an' safe from the weather.

For of all the fine places a heart's ever known,
sure there's none that I love like me dear little home.

Then go find ye someone who will care for ye good,
to sit quiet by yore side at the fire,
an' if he treats ye decent as you hoped he would,
you'll have all that your heart can desire.

For of all the fine places a heart's ever known,
sure there's none that I love like me dear little home.

Let the wind howl outside an' the rain batter down,
with the hearth snug an' cosy indoors,
no Queen in a palace who wears a gold crown,
knows a life full and happy as yours.

For of all the fine places a heart's ever known,
sure there's none that I love like me dear little home.'

Yoofus smiled fondly. 'How would ye like a grand sweet
wife like that now, Doogy Plumm?'

The Highlander rubbed his head thoughtfully. 'Aye, she
could slay all mah enemies by beltin' 'em o'er their skulls
wi' that cookpan o' hers.'

The soup was thick and delicious. They shared it equally,
with a small portion set aside to cool for Rockbottom.

Doogy watched the little creature as Didjety fed him from
a folded dockleaf. 'D'ye reckon he'll ever talk one day?'

The volewife giggled. 'Sure if he ever does, 'twill be only
to ask wot's for dessert! Won't it, me little darlin'?'

The tortoise seemed to smile and nod his head. The Highlander was still curious about Rockbottom, though Yoofus
and Didjety did not seem bothered at all.

Doogy stroked the little fellow's head with his paw, enquiring further, 'Ah wonder, has he ever ventured out o' yon shell?'

The volethief replied, straight-faced, 'He doesn't like anybeast seein' him wearin' only his nightie. I saw him once, but he ran back into the shell.'

Doogy looked as if he believed Yoofus for a moment, then realized the water vole was joshing him. 'Ye wee fibber!'

Yoofus looked innocent. 'No, I'm not!'

Doogy retorted, 'An' I say ye are!'

Didjety raised the empty cooking pan. 'Here now, let's have no more of that. Let's be on our way.'

They continued the journey, Yoofus and Doogy lagging behind slightly, whispering to each other.

The Highlander shook his head. 'Ah wonder if Tam an' the Patrol made it back tae the Abbey.'

Yoofus watched his wife's back as she plodded on with dogged determination. 'Sure we'll never know, mate. We'll be wanderin' this land until we've both got long, grey beards an' walkin' sticks.'

Doogy nodded agreement; his confidence in their pathfinder was at a very low ebb. 'Ah thought when we set out this mornin' that yore wee wifey had some idea o' the route tae go.'

Yoofus hitched Rockbottom up in his harness. 'Mark my words, ould Doogy Plumm, we're well lost. I don't know wot possessed me t'let her lead the way. My Didjety's never been much further than her own doorstep.'

A hill appeared ahead of them. Didjety hurried forward, ascending the steep slope. Yoofus stared up at her before commenting, 'Didn't we go up this hill yesterday? The pore creature's demented, she's dashin' about like a madbeast now. Look!'

The volewife had reached the hilltop. She was dancing up and down, pointing frantically and shouting, 'There it is! Redwaaaaaalllll!'

After a hasty scramble, Yoofus and Doogy joined her on

the summit. The Highlander shaded a paw over his eyes. There in the distance he could see the south side of the Abbey.

The volethief cut a jig. Grabbing his wife, he hugged and kissed her, crying jubilantly, 'Hahahaha! I knew ye'd find it, me own darlin' sugarplum! Ye'd take us t'Redwall ye said, an' sure enough ye did! Wasn't I just sayin' to Doogy here, if'n anybeast can get us to that Abbey, then my Didjety's the one t'do it?'

Doogy sat down upon the great drum, nodding readily. He did not have the heart to speak the truth. 'Och, he's had nothin' but the bonniest things tae say about ye, marm. An' who am I tae doubt yore husband's word?'

The Highlander looked at Rockbottom, who shook his little head and retreated into his shell.

Didjety was slightly flustered by the lavish praise being heaped upon her. But, being the practical volewife, she was quick to recover. 'I thank ye both for yore faith in me. Now, we'd best get marchin'. Sure we don't want t'be late for supper tonight.'

With renewed vigour, they stepped out towards their goal. The great drum trundled easily alongside Doogy, who controlled it like a hoop, with a stout twig. To keep their spirits up he sang an old marching song he recalled from his Highland days.

'Set mah plate an' mah tankard on the table,
an' watch out for me comin' home tonight.
Keep mah supper in the oven if yore able,
an' in the window place a welcome light.

Tramp tramp tramp! Hear what the Sergeant said,
tonight ah'll be sleepin' in mah own wee bed!

No more layin' 'neath the stars in the heather,
no more eatin' what the greasy cook has burned,
no more toilin' through the cold'n'rainy weather,
once tae mah bonny home ah have returned.

Tramp tramp tramp! Hear what the Sergeant said,
tonight ah'll be sleepin' in mah own wee bed!'

On the 'tramp tramp' bits, Doogy hit the drum with his twig. He could not recall any more of the verses, so he sang it twice again, with Yoofus and Didjety joining in on the chorus with gusto. After a while, Yoofus began eyeing the drum. Doogy could tell he was planning to steal it – by one means or the other.

The volethief grinned cheerily at him. 'Ah, sure ye must be gettin' tired an' weary of luggin' an' pushin' that useless ould drum along. Why don't ye let me take charge of the clumsy thing for a bit?'

Doogy left Yoofus in no doubt that he was on to him. 'Ah'll thank ye tae keep yore thievin' eyes off'n this drum. Ye ken 'tis the property o' Redwall Abbey, an' that's where I aim tae deliver it, all in good order. As tae what becomes o' yore goodwife's wee pet Rockbottom, well, the Abbot should be the one tae decide that!'

Didjety looked quite concerned. 'But I couldn't be without dear liddle Rockbottom, he's me own darlin' pet. D'ye think the Abbot will want to keep him, Mister Plumm?' She sobbed visibly and wiped her eyes upon her pinafore.

Doogy patted the volewife's paw comfortingly. 'From wot ah've seen of Abbot Humble, he's a kindly auld beastie. He'd no steal yore pet from ye, marm. Ah'll have a word wi' him mahself.'

Didjety smiled gratefully. 'My thanks to ye, Mister Plumm. Yore a darlin', soft-hearted creature yoreself, to think of me the way ye do.'

Doogy's bushy tail rose in an arc over his head and dropped down to cover his face, a sure sign of embarrassment in any squirrel. 'Och, away with ye, Mrs Lightpaw. Ah only do it cos ah'm so powerful fond o' yore sausage rolls!'

*

The long day was drawing to a pleasant close as the weary travellers emerged from South Mossflower woodlands. Across the grassy commonland in front of them, Redwall Abbey rose majestically, all dusty pink and shadowed by the day's last sunlight. The water voles were walking slightly in front of Doogy, who was still rolling the drum along.

As a born warrior, Doogy had always possessed an inbred sense of danger. As they broke through the trees on to the grassland, the squirrel warrior's neck fur began prickling. The crack of paw upon twig caused him to whirl around, grabbing at his claymore hilt. He saw six vermin stalking through the undergrowth in an attempt to encircle him and his two friends, with Gulo the Savage at their centre.

The Highlander drew his claymore, yelling to the voles, 'Run for it, mates. Get intae the Abbey, now!'

Yoofus and Didjety paused a moment, looking puzzled. Then they turned and saw the vermin.

Doogy launched himself at the enemy, roaring, 'Run! Run! Ye can do no good here! Hawaaaaay the Braw!'

Yoofus grabbed his wife and hustled her wildly along. One of the vermin broke away from the rest, attempting to cut the water voles off. Doogy whirled, slaying him with a sweep of his claymore and as he did so, the Highlander's back was turned from the vermin for but a moment. That was all the time Gulo the Savage needed: he quickly grabbed a hefty rock and threw it at the Highlander. The missile made a clunking sound as it bounced off the back of Doogy's head. He slumped to the ground, unconscious.

Hauling his wife along, Yoofus ran as he had never run before. Neither of the voles looked back as they sped across the commonland toward the south wallgate.

With Rockbottom bouncing around in his backsling, the volethief threw himself at the wicker gate, panting and roaring, 'Attack! Attack! For the love o' mercy, open the gate!'

Didjety joined him, wailing piteously, 'Ah sure we'll be completely destroyed if y'don't let us in! Help! Heeeeelp!'

Fortunately, Ulba molewife was taking a group of Dibbuns for an evening stroll around the Abbey pond before packing them off to their beds. Brookflow the ottermaid accompanied them, lest any should fall into the water, a fairly common occurrence when Abbeybabes and ponds come into contact. The little party was skirting the south edge of the water when they heard the voles' impassioned cries.

Brookflow acted promptly, shouting out a course of action. 'Get the little 'uns back to the Abbey, Ulba. I'll see what's goin' on out there. Send some help, just in case!'

The molewife had her paws full trying to keep the Dibbuns from following the ottermaid. 'You'm h'infants cumm back yurr with oi. Miz Brooky, be ee vurry careful naow!'

No sooner had Brooky shot the bolts back and cracked open the wicker gate than she spied the voles, dancing up and down in agitation.

'Mister Lightpaw, it's you! What's goin' on out there?'

Yoofus shoved the door fully open and dashed inside, pulling Didjety along behind him. He wiped a paw across his brow. 'Sure, an' who did ye think it was, a frog on a frolic? Quick, bar that gate! 'Tis teemin' wid vermin out there!'

Before there was time for further discussion, Tam, Skipper and the Long Patrol hares came charging along.

Yoofus relaxed, quickly regaining his composure now that the danger was past. 'Well now, Mister MacBurl, aren't ye the grand ould sight fer me weary eyes! Oh, I don't think ye've met me darlin' wife. Say hello t'the good creatures, Didjety!'

Tam grabbed the volethief's paw roughly. 'Where's Doogy Plumm, an' what's goin' on here? Speak!'

338

Yoofus winced. 'Ouch! Leave off crushin' me paw t'bits an' I'll tell ye!'

Tam relaxed his grip. 'Hurry up then, an' make it fast!'

The vermin who had been chasing the voles were about halfway across the commonland when Yoofus and Didjety were admitted to the Abbey and the door slammed shut. Gulo looked down at Doogy's senseless form. He eyed the great drum, an idea forming in his mind. Signalling the vermin to return, he waited on them, nodding with satisfaction.

The wolverine issued orders. 'Get ye this captive an' yon drum back into the woodlands. Move sharp now, I have a plan!'

37

Because of the failing daylight, Sergeant Wonwill suggested that they take the water voles indoors for questioning. In Great Hall there was much curiosity about the object strapped to Yoofus's back.

Abbot Humble ventured to touch the hard shell. 'What is this thing, Mister Lightpaw?'

Didjety unfastened the strapping and placed her pet upon the floor. 'Why, that's me darlin' liddle Rockbottom!'

A gasp of surprise went up as the creature poked out his head and legs. He began crawling towards a group of Dibbuns. Squeaking and squealing, they leapt back.

Foremole Bruffy scratched his snout, expressing wonder at the sight. 'Burr, oi never see'd 'owt loike that in moi loife, no zurr!'

Sister Armel knelt down by Rockbottom. He craned his head forward so she could scratch gently under his chin. The Sister obliged, smiling. 'Friends, meet the Walking Stone!'

Recognition dawned in Humble's eyes. 'Of course, the Walking Stone! What a funny little fellow he is. Where did you find him, marm?'

Yoofus swelled his chest out proudly. 'Sure, 'twas meself that found him, Father.'

Sister Armel interrupted Yoofus. 'Wait, don't tell me! You found this creature not far from a lake. It came out of a hole at the foot of an old sycamore, all thick and overgrown with ivy leaves. Am I right, Mister Lightpaw?'

For the first time he could remember, Yoofus was lost for words. He could only stammer, 'Wha . . . Who . . . How?'

Sister Screeve took from her sleeve the copy of the poem which she habitually carried around with her and began reading.

'Where the sun falls from the sky,
and dances at a pebble's drop,
where little leaves slay big leaves,
where wood meets earth I stop.
Safe from the savage son of Dramz,
here the secret lies alone,
the symbol of all power, the mighty Walking Stone.'

Yoofus stared at the Sister and the Recorder. 'How did ye know all that?'

For the sake of manners, Tam had not cut in on Armel and Screeve, but he could hold his impatience no longer. 'Mrs Lightpaw, marm, I'm sure ye can explain all about yore pet to everybeast, but right now I must speak to yore husband on a matter of great importance.'

He nodded towards Cavern Hole. 'Down there, Yoofus, now! Skipper, Cap'n Fortindom, Sergeant Wonwill, I'll need you too.'

The volethief was slightly put out by the fact that he had not eaten in a while, and he wasted no time in telling them so. 'Ah, 'tis a sad thing t'be offered none of the famous Redwall hospitality, so 'tis. Decent vittles haven't passed me starvin' ould lips since I don't know when!'

Captain Fortindom eyed him sternly. 'Talk first, eat later, laddie buck, wot! You tell MacBurl what he jolly well wants t'know, then we'll feed ye!'

Yoofus stared around at the tough faces and shrugged.

'Ah well, here's wot happened. We were leavin' the wood-lands after many a hard ould day's march – meself, the missus an' Doogy. I was carryin' Rockbottom an' rollin' that drum along. 'Twas me who stole it from under the vermins' noses, y'know. Then suddenly, without a by yore leave, just as we made it out into the open, out charges a gang o' vermin!'

Skipper halted him with a gesture. 'A gang, ye say? How many is a gang?'

Lying, like thieving, was second nature to Yoofus. He squinted one eye and scratched his chin as if estimating. 'Oh, I'd say there was at least a score that I could see, an' the ould Gulo beast too. Sure that's one fierce-lookin' creature! Have ye not seen the claws'n'fangs on 'im?'

Tam cut in. 'Never mind how Gulo looked! Exactly how many fightin' beasts were with him? Think!'

Yoofus pursed his lips. 'Well, as I said, there was about a score, sure but I could hear lots of others, hidin' amid the trees they must've been. I can't give ye a number for certain. They was armed to the very teeth, though . . .'

Tam was pawing at his sword hilt. 'And Doogy, what about Doogy?'

The volethief nodded. 'Will ye give me a chance, I'm just gettin' t'that! Anyhow, like I said, out charges the vermin, an' I dealt with the nearest three right away. But I had me darlin' wife t'think of, so I sez to Doogy, "There's far too many of the villains, we'll have to cut an' run fer it. I'll see ye back at the Abbey." I'm sorry about the drum, I had to leave it. But lives are more valuable than some ould drum, now aren't they?'

Wonwill peered closely at the volethief. 'So you an' yore good lady wife ran for the h'Abbey, sah? All well an' good, but wot became of Mister Plumm, sah?'

Yoofus grinned disarmingly. 'Ho ho, I wouldn't be frettin' about Doogy, friend. Now there's a beast who can look after hisself, ye can rely on that!'

Tam's jaw tightened. 'We know that! But what became of him?'

The volethief shrugged. 'Sure, he went one way, an' me wife an' I went the other. That's the last I saw of him. Hah, I wouldn't be surprised if he's not out there now, knockin' at the gate t'come in. I wouldn't worry about him.'

Tam began making for the door. 'I don't like it. Doogy could be in real trouble out there!'

Skipper reached the door ahead of Tam and blocked it. 'Now hold on, mate. Let's think a bit afore we sails off with swords drawn. 'Tis dark out there now, an' we don't know their numbers.'

The Borderer challenged Skipper. 'Doogy Plumm has been my friend through thick'n'thin. I've got to go out there an' help him!'

Captain Fortindom placed himself alongside the otter chieftain. 'Listen t'reason, old chap. It may be a trap.'

Tam shook his head. 'A trap? In what way?'

The hare captain explained. 'Gulo might be doin' this to draw us out an' leave Redwall undefended. Who knows? Perhaps Mister Plumm is hidin', safe someplace, just waitin' for a chance to make a dash for the blinkin' Abbey.'

The sergeant backed up Fortindom's statement. 'Cap'n's right, sah. Best thing we can do is mount a full guard on the walls an' wait, h'at least 'til daylight, eh?'

Tam paced up and down, his paw gripping the hilt of Martin's sword. Then he gave in to the wisdom of his friends. 'Until daybreak, then – but only 'til then. I feel terrible, leavin' Doogy alone out there. I'll be watching from the south walltop if you need me.'

Yoofus patted his shoulder. 'Ah, don't go frettin' yoreself now. Doogy'll be fine, you'll see.'

The border warrior eyed him coldly. 'If anythin' has happened to my mate, an' you've been tellin' a pack o' lies, ye'll answer to me for it!'

*

The hares of the Long Patrol, together with all the able-bodied Redwallers, turned out on the walltops to watch for any sign of Doogy. Even Tergen forgot his depression and came down from the attics to stand on the ramparts.

Inside the Abbey, none of the Dibbuns would go up to bed. They all wanted to stay up and play with their new-found friend, the Walking Stone. To keep the peace, Didjety agreed to sleep in the dormitory with Rockbottom. All the Dibbuns trooped upstairs, following close behind the two.

Didjety allowed Mimsie and Perkle to carry the little tortoise between them. First, however, the volewife laid out specific instructions. 'Go careful now, an' don't drop him. An' don't feed him any more o' those candied chestnuts. He'll get a tummy ache.'

The questions and enquiries came thick and fast at her. She answered each one in turn.

'Do Rockbottims have baffs, missus?'

'Ah no, ye'd drown him by puttin' him in a bath.'

'Hah! Wish't I was a Rockbottim. Doos he come outta dat shell an' have a nightie?'

'Indeed he doesn't, an' don't you try to take him out!'

Abbot Humble chuckled as he watched them disappearing round a bend in the stairway. He turned to old Brother Gordale the Gatekeeper and Sister Armel.

'Poor Mrs Lightpaw! Imagine having to spend the night with our Dibbuns. What do you say we take some supper up to our friends on the walls?'

Burlop was in the kitchens. He wanted nothing more to do with vermin since the day he had slain one in battle. With his help, and that of some kitchen volunteers, they set about making some hot farls stuffed with different fillings – some savoury, others sweet.

Burlop brought up some cordials from his cellars and heated them. 'This should keep the life in 'em. Sometimes the nights can grow chilly up on those ramparts, with nought t'do but stand about.'

*

344

Tam was leaning against the corner of the southwest battlement when Armel approached him with food. He had been peering out into the night and did not hear her come. Startled, the border squirrel turned suddenly.

The Infirmary Sister apologized. 'Sorry, Tam, I didn't mean to surprise you. Would you like some supper?'

He released his grip on the sword hilt. 'I didn't hear you coming because I was concentrating in the other direction, out there.'

Armel placed the food on the battlement ledge. 'Still no sign of Mister Plumm?'

Tam shook his head. 'Not yet, but I've got a feeling in my bones that he's not too far away. I'll wait and see.'

Armel indicated the supper. 'Then you can eat while you wait.'

Tam's eyes never left the woodland fringe. 'I don't feel like eating until I know Doogy's all right.'

The pretty young squirrel placed the tray firmly under Tam's nose. 'You must eat something, Mister MacBurl!'

A stubborn look crossed the Borderer's face. 'I've already said that I don't feel like eating until I know my friend is safe, Sister Armel!'

She spread her paws expressively. 'You'll have to eat sooner or later, Mister MacBurl. Come on now, I made this supper specially for you.'

Tam knew he was going to lose the argument, so he relented. 'Tell you what, let's share it. I'll eat half if you will.'

She smiled. 'There's not much difference between Dibbuns and warriors. Sometimes you've both got to be coaxed into doing what's best for you. Right, we'll share supper!'

Tam bit into one of the farls. 'Mmmm . . . cheese and onion! Why didn't you tell me, that's one of my favourites!'

Armel took a sip of hot cordial and winked mischievously at him. 'I could've tempted you into eating, but I like being bossy. Now eat up, Mister MacBurl!'

Tam laughed as he saluted and took a huge bite of the farl. 'Right you are, marm. Your wish is my command!'

Together they passed the night hours – eating, drinking and talking. All along the walls, hares and Redwallers were doing the same thing in a common bond of friendship as they kept watch on the darkened plain and woodlands.

Dawn's first mystic light stole out of the east, pale shades of misty pastels illuminating the sky as the first birdsong trilled softly over the stillness of Mossflower. Then the big drum boomed out, its echoes reverberating around the Abbey and ramparts of Redwall.

Tergen, who had posted himself on the threshold over the main gate at the western wall, shrilled out a harsh message, arousing every creature to action. 'Yeeekaaaarrrr! This bird sees vermin yonder. Yeekaaaarrrr!'

Tam's sword flashed forth in the dawn light. He thundered along the walkway to the threshold, with Armel dashing behind him.

Skipper and Sergeant Wonwill bellowed out orders to the creatures on the walltops.

'Hold yore positions there, don't leave yore posts!'

'Long Patrol h'archers, up front with Cap'n Fortindom! The rest of ye stay put. Steady in the ranks there!'

Rakkety Tam MacBurl skidded to a halt alongside the goshawk. 'Where's the vermin, Tergen? Where?'

Babooom! Boom! Boom!

Over the deep drum tones, Tergen pointed with his beak. 'Yaaaarrreeeeeekka! See, over there!'

The breath froze in Tam's throat as he looked . . . and saw!

38

It was still dark when Doogy wakened, swimming through the black sea of senselessness into a world of pain. The back of his skull throbbed with one massive headache. The sturdy Highlander could neither move nor cry out. Something scratched against his footpaw. Opening one eye slowly, he craned his head to gaze down. He was bound tight by all paws, neck and chest to a stake, which was driven into the ground. A white fox and an ermine were heaping dead boughs, branches, twigs and dried ferns about him. The white fox saw Doogy's head move.

Checking that the filthy gag was secure around the Highlander's mouth, the fox called out in a hoarse whisper, 'Mighty One, the captive wakens.'

Doogy opened both eyes. In the gloom he saw Gulo the Savage sitting on the drum facing him. The wolverine did not speak for a moment. Doogy swallowed hard. Here he was, helpless, gazing into the insane face of his ferocious foe.

Gulo grinned, his murderous fangs showing through the white-frothed foam that flecked his lips. The wolverine's nostrils flared wide beneath the glinting joy darting from his maddened, red-rimmed eyes as he peered at his captive.

He chuckled wickedly. 'Now we shall see if my brother

will save thee. When 'tis day again, I will lay down my challenge to Askor. He knows he can never rule the lands of ice and snow whilst I live. Askor must face me in combat, that is our law! Hear me, treecrawler, thy life depends on the courage of my brother. Do ye think he will defeat Gulo?'

Doogy could not say anything, though he was gnawing at the gag that stifled his mouth. Surely this crazed beast did not think that his brother was alive and living at Redwall Abbey? Gulo flexed his paws, the long, lethal claws curving out from his heavily matted limbs. 'A pity our father, Dramz, is not here to see his favourite son slain by the one he never looked in favour on. I can see ye are a warrior. 'Twill be a rare sight for ye to witness. Combat to the death, winner takes all. The Walking Stone, this great drum, even the Redwall place yonder – and, of course, thy life. 'Tis a fair wager, is it not?'

Then he seemed to completely ignore Doogy. Leaping from the drum, Gulo raced out on to the western flatlands, clods of earth shooting to either side as he stormed about in a wide circle. With his broad chest heaving, the wolverine gazed about – up, down and around.

His voice became a triumphant snarl. 'Dramz, my father, do ye see me from Hellgates where I sent thee? When thy name is gone and forgotten, beasts will still speak of me. The Mighty One, Gulo the Savage!'

The ermine Duge looked up from a torch she was fashioning from a wooden stave topped with a broom of moss and twigs. She took a cord binder from the aged fox who had served Gulo the longest, remarking quietly to him, 'Only a beast as crazy as Gulo could think that his brother is alive inside that Redwall place.'

The ancient white fox shrugged. 'Who can say whether 'tis true or not? My eyes are still sharp, methinks I saw the Walking Stone last evening. 'Twas strapped to the back of the small, hairy creature who fled into that building. May-haps Askor is truly in there also. There is hope for us few yet, friend. Askor is a better creature than his brother. Life was easier serving under him. Nothing in this world is certain – he may yet best Gulo in combat.'

Duge knotted the cord around the torchhead, tugging it tight. 'Aye, an' methinks fish may fly an' birds swim under the waters. Nobeast could best Gulo in combat!'

The old fox nudged Duge. 'Silence now, Gulo returns.'

Gulo came back to sit upon the drum again, turning his back upon Doogy. He saw the first faint flush of dawn out to the east beyond the treetops. Indicating a spot close by, he ordered the old fox, 'Make fire here. Give me that torch!'

As the fox dug a shallow hole and set steel and flint to tinder over some moss, Gulo began striking the drum with the butt of the torch. *Baboom! Boom! Boom!*

Doogy spat out raggy bits of cloth from the gag. In the breaking day he took stock of his position. They were on the western flatlands in front of Redwall Abbey, just out of bowshot. He blinked hard, focusing his gaze upon the wall-tops. There was Tam, Skipper, a crowd of hares and Tergen the goshawk. Furiously, the sturdy Highlander ripped and tore at the cloth bound across his mouth until he felt it was weakened enough. The binding also went around the stake. With a hard forward thrust of his head, Doogy snapped the gag.

His aching skull felt as though it were lifting off his shoulders as he roared, 'Haway the Braaaaaawww! Ah'm Wild Doogy Plumm! Hawaaaay!'

He slumped forward, stunned, as a swift blow from the torch stave cracked across his jaw.

Holding his head on one side, the wolverine actually smiled at his prisoner. 'Leastways thy friends will know ye are still alive.'

Gulo thrust the torch into the small fire set by the old fox, watching it crackle into flame.

Still smiling, he called out, 'Now it begins, my brother. Now it begins!'

*

349

Tam was struggling wildly in the restraining grips of Skipper, Wonwill and Fortindom. They held him tight as he tried to free himself, calling out, 'Doogy! 'Tis Doogy Plumm that beast has there! I must get to him. Take yore paws off me!'

Sergeant Wonwill whispered sternly in his ear, 'Nah then, Mister MacBurl, just you 'old still awhile. Lookit, ole Gulo's comin' forward fer a parley. Please, sah, calm down. H'I don't want t'give ye a straight left an' put ye asleep, now do I? Be a good h'officer, sah. All the young 'uns are lookin' at ye!'

The sergeant's advice filtered through to Tam, despite his agitated state. He saw Wonwill's hard left paw clenching and took the hint. 'Relax, Sarge. I'm all right now.'

Gulo stood within comfortable listening distance of the walltop. Waving the flaming torch, he peered towards the Abbey and shouted, 'Heed my words an' save thyselves grief an' misery. 'Tis not thee I want, but my brother Askor. Do ye hear me?'

Skipper stood forward, his voice firm and clear. 'We hear ye, Gulo. Now you hear me. There ain't nobeast called Askor at this Abbey. Ye must be mad to think we'd take any brother o' yores inside our gates!'

Gulo laughed, turning hither and thither as though he were consulting others. 'Mad? Nay, waterdog, 'tis thee who is mad! I know that thou art sheltering Askor, aye, an' the Walking Stone. I mean no harm to ye, but this is none of thy business. 'Tis a blood feud. Ye must send out my brother an' the Stone. I will meet him in combat, one to one. The life of that one out there depends upon it!'

Paw on sword hilt, Captain Derron Fortindom came to the battlements. 'An' if we don't?'

The wolverine brandished the lighted torch. 'Then I'll burn thy comrade, an' yonder drum also!'

Fortindom curled his lip distastefully. 'Hmm, about what one'd expect of scum like you. But ye listen t'me, laddie buck. I've got eyes in me blinkin' head, an' I see that the best ye can put in the field amounts to only six vermin. There's about thirty times that number in here, all true blue an' fightin' fit. What's to stop us chargin' out an' makin' short work of ye? Tell me that, sirrah!'

Gulo scoffed, showing his fangs in a cold sneer. 'Numbers mean nought to me! I am Gulo the Savage, I carry no weapons. The Mighty One could slay any ten of ye with just tooth an' limb! But fire can slay thy friend slow an' painfully. It can also destroy the drum which I took from the longears. Then if ye don't send out my brother, fire may destroy the doors of this place, an' I will come in an' get him. So what think ye of that?'

Whilst Fortindom and Gulo were talking, Tam had been cudgelling his brain for a solution, but unknown words kept running through his mind – 'Save my Abbey, thou art the Warrior chosen!' At first he thought it was only tiredness from standing on watch all night. Then he blinked his eyes and shook his head to clear it. Bright lights blossomed throughout Tam's senses, and for a brief moment he saw the speaker. It was Martin the Warrior, whose sword he was carrying. Suddenly he wrenched himself from the restraining paws of his friends and strode to the battlement edge.

As he pointed a paw at the wolverine, Tam's voice rang out, clear as a bell. 'Son of Dramz, thou art looking for a deadbeast. 'Twas I who slayed thy brother! 'Tis me ye want to meet!'

Gulo stared long and hard at the figure on the walltop. 'What foolishness is this? Ye say my brother is dead . . . an' slain by thee?'

The Borderer clenched a paw across his heart. 'Aye, 'twas me, Rakkety Tam MacBurl, an' I'll prove it to thee!'

Tam whispered briefly to Sergeant Wonwill, who saluted and then shot off like an arrow towards the Abbey.

Gulo shook his huge head. 'Nobeast could kill a wolverine in combat. We rule the lands of ice and snow beyond the cold seas!'

Tam nodded at the bulk of the Abbey behind him. 'This

is where I rule. Do ye think this place could be held by a fool? Hah, thy brother did, an' he paid dearly for it. I am the Warrior of Redwall an' its Champion. I stand against anybeast, an' none has ever defeated me! Gulo the Savage, eh? More like Gulo the Fool! Look upon this!'

Wonwill arrived, panting. He thrust Rockbottom into Tam's outstretched paw. Tam held the little tortoise up within Gulo's view before addressing him again. 'If I did not slay Askor, then how did I get this?'

Gulo stood dumbfounded, knowing that, if his brother were alive, he would never have parted with the Walking Stone.

The Borderer's stern tones brought Gulo back to reality. 'When the sun stands at its height, I will meet thee out there on the flatlands. Six will come with me to watch thy vermin lest ye try to play me false. Harm one hair of my comrade before then an' we will charge out an' overwhelm ye. Go now, I have spoken!'

Silence reigned all along the ramparts as the wolverine shuffled off.

Armel grasped Tam's paw as she pleaded with him. 'Oh, you're not really going to fight that monster, are you?'

Tam freed his paw lightly and patted hers. 'Well, of course I am! You can't boss me out of this one, Sister. It's the only solution to the problem, y'see.'

Fortindom muttered out the side of his mouth, 'May I offer my services, Mister MacBurl? Likely you'll need a little help with that flesh-eatin' murderer, wot?'

Tam shook his head. 'No thanks, Cap'n. I've got all the help anybeast could need – the word an' the sword of Martin the Warrior. Is that good enough?'

Skipper gave Tam a pat on the back which almost knocked him over. 'That's good enough for me, mate!'

Sergeant Wonwill saluted. 'H'excuse me, sah, but wot'll we be doin' while all this combat's goin' on?'

Tam took out his dirk and Sgian Dhu, placing them on the walkway along with Martin's sword. 'Just bring me my

352

shield, Sarge. Then leave me alone up here. When the time comes, I'd like you, the Cap'n, Skipper, Tergen, Lancejack an' Ferdimond to go out there with me.'

Abbot Humble stood at one of the top dormitory windows with Armel, Skipper and Foremole Bruffy at his side. They had a fine view of the western flatlands, shimmering gently in the warmth of high summer, brilliant with a profusion of yellow-and-cream pennycress, white clover, red valerian and patches of burnet rose. It would have made a pretty picture had it not been for the presence of Gulo and his six vermin, standing guard with lighted torches over the prisoner bound to the stake and surrounded by kindling material.

Humble stared at the dark, bulky wolverine, whose power and might seemed to dominate all about him. 'Let's hope fortune favours Tam today.'

Armel caught the note of doubt in the old hedgehog's voice. 'It's not fair, Father. I know Tam is a true warrior, but no single creature should have to face that horrible monster!'

Foremole Bruffy shook his velvety head. 'Oi agree wid ee, missy, but they'm says all be furr in luv an' war. B'aint that roight, Skip?'

The otter chieftain leaned on the window sill, nodding. 'That's wot they say, matey. I think our Tam's got a good chance, though. He's small, aye, but light an' speedy. I've seen him fightin'. He's lightnin' wid those blades of his. Don't you fret yoreself, Sister.'

Armel climbed up on the sill and sat by the otter. 'I hope you're right, sir!'

She looked down to the walltop where she could see Tam. He was sitting with his back to them, readying his weapons. Armel listened to the rasp of steel on stone as the warrior honed his blades. When he had finished, Tam took a soft cloth and dipped it in a paste of wood ash dampened with a sprinkle of water.

353

'What's he doing now?'

Captain Fortindom, who had just come into the dormitory, came to the window to see what Tam was doing. 'Burnishing his blades, Sister. Givin' 'em a jolly good old polish, wot! Don't matter whether a chap's a cook, farmer or warrior, marm. Every trade has its tools, y'know, an' if one's blinkin' good at his business, he cares for his implements. I say, just look at MacBurl workin' on that shield of his. He's got the flippin' thing glitterin'!'

Armel and Fortindom blinked at the glint of sunlight which flashed through the window as Tam moved the shield. The captain nodded in admiration. 'Well done that chap, wot. That's the stuff! Nothin' like a smartly presented warrior marchin' off t'meet the rascally foe. Appearances count, doncha know!'

Armel watched Tam labouring away under the bright sun. 'I suppose they do. I've never thought about it, really.'

Fortindom warmed to the subject. 'Oh yes, Sister. When I was a young recruit at Salamandastron, we had a Drill Sergeant, real stickler he was. Had all the new buckoes polishin' night'n'day. Haha, I had a messmate, name o' young Fluffscuttle, as I recall. Well, it seems one day his sword was a mite dusty on parade. By the left! That Sergeant gave him a right old dressin' down, had the poor bloke quiverin' in his fur. The Sarge roared at him, "Yew 'orrible liddle fiddle-pawed, boot-nosed, flop-eared h'excuse for a recruit. H'is that dust h'I sees on yore blade? Sit right down there, laddie buck, an' clean it off. Polish it until the rag wears out! Polish it until y'can see me face in the blade, or I'll 'ave yore tail fer tiffin, yore tripes fer tea an' yore ears fer afters!"'

Armel smiled. 'Oh, poor young Fluffscuttle! What happened?'

Fortindom carried on with his anecdote. 'Happened? I'll tell ye what happened, me beauty. Off marches the Sergeant, leavin' Fluffscuttle sittin' in the middle of the blinkin' parade ground, polishin' away like the clappers at his sword. Of course the Sarge forgets all about the inci-

354

dent, doesn't he! Hah, comes midnight an' the Brigadier's comin' out o' the mess on his way back to quarters. The old boy's crossin' the parade ground when he sees young Fluffscuttle, still sittin' there polishin' away like fury at his flippin' sword. I tell ye, miss, that sword was shinin' like the bloomin' sun on a summer morn. The Brigadier stops to admire it, sayin', "I tell you, young 'un, that's the shiniest sword I've ever seen. Top marks, Fluffscuttle! Come on now, off t'your bed, it's after midnight." But Fluffscuttle just keeps polishin' the confounded sword, an' says to the Brig, "Afraid I can't, sah. The Sergeant said I've got to polish this sword until I can see his face in it. But I've polished an' polished, sah, an' I still can't see the blinkin' Sergeant's face in it!" Wasn't the brightest star in the sky, that young Fluffscuttle! Wot?'

The Abbot, Foremole and Armel were laughing when Skipper glanced up at the sky, announcing, 'Nearly high noontime, mates. Come on, Cap'n, we'd best be on our way. Tam's waitin' on us down there.'

39

Duge saw the Abbey gates opening. Six creatures emerged, three hares, an otter and a hawk, walking side by side, with a squirrel two paces in front of them. Upon her hurried return, the ermine found Gulo and the other five vermin sitting around, their backs toward Doogy and their once well-lit torches now just butts stuck down into the earth. The wolverine was chewing on the raw carcass of a night-jar which the old fox had felled earlier with his sling. Crunching on a bone, Gulo stared up at Duge through hooded lids.

'Do they bring the Walking Stone with them?'

The ermine nodded. 'Sire, the riverdog carries it in a basket around his shoulder. They are all well armed, save for the bird.'

Gulo rose in a leisurely fashion, wiping a few downy feathers from his lips. He swelled his powerful chest and flexed his mighty limbs confidently. 'Come, my slayers! Let us taste the flesh of these fools!'

Doogy Plumm had been gagged three times, but still he had managed to rip and shred each binding.

Not a beast to be silenced, the stout Highlander laughed mockingly. 'Hahaarr, ye scum-faced braggarts, all ye'll taste this day is goin' t'be the soil ye tread on!'

Gulo ignored him, but a white fox climbed up on the wood kindling surrounding the squirrel and struck him a blow to the face. 'Silence, treemouse! Nobeast defeats Gulo the Savage. He could slay twice their number with ease!'

Doogy quickly retorted, 'Hoho, could he now, the saucy great thing! Well, let me tell ye, mah bonnie wee vermin, yer Chief has yet tae meet Rakkety Tam MacBurl!'

Then he bellowed forth, 'Hawaaaay the Braw, Taaaaam!'

Tam answered the cry as he leapt the ditch ahead of his friends. 'Haway the Braaaw, Doogy Plumm! MacBurl for aye!'

Both shouts set off a thunderous roar from the creatures gathered on the high rampart walls. 'Redwaaaaaaallllll! Eulaliiiiaaaaaa!'

At a signal from Gulo, Duge began rolling the drum forward, striking it with the basket hilt of Doogy's claymore as she raised the vermin into a chant. 'Gulo! Gulo! Gulo! Kill! Kill! Kill!'

Both sides marched forward to within six paces of each other, then halted. Gulo and Tam advanced two more paces. They stood facing, eye to eye. Skipper placed the basket containing Rockbottom upon the ground. Then he stood over it, hefting a long javelin. One of the foxes eyed the basket, his paw straying to his curved sword hilt. A swift rasp of steel was all it took, and Derron Fortindom's long blade was out and pointing at the fox.

'Come anywhere near that basket before this contest is finished, sirrah, an' 'tis death to ye. Take my word! We're here to see fair play. This is a one-on-one fight, Tam against Gulo. All others stay out of it. Clear?'

Gulo and Tam began circling warily, each riveted on the other, their eyes unblinking. With his huge, menacing appearance, the wolverine had created immediate fear in all the beasts he had ever faced. He towered over the squirrel warrior, baring his teeth, flexing his claws and breathing heavily. Showing neither fear nor hesitation, and holding the sword of Martin loosely at his side, Tam looked up at his enemy.

Gulo gave a blood-curdling growl, setting up a small cloud of dust as he stamped his footpaws down heavily. He leered at his smaller opponent wolfishly. 'Little warrior, ye are bold to face Gulo. Thy body will add strength to mine. Thy heart belongs to me!'

Normally, this would have set anybeast in a tremble, but Tam's reply was completely unexpected. 'I could not give my heart to one as ugly as ye. 'Tis promised to a fair pretty maid!'

With eye-blurring speed, Tam swung his sword, which produced a pinging sound as it nicked a claw from the wolverine's paw. Gulo let out an unearthly shriek and charged him. The Borderer's shield shook as his enemy's mighty paw struck it. Tam dodged nimbly to one side, avoiding the force of the blow. He swung a counterslash with his blade, but it only shored off a thick bunch of hair. As Tam brought his shield back up into position, Gulo dived headlong. His massive head caught the shield's centre boss, bowling the squirrel backwards, head over tail, and sending him skidding over the grass.

The watchers scattered in all directions as Gulo howled triumphantly and went after his quarry like a thundering juggernaut. Tam recovered quickly. Half kneeling, he held up his shield against an onslaught of blows from both of the wolverine's ponderous paws. Instinctively, he slashed out with his sword and was rewarded by a sharp grunt of pain as it pierced the huge beast's footpaw. Scrambling upright, Tam held the battered shield at shoulder height, sweeping beneath it furiously with the keen blade of Martin's sword as he retreated towards the Abbey.

Gulo came after him, more careful now that he had to avoid the scything blade. He rasped hoarsely at the squirrel warrior, 'Ye can back up an' run, but ye cannot escape Gulo the Savage!'

Retreat, however, was not part of Tam's plan. He suddenly changed tactics. Dropping the shield to his side, the squirrel warrior brought the sword up and forward in a blurring figure-eight movement, forcing Gulo to back off. But he could not keep up the manoeuvre forever. The moment his pace with the blade slacked, the wolverine leapt forward and sideways. The claws on his footpaw raked Tam from knee to paw. He paused, gasping in agony. Gulo swept a swinging crossways strike at Tam's midriff. Only by jumping back a half pace and sucking in his stomach could the squirrel avoid a blow which would have opened him through the middle. Gulo missed, but his paw struck the backside of the shield, ripping it from his opponent's grasp and sending it sailing up and away. The shield landed on the edge of the ditch, side on, its rim buried deep in the earth.

Some of Tam's friends as well as Gulo's vermin had been running forward while at the same time following the progress of the two rivals' life-and-death struggle. To one side of him, Gulo glimpsed the white fox who was carrying Doogy's claymore. The wolverine held out his paw. 'Give me yon blade!'

The fox passed it to his chieftain. Ferdimond De Mayne, one of the least experienced Long Patrol hares, made as if to stop him, but Sergeant Wonwill pulled him back. 'Stay out of it, young 'un. No rules say they can't be armed!'

Now Gulo came after Tam with the claymore, bludgeoning and hacking. The squirrel was hard put to defend himself.

All along the western walltop, silence had descended on the onlookers. It seemed that fate had placed Tam on the losing side. Steel clanged upon steel as the Borderer was driven back by the relentless blows Gulo rained upon him. Back, back he went, countering and parrying as the long-bladed claymore hammered against his own, shorter sword.

Tam could not look to see where he was being driven, but he knew he was being forced towards the ditch, which ran alongside the path outside the Abbey wall.

Gulo began roaring as he delivered each crushing blow. 'Gulo! Kill! Gulo! Kill!'

Then Tam tripped . . .

He fell heavily backwards, striking the ground with a force which almost knocked the wind from him. The last thing he saw was Gulo, flinging himself forward with the claymore upraised.

For a brief moment, time seemed to freeze. Then, none too soon, Tam sighted the wolverine in mid-air, falling towards him, with claymore raised for the fatal blow. Blood-red eyes ablaze, the Border warrior seized his final chance with the speed of chain lightning. Gripping the sword of Martin, hilt and blade with both paws, he held it up horizontally. A fierce spirit possessed him as he shot both footpaws up rigid at the descending wolverine. A wild howl of rage ripped from Tam's throat – 'Haway the Braaaaaaw!' Then the weight of his adversary fell upon him as Tam thrust upward with the sword and all four paws in a stupenduous burst of power.

Like a stone from a slingshot, Gulo was carried through the air by the impetus of the mighty effort. He slammed to earth, just short of the ditch. His own massive body weight sent his outstretched neck right on to the edge of Tam's shield, which was buried upright in the earth at the edge of the ditch. Gulo was transfixed for one horrifying heartbeat, his body at the ditch's edge. *Clunk!* His head fell into the dried leaves on the ditchbed.

Gulo the Savage would never return to rule the lands of ice and snow beyond the cold north seas!

40

Tam recalled distantly his very young days, when he had grasped a thistle whilst picking flowers for his mother, or *was* it his mother? He could not recall who, but it was a creature with deep, dark eyes, murmuring to him, soft as a summer stream, 'Hold still now, it's nearly done. There, that did it!'

Opening his eyes, he found himself lying in Redwall Infirmary on a spotless white-sheeted bed. Sister Armel shielded his eyes from the midnoon sunlight pouring in through the open window. She put aside a length of fine flax and a small thorn needle, reaching for some warm water, ointment and dressings.

Still dazed, the Borderer murmured dozily, 'Did y'get all the prickles out? I didn't cry, did I?'

Doogy Plumm's voice answered him. 'Nay, ye didnae cry, ye were a good wee babe. Hahahaha!'

Sister Armel spoke severely to the Highlander. 'Mister Plumm, stop moving his paw and hold it still, or I'll never get this dressing on!'

Tam came fully awake now. He tried to sit up, but was pushed back down firmly by the Infirmary Sister. Craning his neck, he could see the crowd gathered in the passage beyond the open door. Sister Armel, Doogy and Abbot Humble were the only ones allowed inside the room.

Slightly bewildered, Tam looked questioningly at Doogy. 'What happened? Oooh, my leg feels stiff!'

Armel tied off the paw bandage, explaining briefly, 'Your leg *should* feel stiff, Mister MacBurl. It was cut to the bone by that creature's claws. I've put it in a splint. Your left paw was almost sliced through by Martin's sword. You were holding the blade when that awful beast fell upon you. I've stitched it up and it should heal properly, providing you keep it still and get lots of rest!'

Tam wrinkled his nose at Doogy. 'She's being bossy again, mate. I can always tell when she's in that mood, cos she calls me Mister MacBurl. All I can remember from out there is passing out. Tell me, what really went on?'

Doogy began playing their old game, speaking to Tam in mock bad temper. 'Ah'll tell ye what happened, laddie. Ye ruined mah best an' only claymore! Och, ah don't know what sort o' steel Martin's sword is made of, but it cut great chunks out o' mah blade. When ah picked it up, mah poor claymore fell in two pieces! Oh, an' another thing, yore shield will nae go intae battle again. 'Tis battered an' holed an' bended a'most in two halves. An' what possessed ye tae sharp its edge all around like a blade, eh?'

Tam laid his head back on the pillow. 'Oh, that was a little tip I got from Martin the Warrior.'

Doogy Plumm threw up his paws in resignation. 'Och, that explains everythin'. He should've been called Martin the Destroyer o' Weapons. That's a bonny claymore an' a fine buckler completely destroyed, thanks tae him!'

Abbot Humble and Armel could not help smiling as they listened to both warriors wryly arguing.

'Yer a terrible beast, Doogy Plumm! Sittin' tied nice an' comfy to a stake whilst I'm left fightin' Gulo. By the bye, did I win, or did ye take a nap an' miss it all?'

'Aye, ah took a wee doze, but they tell me ye cut off ole Gulo's head wi' yer shield edge. Personally, ah don't believe it. Ah think he slew hisself, cos he was a-feared ah'd break loose tae teach him a lesson. His head's still in the ditch. Ye can go an' ask him yerself, though ah dinnae ken he'll want tae talk to ye any more!'

Tam grimaced. 'Aye, he must be a bad loser, Doogy. I suppose ye let the other vermin escape?'

The Highlander scratched his tail. 'Well, we were considerin' it. The rest of the vermin fought hard, but that Cap'n Fortindom, he's no' very fussy on vermin. Him an' Wonwill finished 'em afore we got the chance. Och, ah'll tell ye, Tam, those shrews were no' pleased at all!'

Tam looked mystified. 'What shrews?'

Doogy gave him a jaundiced glance. 'Do ye not recall Log a Log Togey tellin' ye he was goin' tae fetch help when ye parted company? Ye've got some explainin' tae do, laddie. The Cap'n an' Wonwill had no sooner put paid tae the last vermin when who comes chargin' oot o' the trees but Togey an' tenscore o' Guosim, armed tae the teeth an' roarin' blood'n'slaughter! Mind, that was nothin' compared tae auld Friar Glisum when he saw he had two hunnerd more mouths tae feed fer a few days. So that's mah bad news. Now, have ye got any good news fer me?'

Tam winced as Doogy patted his injured paw absently. 'Good news, aye. Did ye hear I got my claymore back, an' Araltum's Royal Banner too? Skipper found a hole in the streambank where that thievin' volerobber had hidden 'em!'

Doogy grinned. 'So ah heard. As a matter o' fact, ah talked the good Sister Armel intae givin' me yore claymore, seein' as how ye ruined mah claymore wi' yon hard-steel sword ye were carryin'. Ah thought 'twas only fair!'

Tam sat up, outraged, but Armel pushed him back down before explaining herself. 'I was only acting for the best, Mister MacBurl. Besides, what would you be needing two swords for?'

Tam spluttered, 'But one of 'em belongs to Redwall. It's Martin's sword, not mine!'

The Infirmary Sister shrugged. 'Well, it's always there, should you need to defend Redwall against foebeasts. Oh, I sewed the tears in your banner and I washed and pressed it. I must say it looks a bit more acceptable now.'

Tam, however, was not listening to Armel. He was raving on at Doogy Plumm. 'Hah, some mate you are! Yore worse'n that Yoofus Lightpaw, wheedlin' my best claymore off an innocent Infirmary Sister. Shame on ye! There's nobeast more disgustin' than a claymore thief. Huh, I'd best hide my dirk an' Sgian Dhu before ye take a fancy t'them too!'

Armel waved her paws sternly. 'Enough, I've heard enough! Clear this room so that my patient can get some rest. Out you go, Mister Plumm, and you, too, Father Abbot. Be off with you! And the rest of you hanging about that passage outside, have you no chores downstairs? Begone everybeast!'

Humble protested, 'But I was just sitting here quietly!'

Tam winked at him. 'I'd go if I were you, Father. She's in one of her bossy moods. See how her chin sticks out?'

The pretty young squirrel tried not to smile. 'One more word out of you, Mister MacBurl, and . . . !'

Tam scowled fiercely. 'And you'll what?'

She smiled sweetly. 'And I'll have Friar Glisum make us a nice tray of afternoon tea for two. So what do you think of that, Mister MacBurl, eh?'

Rakkety Tam MacBurl gave a deep sigh of satisfaction. 'I think that's a wonderful idea, Sister Armel!'

Epilogue

It is now fifteen seasons since Gulo the Savage was slain by my father. Fallen green leaves are turning to gold and brown, covering our orchard with a thick carpet, which is deliciously crisp underpaw. But what a beautiful summer it has been! Let me tell you of the trip I made, quite an adventure for a maid who has never strayed far from Redwall Abbey. What excitement!

Armel, my mother, finally persuaded Tam, my father, and my uncle, Doogy Plumm, to return the great banner to its owners. Father was willing, but Uncle Doogy did a lot of grumbling – 'Och, ah'd let the auld fusspots stew in their own juice, an' weep salty tears tae get their flag back!' Those were a few of his words.

But Mother became very bossy and had her way in the end. Dad laughs a lot when she gets like this. Soon we were on our journey – Dad, Mum, Uncle Doogy, Tergen and my mother's dear friend, Aunt Brooky. I'd never imagined Mossflower Wood was so vast! But we were in no hurry. I was fascinated to see the campsite where my dad stole the sword of Martin back from the vermin. Oh, incidentally, Old Abbot Humble let us take the sword along in case it was needed. Uncle Doogy insisted that I wear the sword – from the day I took my first steps, he and my dad were the ones who taught me the ways of the blades. I'm told I used to wield the little Sgian Dhu; I learned to fence with it. Then, as I grew taller, I was given the dirk to use; then, finally, at the end of my eleventh season, I could use two swords – either the blade of Martin or Uncle Doogy's claymore (which my dad still claims is his).

Mother was slightly worried about me being the sword carrier, but I remember exactly what Uncle Doogy said to reassure her – 'Och, cease frettin', Armel. The wee maid's a better swordbeast than mahself or her great lump of a daddy. Ah ken she'd draw rings aroond us wi' one paw!'

Well, the first stream we came to, guess what happened? We were met by a fleet of logboats! I've got another uncle now, a fine old fat, bearded shrew everyone calls Log a Log Togey. I like him! He told me I'd make a good Guosim, and let me steer his big logboat. Have you ever been on a stream for a few days? Sailing along peaceful, shaded waterways, letting your paw run through the water. Especially getting to sleep aboard under a canopy, lulled by the murmuring current . . . It's a dream! And the delicious Guosim food, what a treat!

But we did have some hair-raising moments fighting our way up a stretch of very rough rapids. Finally, though, the water calmed, and on the fourth day we said goodbye to the shrews. They were sorry to see us go, but they looked relieved to be rid of Tergen. I think shrews are not great lovers of fierce goshawks.

Not far from the stream was an abode where we spent another few, very happy days. The dwelling was the home of Yoofus Lightpaw and his wife, Didjety. What a jolly pair! I even saw the famous Walking Stone, though at first I thought Rockbottom was a pawstool (silly me!)! What an extraordinary creature little Rockbottom is, and what fun his owners are. On the first night we were there, Didjety made us a huge batch of her famous sausage rolls. (I say 'famous,' because she gave the recipe to Friar Glisum, and now they are the favourite food of Redwall Dibbuns – and most elders too.) I never laughed so much in my life, and neither did Aunt Brooky (and she's laughed a lot in her life, I can tell you). We had a feast, a real celebration: Didjety sang us funny songs and did comical dances, Yoofus told us hilarious tales of his thieving adventures and Rockbottom sat on my lap all evening.

On the morning we were going, the great banner and Uncle Doogy's claymore were missing. My mum and Mrs Lightpaw gave poor Yoofus such a scolding that he returned them immediately, saying, 'Ah sure, I was only havin' a liddle borrow of the grand flag an' the big ould sword. Wasn't I now, Rock, me ould icecake?' And do you know what? Rockbottom nodded and smiled, I'll swear he did. Really, the nerve of those two!

Early one sunny morning, we crossed some heathlands, climbed a lot of dunes and came to some lovely tree groves. Beyond them I could see the sea, a first-time experience and a real treat for me.

Uncle Doogy began grumbling again. 'Och, ah'd as soon fling this flag intae the waves than return it tae those two snooty-nosed wee braggarts!'

For a moment I thought my dad was going to do it, but Mum took Uncle Doogy by the ear and wagged a paw at them both. 'If either of you two rogues even dare, we'll chuck you in straight after it. Right, Brooky?'

Auntie Brooky enjoys anything like that. 'Whoooo-hooohooohaha! Let's do it, Armel. Hahahahaaa!' See what I mean?

We sat down and had lunch on the fringes of the trees. Uncle Doogy whispered to Tergen, who flew off into the groves. (The high-strung bird has been flying since the autumn following the death of Gulo the Savage.) No sooner had we finished eating than we heard a lot of scurrying and squealing from within the trees. Out tumbled a score of squirrels. Our fierce goshawk came swooping behind them. As they huddled in a terrified mass, Tergen stood over them.

Uncle Doogy clashed his claymore upon his shield and shouted, 'Ah can see two wee maggots in there called Araltum an' Idga. Shove 'em out! We want tae have words with 'em!'

The pair were pushed out by the other squirrels. Honestly, I had never set eyes on two more fat, wheezy, overdressed little beasts. Tear-stained and wailing, with both their home-made crowns askew, they grovelled on the ground in front of us. A moment later, a young squirrel, almost as fat as the two of them put together, strutted out. He was fearfully ugly and had a squeaky, petulant lisp.

'Who are these cweatures? Thwow them in pwison an' give them no bwead or dwink for thwee days!'

Uncle Doogy scowled at him. 'An' who are ye, mah bold wee barrel-bottomed babe?'

The young squirrel stamped a podgy footpaw angrily. 'Insolent squiwell, you are addwessing the Cwown Pwince Woopurt. Show some wespect, an' bow before me, wetch!'

My dad ignored him. Taking the banner, he rolled it lengthways into a long scarf. This he knotted loosely about the necks of King Araltum and his Drayqueen Idga.

Dad sounded very stern when he spoke to them. 'I bring ye back the banner now, as I vowed I would. Doogy and I were fools to ever swear our oaths to ye. Release us from our bond now, Araltum. Keep your promise!'

Dad and Doogy both drew their swords. Araltum arose, trembling. He placed his paws on both blades and said, 'I release you from your bonds and pledges, from hereon you may use your swords as freebeasts!' All the squirrels – including more who had emerged from the groves – drowned out any further speeches by the pompous king with their cheering and leaping about.

Little Crown Prince Roopert kicked the nearest squirrel,

shouting shrilly at him, 'Tweason, you're all under awwest for tweachery!'

Pinetooth, the old squirrel he had kicked, was a longtime friend of my father. He kicked Roopert back, right on his fat little rear end. Then he winked at my dad and Uncle Doogy. 'I've been wantin' to do that for a while now, mates. 'Tis time Araltum an' Idga's rule came to an end!'

Amid happy celebrations, the squirrels marched with us from the groves down to the sea. Pinetooth, and another old squirrel named Hinjo, offered the twin crowns of Araltum and Idga to my mum and dad. Mother was magnificent. After taking both crowns and throwing them into the sea, she made a speech.

'Friends, there will be no more tyranny. From now on, you must live together in harmony. We wish you peace and long life!'

Setting our faces toward the mountain fortress of Salamandastron, which loomed to the north like a silent sentinel guarding the shores, we marched off. The jubilant squirrels cheered us until they were mere dots on the tideline, far behind us.

I always thought Redwall Abbey was a big place, but the sight of Salamandastron, from close up, took my breath away. Simply colossal! What a delegation came out to meet us! Though I had never seen the hares before (they had left Redwall long before I was born), I was able to put names to some of their faces – Sergeant Wonwill, Captain Derron Fortindom, Lancejack Wilderry, Flunkworthy, Folderon and a couple who had been wed for five seasons now, Ferdimond De Mayne and Kersey. These two had their infant son with them, a chubby creature named Dauncey De Mayne (Dauncey, in memory of Kersey's twin brother). The Long Patrol put on a Guard of Honour, escorting us into the large Banquet Hall. A feast was held to welcome us – and, I must say, those regimental cooks did us proud! I was especially overawed by Lady Melesme; she was every bit the Badger Ruler of Salamandastron. Tall, stately and dignified, dressed in only simple homespun robes, she radiated serenity and respect. Now I know why badgers are regarded as such special creatures.

We spent six glorious days at the mountain. In my spare time this winter, I plan to write a journal to recount this experience, though it will be difficult to properly describe what a fascinating place the mountain is – so shrouded it is in grandeur, legend and mystery.

I was loath to leave when the time came, and I promised to visit them in the future. We left there with an escort of twoscore Long Patrol hares to guide us back home. Actually, it was twoscore and three – Ferdimond and Kersey, together with baby Dauncey, are coming back to the Abbey as our resident hares. Sadly, we left minus one of our number: the goshawk Tergen had elected to stay on at Salamandastron as lookout and scout to the regiment. Such a fierce heart as he will, I'm sure, find his true destiny there among the warriors.

What more can I tell you, my friend? We are back once more in our beloved home, and the autumn season is upon us. Burlop Cellarhog has predicted the harvest will begin to-morrow at dawn. Tonight there is a beautiful harvest moon. Mother and I will be taking all the Dibbuns, including little Dauncey De Mayne, out to our Abbey pond. There we will cast pebbles at the moon's reflection in the water. They say that if you make a wish before the ripples reach the pond's edge, your wish will be granted. So I will cast my pebble right into the centre of the moon's reflection and make a wish for all of us – the creatures of Redwall, my family and friends, and a special one, just for both of *us*. I wish for the harvest to be an abundant one, and I wish that the feast we have tomorrow night in the orchard will have the most beautiful decorations of flowers and many-hued lanterns. I wish for peace and prosperity, love and happiness for all. I know I will not have to wish that the food will be at its most delicious. How else could it be at our Abbey? I will lay a place at our table for you and hope you can join us, if not in body, then in the world of your imagination, where you can visit us any time.

Melanda MacBurl. Recorder of Redwall Abbey
in Mossflower Country

He lost a sword an' gained a sword,
tae triumph at the slaughter.
He's met a Sister, found a wife
an' gained a bonny daughter!

Tam took his bond back off the fool,
he left him sore an' grievin'.
An' gave tae friends o' former days,
a grand auld taste o' freedom!

Rakkety Rakkety Rakkety Tam,
the drums are beatin' braw.
Och, now ye've gained a heart's desire,
ye'll no more march tae war!